"My dragon is coming loose!" Tas called to the gnome.

Tasslehoff felt his grip slipping even further. He pressed his chest to the dragon's back, locked his arms around its neck, and wrapped his legs around the pole behind him. Why wouldn't that silly gnome stop the ride? Had he forgotten where the off switch was again?

Just then, there was a sharp sound of splintering wood, and the poles connected to the dragon statue ahead of Woodrow tore loose. Woodrow opened his mouth to shout a warning to Tas. Then his blood froze as he saw the red dragon's head swing around to look at the kender on its back. The human's jaw dropped when he saw the dragon flick its tail and flex its wings. The muscles in the monster's back rippled beneath its red scales!

The dragon was alive!

Woodrow shook his head, unsure whether he'd imagined the dragon's movement or really had seen it. When he looked up again, the centaur he was riding was staring into his face. "The dragon is getting away with your friend," it said.

The DRAGONLANCE® Saga

Chronicles Trilogy
Dragons of Autumn Twilight
Dragons of Winter Night
Dragons of Spring Dawning

Legends Trilogy
Time of the Twins
War of the Twins
Test of the Twins

Tales Trilogy
The Magic of Krynn
Kender, Gully Dwarves, and Gnomes
Love and War

Tales II Trilogy
The Reign of Istar
The Cataclysm (July 1992)
The War of the Lance (Nov. 1992)

Heroes Trilogy
The Legend of Huma
Stormblade
Weasel's Luck

Heroes II Trilogy
Kaz, the Minotaur
The Gates of Thorbardin
Galen Beknighted

Preludes Trilogy
Darkness and Light
Kendermore
Brothers Majere

Preludes II Trilogy
Riverwind, the Plainsman
Flint, the King
Tanis, the Shadow Years

Meetings Sextet
Kindred Spirits
Wanderlust
Dark Heart
The Oath and the Measure
Steel and Stone
The Companions (January 1993)

Elven Nations Trilogy
Firstborn
The Kinslayer Wars
The Qualinesti

The Art of the DRAGONLANCE Saga
The Atlas of the DRAGONLANCE World

DragonLance Saga

PRELUDES

VOLUME TWO

Kendermore

Mary Kirchoff

Cover Art
JEFF EASLEY

Interior Illustrations
VALERIE VALUSEK

Poetry
MICHAEL WILLIAMS

DRAGONLANCE® *Preludes*

Volume Two

Kendermore

Copyright ©1989 TSR, Inc.
All Rights Reserved.

First Printing: August 1989
Printed in the United States of America.
Library of Congress Catalog Card Number: 88-51719

9 8 7 6 5 4

ISBN: 0-88038-754-8

TSR, Inc.
P.O. Box 756
Lake Geneva, WI
53147 U.S.A.

TSR Ltd.
120 Church End, Cherry Hinton
Cambridge CB1 3LB
United Kingdom

To Steve, who helped me immensely and without complaint and exhibited considerably more patience than I might have managed if the roles were reversed.

And to Alexander, the light of my life, who, despite seeing me only at dinner for months on end, still remembered to call me Mommy.

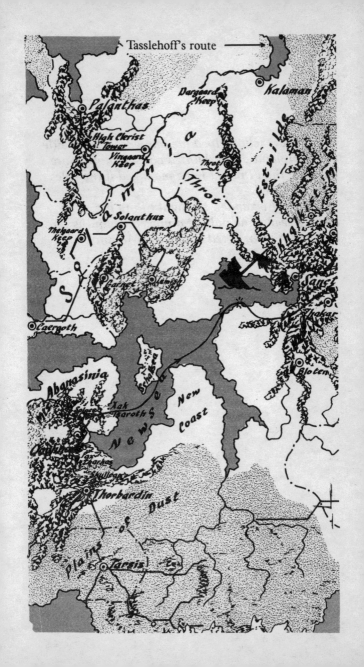

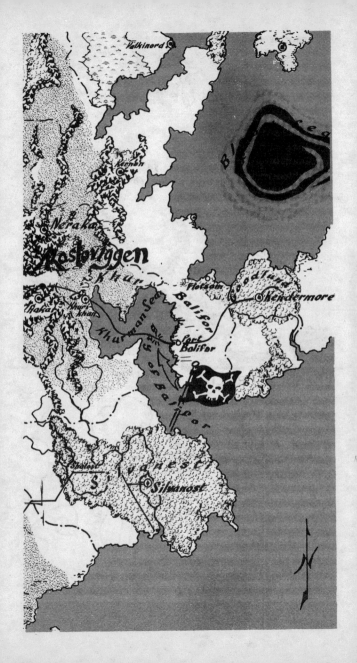

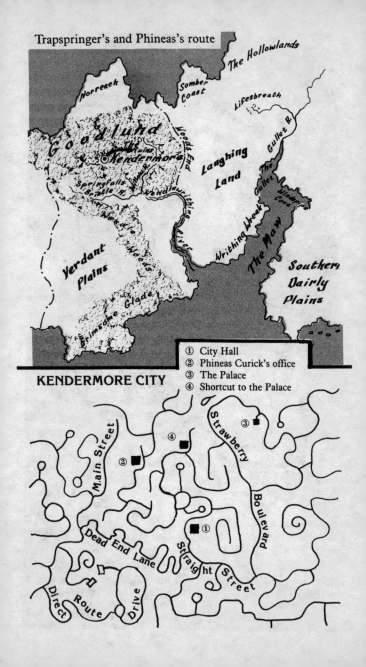

Trapspringer's and Phineas's route

The Hollowlands

Norreach

Somber Coast

Lifesbreath

Goodlund

The Plains
Kendermore

Woods End

Laughing Land

Gullet R.

Springfalls

Bristle R.

Windlewithing

The Gullet

Gullet

Willow Cove

Writhing Wreak

The Maw

Verdant Plains

Nettle Woods

Southern Dairly Plains

Grimstone Glade

① City Hall
② Phineas Curick's office
③ The Palace
④ Shortcut to the Palace

KENDERMORE CITY

Main Street

Strawberry

③

④

②

Boulevard

①

Dead End Lane

Straight Street

Direct

Route

Drive

Prologue

Late afternoon was a peaceful time at the Inn of the Last Home in the village of Solace. Three friends sat at their favorite table near the inn's fireplace, making plans.

"Where do you think you'll go first, Tas?" The speaker was Tanis Half-Elven, who relaxed with his chin cupped in his hand and his elbow propped on the dark, oak table.

Across the table from Tanis sat his kender friend, Tasslehoff Burrfoot. Next to Tasslehoff was the burly dwarf, Flint Fireforge.

The smell of smoke hovered about the kender's nose. It clung to all forty-eight inches of his childlike frame, from the toes of his blue leggings to the very tip of his topknot of ginger-colored hair. The familiar scent comforted him, for he was just a smidgeon sad; soon he would be leaving his closest friends for five years, which was a very long time. Their tight-knit group of seven had decided to part and meet again—five years to the day— after they'd learned what they could about rumors of war in the land, as well as solve some personal problems.

"I haven't thought much about where I'm going yet," the kender said vaguely. "Wherever the wind blows me, I guess." Raising an empty flagon upside-down, Tasslehoff threw his head back and waited for the last dollop of flavorful foam to slide slowly into his waiting mouth. At last, the froth drizzled out with a "plop!"

Smacking his lips in satisfaction, he wiped them with the edge of his fur-trimmed sleeve. Squinting against the haze in the dimly lit taproom, he looked at Tanis. "Friends all over Krynn have been waiting for my next visit, though!" Tasslehoff pushed his empty mug to the edge of the table for refilling.

Flint's eyes twinkled merrily under his bushy, gray-black brows. "I'll bet they've been waiting! And I'll bet they've kept busy, too, working on kender-proof door locks!" Beneath his huge bulb of a nose and wild, peppery moustache, the old dwarf's mouth opened wide with laughter, setting his fleshy cheeks to jiggling. Even Tanis, ever the peacemaker, could not help smirking behind his hand.

"Oh, do you think so, really?" Tasslehoff cried earnestly. As he smiled, his young face broke into a thousand tiny, spreading creases, like a shattered pane of stained glass. Facial wrinkles were a characteristic shared by all kender, which made it very difficult to accurately guess a kender's age. "Most locks nowadays are so flimsy—no protection at all! I don't know how anyone expects to keep anything safe anymore."

"No one does if kender are about," Flint snorted under his breath. He could tell from Tanis's warning glance that the elf's sharp ears had caught his words. Tanis liked to defend the kender against Flint's gratuitous insults, even if Tas was never in the least truly offended.

Two of Flint's fingers, tightly pressed together, disappeared under his moplike moustache, and he blew a loud, sharp whistle. The inn was not busy, so in no time the innkeeper's adopted daughter appeared. She was a rosy-cheeked girl with eager eyes and short-cropped, dark, curly hair. Though a slight breeze blew through large cracks in the inn's few arched, stained-glass windows—in a few weeks they would be doubly covered with oiled parchment to keep out the winter—the weather on this day was unseasonably warm for early fall. Flint called it "summer's last dance." Coupled with the heat from the ever-present fire in the hearth, the heavy air had pasted the girl's hair to her forehead and moistened her coarse, graying tunic to her back.

"Yes, sir?" she inquired eagerly. Her voice carried none of the weariness so common among seasoned serving wenches. In a few years, Flint thought sadly, when the impertinence and unwanted attentions of too many men wore her down . . .

"Tika, isn't it?" he asked, and she nodded. Flint smiled encouragingly. "Then, Tika, I need two more—" Tanis quickly drained the last of his own mug and pushed it forward. "—make that three more mugs of Otik's fine ale," Flint corrected himself. "On me."

"Very good, sir." Tika's willowy form bobbed once, then darted skillfully through the closely spaced tables to the bar.

The Inn of the Last Home was shaped like the letter "L." The ceiling was low, making the room cozy for small groups, though sometimes on very busy nights it just seemed cramped. The walls were built of thick, dark beams sealed with a thin mixture of tar, which gave off a heavy, musky scent that was pleasantly familiar to the inn's regular patrons. Small, round tables filled the room, though Otik had also included one long table with benches to encourage conversation among strangers.

The kitchen, a noisy, bustling place, was at the foot of the L. The sounds of pans rattling and the cook screaming, and the enticing scent of Otik's renowned spiced potatoes, were not unusual at any hour.

What was unusual was that the inn was built in the mighty branches of a vallenwood tree, a graceful, fast-growing giant that seemed to thrive around Solace. In fact, the entire town, except for the stables and a few other buildings, was all located high above ground in vallenwood trees. The village was unlike any other—breathtakingly beautiful, yet practical for defense. Bridgewalks spiraled to the ground around the trunks and swayed gently in the air between trees, linking together businesses, families, and friends.

The three friends seated before the fire seemed lost in thought as Tika returned with their drinks. The young girl's eyes lingered on Tanis's attractive face—the dark, wide-set, brooding eyes, cheekbones seemingly chiseled from marble, and his thick, wavy, red hair, carelessly uncombed. But when her gaze dropped unconsciously to his lean, muscled torso, obvious even through his shirt, her hands grew clumsy and she slopped a bit of ale across the table.

"Oh, I'm sorry . . . it must be the heat!" she mumbled, jabbing at the spill with the hem of her apron.

"No harm done," Tas assured her. "It's really a very small puddle. Actually, I'm impressed that you hit the table at all, considering the way you were staring at—"

"Thank you, Tika," piped Flint, drowning out the rest of the kender's all-too-honest proclamation. Tika flushed crimson and, grateful for the dismissal, dashed into the shadows of the kitchen.

"Tas, you shouldn't have embarrassed her like that," Flint scolded the kender.

"Embarrassed who? Whatever do you mean? Oh, Tika!" Tas finally caught Flint's meaning. "It's not *my* fault if she fills mugs to the brim, although"—he shrugged—"personally I like that in a girl." Tas scooped a fingerful of foam from the top of one of the mugs and guided it into his mouth.

Flint rolled his eyes in mock disgust. "There's not a bit of common sense in that head of yours sometimes. You shouldn't have pointed out that she was *staring* at Tanis."

Tas looked puzzled. "But girls always stare at Tanis. Have you seen some of the looks Kitiara gives him? Why, sometimes I get so embarrassed it's hard to watch! Kit never seems to feel ashamed, though. I wonder why . . ."

"Uh-hmmm!" Tanis cleared his throat loudly, his face suddenly hot. "Would both of you mind not talking about me as if I weren't here?" He frowned sternly, turning to the unabashed kender. "Tas, what Flint meant was—" Tanis groped for words that might persuade the kender.

"It doesn't matter," he sighed at last, seeing Tas's attentive, childlike expression, curious yet uncomprehending.

"So, Tanis," Flint said, striving to change the subject, "you haven't told us where *you're* going." Pulling a chunk of wood and his whittling knife from the depth of the brown leather vest he insisted on wearing in every type of weather, Flint leaned back and began carving details into the miniature form of a half-finished duck.

Tanis stroked his clean-shaven chin and contemplated the fire's blue flames. "I don't know . . . I thought I might wander toward the city of Qualinost," he said ambiguously, his unblinking eyes burning.

Flint looked up and gave Tanis a meaningful stare. Tanis's entry into the world had been more difficult than most. His mother, an elf woman raped by a human, had died giving birth to Tanis. The half-breed child was raised by his mother's brother. Though his uncle treated the boy as one of his own, Tanis never felt truly welcome among humans or elves. And as Tanis grew into manhood, his mixed heritage became even more physically apparent; he was smaller than most humans and larger than most elves.

It was then that he felt the attitude of his elven family

change. Everyone except Laurana, that is, whose girlish attentions were not completely unwanted. Which made the tension between Tanis, his uncle, and his uncle's sons—Laurana's brothers—even more apparent.

So he had left. The void haunted him, and he knew he must face his uncle—and Laurana—one day. The task was complicated by the fact that the man was not only his uncle, but the Speaker of the Sun, the leader of the Qualinesti Elves.

Flint reached out and squeezed Tanis's shoulder reassuringly. "You'll always have a home here, lad."

Tanis looked away from the flames, giving Flint a smile that was not reflected in those brooding, dark eyes. "I know." But this was to be a happy parting, and Tanis did not wish to think of Qualinost just now. Not yet.

He flashed Flint a cheery smile. "And if I know you, Flint Fireforge, you'll spend the whole five years whittling before your hearth."

Flint sliced an over-large chunk from the wood in his fingers. "And what would be wrong with that?" he asked indignantly. Tanis was sure now that the dwarf intended to do just that.

"Nothing, except that it would be awfully boring after an hour or so," interjected Tasslehoff, sending sparks flying as he stirred up the fire in the hearth. "You know, Flint, I could stay for a while and keep you company and—"

"And nothing!" Flint cut in, glaring at the kender. "I don't need any lame-brained kender underfoot! Did it occur to you that maybe I'd *like* to be a little bored after having you kids cluttering up my hearth for so long!" Tanis found the term "kid" amusing since he was nearly one hundred years old by human reckoning, though he looked twenty. Of course, Flint was no youngster himself—he was in his early one-hundred-forties, which translated to late fifties for a human.

The grizzled dwarf wasn't finished yet. "Raistlin always brooding, Sturm so blasted stoic, Kitiara forever arm-wrestling with Caramon, or wrestling of another sort with Tanis. . . ." His gruff expression softened, and he gave the half-elf a good-natured poke in the ribs.

Tas leaned back his chair and propped his feet on the table. "Do you think Sturm has a chance of finding his father in Solamnia?" he asked, suddenly reminded of their friends who had already left. Sturm Brightblade and Kitiara Uth-Matar had left Solace earlier in the day, headed for Solamnia to the north. Sturm was searching for the father he'd been forced to leave as a child, and Kitiara had gone along for the adventure.

"If Sir Brightblade is still alive, I'm sure Sturm will find him," Tanis said firmly. "He can't miss with Kit along to help."

The fire crackled and popped, spitting a hot ember onto Tas's left leg. With a yelp he was on his feet, leaping around madly. "Ouch! Ouch! Is that why Kit went—to look for Sturm's father?" he asked, slapping furiously at his smoldering legging.

Tanis, scarcely taken aback by the kender's acrobatics, replied seriously, "I don't think Kit knows what she's looking for."

The ember extinguished, Tas poked his finger through the black-rimmed hole in his blue leggings. "Well, whatever it is, I'm sure she'll find it," he said. "She's so . . ."

"Driven?" Tanis completed the sentence.

"Determined, I was going to say," said the ingenuous kender.

"She is that," said Tanis with a knowing smile.

"I'm worried about those darn fool brothers of hers," Flint muttered, "although I don't know why I bother. And I don't care what anyone says, Raistlin is too young to be taking that magical test in the Tower of High Sorcery. Gonna get himself killed is all. And poor Caramon—I don't know what he would do without him." The twin brothers, Caramon and Raistlin Majere—Kitiara's half-brothers—had already left as well. Frail Raistlin intended to take the dangerous magic-user's test in the Tower of High Sorcery at Wayreth, and his burly brother Caramon had insisted on accompanying him for protection.

Tasslehoff looked thoughtful. "I think it's the other way around," he said, not intending to sound unkind. "I don't know what Raistlin would do without Caramon. Unless, of course, he's dead."

"Family. . . ." was all Tanis said, his thoughts remote.

"That's it!" Tas exclaimed, jumping to his feet, his eyes sparkling with excitement. "That's what I'll do! I'll go visit my family. Gee, I wonder where any of them are."

"You don't know?" Flint asked, looking up from his whittling. "How about your parents?"

"Not exactly, no. Not lately, anyhow."

"Then, how do you even know whether any of them are still alive?" Tanis asked, sipping his ale.

"Someone would have told me if they weren't, I guess," Tas reasoned.

"But if you don't know where they are, how would anyone know where *you* are to tell you that someone whose whereabouts you didn't know had died?" Flint sputtered awkwardly. The dwarf paused for a moment, then shook his head. "Listen to me, now I'm starting to sound like a kender!" he spat.

But Tas was too busy listing off relatives to notice. "There's Uncle Remo Lockpick, my father's uncle's second cousin, I think. He has a wonderful collection of keys—big ones, small ones, heavy ones, ones made of bright blue gems as big as your head." Tas scratched his chin. "What would anyone use a key like that for?"

Both Flint and Tanis wondered why any kender had need of a key, considering their light-fingered tendencies, but each remained silent.

"And then there's Uncle Wilfre," Tas continued thoughtfully, "but no one's seen him in, oh, well . . . I guess I've never seen him, actually." He took another pull on his ale before continuing.

"My favorite uncle, though, is my mother's brother—I

think," Tas said, happily remembering. "He's a Furrfoot, not a Burrfoot, which is very confusing at family picnics, as you might guess. Anyway, Uncle Trapspringer moved in with my family after his bride died on their honeymoon. At least he assumed she was dead."

"What do you mean, 'assumed'?" Tanis exclaimed. "That sounds tragic."

"Oh, it's all very romantic, the way Uncle Trapspringer tells it," Tas began, holding up his mug for a refill. The kender was obviously gearing up for one of his long stories.

"The short version, if you please," Flint warned him. "I don't want to be sitting here, listening to your tale, when the others return five years from now."

Tasslehoff rolled his eyes. "Very funny, Flint. I've never told you a five-year story. Not that I don't know a few. . . .

"Now," he continued as if uninterrupted, "Uncle Trapspringer and his bride decided they didn't want to go just any old place for their honeymoon, so that's exactly where they went. Or tried to, anyway."

As usual, Tas was proving obtuse. "Where *did* they go?" Flint asked, feigning patience. He was sorry almost the second the words left his mouth.

Tas looked exasperated. "Really, Flint, you're not listening. Where else would you go on your honeymoon but the *moon*, of course? That's the point!"

Tanis's eyes narrowed. "They went to the moon?"

"No," Tas corrected him, "but they sure tried to. They bought a magical potion at the Spring Faire in Kendermore. They both drank half, closed their eyes, and thought about the moon, just like the salesman told them to. But when Uncle Trapspringer opened his eyes, he was still at the faire and his bride was gone! Her wedding dress was in a heap next to him on the ground." Tas's eyes misted over. "Golly, that story always makes me sad. Do you suppose he just didn't think about the moon hard enough?"

"He didn't think hard enough all right, but not about the moon," snorted Flint as he shook a handful of wood shavings from his beard. "She probably knew what she was getting into and ran off while his eyes were closed, before it was too late. Surprising insight, for a kender."

"Uncle Trapspringer says she must be dead," Tas said, "because if she weren't she would have found a way back to him by now. But I think she's on Lunitari right this minute. I bet she's awfully lonely. I wonder what we look like from up there?"

"At least she won't be going hungry," said Flint. "Everyone knows that the moon is made of red cheese!" He forced the smile from his twitching face.

"I'm not so sure," Tas said soberly. "I don't know what Lunitari is made of, but red cheese is most unlikely. Red something, I'll wager, but nothing so mundane or squishy as cheese—"

Flint burst into a loud guffaw.

Tas's monologue was cut short when the heavy, oak door at the entrance to the inn blew open and slammed against the wall with a bang, sending early autumn leaves swirling through the taproom. Through the doorway stepped the most unusually vivid creature any of the three companions had ever seen. The woman, a dwarf judging by the squatty proportions of her body, was incredibly voluptuous by that same standard. A silky, raspberry-colored blouse that gathered at the wrists was stretched tight across her sizable bosom, straining the criss-crossed front laces. Below it, a canary yellow braided leather belt cinched in her waspish waist. Her pants, made of skin-tight purple leather, were tucked into leather boots that matched perfectly the color of her blouse. Her lips and cheeks glowed with the same impossibly brilliant, unnatural shade of pomegranate as her long, wavy hair. Perched upon it at a jaunty angle was a small, plumed purple and yellow hat.

"At last, we're here," she sighed contentedly, looking around the inn. Hands on her hips, she struck an imperious pose that made her appear taller than she was. The inn fell silent. Even the pans in the kitchen stopped rattling. "Woodrow, come in here!" she called as an afterthought over her shoulder.

"Yes, ma'am," croaked a nervous voice. A young man stepped from behind her, carefully squeezing around her bulk so as not to intrude on her magnificence. His sun-bleached hair looked like straw that had been cut with a bowl around his head. His nose was hawkish and strong, as was his tall, sinewy frame. He was dressed, oddly, in gray, quilted cotton pants and a long-sleeved, padded shirt of a type commonly worn as protection under chain mail. His pants, obviously past their prime, were torn at the seams and faded. The young man's wrists dangled more than an inch below the cuffs.

"Do stop calling me ma'am," she chided him good-naturedly. "You make me feel so *old*. And let me assure you," she continued, giving him a seductive wink, "I'm not *that* old yet!"

The young man named Woodrow blushed furiously. "Yes, ma'am," he gulped.

She looked at him for a long moment and touched his cheek briefly. "So young . . . but I like them young. . . ." She looked away abruptly and peered into the depths of the inn, spotting Otik behind the bar in his apron.

"Yoo-hoo!" she called, fluttering her hands in his direction. His eyes transfixed, Otik scurried to her side. "A man so important-looking and dignified as you must be the barkeep," she purred.

Otik's stout body jiggled to a stop, and he grinned like a lovesick fool. "Uh, yes, I guess I am. Can I be of some assistance? A room, perhaps? Dinner? Our food is the best in Solace—all of southern Ansalon!" he blathered.

"I'm sure it is," she said smoothly, "but perhaps later. Actually, I'm looking for someone. A kender named Tasslehoff Burrfoot. I was told I might find him here."

The three companions had been watching the whole display. At the sound of his name, Tasslehoff jumped excitedly to his feet and raced up to her. "That's me! I'm Tasslehoff Burrfoot! Did I win something? Are you here to give me my prize?" He paused for a new thought. "Or did I lose something? Did you lose something?"

"You could say that," the voluptuous dwarf said, running her gaze over his childlike form. "Can't say I understand what all the fuss is about," she muttered mysteriously, then latched her surprisingly strong fingers around his bony wrist.

"You'll have to come with me now, and I'm in a bit of a hurry," she said, stepping toward the door. Not quite sure what was happening, Tasslehoff draped behind her like dead weight. He dug his heels into the floor. "Well, come along," she chided, "I haven't got all year." With that she tugged him toward the door.

"Wait a minute!" he blurted. "Who are you? Where are you trying to take me? You're not at all polite." The dwarf's outburst brought Tanis and Flint to their feet, and they began making their way to Tas's side.

The stranger seemed to recollect something. "Oops, sorry. I forgot that part." She adopted an officious tone. "Tasslehoff Burrfoot, you're under arrest for violating section thirty-one-nineteen, code forty-seven, paragraph ten, sub-paragraph something or other, of the Kender Code of Conduct." She gave Tasslehoff's wrist a sharp yank, leaning toward the door.

"That certainly sounds serious," Tas agreed grimly, keeping his heels planted. "What does it mean?"

"It means you broke your marriage oath. You're in big trouble, Burrhead."

PART I

Chapter 1

"*Oh, that!*" *exclaimed Tas, dismissing concern* with a wave of his hand. "I forgot all about it."

"Obviously. However, the Kendermore Council didn't. Now, stop stalling!" the brightly clad dwarf complained, giving the kender's wrist another sharp tug. Tas dug the fingers of his free hand into the edge of a heavy table and refused to budge.

The red-haired dwarf stopped and turned around to face him. "I don't want to do this, but you're really giving me no choice. Woodrow, pick him up and carry him." But the blond young man took only one step before Tanis's voice halted him.

"I wouldn't if I were you, boy." Stepping forward with his fists clenched before him, the powerfully muscled half-elf looked as if he outweighed Woodrow by at least fifty pounds. Standing next to Tanis, Flint's face was grim and his hand rested reflexively on the hammer that always hung at his thick waist.

"What's this all about, Tas?" Tanis asked in his sternest voice.

"I'd like the answer to that as well," Otik demanded, focusing his irritation at the kender. "You're disturbing the peace of my inn." He looked at his kitchen staff, including his daughter Tika, all of whom had gathered around the bar to see what was happening.

Tas stopped his struggling. "I think this lady wants me to go back to Kendermore and get married," he said, avoiding his friends' eyes.

"To her?" Flint asked, his brows raised in amazement.

"Don't be insulting!" the female dwarf cried, drawing back.

"Of course not, Flint," Tas sniffed. "She's not even a kender."

"Look," Tanis said impatiently. "Would somebody tell us what's going on?" He gazed directly at the unusually vivid-looking dwarf. "Who are you, and what's the real reason you want Tasslehoff?"

The woman regarded Tanis's handsome face with interest. Suddenly she thrust out her hand, palm down, and said sweetly, "My name is Gisella Hornslager. Yours?"

"Tanis Half-Elven," he responded, awkwardly returning the woman's crushing handshake.

Gisella withdrew her hand. "As I was saying, Buzzfoot is under arrest for breaking a marriage oath according to some kender law or another," she said vaguely. "Now, as much as I'd like to stay and chat," she continued, letting her gaze wander down Tanis's lean form, a smirk on her lips, "I really must be going. Schedules to keep, places to be, you know how it is."

Flint, who had been quite obviously staring at the woman since her arrival, gulped in surprise. "You're a bounty hunter?"

"Oh, not specifically," she said, spinning on her heel. "I'm in the import-export business; my motto is 'You want it, I got it.' The Kendermore Council asked me to do this job, and I thought 'fabric, a kender—what's the difference as long as it's portable?' "

She lifted her broad, raspberry-colored shoulders in a weary shrug. "Now, I don't mean to be rude, but I really must be going. I've got two bags of rare merganser melon out in my wagon getting riper and costing me more money every second I delay. Kendermore's Autumn Harvest Faire opens in a little more than a month, and that load is worth a half-year's profits to me there. Woodrow?"

The young man stepped forward obediently and wrapped his strong arms around the wriggling kender. "Sorry, little fella," he mumbled.

Tanis stopped Woodrow again, this time with a hand on his arm. The kender slid to his feet once more, twisting his vest back into place with a disgruntled "humph!"

Gisella pulled Tanis to the side, batting two small, kohl black-lined eyes at him. "Look, friend, if it's money you want, I'll give you half of my take for him. Fifteen new steel pieces," she said, biting into each word as though she enjoyed their taste.

"You've got to be kidding!" Tanis sputtered, unable to comprehend that someone was trying to *buy* Tasslehoff from him.

"That's more than fair!" She dropped her voice abruptly. "OK, twenty, but that's my final offer."

"My good woman," Tanis growled, his eyes flashing black, "you cannot buy and sell a kender like horseflesh!"

"You can't? Why not?" she asked, genuinely surprised.

"Because some things just aren't for sale!"

"Honey," she purred, letting her tightly clothed thigh rub against his for a moment, "everything has a price."

Tanis jerked his leg away and took a deep breath,

throwing a withering look at Flint, who was jiggling with silent laughter. Groping for a new approach, Tanis suggested, "Let's ask Tas what he wants to do."

Everyone turned toward the kender. "Well, Tas?" Tanis asked. "What's this about getting married, anyway? You never even told us you had a sweetheart."

Tasslehoff shuffled uncomfortably. "I don't, exactly," he confessed. "See, a long time ago, somebody suddenly noticed that there weren't many kender left in Kendermore—people just never got around to getting married. So some other somebody came up with the idea of randomly assigning mates at birth. You know, a boy and a girl are born near each other timewise in the city, and they have to get married sometime near their thirty-fifth birthdays. It's one of the few rules that any kender can remember. Except me. I just forgot it."

"So there's a girl waiting in Kendermore for you to marry her?" Flint asked, struggling to keep the smile he felt growing inside him from showing on his face.

"I guess," Tas said morosely. "I've never met her. I think her name begins with a 'D,' or at least it sounds like 'D.' Dorcas . . . Dipilfis . . . Gimrod . . . Something like that."

Flint could contain himself no longer; he burst out laughing. "I'd like to see the look on her face when she sees what she's getting! Ha!"

"Tas," Tanis said kindly, looking into the kender's crestfallen face, "do you want to marry this girl?"

Tas pursed his lips in thought, watching leaves swirl in Tika's wake as she marched by with a tray of drinks. "I've never thought about it, really. I always figured I'd get married someday . . . someday later . . . much later."

"If you don't want to marry her, the honorable thing to do is to go back and tell her so," Tanis suggested reasonably. "Or send a message through Miss Hornslager here. I'm sure the girl will understand."

Tas brightened slightly. "I suppose I could do that."

"Well, let me just tell you that *Miss Hornslager* won't

understand," Gisella grumbled. "I get paid for delivering a kender, not a message. Bundle him up, Woodrow," she instructed abruptly.

"You don't need to treat me like a sack of potatoes," Tas pointed out, his face dark.

"I don't know," Flint said mischievously, a twinkle in his eye. He was enjoying Tas's discomfort immensely. "I'd keep my eyes on him every minute. He may intend to return with you today, but a butterfly might cross his path tomorrow, and off he'll go."

Gisella looked directly at Tas and clicked her tongue. "Any old time you think about wandering off, just remember this: The council is holding your Uncle Trapspringer prisoner until you return. They want you back real bad."

"Prisoner? Poor Uncle Trapspringer!" Tas cried. Suddenly his eyes narrowed suspiciously. "Wait a minute, how do I know they really have my Uncle Trapspringer?"

Gisella's cheeks colored for the first time. She scratched the back of her neck, looking uncomfortable. "Well, it wasn't my idea, but they told me to show you something if you gave me any trouble." She pulled a tiny pouch from the depths of her blouse and tugged open the strings. Wrinkling her nose, she held up a two-inch, jointed piece of polished white bone. "Here's his finger!"

Tas peered at the fragment closely. "Yep, that's Uncle Trapspringer's favorite one," he said, unperturbed. "I'd recognize it anywhere."

Tanis's face wrinkled in horror. "They cut off your uncle's finger? But why would they do that over such a small matter?"

"I thought it was unusually nasty, myself," Gisella agreed, dropping the bone back into the pouch.

Tasslehoff's expression turned from confusion to sudden amusement. "You thought this was one of *his* fingers? Oh, that's funny!"

"Well, that's what you said it was, you doorknob," Flint growled, shuffling his feet angrily. Tanis looked merely bewildered.

"Oh, that's *really* funny!" Tasslehoff shrieked. He clutched his stomach and doubled over with high-pitched laughter, oblivious to the irritation of his friends. "Uncle Trapspringer collects bones," he gulped—"of animals and such," he managed to gasp at last. "That's the one he carries for good luck!"

"Obviously it's not working," observed Gisella dryly, tucking the purse back into her blouse.

Tanis sighed heavily. "I should have known better than to try helping you out of a jam, Tas. I give up; you're on your own." The half-elf shook Tas's small hand and backed out the door. "Good luck, friend. See you in five years."

Chuckling aloud, Flint stepped after the young half-elf. "Have a nice wedding, Tas!" he said, clapping the kender affectionately on the shoulder as he passed him.

"Wait!" Tas called. "Of course I'm terribly concerned about Uncle Trapspringer—" But his friends were already gone. Tasslehoff took a step after them, but Gisella and Woodrow blocked his way. Feeling just the tiniest bit forlorn, he chewed his lip and looked expectantly at the red-haired dwarf.

Gisella Hornslager arched her eyebrows in a hopeful gesture. "Well, that's that, hmm? Those melons aren't getting any greener."

Tasslehoff hesitated.

Just then, Otik emerged from the kitchen, carrying a parchment sack. "I, uh, just wanted you to have something to remember your trip to Solace," he said shyly, placing the sack in the dwarf's outstretched hands. Then he wiped his own greasy ones on the front of his apron.

Gisella flashed the tubby barkeep a brilliant smile. "You wonderful, thoughtful little man!" she cooed, planting a red-lipped kiss on his plump, blushing cheek. Behind him, Tika crossed her arms in disgust, a baleful glare on her young face.

"Well, Burrfoot, are you going to come with us easily,"

Gisella began, her arms crossed in challenge, "or is Woodrow going to have to carry you?"

Tasslehoff thought about his uncle locked up somewhere because of him, and he realized there was no choice to be made. "I'll go easily," he said. "Just let me get my things."

"Fine. Ta-ta!" Gisella called grandly to Otik, sweeping out through the open door. Under Woodrow's watchful eye, Tas hurried back to the table he'd shared with his friends and snatched up his hoopak, the fork-shaped, slinglike weapon no kender would be without. Waving good-bye to the preening Otik and scowling Tika, Tas followed Gisella down the bridgewalk that spiraled around the trunk of the inn's supporting vallenwood tree.

"Wow, what a wagon!" Tas breathed, catching sight of a large, enclosed, wooden wagon hitched at the base of the tree. The roof was arched instead of flat, showing intricate carving and workmanship. Even the wheels looked expensive: thick, with wrought iron spokes. Painted on the side in bright red were the words: "Mr. Hornslager's Hypermarket: You Want It, I Got It."

"Where's Mr. H?" Tas asked.

Gisella smiled broadly and slapped her thigh. "Right here, Bramblefoot. It's good for business if people think I'm a Mrs. They just assume I'm Mrs. H. It makes the poor saps think they got a better deal by bamboozling the owner's silly wife." Gisella widened her eyes and raised her voice an octave or two. "Oh," she mimicked, "I couldn't sell it for that! We paid more than that! Well, if you really like it . . . it looks so nice on you. But please don't tell my husband!"

Tas giggled helplessly. He raced down the remainder of the bridgewalk and skidded to a halt before the wagon. "I can't wait to see the inside! You collect stuff from all over the place, right? Gems and steel pieces and candy—"

She laughed. "No, that's what I get when I sell my

goods. Right now I have some spices, a few bolts of fabric, and some melons growing riper by the minute."

The dwarf hurried up to the buckboard and rummaged through a large leather pouch at the side. "Now, where is that thing . . . ," she muttered, pushing a loose sheaf of papers around impatiently. "Woodrow!" she yelled without looking up.

"Yes, ma'am?" he said quietly at her side.

"Oh!" she cried, startled. "Don't creep around like that, dear," she scolded. "Get the kender settled in the wagon while I find that blasted map. I've got to see if I can't shave some time off the return trip, or we may as well throw some of this stuff out right now."

Tas's ears perked up. "Map? You're looking for a map? I've got lots of maps. My family makes maps." He thumped his chest proudly. "I'm a mapmaker. It's what I do!"

"Really?" Gisella asked, looking up, her face half hopeful, half dubious.

"Yes. Here." He reached into his fur-trimmed vest and pulled out a surprising number of rolled pieces of parchment.

Peering closely at the numbers and shapes scribbled on the upper left corner of each, he finally selected one and unfurled it on the ground. It was slightly faded and the corners were torn, but otherwise the map was in good shape and readable. "That's odd," Tas said, blinking at the page. "Solace isn't on here. Well, it's a small village, and everyone knows where it is," he concluded. "It's just west of Xak Tsaroth, which *is* marked. He traced his finger from that city to where he knew Solace was.

"Now, I'll bet you came up the Southway Road from Pax Tharkas, right? Everyone does." Gisella nodded, studying the map over his shoulder.

"Look at this." Tasslehoff drew an invisible line to the right edge of the map. "The region of Balifor is almost seven hundred miles straight east of here, and that's right next to the city of Kendermore. We'll have to climb a few mountains and travel through some thick forests, but we should save a lot of time over going the long way to the south." He did some quick figuring in his head. "If we really hurry, we should be able to make it to the city in near to a month."

Something about the plan bothered Gisella. "Let me see that," she said, indicating the map, her expression puzzled. "I know what's different! I don't see any of the landmarks here that were on my other map."

"Was it made by a kender?" Tas asked. She shook her head. "Well, that's it, then," Tas said definitively. "Kender often use their own sorts of landmarks, symbols, and elaborate measurements."

"Like 'Uncle Bertie's foot'?" she asked, pointing to words toward the top of the page. "And what's this one?" Her eyes were left of center. " 'Where I found the pretty stones'; 'shop with great candy'; 'monsters with big teeth here'." She looked up at Tas. "These are important landmarks?"

Tas shrugged. "They were to Uncle Bertie."

"I don't know, Tasslefoot," Gisella said slowly, still looking closely at the sheet. "I don't recognize the names of very many cities on this map."

"All the major cities are here—Xak Tsaroth, Thorbardin, Neraka. You name it!" Tas said, stomping his foot in frustration at her reluctance. "Your map must not have been as detailed as mine," he sniffed, then had a thought. "Do you want to get to Kendermore before your melons rot or not?"

Gisella frowned. "Of course I do."

"Then leave everything to me," the kender said grandly, rolling up the parchment and slipping it back into his vest. "If there's one thing I'm good at, it's getting to where I'm going." With that, he climbed expectantly onto the buckboard. Gisella excused herself and slipped for a moment into the back of the wagon, giving Woodrow last-minute instructions to quickly finish feeding the horses.

Woodrow's straw-blond head bobbed absently ahead of the wagon, where he stood feeding the two horses, one dirty-white, the other dove-colored. He stroked their thick necks softly as they nibbled their dinners. The young man didn't know much about kender, but the one thing he had learned from the few he'd met was that it was a rare kender who knew where he was going in the first place. Woodrow didn't contradict Tasslehoff's claims, though; he was in no hurry to get anywhere.

Chapter 2

"Now remember, keep those beeswax plugs in your ears for two weeks, and when you take them out you'll be able to hear much better."

The kender, a sawyer named Semus, cocked his head to the side and looked at Phineas Curick with a puzzled expression, then tapped his ear with his hoopak. Phineas placed his mouth next to the kender's ear and shouted, "Keep them in for two weeks!" Semus smiled.

"Thanks, Dr. Ears," he shouted. "Can you hear me OK?"

"Fine, fine," said Phineas, ushering the beaming kender out of the chair and steering him back through the waiting room. "That'll be ten copper," the doctor said, holding his hand out for payment.

The kender patted his pockets, then reached in and pulled out a fistful of sticky candy. "I seem to be a little short today. Could you maybe use some scrap wood? You could fix up this dump real nice, add a few more shelves, you know—"

"No, thank you," Phineas said, snatching the plugs from the startled kender's ears and booting him out of the door into the cobbled street. The balding, middle-aged human dusted off his hands, scratched his red-veined nose, and turned to the waiting throng. Ten kender were seated on the long wooden bench that ran along the north wall of the office.

For a year and a half Phineas Curick had been practicing his peculiar brand of medicine in Kendermore. And if he lived to be one hundred years of age, he thought, he would never understand kender. Day after day they crowded into his front office with their aches and pains and imaginary ills, and day after day he dispensed sugar pills, beeswax, curdled milk, and mustard to his faithful patients. The only real medical procedure he knew was pulling teeth, and there was some call for that, too.

To kender with toothaches he was Dr. Teeth. To those with ear problems, Dr. Ears. If someone's joints hurt, Dr. Bones. No ailment was too acute or too minor.

"Who's next?" All ten of the seated kender jumped to their feet—or tried to. Only one stood up and strolled confidently into the examination room. The other nine flew to the floor, arms and legs akimbo, shoelaces mysteriously tied to their chairs. Phineas had seen many things in his kender-filled waiting room. Most of his patients with genuine ailments received them in his office. Fights broke out regularly— he made a lot of money off those, removing broken teeth and plugging bloody noses—but he admired this particular kender's ingenuity.

Stepping gingerly through the thrashing, flopping bodies and dodging their famous kender taunts, Phineas followed his next patient into the examination room.

Washing his hands in a stoneware pitcher of cool, murky water, he smiled at his patient. "Just hop up in that chair," he invited. "What can I do for you today? Teeth, ears—a haircut, maybe?"

"I have those, yes, and I could use a haircut," replied the kender—a young one, judging from the deep brown color of his hair and wrinkle-free skin. "But it's my eyes. When I step into bright sunlight, I can't see anything, and when I step out of the sunlight and back into the shade, I can't see either."

"This is a problem?" the doctor asked, readying some large calipers, pliers, and an ice tong on a wooden tray next to the chair.

The kender glanced uneasily at the tools arrayed on the tray. "That's a bit of a problem, as I'm the doorman at the Kendermore Inn. What are you going to use that for?" he asked, fidgeting into the farthest corner of the chair.

"Don't worry," Phineas said, opening the ice tongs and placing a point against each of the kender's temples. "I just have to take a measurement." He closed the tongs slowly against the patient's head, then sighted carefully along both temples, with a "hrrmmm" and a "hummm.

"There!" he announced. Careful not to jiggle the open tongs, he held them up to a row of wire eyeglasses on the wall behind him. "Here we are," he said, satisfied at last that he'd found the right fit. He placed the spectacles on the tray, then turned away again and rummaged through one of many drawers in a large wall cabinet. He removed two rectangles of dark, oiled parchment and slipped them into the spectacles where the lenses should be. Finally, he set them on the bridge of the kender's nose and hooked the horns around his ears.

"You must wear these spectacles for two weeks, and when you take them off you'll be able to see much better."

"But I can't see at all, Dr. Eyes," the kender protested, struggling to find the arms of the chair so that he could climb down.

"If you could see, you wouldn't have come to me," Phineas noted patiently.

The kender's face brightened under the dark glasses. "That's true! Oh, thank you, Dr. Eyes!" Arms held before him, the kender bumped into the doorjamb, then banged into a hanging skeleton on the way out of the examining room, sending bones rattling. Phineas guided him to the front door.

"Just doing my job," the doctor said modestly. "That'll be twenty copper." It was a bit steep for parchment spectacles, but he had to make up for lost revenue from the sawmill worker.

"I'm afraid I can't see very well," the kender apologized. "Could you?" He held open the pouch dangling from his belt by a string.

Phineas helped himself to twenty-three copper pieces and two of his own pliers. "Thank you, do come again."

Only two of the previous nine patients were still in the waiting room, the rest having apparently wandered off after untangling their shoelaces. Or perhaps they all trooped out in one big knot, mused Phineas. One of the two patients was a young woman whose fingers had somehow got caught in opposite ends of a hollow stick and a construction worker who had nailed his own pant leg to a board. Eyeing the reflection of the setting sun in the shop windows across the street, Phineas decided to call it a day.

Ushering out the unhappy kender, he advised the two of them to try again tomorrow. Locking the door behind them, he extinguished the one source of light in the room, a small, dim oil lantern with a greasy, black mantle.

Phineas Curick commended his good fortune as he cleaned his tools in the examination room at the back of his "Doctor's Office." Kender were such wonderful patients, even for someone who wasn't a doctor! And while he seldom cured anyone outright, he assuaged his guilt with the knowledge that he provided a great psychological balm to people in distress. And that should be worth something, shouldn't it?

"Ten copper pieces per examination!" he chortled happily under his breath.

Hearing a noise in the outer waiting room, he wiped his hands on his spattered apron and called out in irritation, "I'm closed, didn't you see the sign?" There was no telling what might be going on, since even locking the front door was no guarantee against a kender just strolling into the office. "You'll have to come back tomorrow."

Many moments passed, and he heard no response. Puzzled, Phineas stepped into the shadows of the waiting room.

"Hello!" said a deep voice in the darkness.

Startled, Phineas fell back against the wall, setting up a chorus of rattling glass bottles. "Who are you," he demanded, "and what do you want? You scared the wits out of me!"

"Trapspringer Furrfoot. Pleased to meet you." Phineas felt a small hand shake his. "My friends call me Trapspringer. I'm truly sorry I frightened you; humans are such a jumpy bunch, but I guess you can't help what you are. Did you know your door is stuck?"

Phineas strained his eyes in the darkness to discern his visitor. "It's not stuck; it was locked," he said sternly, having composed himself. "And you're supposed to be on the other side of it. You'll have to come back tomorrow."

"Could you light a candle or something?" asked the

kender. "I can't see a thing!"

"Didn't you hear me? I said the office is closed."

"I heard you, but I was certain you didn't mean me, since this is a matter of life and death!"

Phineas sighed; emergencies like these came up daily in Kendermore. "What is it this time?" he asked wearily.

"I've just lost my finger and—"

Phineas's eyes went wide with alarm. "Good gods, man, why didn't you say so?" Phineas didn't know much about medicine, but he knew that a kender bleeding to death in his office would be bad for business. Groping for the kender's shoulders in the darkness, he ushered him into the candlelit examining room. "Get up in that chair and hold your hand above your head!" he ordered, collecting a large roll of white cloth strips he used for bandages.

"This is awfully nice of you," Trapspringer said.

With the roll of bandages under his arm and clean water sloshing from a bowl in his hand, Phineas turned to the kender, expecting to be greeted by a fountain of blood.

Trapspringer Furrfoot sat in the chair, his hand—with all five digits—held high above his head, as instructed. There was not a drop of blood on him.

"All right, get out of here," Phineas growled, grabbing Trapspringer by the scruff of the neck. "I'm not in the mood for practical jokes."

Genuinely surprised, the kender twisted out of the human's grasp. "I wasn't joking. I lost my finger. It was from a minotaur, or maybe a werewolf; they're hard to tell apart. I collect interesting bones, and this was my lucky one, a beautiful, polished white joint—it looked just like alabaster. Actually, I didn't lose it. The Kendermore Council borrowed it, but that's another story entirely and part of the reason I can't come back tomorrow. So can you help me? It's really very important, and I'm certain my life is probably in danger."

Totally bewildered, Phineas stared at the kender for a long time. This Trapspringer Furrfoot looked very cosmopolitan for a kender. Phineas judged him to be late middle-aged, from the advanced network of lines on his face, the gray streaks in his copper-red, feather-studded topknot of hair, and his deepish voice. He wore a very expensive, flowing cape of purple velvet, so dark it looked black, with leggings of the same, unusual color. His tunic was pea green, and a wide, black leather belt hid the beginnings of a paunch. Around his neck hung a necklace of small, gray-white bones— from what, Phineas did not wish to contemplate. Trapspringer's red-and-gray-streaked eyebrows twitched in curiosity above his almond-shaped, olive-colored eyes.

"Well?" Trapspringer said expectantly, tapping a toe. "Will you help me or not?"

Phineas was still confused. "You want me to get this bone back from the council?" he asked stupidly.

"Oh, no, that wouldn't be possible," the kender said firmly. "What I really need is another minotaur finger bone."

Phineas rubbed his face wearily and plopped down on his padded stool. He'd lived around kender long enough to know there was going to be no easy way out of this conversation. "You want me to give you a mino-taur bone," he repeated dully.

"From a finger. I would be most grateful," Trapspringer said, holding out his hand expectantly. "You see, my old one was my good luck charm, and I'm certain something dreadful will happen to me unless I replace it soon."

"You're afraid you'll die without it?" Phineas asked.

"Perhaps, though that's not the most dreadful thing that could happen. Actually, it might be interesting, depending on how you, you know, died. Getting run over by a farmer's cart wouldn't be nearly as fascinating as, say, falling off a cliff into the mouth of a lion who's on fire. Now *that* would be interesting!" His eyes glowed at the concept. "Just the same, I don't want to take any chances."

Phineas gave the eccentric kender an odd look. "But I'm not an animal doctor, or even an apothecary. What makes you think I'd have such a thing?"

"Well, to be honest, you weren't my first choice. I couldn't find anything that looked like my bone in those places—" he pulled a wad of string, four pointy teeth, and a small vial with blue liquid from inside his cape—"though I found some other things I've been needing. But there was no one around to ask about bones."

"Won't any of the bones around your neck do?" Phineas asked, suppressing a shudder.

"If they were finger bones, sure," Trapspringer said irritably, "but they obviously aren't."

Now that he knew what the kender wanted, Phineas regained his composure and opened a cupboard. He removed a flat-edged wooden tray carefully, so as not to dump its contents of numerous thin, white bones. He picked up the largest of the bones and cupped it tenderly in his hand.

"Well, this must be your lucky day, Mr. Trapspringer. I just happen to use minotaur finger bones in the preparation of one of my most potent and expensive health elixirs. In fact, I have here the finger bone of a minotaur that was also a werewolf, one of the rarest and most exotic creatures in the world. Lycanthropy is a strange thing. There are those who say it can't affect creatures like minotaurs, but right here we have the proof. Quite an indispensible item. Being a collector yourself, you must know that such a bone as this is very valuable. But, if it means so much to you—saving your life and all—I'd be willing to part with it. I ask only that you reimburse me for my cost." He held the bone up for Trapspringer's inspection and sucked in his breath.

"It's marvelous!" Trapspringer cried, elated. He picked up the bone gingerly and cradled it in his palm. "I couldn't possibly pay you what this is worth," he lamented. "But I would gladly give you my most valuable possession in trade!" The kender reached into the depths of his cape.

Phineas's eyes lit up with greed as he watched Trapspringer's hand create waves in the rich velvet of his cape. When the kender's hand emerged, he pressed a folded, old parchment sheet into the doctor's outstretched palms. A bank note! What else could it be? Phineas nearly leaped out of his skin with excitement. At last he had met up with a rich kender! He forced himself to not appear too anxious or gauche.

"Thank you. You are most kind," Phineas said, pocketing the note. "If I can ever be of service again . . ."

"Yes, I'll remember," the kender assured him, stepping back into the dim waiting room, happily holding his "minotaur" bone. "Well, I really must be getting back to the prison now. It's not a prison, really. It's actually very nice, if you like overstuffed chairs and floral prints. I don't want to be gone too long or they'll worry over me. If I can ever be of any help to you, just ask. I'm a close personal friend of the mayor's, you know. My nephew is going to marry his daughter. Ta-ta!" With that, the kender slipped through the darkness and out the front door.

Phineas stood, stunned and slack-jawed, staring after Trapspringer Furrfoot for several moments. He'd been had! But by the time he could react, he knew it would be too late to catch the kender. Furrfoot was obviously an old eccentric who had escaped from the city jail. Bank note, indeed! Marrying the mayor's daughter, bahh! Strangely, Phineas wasn't very annoyed at Trapspringer for having tricked him. In a way, he admired the kender's ability to get what he wanted, just like he had admired the kender who'd tied everyone's shoelaces to the bench.

With a shrug, Phineas blew out the candles and headed for the stairs at the back of his shop that led to his quarters above. On the way back, he took the worthless "bank note" from his pocket and tossed it on his tool tray without looking. He'd throw it out in the morning, along with the remaining rat skeleton he'd "sold" as minotaur bones to the kender a few minutes before. Phineas had found the dried rodent husk, long dead, in his medicine cupboard. He'd swept it into his wooden dustpan and had been meaning all week to throw it out. But when Trapspringer had begged for the finger bone of a minotaur, Phineas, ever the con man, remembered the rat bones and thought the ploy worth a try.

And Trapspringer had fallen for it!

Phineas smiled. Trapspringer Furrfoot was quite the shyster, but he wasn't the only one who'd be laughing tonight.

Mr. Hornslager's
Hypermarket
You Want It ~ I Got It

Chapter 3

A light rain began falling at dusk as Tasslehoff, Gisella, and Woodrow rode due east of Solace. The forest surrounding the village quickly gave way to the foothills of the Sentinel Peaks. The wagon traveled steadily uphill past low scrub pines and aspen, the air scented with wet worms and bitter-sweet wild chrysanthemums. The road ran through a narrow valley between two spurs of the mountains, but it was clear and relatively rut-free. The horses plodded amiably, away from the setting sun.

Seated between Tasslehoff and Woodrow on the buckboard, reins in one hand, Gisella mopped her damp brow with a vivid, orange silk scarf.

"Gods, it's warm," she sighed. "That rain helps,

though. Shouldn't be so warm this time of year." Rain-drops gathered in shimmering pools on her unusually red hair and ran through it in wavy streams.

"It's a bad omen, I think," said Woodrow, voicing the first opinion either the kender or the dwarf had heard from him. His almost-white hair clung to his head in wet, arrow-straight clumps. He pushed his bangs aside, sending drops of water flying in a shower.

"A bad omen?" asked Tas, whose braided topknot of hair looked the same wet as dry. Looking up at the fall-ing rain, he tucked his parchment map into his vest to keep it dry. "What do you mean, exactly?"

"When it's this hot in late autumn," Woodrow be-gan, "we're in for a harsh winter."

"That's a trend or a cycle, not an omen," Gisella commented. "I don't believe in omens and supersti-tions."

"You don't?" said Woodrow, looking at the dwarf with an odd combination of disbelief and pity. "You mean you would actually walk past a nesting bird dur-ing a full moon? Or drink ale from a chipped flagon? Or . . . or even use a candle that had been lit in the presence of a dead body?"

"I don't take any pains not to," said Gisella. "What's supposed to happen when I do those things?"

"Oh, terrible things *will* happen!" Woodrow gasped. "If you walk past a nesting bird during a full moon, all of your children will be hatched from eggs. Drinking ale from a chipped vessel means you will be robbed before the day ends." Woodrow nibbled at his nails nervously.

"But worst of all, whoever lights a candle that was used in the presence of a dead body after the body's been buried or burned will be visited by the spirit of the dead person." Woodrow's young face grew even paler. "Sometimes, if the soul is newly dead, it will take over the body of the living person!"

"That's ridiculous!" Gisella snorted indelicately.

The horses were having a difficult time avoiding ruts in the growing darkness; she gave the reins an impatient tug.

"It's the gods' own truth, ma'am," Woodrow vowed solemnly.

"I don't believe in any such things, including the gods," Gisella mumbled under her breath. "Tell me, Woodrow," she said more loudly, "have you witnessed any of these curses yourself?"

"Of course not, ma'am," he said, suppressing a chill. "I've been very careful to avoid those things."

"It would be interesting to hatch from an egg, if you could remember it, don't you think?" remarked Tas. But then he frowned. "I shouldn't like to be robbed, though. But I wouldn't mind talking to a spirit. Maybe it would tell you where its jewels and things were, since it wouldn't need them anymore. At the very least, it could tell you what it felt like to be dead—whether you're happy or sad all the time, or what."

"No spirit is ever going to talk to you, Burrfoot," Gisella laughed. "At least not while I'm available as the preferred party."

"You shouldn't joke about such things, ma'am," Woodrow said softly. "Spirits don't like that."

"And I don't like this discussion," the dwarf said uncomfortably. She held a hand out, palm up. "I think the rain is beginning to let up. But it's getting too dark for travel." She steered the horses off the road to the right and jumped from the buckboard. Taking the horses by the bridles, she led them away from the road to a clearing that was partially screened by a high hedge of red-leafed bushes.

"Feed the horses, will you, Woodrow?" she instructed, walking past them to the back of the wagon. "And keep an eye on Burrfoot. I'm going to find someplace to take a bath." The front of the wagon pitched up suddenly as Gisella stepped inside.

Dutifully, Woodrow slid from the wagon and unharnessed the horses. Pulling a burlap bag of dry grain from under the seat, he crooned softly to the animals and petted their silky noses. They nuzzled his hands affectionately. Setting the bag on the ground, he dipped both hands into it and pulled out two fistfuls of grain. The horses nibbled eagerly from his open palms.

When each had finished a handful of grain, Woodrow said, "I've got other chores that need tending, my friends." He set out enough grain for the horses' dinner and called, "Enjoy your food. I'll bring you some water later." Both whinnied contentedly.

Tas had been watching Woodrow unabashedly the entire time. "They really seem to like you," the kender said admiringly.

Woodrow shrugged, but there was pride in his smile. "I've grown fond of them, too, in the few weeks I've been Miss Hornslager's hired hand." He peered around the campsite. "Help me find some big rocks to block the wagon wheels with, would you?" He strolled back toward the road, eyes scanning the ground, and Tas scurried after him, trying to help.

"Can you speak with animals?" Tas grunted as he struggled to lift a rock almost as big as his torso. "My friend Raistlin can sometimes, when he casts a spell. It's funny, though; animals still don't seem to like him very much."

Woodrow shook his head. "I can't speak to them with words, no," he said. "I do seem to understand them—their feelings and such—except I have trouble with lizards and some birds." Wordlessly, the human lifted a small boulder from Tasslehoff's straining arms. "We don't need rocks quite this big. Why don't you gather some wood?" The young, wiry man strode over to the wagon and dropped the stone behind one of its rear wheels. "There, that one ought to do it," he said, kicking the stone into place. "This area is mostly level."

Using some smaller rocks, Woodrow made a large fire circle about six feet from the wagon. After completing the circle, he found the kender at the edge of the clearing, gathering handfuls of dry pine needles for starting a fire. Woodrow collected an armload of small sticks and dry branches.

"How did you learn to do that?" Tas asked him. "Understand animals, I mean."

"I dunno," said the young human, shrugging. "I just watch and listen. Always have. I think anyone can understand animals. Most people just never pay enough attention."

"Of course, Flint says I talk too much," Tasslehoff reflected pensively. "Maybe that's why I've never heard an animal talk."

"I guess," Woodrow said. "Anyway, I hope you can cook something. Miss Hornslager can't even boil water. I try, but . . ."

"Oh, I'm a great cook!" Tas proclaimed modestly. "Why, I can make rabbit gumbo and turnip dressing and even acorn pie!"

"I'm afraid we don't have any of those ingredients," Woodrow said sadly. "Miss Hornslager lives in the wagon year-round, so she travels light—just her possessions, and what she has for barter or as payment. I haven't seen her do a lot of trading in the few weeks I've been with her—at least not for goods." Woodrow blushed, remembering the lusty dwarf's advances.

But Tas didn't notice. "So what do we have on hand?"

"At the moment, we're down to one skinny chicken, a bag of dried beans, three bolts of fabric with gold threads, two crates of merganser melons that we don't dare touch, two live pug ferrets—which will stay that way," he warned through narrowed eyes, "and some odd spices, most of which have to be scraped off the floor of the wagon, though there are some in jars."

"That's not much to work with, but I think I can do something with the chicken and the beans," Tas replied.

Woodrow looked skeptical. "You'll find everything inside the wagon, in a cupboard toward the front. If it looks edible—except the ferrets and the melons—it's fair game." With that, he dropped to his haunches and set about building a cookfire.

Tas sprang into the back of the wagon, expecting to find Gisella, but the wagon was empty. Fortunately, a lighted lantern hung from a hook by the door. He looked around in astonishment. The interior looked much larger than the outside would suggest. From floor to low ceiling on the right side of the wagon were narrow shelves containing neatly stacked, corked, green apothecary jars, some empty, most full of dried herbs. The shelves held various and sundry other items, from pale yellow beeswax candles to a black velvet-covered board crammed full of rings studded with winking, colorful gems. Tas reached out a hand eagerly.

"Don't touch the rings, whatever you do," Woodrow called to him suddenly from outside the wagon. "The gems are fake, but Miss Hornslager trades them as real ones. She knows exactly how many she has and where each one's place is in the velvet display board."

Tas snatched his hand back abruptly. "I wouldn't," he said, flustered, wondering if the young human could read minds as well as understand animals. "She shouldn't leave them out where just anyone can get at them," he murmured.

Tas dragged his eyes away from the sparkling rings and examined the rest of the wagon. Except for the far front corner, the entire left side of the wagon was covered with fluffy, overstuffed, brightly colored pillows atop a thick-piled, midnight-black fur—probably Gisella's bed, Tas decided. In the far corner was an ornate, black-lacquered dressing screen folded accordian-style. At the rear of the wagon Tas spotted Gisella's clothes where they were piled neatly on a stack of pillows.

His stomach growled, and he remembered why he was in the wagon. As promised, he found a wide, shallow cupboard and opened the door. Inside was a headless, unplucked chicken hanging from one leg, a small bucket placed beneath it to catch drops of blood. The chicken seemed pretty well drained, so Tas took it down and snatched up the bag of dried beans. He located what smelled like fennel and sage in two of the green, corked jars (but only after testing all of them, just to be sure). He also nabbed a dried-up lemon—a treat, despite the mold—and a few pans and bowls, and then left the wagon to join Woodrow by the small fire.

"Miss Hornslager is bathing in a stream on the far side of that grove of trees." Woodrow pointed, handing a half-filled bucket of water to Tas. "Here, the horses didn't drink this water. You can use it to flavor your cooking."

Wrinkling his nose, Tas took the wooden vessel. He was relieved to find no foam on top, and even more so to see that the horses had their own bucket. He dumped half of the beans into a bowl, added enough of the cold, clear water to cover them, and set the bowl near the fire to warm the water and soften the beans. Finally, he stretched the chicken across his lap for plucking.

"Where did you learn to cook?" Woodrow asked, adding a few larger sticks to the flames to encourage the coals.

"Watching my mother, I guess," Tas said. "She was a great cook," he said fondly. "She could turn a week-old loaf of bread into a feast! One whiff of her mongoose pie caused riots in our neighborhood in Kendermore. In fact, she was forbidden, by order of the Kendermore Council, to make it anymore." Tasslehoff's eyes shone with pride.

"Was?" Woodrow said gently. "Is she dead?"

"I don't think so," Tasslehoff frowned, "but I haven't seen her in a long time."

"If my mother were still alive, I'd visit her as often as I could," Woodrow said wistfully, stirring the coals a little too vigorously. "My father, too."

"Both your parents are dead? Gee, I'm sorry," said Tas kindly, tearing out a handful of black feathers. "How did it happen?"

Woodrow blinked frequently. "My father came from a family of Solamnic Knights. He was raised to it—he didn't know anything else. He didn't care so much about the knighthood as he did about helping people, though. And that was his downfall."

Tas could almost guess Woodrow's next words. He knew, from his friend Sturm Brightblade, that the Knights of Solamnia, once the peacekeepers of the realm, had lived in persecution and fear from the common people in the region of Solamnia. Many of those people wrongly blamed the knights for the Cataclysm, which Tas found difficult to understand, no matter how many times Sturm explained it. Sturm's father was a knight who had sent his wife and then young son to the south until things quieted down. Sturm never heard from his father again.

"About ten years ago, my father came to the aid of a neighboring farmer," Woodrow continued. "The man was wounded and claimed that several men who looked like knights had looted his home and left him for dead. My father was trying to help the man to his feet when other neighbors, alerted by the farmer's cries, as had my father, came storming into the cottage, bearing pitchforks and axes. They saw a Solamnic Knight standing over the injured farmer, and without a question, they struck him down." Woodrow's voice was even and clear, but his eyes watered. "The farmer tried to stop them, but he was too late. He tearfully told us later of my father's senseless death."

Tas's tender heart was near to bursting. "And your mother?" He blew his nose on his sleeve.

"She died miscarrying my brother shortly after." Woodrow stared into the flames.

For once Tas didn't know what to say. Then he had an idea. "You could visit my parents with me when we get to Kendermore—if they're still there, that is."

"That's awfully kind of you," Woodrow said, "but it wouldn't be the same."

Tas frowned. "I suppose not. Is that why you're with Gisella?"

"Sort of," Woodrow said slowly. "After my parents died, my uncle—Father's brother—took me in."

"That was nice of him," interjected Tas, trying to sound cheerful.

"Father and Uncle Gordon were very close." Woodrow added another log to the fire. "I've thought about it a lot, and I believe he hoped to bring my father back through me. He was always saying how much I looked like Father. Anyway, he wanted me to be his squire, and day after day we trained." Woodrow shook his head sadly. "But I knew how—and why—my father had died. I wanted no part of the knighthood, and I told Uncle Gordon so as nicely as I could. But it was as though he hadn't heard me. He just kept reciting the Oath and the Measure. So I had to run away."

"Yes, I suppose you did," Tas agreed awkwardly.

The story seemed to have drained Woodrow. He sighed heavily. "To answer your original question, I met Miss Hornslager at a fair in Sanction. I needed a job, and she needed an assistant. So here I am."

They were quiet for some time. Tas's thoughts traveled back to his own family. "I have an uncle. He's my mother's brother, and his name is Trapspringer. You know the one—the Kendermore Council locked him up and took away his lucky finger bone because of me." Tas looked up from the chicken at Woodrow earnestly, white and black feathers clinging to his fingers. "Would you say that's a bad omen—having his lucky bone taken away?"

Woodrow smiled for the first time since the conversation began. "I wouldn't say it was a good one."

"Poor Uncle Trapspringer," Tas said sadly, shaking his head as he pulled the last of the feathers from the bird.

"I'll gut it for you," Woodrow offered, holding out his hand for the chicken. "If I learned anything from my time as a squire, it was how to dress game."

Tas handed him the chicken. "I'll need a spit, too," he

said to Woodrow. After wiping his palms on the grass to remove the feathers, Tas rinsed his hands with the clear water he'd set aside earlier. Next, he drained the water from the bowl of beans. Tossing in a handful each of fennel and sage, he stirred the mixture with his hands.

Woodrow returned with the bird. "All clean and shiny and pink," he said, handing it over by the neck.

Tas split the lemon in half and rubbed what little juice there was over the chicken, inside and out. Next he stuffed the bean mixture into the cavity of the bird while Woodrow drove two sturdy, fork-shaped branches into the ground on either side of the fire. Tas held the stuffed chicken up and Woodrow ran a straight, thin stick through it from one end to the other. Wordlessly, he set it on the two forked sticks with the chicken centered over the glowing coals.

"Perfect," Tas sighed. He leaned back against a sturdy wagon wheel and closed his eyes.

"I'll keep an eye on dinner," Woodrow offered, but he knew the kender was already asleep. The human sat cross-legged before the fire, absently staring into the red-hot coals.

Meanwhile, Gisella scampered barefoot up the slope toward the light of the fire, stopping occasionally to pluck pine needles from the tender pads of her feet. She knew Woodrow was scandalized by her nightly forays to the nearest body of water—and to bodies of another sort when the option was available—she thought with a girlish giggle. He'd said it was rather bold of her to traipse around in the woods unclothed. But Gisella Hornslager was accustomed to taking care of herself. She found the damage from a day's dirt and sweat grinding into her skin more upsetting than any possible encounter with a wild animal. The frigid bath by moonlight had felt divine, though now her damp skin felt cool against the night mountain air. She drew her thin wrap closer and hurried toward the promised warmth of the fire.

Gisella stopped in her tracks at the edge of the clearing; the most delicious aroma assailed her nostrils.

"Tasslehoff's recipe," said Woodrow, noting the pleased expression on her face. He had removed the chicken from the fire and was in the process of sliding the bird from the stick.

Gisella rushed foward and turned over the bucket of water for a seat. Gingerly testing the temperature of the rocks around the fire with her icy toes, she found a comfortable spot. Sighing contentedly, she looked at the kender, who had woken and was holding a large tin plate under their dinner.

"Perhaps your friend, that cute half-elf, was right about one thing: maybe you *are* worth more than a bolt of fabric." She snatched up a smaller plate and held it out eagerly to receive her share. "I'm starved!"

"Thank you," Tasslehoff said, though he wasn't sure if that had been a compliment or not. He tipped the platter so that tender, crumbly bits of chicken rolled onto Gisella's plate, and then added a helping of bean stuffing. Tas sat back to enjoy his own meal.

Woodrow ate his share in silence, watching his employer. Gisella's hands were a flurry of activity, and her mouth never stopped chewing. Before Woodrow had eaten more than two bites, Gisella was finished with hers. She sat with her arms clutched tightly about her waist, holding her wrap closed, her eyes the half-closed slits of a sleeping cat.

Woodrow had not met many women, and had come to know only a few of them, but he felt that Gisella Hornslager was not typical of her sex. She had her own rules about everything, and she seemed to care not one whit what anyone thought of her. She had a voracious appetite for food, among other things. He blushed, remembering the sound of her "trading" with men these last weeks. He'd tried not to listen to the grunts and groans coming through the wagon's windows, but it was impossible since on those occasions she posted him right outside as watchman. Afterward, she seemed not the least ashamed to face him and, in fact, seemed to delight in bringing a flood of red to his cheeks with some earthy remark.

She was afraid of nothing—except the possibility that something she wanted could not be bought. Woodrow concluded that, although he strongly disagreed with her freewheeling lifestyle, he respected her for having the courage of her convictions.

"What are you staring at?" she demanded suddenly, her eyes wide open. She looked over his lean, muscled body with a suggestive smile on her face. "You haven't changed your mind about my preferred payment plan?"

His gaze flew back to his plate, and he concentrated madly on his meal. "N-no," he stuttered, blushing as usual. "I still need the steel pieces, ma'am."

She shrugged, unoffended. "Suit yourself. You know I prefer to barter for services, whenever possible." Gisella picked up a twig and poked it into the fire. "Let me see that map, Burrfoot," she said.

Looking up from his plate, Tas sucked his greasy fingers loudly and reached into his vest. He handed the dwarf a folded piece of parchment. "We've traveled for little more than a half-day. Given that, I think we should be able to reach Xak Tsaroth by late tomorrow," the kender predicted.

Ignoring him, Gisella tipped the map toward the firelight and peered closely.

"We're right about here," Tas said helpfully, jabbing at the back of the map toward the top center, at a point near the city marked Xak Tsaroth.

Gisella could see the shadow of his finger through the parchment. "Hmmm, yes," she said. "It looks like a nice, straight shot from here to—" she looked closely all the way to the right edge "—well, all the way to Balifor."

Tasslehoff puffed himself up. "I told you I'd get you back before your melons went bad. If there's one thing a Burrfoot knows, it's maps."

But Gisella was still looking closely at the map, shaking her head slowly. "I guess . . ." she mumbled. But the dwarf continued staring at the piece of paper, wondering what it was that she was missing, until the coals burned black, long after Tasslehoff and Woodrow had both curled up to sleep.

The map shows various labels including: KENDER, Old Dead Stump, To Get Here, Bertie's House, Short Cut Blvd, Main Street, That Way, Road Curve, Big Rock, TREASURE SEE Directions, Dead End Lane, Broad Ave, Dizzy Court, One Way Street, Main St, Straight Street, Here's where the robin's nest is, Tracy Pl, Here End Drive, Violet Patch, Direct Route Drive, Nothing Drive

Chapter 4

PHINEAS WIPED THE NIGHT'S GRIT FROM HIS EYES with a corner of his white smock as he clomped down the wooden stairs, headed for his office below. Grimacing, he smacked his lips. His mouth had an awful, metallic taste, as if he'd been sucking on a rusty sword. Undoubtedly residue from the pitcher of kender ale he'd drunk before falling asleep last night, he decided.

After opening the door to his examination room at the foot of the stairs, he quickly lit the stub of a candle in the darkened room and headed straight for the counter that contained the green glass bottle of his own special elixir. It was Phineas's cure for anything that couldn't be covered up with a bandage, ear plugs, or oiled parchment glasses, or pulled out like teeth or in-grown toenails. He prescribed it for headaches, stomachaches, foot aches, joint aches, sore throats, bulging eyes, rashes, bad breath, swollen tongues, ir- regularity, and a host of other ills that seemed to plague the citizens of Kendermore. Oddly enough, he'd found that the sharp-tasting liquid was actually effective against stomachaches and bad breath. He charged a dear price for his elixir, claiming that its mystical ingredients came "from dangerous lands far away, where strangers are met with the sword and the flame and seldom escape with their lives." Kenders' eyes would open wide as they contemplated the green bottle, and a low whistle would often escape their lips as they reached greedily for the exotic medicine.

Taking a swig now and swishing it around in his mouth, Phineas's full cheeks jiggled with mirth. The special ingredients of his elixir were a few crushed cherry and eucalyptus leaves that he scavenged from the trash behind the neighborhood apothecary's shop. Nothing mystical about that. Certainly he had never put a bone from a lycanthropic minotaur in any batch, as he'd told the kender the night before.

Thus remembering his visitor, Phineas's eyes fell across the folded paper on the nearby wooden tray. "That Trapspringer was a con artist—maybe even bet- ter than me!" the human admitted aloud, unfolding the sheet absently. It was a map. He was about to crumble it between his fists when a word on one corner fleetingly caught his attention.

The word was "treasure."

Frowning in thought, Phineas thumbed the map open and spread it out on the counter, allowing the glow of the candle to fall over it. He squinted in the flickering light and deduced from a smudgy title at the top that this was a map of Kendermore. But he couldn't make out any fine details on the aged, deli- cate map. He needed more light.

The window in the examination room faced west, so

Phineas didn't even bother opening it; he knew he wouldn't get any appreciable light from that direction so early in the morning. Instead, he stepped into his small waiting room and opened wide the shutters, which faced the east and the rising sun. Morning sunlight filtered in beneath a heavy canvas awning. Phineas dragged a rickety stool to the open window, spread the map out on the waiting bench, and parked his bulk on the stool. The wood creaked in protest, which usually happened when Phineas sat in anything made for a kender.

Not that he was heavy, at least by the standards of his own race. He was of average human height, with a barrel-shaped chest and rather sticklike arms and legs. His hands were lily white, and there was not an ounce of muscle on his bones. He had always been considered slight and nonthreatening among his own people. But compared to kender, he was large, which was one of the reasons he liked living in Kendermore.

Nibbling at a fingernail now, Phineas scanned the old parchment map for the word "treasure." He scanned it again, and then a third time. Had his eyes somehow played a trick on his mind? He was sure he'd been looking at the right side of the map, near the edge. Phineas concentrated his gaze there.

"Hey, it'th Dr. Teeth!" called a high, lisping girl kender's voice. Phineas started so violently he almost fell backward off the groaning stool. The voice's owner poked her head under the awning to peer in the window. "Are you open?" she asked. "I have thith terrible toothache, and thinth there'th no waiting right now, you could . . ."

"No, I'm *not* 'open' yet," snapped Phineas, his eyes drawn back to the map. "Do you see an 'open' sign in my door?"

"Well, no, but your window ith open and I thought maybe you hadn't turned the thign yet, and my tooth hurtth real bad. Thay, what'th that? A map?"

Phineas instinctively jerked the paper from the kender's prying eyes, then looked up. A white strip of cloth was stretched around the kender's jaw and tied to the top of her head.

"This? Why, yes, it is a map. I'm thinking of moving my shop, and I'm simply considering new locations," he improvised hastily. "And yes, my window *is* open, but I am not."

"Well, when will you be open?" she asked, laying a hand gingerly to the left side of her jaw.

"I don't know!" he growled impatiently. "Come back this afternoon!"

"Should I come here, or should I go to your new shop?"

Phineas looked at her strangely. Ordinarily, kender didn't bother him, like they did most humans. But for some reason, this kender was annoying him to distraction. Perhaps it was simply a reaction to the previous evening's excessive nightcap.

"Here!"

"OK!" she said merrily. "Bye! Thee you thith afternoon!" Waving, she grinned, but her smile disappeared immediately. Holding her sore jaw, she drifted away down the uneven, cobbled street.

Quickly, before more snooping kender could appear and pester him, Phineas pulled the map back onto his lap and studied it closely. A street map of Kendermore looked like a box filled with writhing snakes. No two roads were parallel—or even straight—and all but the thicker, main avenues were dead ends. Phineas noted that the names on those main thoroughfares seemed to change at random. He focused his attention on one whose name he recognized as being near his shop; there it was called "Bottleneck Avenue," two irregular blocks to the east, the same road bore the name "Straight Street" (and appeared to be anything but), and just beyond that word, the street was renamed "Bildor's Boulevard."

If all that weren't confusing enough, the mapmaker had used his own symbols, which depicted such important landmarks as "Bertie's house," "here's where the robin's nest is," and "violet patch."

Looking at the map only made the city more confusing, Phineas decided. But asking directions from a kender was hopeless, too. "Turn right—or is it left?—at the big, green tree, then spin in place twice, go past the red geraniums—beautiful, have you seen them?—and before you know it you're where you are!"

Again the word seemed to leap from the right edge of the map, this time hitting him squarely in the eyes. Actually, "treasure" was part of a phrase, which may have made it difficult for him to see. In full, it read, "Here be a treasure of gems and magical rings beyond compare." Phineas's pulse throbbed in his temples. Snatching up a bit of coal from the small pile near his heating brazier, he circled the phrase with shaking hands. Then he noticed the symbol below it.

Beneath the glorious words was an arrow pointing to the right edge of the map, its chevron point catching exactly the lip of the sheet. With his nose less than an inch from the page, he noticed that the right edge of the map was slightly frayed, as if it had been torn along a fold.

The map had been ripped in two, and the location of the treasure was on the other half!

"No!" Phineas cried. His head moved quickly from side to side, his eyes scouring the map for a different answer. Maybe the arrow didn't apply to the treasure. But after a few frantic moments, Phineas had to admit that it did. There *was* nothing else on that edge of the map. Strangely, he was fairly certain that all of Kendermore, as he knew it, was represented on the map in his hand.

Then what was on the other half of the map?

And where was it?

Phineas forced his mind to slow down. He might

possibly have in his possession the find of a lifetime.
He could live a long time on the sale of gems and magical rings. But he had to have the whole map to find this
treasure.

Trapspringer! The kender had told him the map was
one of his most prized possessions, so he obviously
knew its value. Surely the odd, elder kender had the
other half. But how would he find Trapspringer in the
vast city of Kendermore? Phineas's heart pounded like
the sound of a hundred horses' hooves.

Frowning, he craned his neck through the open window, then snorted at his own foolishness. The ringing
in his ears wasn't his heart at all, but an early morning
parade coming down his street.

Parades—if the term were used loosely—were a
daily event in Kendermore. The occasions they cele-
brated ranged from the ridiculous to the sublime. This
one was shaping up to be the former, Phineas thought
sourly, taking note of the band. Five squealing fifers
and three thundering cymbalists provided background noise for a middle-aged kender with a black
topknot, who yelled through cupped hands from a
bench atop a seriously listing wagon. A banner,
stretched between the hands of two scantily clad
young female kender in knee-high boots, short skirts,
and low-cut blouses, proclaimed that they were pro-
moting the election of someone or other into the may-
or's office.

"And why do we want a gynosphinx for mayor?" he
yelled. "Because we've never had one, that's why!
Kendermore was founded on freedom and equality—
well, maybe no one said those things specifically—but
we say that a gynosphinx deserves a chance! Besides,
they tell good riddles!" The fifes struck a piercing trill,
the cymbals crashed, and the ensemble continued
down the street, yelling and cheering for the spokes-
man's words.

Distracted from the map, Phineas shook his head in

amusement. A gynosphinx for mayor, indeed. As far as he knew, gynosphinxes were the female of the species of creatures with lion bodies. They were almost as large as ogres, though vastly more intelligent, and they tended to devour anything that offended them. Only in Kendermore would anyone suggest such a thing. Besides, Kendermore already had a mayor, and Phineas had heard of no scheduled elections. Of course, kender seldom scheduled anything.

Kendermore already had a mayor. Phineas's eyes darted from side to side as a thought—a recollection, really—congealed in his brain. Trapspringer had said some very strange, contradictory things the night before. He'd said that he was being held in prison. But he'd also said that his nephew was marrying the mayor's daughter. Had one or both statements been the rambling of a crazy old kender? The two could not possibly be connected. Nevertheless, in the absence of any other clues, it seemed that Phineas's best chance to find Trapspringer might lay with the mayor, whoever he was. A smile of pure delight and anticipation spread across his middle-aged face.

In the wake of the parade, kender had begun appearing before his window.

"Dr. Bones—"

"I need a haircut and—"

Forced to acknowledge their raucous presence, Phineas asked abruptly, "Say, do any of you know where I might find the mayor?"

"City Hall!" they sang out.

"Thanks," he said tersely. "I'm closed today, because of the holiday—the parade, and gynosphinxes, and all that." With that he swung the shutters closed in the kender's tiny, surprised faces. He could hear their sputtering taunts, but his mind was already on its way to City Hall to locate either a crazy man or—

Phineas couldn't think of an 'or.'

Chapter 5

"*I don't get it,*" Tasslehoff said for the tenth time that morning. He was seated on the buckboard between Gisella and Woodrow, his map unfolded and spread wide. "The village of Que-shu was where it should be, smack in the middle of the plains. We're riding on the Sageway East Road—right where it should be, too—but this should be more plains, right?" He flung his arms at the scenery around him. "So where did these mountains come from?" He thumped the map and shook his head. "Has there been an earthquake or something? Everything is turned around."

"You tell me," Gisella said, clicking her tongue at the horses to spur them up the incline. "After all, you're the sport who made the map."

"I said I made maps, all right. But I never said I made *this* one," Tasslehoff said, fidgeting.

"Mr. Burrfoot's Uncle Bertie made this map," Woodrow said innocently.

"Well, I'm not exactly positive Uncle Bertie made it," Tas said. "That's just what my Uncle Trapspringer told me when he gave me a bunch of maps for my coming-of-age present. Come to think of it, I've never met an Uncle Bertie. I wonder if he's even *my* Uncle Bertie."

"How did you get to Solace in the first place?" Gisella demanded, ignoring his chatter. "You must remember the route, being a map aficionado and all."

"Of course I remember. I came up from the south, through Thorbardin and Pax Tharkas, just like you did," the kender said simply.

"Pardon me for asking, but why didn't we just go back that same way?" said Woodrow.

Tas looked a little exasperated and held up his hands. "Don't look at me. Gisella's the one who was in a hurry and wanted to take a short cut. I simply suggested the direction!"

Gisella scowled. "I'm not sure what we're bickering about," she said. "So Tasslehoff's map is missing a few cities, some mountains—no ill has come of it. The road is clear, we're making good time. Let's keep on!"

At that, the miffed expression on Tas's face was replaced by satisfaction, and Woodrow drifted off into silence again.

Their morning had, in fact, been peaceful, uneventful. They had woken to find the gray, rainy sky replaced by a cloudless, azure one. Tas had risen early, drawn to the sounds of rushing water. Removing his grease-stained leggings, he scrubbed them on a rock in a cold, clear stream, and they dried quickly on a branch in the early morning sun.

A light sleeper, Woodrow had meanwhile quietly slipped the bag of grain from under the buckboard and fed the horses in anticipation of the long day ahead. After filling their bucket with fresh water, he ventured into the woods and found a late crop of wild blackberries.

Before long, Gisella had slipped from her bed of over-stuffed pillows in the wagon, wearing her raspberry-colored boots and a vivid orange, long-sleeved tunic with matching pants so tight they looked like they had been painted on. The sun gave her hair red hotspots of light as the three sat by the ashes of the fire and breakfasted on cold, leftover bean stuffing, fresh black-berries, and mountain spring water.

Spirits had been high as they rolled away from camp. Within an hour, they had left the mountains, and the barbarian village of Que-shu shimmered against the blue-gray horizon. Though the road they traveled passed very near—easily within one thousand yards of Que-shu—a clear view of the village was blocked by the perfectly circular stone wall surrounding it. Still, the up-per levels of several huge stone temples and a spacious arena could be seen against the blue sky in the late-morning sun. Barbarian eyes, apparently accustomed to traffic on the road, watched from atop the wall, but there was no effort to hail or molest the travelers.

After passing Que-shu, they had stopped for lunch. Gisella reluctantly dipped into her secret stash of trade goods and produced a small haunch of expensive Tarsi-tian smoked ham. While munching his portion, Tas had looked to the east and was the first to spot the jagged spines of the mountain range about which they were now bickering.

"We're traveling downhill now," Woodrow said, de-tecting a slight decline. "Maybe this mountain range wasn't included on your map because it was relatively small," he suggested to Tas.

The kender brightened considerably. "That's probably it!" He liked finding the answers to mysteries.

Soon their descent became more obvious. Gisella had to strain mightily on the reins to keep the horses from galloping pell-mell down the mountain. But before long, mountain evergreens gave way to the leafy maples and oaks of the foothills.

"It's a straight shot from here to Xak Tsaroth," Gisella announced, giving the horses their heads. The wagon swayed and bounced and kicked up clouds of dust as the horses bolted down the road. Tasslehoff's slight frame was tossed about like a ball, but the kender giggled with joy at the madcap dash, though he clutched the buckboard to keep from being tossed to the ground. Brisk wind stung his eyes into tears of laughter.

But suddenly, looking beyond the horses, Tasslehoff blinked hard. Were his eyes just blurry, he wondered, or did—?

"Look!" he cried, pointing ahead down the road.

Gisella squinted in the direction of his finger. But her day vision was not as keen as her night vision when, like all dwarves, she could see partially into the infrared. Her vision got fuzzy some twenty feet ahead of the horses. She saw nothing untoward, so she continued on.

What Tasslehoff was trying to point out but she could not see was that the road simply stopped, as if the builders had walked away before finishing it, some fifty yards ahead.

Abruptly the galloping horses skidded unceremoniously into a swamp, dragging the wagon bearing three unwitting passengers. Tasslehoff sailed through the air, leggings over topknot, to land between two squishy lumps of grass-covered ground known as bogs. Lifting his hands out of four inches of cold, muddy water, he shook the slimy green swamp gook from them and stood up. The kender looked sourly at his once-clean leggings. Taking a step toward the wagon, he tripped over an underground bog and landed face-first in the water. Gods, it was cold! he thought. Jerking himself out and up again, he held on to the wagon and shook his head like a wet dog.

Woodrow had managed to stay with the wagon when the road stopped. Now he was scrambling down to calm the hysterical horses, who were up to their fetlocks in water, their eyes wide with fright.

"My outfit! It's ruined!"

Gisella's shrieks came from the other side of the horses, to the left of the wagon. Woodrow carefully picked his way through the bogs, sometimes sinking as high as his knees in the mud, until he found the female dwarf.

Gisella was sitting in the swamp, legs sprawled, arms propping her up from behind. She was covered to her ample chest with murky water. Only two inches of her outfit was still orange. The dwarf gave a start as a frog leaped from her shoulder into the dark, sludgy water.

Spitting a thick strand of wet, red hair from her mouth and eyes, she spotted the kender, who had stepped around the wagon next to Woodrow. Gisella glared at him. "I don't suppose this swamp was on your map, either? Or is this your idea of a fun little surprise?"

* * * * *

Gisella sat on the top step at the back of the wagon, resignedly pouring muddy water from her raspberry boots. "They'll never be the same," she said morosely. "And I traded one of the best nights of my life—" she caught the kender staring at her "—uh, never mind what I traded."

She had changed her clothes, putting on a conservative (for Gisella, anyway) purple tunic with pants and plain black work boots. Tasslehoff's leggings were clinging to his skin and they itched horribly, but he did not have a spare pair.

"I guess we'll have to turn around and take the southern route after all," Gisella grumbled. "We can't possibly reach Kendermore in time for the fair now." She sighed. "My melons, my melons . . . I could have replaced my wardrobe with the money they would have brought me. . . ."

"I'm not so sure, ma'am," Woodrow said suddenly,

coming around from the front of the wagon. "About turning back and going south, I mean. I unhitched the horses and led them forward into the swamp for quite some distance, and the water didn't get any deeper. In some places it was even drier." The young man shook his shaggy hair from his eyes and regarded Gisella.

"And?" Gisella's patience was strained. "What does that mean, Woodrow?"

"It means the water doesn't appear to get much deeper than four or five inches in most places. It means that it would be tough with these heavy wheels, but if we take it slow and steady, I think we can make it through."

"Through to where? To Xak Tsaroth? How do we know if we're anywhere *near* Xak Tsaroth? How do we know this swamp doesn't go on forever?"

"Nothing goes on forever, ma'am," said Woodrow.

Gisella gave a rueful smile at the young man's unintentional philosophy. "My head is splitting."

"I know how to fix that," Tasslehoff said helpfully from inside the wagon, reaching toward her temples. "You just tie two dead—"

"Thanks, but no thanks," Gisella said quickly, ducking from his grasp and out the back of the wagon.

"—eucalyptus leaves," Tas finished vacantly. "But suit yourself."

Woodrow pointed the horses toward a distant grove of trees. Holding the horses by their bridles, he kept his eyes on his feet as he picked a path through the bogs and the bush-topped cattails. Muck and mud latched onto him with each step. He curled his toes inside his boots to keep them on his feet. Humidity was high in the wake of the previous day's rain and heat. Woodrow's dirty-gray tunic clung to his wiry frame, the hem hanging ragged where he'd ripped a strip of cloth to use as a sweatband. Between swatting at flies, kicking at water snakes, and staying on his feet among the slippery bogs, he was keeping busy.

Tasslehoff sat next to Gisella, who held the reins and

made a show of steering the horses, despite the fact that Woodrow led them.

The terrain alternated between marshy areas that looked deceptively dry and large expanses of shallow water. Ahead about five hundred yards was a low expanse of shrubs and trees, which everyone hoped meant the end of the swamp.

"I'd like to know where all this water is coming from," said Gisella. "We haven't seen any lakes, or even any streams since we passed Que-shu."

Tas rolled out his map. "It's got to be coming from a stream in this small mountain range just north of Xak Tsaroth," he said, pointing.

Gisella snorted indelicately. "I wouldn't trust *that* piece of junk," she said, thumping the back of the map, "for anything more than wrapping mackerel."

Tas was about to retort when Woodrow stopped suddenly and cocked his head. "Do you hear that?" he asked.

Both Tasslehoff and Gisella fell silent and listened. From ahead came the distinct sounds of crashing waves.

"Ah, ha!" Tas exclaimed. "There's the stream I predicted."

But Woodrow looked skeptical. "It sounds bigger than a stream."

"There's only one way to find out," said Gisella, clicking her tongue at the horses. Woodrow held steady to their bridles again, until they reached the grove of trees, when he disappeared into the dense shrubs.

He was back in a flash, his face as white as his quilted tunic must once have been.

"What is it, Woodrow?" Gisella asked.

"It's no stream, ma'am," he gulped. "There's water as far as the eye can see."

Gisella's gasp was her initial reply.

Human and dwarf turned questioning eyes to the kender. Gisella poked him in the chest. "Your Uncle Bertie forgot an ocean, too?"

Chapter 6

"Order! Order!" Mayor Meridon Metwinger's gavel bounced off the hard wooden table that served as the Kendermore Council's Bench of Authority. The council met every fifth Thursday, and every Monday with a two in its date. Every Friday with an odd-numbered date, the mayor held Audience, the day when criminal cases were tried and domestic and community disputes were settled. Today was such a Friday.

Rounding up council members to serve as the jury for criminal cases on Audience Day was a mayoral duty. Though the city books listed sixty-three elected council members, representatives of the most important trades in Kendermore, Mayor Metwinger was seated beside just five council members today. He'd managed to find six of them during his morning roundup, but one had apparently wandered off on the way to City Hall.

The venerable kender rubbed his forehead distractedly and let his hand wander up to scratch the scalp under his graying topknot. Beneath his cheek braids, which marked him among kender as having noble blood, his skin was flushed from his council member search and the exertion of calling the meeting to order. Still, he felt chilled and damp from a draft and pulled his purple, fur-lined mayor's robe up closer to his pointed chin. Glancing to his immediate right, two feet beyond the end of the Bench of Authority, he eyed the source of the draft.

The council chamber was missing its exterior wall. At that moment, light autumn rain and damp leaves swirled around the mayor's feet. Before too long, snow would blow in and form a thick bank on the edge where the wall should be, making it difficult to determine where the building started and stopped. Metwinger made a mental note to have something done about it eventually, although he would surely miss the view.

The chamber was only one of many rooms on the second floor of the four-story building, housing all of Kendermore's public works and government offices. Located near the city's center, the structure had been built more than a century before. Following a kender tradition—or building tendency—each floor was less finished than the one below it, so that the top floor looked as if it were still under construction. The first floor—two grand ballrooms—were intact though had long ago been stripped of anything valuable. The second floor was basically complete, except for the missing exterior wall in the council chamber. The third floor had all the necessary outside walls, but was without a number of crucial doors: kender builders preferred to complete a room before allowing for doorways, so that openings might be located for the convenience of the occupant rather than arbitrarily placed. (More than one kender builder has found himself trapped inside a room with no doors!) The fourth floor was mostly exposed beams, window frames, and the occasional interior wall.

Not surprisingly, a problem arose with the design of the building shortly after its completion. The original builders had forgotten to include a stairway linking the four floors. Occupants of the upper floors were forced to scale the stone walls and climb in through tiny windows, which made the missing wall in the council room something of an asset. Complaints of deaths, though, particularly among mayors, brought about the construction, some ten years later, of a very elegant, polished wood central staircase that spiraled upward in an ever-decreasing circle (things got pretty tight up on the third floor).

Kender were a very political people, but they were dedicated to no cause as stridently as their need for constant change. Mayor Metwinger was Kendermore's 1,397th mayor. Not all of them had been kender. Nailed to the wall in the council chamber was a portrait of the 47th mayor, a leprechaun named Raleigh who reportedly had been an excellent mayor, having successfully held the post for nearly a year. Rumor had it that Raleigh resigned after a dispute when a pot of his gold mysteriously disappeared. Thirteen hundred fifty mayors had worn the coveted purple mayoral robes in the intervening three hundred or so years. Merldon Metwinger had been in the position for a little more than a month, which was longer than average, if no great achievement.

Accidentally elected when the populace confused his moneylending advertisements for campaign posters, he found that he enjoyed the vaunted position. He particularly liked the purple velvet mayor's robe with its many secret pockets.

Looking out at the occupants of the council chamber, Mayor Metwinger rubbed his hands in gleeful anticipation; it promised to be an exciting Audience Day. Two old, white-haired kender were struggling over a bony, wide-eyed-with-fright milk cow, each tugging on one of the animal's ears, which poked out of holes in a ratty straw hat. Metwinger would liked to have watched them get the cow up the narrow flights of stairs to the council chamber, which no doubt had contributed to the cow's anxiety.

Also waiting for a turn with the mayor were a male and female kender, obviously married from the way they were glaring at each other. A matronly looking kender angrily shook a floury rolling pin at a red-faced child, whom she held by his pointed ear. While Metwinger watched, another kender, probably in his mid-fifties and looking strangely content, straggled in and sat quietly. Behind him came two attractively dressed, angry-eyed misses, clomping and bobbing awkwardly, since each wore one of an obvious pair of red shoes. Metwinger couldn't wait to hear *their* story.

"This Audience is now in session," the mayor proclaimed, giving the table another rap with his gavel. "Who's first, then, hmmm?" he asked eagerly.

"Me!"

"Me!"

"Us!"

"Them!"

"I'll take the two with the cow first," Mayor Metwinger instructed. The others sat down with grumbles and thinly veiled comments about the mayor's mother.

The two farmers stepped forward respectfully, both insisting on keeping a hand on the cow's collar. They introduced themselves as Digger Dunstan and Wembly Cloverleaf.

"You see, Your Honor, Dorabell is mine—" Digger began.

"Bossynova is mine, Digger Dunstan, and you know it!" the other protested, giving the cow's collar a possessive tug. "Dorabell—what a silly name for a cow! And take that stupid hat off her! She prefers feathers tucked behind her ears!"

"Well, you should know about stupid, Wembly Clo-

74

verleaf," the first taunted, "you lame-brained, drain-brained excuse for a farmer. You borrowed her from my field—"

"Only after you took her from mine!"

"Did not, you oaf!"

"Did too, you ogre-lover!"

"DID NOT!"

"DID TOO!"

Rather predictably, a scuffle broke out. The farmers reached for each other's throats over the bony back of the frightened cow. Soon, the audience chose sides and got in on the fight; the members of the council and the mayor cheered them on.

It was the cow herself who settled the matter. Mooing frantically, she bolted through the throng of kender, right past the Bench of Authority, heading toward the open wall. Splaying himself on his stomach across the right corner of the table, the mayor managed to get a hand on her collar and jerk her to a stop just inches before the precipice.

"So," he panted, "you both claim you own her."

"She was mine, first!" both of them howled, hurrying forward to calm their cow.

Metwinger straightened his robes and sat back down, wheezing heavily. Watching them fawn over the cow, he was struck with an idea. "Then you shall both have part of her," he proclaimed, thinking his decision not only brilliant, but incredibly fair.

The two kender looked at him, puzzled. "You want us to cut her in half?" Digger finally managed.

"Oh!" the mayor looked startled. "I hadn't thought of that solution. Hmmm—well, anyway, what I meant was that you must share her. You, Digger, will have her on odd days, and you, Wembly, shall have her on the even ones."

"But her birthday is on an odd day!" protested Wembly.

"And All Cows Day is on an even day!" complained

Digger.

"Well, then I'd say that makes you even," said the mayor, with an apologetic smile at Digger. "Next!"

"Brilliant judgment," whispered council member Arlan Brambletow, who secretly thought he would look nice in the velvet mayoral robes.

Mayor Metwinger beamed with pride at his own cleverness. Never before had such a brilliant and impartial mayor presided over Kendermore's council, he told himself. Fairly bursting with self-importance, he waved forward the next case, the contented-looking kender, who began to state his complaint against the city.

"Well, it's not really a complaint, Your Highness," the kender began, clearly nervous now in the presence of the mayor.

Metwinger flushed with pleasure. "You may call me Your Honor. I'm not a king, you know. Not yet, anyway." He chuckled modestly. "Continue with your story."

"Well, you see, the city recently completed cobbling a new street near my home—*extremely* near my home."

"Let me guess," the mayor began, having heard such complaints before. "The construction crew was too noisy, too quiet, or too sloppy. Or perhaps your taxes were raised too much?"

The kender looked surprised. "Oh, no, none of those things. Well, maybe the taxes *were* a bit high. . . . But the workmen were most pleasant, considering that they built the street through the middle of my home."

The mayor slumped back in his chair, suddenly bored. "So what's your point?"

"Your Honor, I don't think the street was supposed to go *through* my house," he said. "At least no one mentioned it to me."

The mayor sat forward. "The city is very busy, you know, and can't be expected to contact just anyone about every little thing." He sighed. "I suppose you expect the city to disrupt its plans and reroute the street?"

The kender looked alarmed. "Oh, no, Your Honor!

I've never had so many friends! In, out, in, out—carriages from all over the world! What I'd really like is a permit to open an inn."

The mayor shook his head sympathetically. "You're in the wrong place, then. What you want is the Department of Inn Permit Issuing. Up the stairs, first room on the right—or is it left?" The mayor waved toward the door at the back, in the left corner of the room.

But the kender did not move. Instead he shook his head. "Oh, no, you're wrong. I went there and they told me that *you* issue permits."

"They said that?" the mayor squealed. "Well, what do *they* do, then?" He turned to the council members, who all shrugged, except for one.

"Aren't they in charge of new streets?" Barlo Twack-dinger, the bakerman council member, ventured helpfully.

Metwinger shrugged. "Well, if they say we do it, then I guess we do it. OK, you can have a permit. Next?"

While the kender with the permit danced happily out the door, the domestic case shuffled forward, and a balding, paunchy human slipped inside the room. Phineas Curick sat at the back of the chamber and tried to calm himself. It had taken him hours to reach this spot. He thought he knew where City Hall was, but somehow he'd got turned around and had to stop and ask for directions. Those directions had led him to the outer fringes of Kendermore—practically out of the whole region of Goodlund, he fumed.

But he was most perturbed, because his desperation had caused him to lose his own good sense. He knew better than to ask a kender for directions!

It also galled him that, in the end, he'd only found City Hall because he nearly ran into it. Head bent, mumbling in disgust as he marched back toward where he thought his shop was, he'd nearly smashed into the side of the building. Somebody had run a street right up to City Hall's west wall! Dazed, he didn't even realize where he was until a concerned kender, wearing a badge and a uniform that was so small its buttons were straining, scraped him up and brought him into the building for a drink of water.

"Who in Hades put a building in the middle of a street?" Phineas had growled.

"Oh, all roads lead to City Hall," the kender guard had explained.

Phineas had shaken his head stupidly. "Never mind. Where do I find the prison?"

"Kendermore doesn't have a prison—no point in it," the guard said mildly. "Why, are you a prisoner?"

"No, I am not!" Phineas sputtered, more than a little aggravated. The human was *sure* Trapspringer had said he was a prisoner! Frowning, Phineas decided to take a different approach.

"If Kendermore had a prisoner, where would he be held?"

"Well, that depends . . . ," the kender said. "Say, you wouldn't have any candy, would you?"

If it hadn't been for the guard's genuinely innocent expression, Phineas would have thought he was being asked for a bribe. In the end, it amounted to the same thing. "I'm not sure, let me look." Phineas reached into his pocket and pulled out its contents: two steel pieces and a pocket knife. Sighing, he placed them in the guard's outstretched palm anyway. "Sorry, no candy. Now, what does it depend on?"

"Huh?" the guard said, his attention riveted by the spring-action latch on Phineas's knife. "Oh, where he'd be at depends on what he did and who he did it to. What's his name?"

"I believe his name is Trapspringer Furrfoot, but I don't know what he did to get thrown in prison."

The kender looked at him. "You're not sure where you're going or who you're going to see, and you don't know what he did."

Phineas felt stupid and annoyed at the same time. The

only thing Trapspringer had said, other than that he was in prison, was that his nephew was going to marry the mayor's daughter. Phineas brightened. "I think it may have something to do with the mayor."

"Considering how little you know, you're lucky I'm around to help you sort through this," said the guard, puffing up his chest, straining the buttons to the bursting point. "Today is Audience Day, so Mayor—let's see, it's Metwinger this month, isn't it? I'm not sure, since I'm just sitting in for my brother today. Our honored mayor is holding Audience on the third floor. If you hurry, per-haps you'll be allowed to address him." With that, the kender wandered back outside City Hall, Phineas's knife in his small hands, Phineas's coins jingling in his pocket.

Glowering at the guard's retreating back, Phineas gulped down his water and rushed up the ever-narrowing circular stairs to the third floor. He searched every room there, growing more desperate with each, until he reached the last. There he found a kender clean-ing woman, from the mop at her side and the overturned bucket upon which she sat, who seemed more intent on her game of marbles than tidying. She told him Audience was being held on the second floor, not the third. Sure enough, on the second floor Phineas found the council chamber where Audience was being held.

He was not sure how things proceeded, so he sat back to observe. There appeared to be a number of cases be-fore him anyway, including a married couple who was presently stating their complaint.

"—So, I said, 'these are my special rocks—my agates, my amethysts, and my very reddest rubies'—I collect them, you see—'so don't touch them,' " said the wife, a dower-looking kender whose age was difficult to guess, since her face was very wrinkled but her hands were smooth. "So what does he do?"

"He touched them," the mayor supplied.

"Not only did he touch them, but he put them in his rock tumbler!" Her face was a mixture of outrage and astonishment.

"He put them in an ale flagon?" asked the mayor, perplexed.

"You know," the husband said merrily, "everyone thinks that when I tell them I collect rock tumblers." His age was no more discernible than his wife's. His hair was dishwater brown and wisps poked out of his tightly stretched topknot, giving him a disheveled look. He had a slight, stubbly beard, unusual for kender.

The husband stepped up closer to the Bench of Authority, addressing the mayor directly. "Did you realize that the history of the rare gnome rock tumbler—a drum-shaped, crank-driven device used to reduce stones to sand—is long and very interesting? No, I'm sure you didn't. In fact, many experts believe that throughout the ages, rock tumblers have played a large part in the development of the world as we know it. None of us might be alive if there weren't rock tumblers! Many people don't know that, but—"

"*I* know it!" the wife complained, clapping her hands to her ears. "It's all I ever hear, especially after he pulverizes my prettiest rocks!"

The man turned to his wife. "It wasn't *my* fault that your rocks got tumbled," he said defensively. "You left them sitting out where just *anyone* could take them, so I put them in my tumbler for safe keeping. Only I forgot they were in there the next time I tumbled some rocks."

"Out where just anyone could find them? They were locked up in two boxes and hidden under a loose floorboard before the fire!" she cried, giving his arm a vicious punch.

"Exactly!" he exclaimed, rubbing his arm and pulling away. "Everyone knows to look under floorboards! Nobody would think to look for gems in a rock tumbler! Don't you agree, Mayor?"

"Huh? What?" Metwinger asked, looking up guiltily from under the table. He'd found their argument tedious and had turned his attention to the shiny buckles on councilman Barlow Twackdinger's boots. "Oh, yes. It's obvious to me that one of you must develop another hobby. Perhaps rock gathering isn't the wisest hobby for a woman whose husband collects rock tumblers."

The mayor was about to suggest a specific solution when, to his surprise, the couple proclaimed in unison, "A brilliant idea!" Hand-in-hand they walked through the door at the rear of the chamber, though their voices could be heard rising even as they descended the stairs.

"Now, honey, you should be the one to find a new hobby," the wife could be heard saying brightly. "At least my gems aren't worthless!"

"Worthless, dear! Why, rock tumblers are the most valuable investment—"

But the council was on to other business. Phineas looked up as a kender burst through the door, pushing a wheelbarrow full of bricks, his brow sweating. The kender began to explain how his neighbor had been tossing the bricks from his window and into the kender's own house one story down. It seemed he didn't mind, since he could use the bricks. However, they had not stopped at his home, but had fallen through his apparently thin floor to the house below his, and he was having a difficult time getting them back from the neighbor below. Phineas let his chin drop onto his chest, and he promptly fell asleep.

"Hey, where are my boots?" Barlo Twackdinger demanded suddenly. He glared down his red-veined, flour-dusted nose at the mayor seated to his right on the Bench of Authority.

"Oh," mumbled Mayor Metwinger, surprised to find the thick, furred boots in one of his many pockets. "You must have put your feet in my vest, and somehow your boots fell off." He handed them over, letting his fingers linger on the shiny buckles near the plush toes. "They're very nice, even with the flour on them."

"They ought to be," said council member Windorf Wright, snatching them from Barlo's expectant hands.

"They're mine!" claimed the leader of Kendermore's farmer's union. Stockier than the average kender, his bright red vest looked too tight to be comfortable. His head was shaved right up to his thinning topknot to show his delicately pointed ears to their best advantage.

"Not until I get those chickens and turnips you promised me for these boots!" said Feldon Cobblehammer, a blue blur as he leaped across the meeting table to pluck the coveted boots from Windorf's hands.

A scuffle broke out on the table, and soon three pairs of boots were flying. Scrabbling happily among the throng, the mayor found some pointy animal teeth, six-sided, wooden gaming dice that looked just like a set he'd been missing, and some tasty-looking sweets. He barely had them in his pocket before someone grabbed him by the topknot and conked him soundly on the head with his own gavel. Metwinger sank to the floor behind the Bench of Authority.

Phineas awoke with a startled snort. Looking around quickly, he realized that he was the only one in the room not involved in the brawl, which was rolling like a huge, living ball, toward the door—and his chair! Standing, he dove to his left, away from the door, and landed on his stomach between the last two rows of chairs—a scant distance from the precipice of the open wall.

Propping himself on his elbows, he looked behind him toward the door. The chair he had occupied was smashed into firewood in the wake of the melee. Bottle-necked by the door, the mass of bodies tumbled apart, arms and legs flailing to the accompaniment of savage, joyous shouting. Leaping to their feet in unison, the constituents of the living ball threw the door open and dashed out into the hallway to resume the riot.

Alone in the chamber, Phineas stood slowly and tried to shake away the fuzziness inside his head. He'd been led a merry chase, then nearly crushed by kender, and for what? Nothing! He still had no idea where Trap-springer might be!

"I say, what a splendid Audience Day!" a voice said weakly from behind the Bench of Authority. A small hand grasped the edge of the bench and pulled up the owner of the voice. Phineas recognized the disheveled head of Mayor Metwinger, his topknot completely undone. "Oh, hello!" he said, spotting Phineas at the rear of the room.

"Hello, Your Honor," the human said politely. "You mean the fight wasn't so very unusual?" His tone was incredulous.

"Oh, it certainly was. The brawl usually starts after the second or third case," the mayor responded, his voice breathy as he smoothed his tangled hair. His head was throbbing, and he didn't feel quite right. "The last thing I remember is getting thumped on the noggin with my own gavel." Drawing himself up, Mayor Meldon Metwinger brushed off his sleeves and noticed that his purple mayoral robe had somehow been exchanged with a bright blue cape that looked just like one Feldon Cobblehammer had worn at the start of the Audience. Straightening the collar, the mayor decided the color looked very nice on him.

Phineas hurried forward to take advantage of this unexpected turn of luck. "Your Honor, I understand you might know the whereabouts of a, uh—" he treaded lightly, in case the mayor was sensitive on the subject— "a person named Trapspringer Furrfoot."

"Trapspringer, Trapspringer," the mayor muttered. "I know quite a number of Trapspringers. Can you describe him?"

Phineas's eyebrows puckered as he concentrated. It had been dim during much of his talk with the eccentric kender. "Um, he wears a topknot, his face is very wrinkled, I guess, and he's short." Which describes every kender ever born, Phineas realized with dismay. "I believe he collects rare bones," he added desperately.

"Oh, *that* Trapspringer!" the mayor said cheerfully. "Why didn't you say so? He's my dear friend and soon-to-be in-law! His nephew is birthmated to my daughter Damaris, you know. Yes, I know where he is. I had to put him in prison." Only Metwinger didn't sound the least bit concerned or remorseful.

"You put your daughter's future uncle in prison?" Phineas asked the question despite the little voice in his head that told him he probably wouldn't understand the answer anyway. "What did he do?"

"Oh, *he* didn't do anything," Metwinger said lightly. "His nephew is late for the wedding, so we sent a bounty hunter after him—standard operating procedure concerning wayward bridegrooms, actually. We had to do something to ensure that he would return, so we locked up his favorite uncle. Now, if you don't mind, I think I have a concussion." The mayor looked toward the door and swayed unsteadily.

"I'm sorry to bother you with this, Your Honor," Phineas said quickly, blocking his path. "But there's a small matter of a debt which is owed me."

The mayor looked up, his eyes glassy. "If I have a bill, then I should pay it." He reached into his robes. "How much—"

"Not you, Your Honor," Phineas said, willing himself to remain calm. "Trapspringer Furrfoot. If I could just speak with him, I'm sure we could clear the matter up."

"He's not here," the mayor said, grabbing the edge of the table as the room began to swim. What pretty colors! he thought.

"Yes, I know that, Your Honor," Phineas said with forced patience. "Where is he being held?"

"Prison, dear," the mayor mumbled incoherently, crawling onto the table. "At the palace. We're having a party tonight. Wear your blue dress to match my new cape. . . ." Laying his cheek on the cool wood, he closed his eyes.

"Thank you, Your Honor," Phineas breathed in relief. He was about to dash out the door when he felt a twinge of guilt. He looked at the snoozing mayor—could he leave him like this? He was a doctor, after all—well, sort of. Phineas didn't think Metwinger would die; at worst, the mayor's head would feel like a pumpkin when he woke up. Still . . .

Just then, several giggling kender padded through the door; Phineas recognized them as council members who'd been seated with the mayor. Thinking fast, he bolted by them and shouted, "There's been a terrible accident! The mayor struck his head. Keep an eye on him while I get help!"

Phineas rushed out the door, knowing full well that they'd do no such thing; waiting patiently was not one of their better skills. Before long, they'd decide the mayor needed to be submerged, or perhaps needed a slice of wumpaberry pie, and they'd hustle him off. Metwinger would be all right. Phineas flew out the door and down the stairs.

He was going to find Trapspringer after all.

Chapter 7

"Gee, an ocean?" Tas repeated Woodrow's words. "Are you sure, Woodrow?" He scrambled down from the wagon and headed for the dense screen of shrubs and trees.

"I wouldn't bet my last silver piece that it was an ocean," Woodrow conceded. "It might be a sea," he continued seriously, following on the heels of the kender. "How do you know, unless you have a map?"

Gisella pushed her way past Woodrow to dog Tasslehoff through the brush. "Ouch! These damned branches are tearing my sleeves!" she complained bitterly, swatting foliage from her path. "The last few miles have almost wiped out my wardrobe!"

Tasslehoff burst through the last of the shrubs. He

stood on a flat, dirt-caked, cracked expanse of slate, which met the horizon about thirty feet away. Waves crashed far below in the distance.

The kender hastened to the brink of the barren, rocky cliff and looked over the edge. Below was the shoreline of a vast body of gray-green water. Tas scooped up a piece of chipped slate and flung it out to sea. He lost sight of the stone, and thus concluded that the water was very far off indeed.

Looking to his left, the kender saw that the cliff cut back farther inland, obscuring the view of the coastline to the north. Gulls, their wings tipped, soared and dived around Tasslehoff's head.

"Woodrow has a good point," Tas said at last. His eyebrows shot up. "How does the first person to make a map know if it's a sea, an ocean, or just a really big lake?"

"You're the mapmaker," Gisella growled near his side. "Why don't you tell me? While you're at it, tell me where this body of water came from? Maybe it was hiding behind the mountain range your Uncle Bertie overlooked! And while you're explaining things, tell me how we're going to cross this really, really big lake with a wagon?"

"Let me think," said Tas soberly, his young face scrunching up in thought.

"Indeed," Gisella snorted humorlessly.

"You know, I believe that trek through the swamp caused us to turn a bit south of Xak Tsaroth," Tasslehoff said. "Maybe someone in the city knows where this water came from—"

"You think that ocean is going to dry up a few miles north of here?" Gisella shrieked. She immediately regretted showing a crack in her composure. Painfully digging her fingernails into her fists, she regained control. "Perhaps someone in Xak Tsaroth could tell us where we are, and direct us to the best east-bound road. If we can actually find Xak Tsaroth, that is."

Gisella wiped her eyes with the back of her hand in a gesture of fatigue. "But I can't move another inch tonight. We'll make camp here," she said, indicating the wide expanse of level slate with a wave of her hand. "Woodrow, be a dear and get the wagon. My head is splitting!"

"Yes, Miss Hornslager." The straw-haired young man sprinted across the ledge to the row of shrubs and disappeared.

One arm hugged tight to her waist, the other supporting her chin, Gisella looked down at the distant shore. She smirked mirthlessly and shook her head. "Isn't it ironic? All that water, and I can't even get to it to take a bath."

*　*　*　*　*

Tasslehoff first heard the noises before dawn. Curled up by the smoldering remains of the fire across from Woodrow, he was having the most delightful dream, and he did not want to wake up before it ended. He was in a merchant's shop, and its walls were lined from floor to ceiling with jars of all sizes and colors, each crammed with more interesting objects than the last. There were jars of stained-glass marbles and pretty stones, jars with balls of brightly colored string, jars overflowing with confections and wind-up toys. There was a whole shelf devoted to jeweled rings, and another just for ruby-studded brooches.

The owner of the shop, who hadn't been in the dream just a moment before, turned to Tasslehoff and said, "You must take everything and hide it, before someone steals it. I can trust only you!"

And then Tasslehoff heard the noise again, just at the edge of his consciousness. He scrunched up his eyes and focused his mind on the shelves in the shop.

But there was that noise again, like raccoons rattling a trash barrel. He jerked awake against his will, irritated and out of sorts.

In the dim light of dawn, the kender saw three sets of dark, overly large eyes peering at him from around the edge of the wagon. Infiltrators! Bandits! They were under attack! Tasslehoff jumped up and assumed a kender fighting stance, legs spread and braced. Holding the "v" of his hoopak in his left hand, he pivoted his hips and swung the straight end of his weapon around with his right hand.

"Stay back, whoever you are!" he warned. Suddenly, more sets of eyes appeared. Without looking down, Tas drove a toe into Woodrow's ribs.

The sleeping human snorted, raised himself on his elbows, and finally looked up through bleary eyes. He saw only Tas's battle stance before jumping to his feet and reaching for the first thing at hand, which was the unlit end of a small, smoldering branch in the fire. Only then did he spot the eyes, glowing like the neutral, golden moon, Solinari, in the dim light of dawn. There were eyes under the wagon, at the back of the wagon, on top of the wagon.

Suddenly the wagon's back door flew open and Gisella stepped out in a thin, silky, red wrap. Whatever stood at the rear of the wagon jumped back and giggled.

"Oh, for heavens' sake," Gisella moaned. "What's this, now? Shoo, shoo, you little beasties!" she clucked, taking a step down and waving the backs of her hands toward where the eyes had stood.

"Miss Hornslager, get back in the wagon!" Woodrow called. "We're under attack!" He swung his branch at the eyes in a gesture meant to look brave.

"By gully dwarves?" Her voice cracked on a high note. "Don't be ridiculous. They're as annoying as horseflies, I'll grant you that, but they're harmless." She turned back to glare in the direction of the still-aproaching eyes. "I said shoo!" She waved the hem of her nightshirt at them like a farmer's wife scattering chickens with her apron.

"Gully dwarves?" Tas asked, lowering his hoopak. He took a step toward the wagon and squinted into the darkness. The air was filled with the sound of uncontrollable giggling. Finally, Tas could see eleven or more short creatures who looked vaguely like dwarves gathered before the door. Instead of "shooing," they were looking up at Gisella expectantly, like pigeons waiting for breadcrumbs in a city square.

Tas knew from his mountain dwarf friend, Flint, that gully dwarves, or Aghar, were the lowest caste in dwarven society. They were very clannish, keeping to themselves and living in places so squalid that no other creatures, including most animals, would live in them. Which would leave them with a lot of privacy, Tas supposed.

Tasslehoff hadn't seen many gully dwarves up close, except for a few who had been cleaned up and recruited into domestic labor by ambitious but notoriously cheap merchant middle-class Kendermorians, as they called themselves. (Gully dwarves made miserable servants, as they tended to pick their noses continually and attracted dirt as if by magic.) Their features varied little from one to the next. They shared a typical thick, bulby nose, scruffy whiskers—even the females—and sported ratty, wild hair that looked like it had been combed many years before with a stick. The males wore torn, dirty vests and pants cinched up with frayed rope, and the females wore torn, dirty, sack-shaped dresses, and they all wore shoes that were three sizes too big.

"Get rid of them, will you, Woodrow dear? The little beggars will undoubtedly steal us blind," Gisella said, drawing her wrap closer. "And we really must be on the road."

In the growing light, Woodrow looked helplessly at the crowd of gully dwarves continuing to gather around the wagon. They stared with awe at Gisella. "What would you like me to do, ma'am?" asked the bewildered human.

Gisella, looking exasperated, took a step back from the pressing throng of gully dwarves. "I don't know! Do something manly, like wave your sword at them."

The human looked dismayed at the suggestion.

Vexed by his hesitance, Gisella jammed her hands on her hips. "So, belch in their faces; that's manly!" she added with disgust.

Woodrow looked from the stick in his hand to the two dozen or more curious, grubby gully dwarves. They looked at Gisella reverently. The boldest of the bunch, a male, judging purely from the fact that he wore shapeless pants rather than a shapeless dress, reached up a hand to the dwarf's red hair.

"Stop that!" Gisella said, slapping his hand away. Holding her wrap closed, she nearly tripped while scrambling backward up the steps into the wagon.

"Where you get hair?" the gully dwarf spoke at last, not the least put off by her slap. He leaned forward, his stubby fingers reaching out. The silly grin on his smudgey face revealed that he had a big, dark hole in his mouth where one front tooth should have been.

"What do you mean?" she snapped. "I grow it, of course!" She slapped his hand again.

The gully dwarf shook his head stubbornly. "Not that hair. Hair not come that color."

Gisella bristled. "I assure you, this is my natural hair," she said staunchly, giving him an appraising glance. "I might add that yours would look better if you washed it instead of ripping it out in clumps."

The gully dwarf smiled up at her hair. "It pretty. You pretty."

Gisella's eyes shifted. "You like it?"

"It pretty," he repeated reverently. The crowd of gully dwarves chorused his words, then giggled.

"Thank you," Gisella said hesitantly. "Your hair ain't so bad, either," she added generously.

"Should I get rid of them now for you, Miss

Hornslager?" Woodrow asked.

"I've been meaning to ask you about your hair myself," Tasslehoff chimed in. "Is it real—the color, I mean? Personally, I see nothing wrong with a little cosmetic overhaul. Why, once, when I was younger, I drew some lines on my face because I was embarrassed that I had no wrinkles yet. Of course, they weren't *red* wrinkles. But it's the same difference."

Gisella only glared at Tas and announced in an icy voice, "I'm going inside to get dressed now. And when I come out, we're leaving."

"Leave?" The male gully dwarf's ears perked up. "I thought maybe you here for pulley job," he said.

"A pulley job? Why, I haven't had one in—" Gisella got all tingly at the memories of an inn long ago and far away. Well, at least a week and a hundred miles. . . . Abruptly she caught the human's and kender's innocent expressions, and she realized that the gully dwarf couldn't possibly be talking about the same kind of pulley job.

"Pulley job?" she repeated.

"Oh, boy!" The head gully clapped his hands in delight, taking her question as confirmation. "Pulley job! How you pay?"

"No, no! I'm simply asking, what *is* a pulley job?" she explained with forced tolerance.

"Fondu show you," he offered, taking her hand before she could protest. He led her off the steps, directing her to the north, where the cliff cut back farther inland, obscuring the view. Woodrow and Tasslehoff followed closely, the rest of the gully dwarves dancing in joyous circles around them, their big, floppy-toed shoes slapping noisily on the slate cliff. A short distance up the coast, out of view of their camp, Fondu pointed to a huge, lone cypress tree that dangled out over the edge of the cliff.

"So what?" Gisella said, starting to get annoyed. "You led me barefoot over rough ground to look at an old tree?" Wincing, she steadied herself with one hand on Fondu's shoulder while she plucked pointy pebbles from her tender heel.

Tasslehoff scampered to the base of the tree. Looking up, he launched himself at a low, sturdy branch, and began scrambling up hand over foot like a monkey.

"Tasslehoff, you get down from that tree this minute!" Gisella cried in alarm. "You'll plunge to your death, and I'll have nothing but bloody bones to trade to the council."

"So nice of you to be concerned about my health," he said sweetly.

"What do you see up there, Mr. Burrfoot?" Woodrow asked.

There was a brief pause as Tasslehoff swung from branch to branch in the tree. "Well, it's three pulleys . . . no, it's four pulleys. Hooked together in pairs. Only really it's six pulleys, because two of them are two pulleys hooked together side by side. And they're all linked with ropes as thick as my wrist, only real short. My guess is it's Fondu's pulley job."

Gisella turned to Fondu. "No doubt." But she was doubtful. Gisella could not believe that a bunch of gully dwarves could have rigged up such an apparently elaborate system.

Fondu's face crinkled up into a glassy-eyed smile. "Many men come and build pulley job. They funny little men." Imitating them, Fondu frowned up at the tree, stroking an imaginary beard. Abruptly he marched around, stumbling over his floppy shoes and swinging his arms. Giggling, the crowd of gully dwarves marched in small circles, slapping their feet up and down.

"They sound like gnomes, because gnomes like to build things like this, but they look like dwarves," Tas said, laughing at the antics of the gully dwarves. He swung down out of the tree.

"No self-respecting dwarf looks like *that*," Gisella scoffed, watching their parade out of the corners of her narrowed eyes.

"These 'men' just put up the pulleys and left?" Woodrow asked Fondu.

The gully dwarf gave Woodrow a calculating stare. "No, they bring up big boxes from there." Fondu pointed to the cliff and downward. "Then they leave." He suddenly looked suspicious. "Too many questions! You want pulley job or no?"

Gisella shuddered, stretched her wrap tightly around her curves, and turned back toward the camp. "I hardly think so. Now, if you'll just point us toward Xak Tsaroth, we won't trouble you further."

"You want come to Zaksarawth? You meet Highbulp! No one come to Zaksarawth since so long!" cheered Fondu. The rest of the gully dwarves started yelling and flinging handfuls of dirt in the air.

Gisella, Tas, and Woodrow ducked away from the whirling dust cloud. "Why are you acting like that?" shouted Gisella.

"We happy," said Fondu. "No one come to Zaksarawth anymore except Aghar, but you special. You like our city under ground. It beautiful."

"An underground city?" Gisella gulped, turning to Tasslehoff. "I thought you said it was a big, bustling place!"

"It is!" Tasslehoff cried defensively. "At least that's what my map indicates." He pulled the map from his vest and spread it out on the ground.

Gisella glowered. "Oh, yes, your wonderful map."

Woodrow crouched down next to Tasslehoff. "What does 'P.C.' mean?" he asked, pointing to the letters inked after the title "Krynn."

Gisella snatched up the map and stared at the letters. " 'Pre-Cataclysm,' you idiots! It means pre-Cataclysm! We've been following a map that predates the Cataclysm!"

"Really?" Tas said dubiously. "I thought it stood for 'positively confirmed'."

Dazed, Gisella just shook her head. "Serves me right for listening to a kender. Pre-Cataclysm, indeed!"

"That changes things, does it?" Woodrow asked innocently.

"A little," Tas gulped.

"A little?" Gisella gaped at the kender. "New mountain ranges erupted, and whole sections of land slipped into the ground and formed seas!"

Tasslehoff looked subdued. "Well, *most* of the cities stayed in the same places," he moaned.

"Yeah, those that weren't sucked up by rushing waters, mountains, and volcanoes!" Gisella rolled her eyes and sighed heavily in resignation. "Well, that about hangs it—we can't sail this wagon on the sea. We're going to have to backtrack, and there's not a chance on Krynn that we'll reach Kendermore in time for the Autumn Faire. This is going to set me *way* back."

"Sail wagon on sea," Fondu remarked.

Gisella ignored his mocking voice. "Come on, Woodrow," she said wearily, starting for camp. "We've got a long trip ahead of us."

But Fondu stumbled along at her side, tugging at her wrap. "Sail wagon on sea!" he repeated.

She stopped and brushed him off. "Wouldn't that be nice, Fondu," she said patronizingly. "Come on, Woodrow, Burrfoot."

But Fondu would not be put off. "Wagon no float, but boat float!"

"What are you trying to tell us, Fondu?" Woodrow asked.

The gully dwarf scowled at Woodrow. "I tell pretty lady. Your hair weird—look like noodles." Fondu grabbed Gisella's hand again and tugged her to the ledge. He pointed down. "See? Boat."

Gisella brushed off her hand disdainfully. "Well, I'll

be!" she exclaimed, looking over the edge quickly. "The little bug-eater—uh, gully dwarf—is telling the truth! There *is* a boat down there."

"Let me see!" cried Tas, moving to Gisella's side, along with Woodrow. "But why would anyone leave a boat anchored here?"

"I don't know," answered Gisella, "and I don't know what difference it makes, anyway. Everything I own is in that wagon, and I'm not going to leave it here," she finished firmly.

Fondu tugged at Gisella's wrap. "Take wagon on boat."

"Woodrow," said Gisella, "would you please try to explain that we can't possibly get this fully loaded wagon down a sheer, five hundred-foot—"

"Oh, it's got to be at least eight hundred feet—at least," chimed Tas, on his stomach, looking over the cliff.

"—six hundred-foot cliff and onto a rocking boat," finished Gisella. "You're making me terribly nervous, dear," she added, addressing the human.

Woodrow, who had crawled out on a cyprus limb overhanging the ledge, cleared his throat. "Excuse me for saying so, Miss Hornslager, but I'd bet that whoever—"

"—whoever owns that boat made the pulley job!" Tas finished for him. "They had to get up here somehow, and I'll bet they used the pulleys. We could use their equipment to go up and down the cliff!"

"Exactly," said Woodrow.

"Pulley job! Pulley job!" screamed Fondu, jumping up and down beneath the cyprus tree.

"Wait just one minute," Gisella said, refusing to get caught up in the excitement so easily. "Do we have enough people to lower a swinging wagon six hundred feet? And do you think we could then load the wagon onto the ship and sail it away?"

"Maybe," Woodrow said. "But I don't think we

should. That would be stealing."

"It wouldn't be stealing!" Tas disagreed. "We would just be borrowing it. They're not using it now, and we don't know when they'll be back. When *will* they be back, Fondu?"

"Two day," the gully dwarf said simply, holding up four fingers.

"How long have they been gone?" Gisella asked.

"Two day." He held up all his fingers.

Gisella, Tas, and Woodrow looked at each other.

"How many of you are there?"

Fondu looked at the dozens of gully dwarves and smiled broadly. "Two."

"Oh, boy," breathed Woodrow.

"We don't seem to be getting any real information out of this," drawled Gisella. "Woodrow, you're good at technical things. What would we need to do this 'pulley job'?"

Woodrow squatted on his haunches and poked at the ground with a stick, scratching lines at random on the slate. Within moments, all of the gully dwarves were down on their haunches, scratching and doodling on the rock in imitation of the human. Tas was enormously amused and strolled among the pondering gully dwarves.

Gisella stood over the human with her arms folded expectantly. "Well?"

After a minute or two, Woodrow tossed his head back and looked up at Gisella. "Ma'am, I figure we'll need the pulleys there in the tree, at least four thousand feet of rope, and for muscle, the team of horses— plus about a dozen good men. But that's just a guess," he added modestly.

Looking somber, the gully dwarves all nodded their heads in agreement, pointing at each others' scratchings and chattering among themselves.

Gisella threw her arms into the air. "Well, I guess that's that. We don't have a dozen *good* anything, and we certainly don't have four thousand feet of rope. If I didn't have so many steel pieces tied up in those rotting melons, I'd push the wagon off the cliff myself and smash that lousy boat into splinters." She flopped down on the ledge where she stood, her chin in her hands.

Tasslehoff skipped back to the sullen Gisella. "As far as muscle is concerned," he said, "we've got all the gully dwarves we could ever want."

"And how many is that?" Gisella quipped. "Two?"

"I know they're not much to look at and they don't smell very nice, but I'm sure they'd be willing to help," prodded Tas. "After all, this was Fondu's idea."

Fondu grinned broadly. "We glad to heave-ho. Heave-hoing fun! We heave-ho lots for funny men. 'Heeeeave ho'," he mimicked, drawing on an imaginary rope.

"That's very nice, Fondu," Gisella said flatly. "Now I don't suppose you can tell us where to find four thousand feet of rope, can you?"

The gully dwarf's chest swelled with pride. "Fondu have rope. Big rope. Pulley rope. I show pretty-hair lady."

The three travelers stared at Fondu, then looked at each other. "You don't suppose," mouthed Gisella.

"Funny men hide pulley rope," explained Fondu, "but Fondu find it. Me smell rope, my nose smell big."

Gisella batted her eyelashes at Fondu. "And would you show *me* where it is?"

Fondu grabbed Gisella's hand and yanked her to her feet, nearly tripping himself in his excitement. "Come come come!" he shouted, dragging the object of his infatuation behind. Tasslehoff and Woodrow ran behind the stumbling pair, followed by a tumbling, sweating mass of gully dwarves.

Fondu led the pack to an enormous, hollow tree not quite five hundred feet from the edge of the cliff. With a quick scramble, he was up on the lowest branch, and then disappeared through a basket-sized hole into the tree. His fuzzy head reappeared moments later, and he thrust the end of a coarse hemp rope back out through the opening.

"See?" he shouted. "Pulley rope! You no worry, pretty lady," Fondu said, petting Gisella's hair. She batted his hand away, shivering.

In a moment, Tasslehoff was up the tree and had stuck his head through the hole for a look. When he pulled it back, he was grinning from ear to ear.

"The entire tree is full of rope!" he gushed. "Coils and coils of rope! I've never seen so much rope in my life, except maybe on the docks at Port Balifor. Wow! I wish my Uncle Trapspringer was here to see this."

Gisella clapped her hands and rubbed the palms together. "All right, crew, it looks like we've got ourselves a pulley job."

*   *   *   *   *

It took the dozen gully dwarves three and a half hours to drag all the rope out of the tree and arrange it in two orderly lines leading away from the cypress tree. Meanwhile, using a small length of rope from the wagon to practice with, Woodrow figured out how the pulleys had to be set up. When the longer rope was ready, he rigged two stout loops of rope around the wagon, one lashed to the front axle and the other to the rear axle. All of that was simpler than explaining the system to Gisella.

"We connect the two single pulleys to the ropes around the wagon. The two double pulleys are connected to the overhanging branch of the tree. You've got that part, right?"

Gisella nodded. "Of course. I'm not dense." But darned if she understood it anyway!

"We used to rig up a hoist like this on my cousin's farm when I was a boy," Woodrow said.

The dwarf, who was now wearing a simple, green

working outfit and leather gloves, sat down on the wagon next to Woodrow. She looked at the wagon, then up at the pulleys, and then back at the wagon. "This is everything I own, Woodrow. Are you sure?"

Woodrow looked up. "Reasonably sure, Miss Hornslager."

Gisella glanced up at the pulleys again and contemplated the mass of ropes connecting them to the tree, and the wagon to them. Her gaze moved on to include the ropes that had been strung to several boulders to anchor the tree. Then she cleared her throat.

"I haven't had much practice trusting people," she said to Woodrow. "The few times I've tried it, it hasn't worked out too well, personally or financially. I don't have a lot of choice here, though. If we go south, I'm ruined by the delay. If we go down the cliff—well, maybe I'm ruined and maybe I'm not. It sounds like a plan to me. Fondu! Where's Fondu?"

The gully dwarf tumbled out of a knot of his fellows that were wrestling over someone's grimy cap. "Fondu here," he announced. "You ready for pulley job?"

A pair of hands reached out of the melee and hauled Fondu back into the writhing mass before Gisella could answer. Careful not to get too close, Gisella approached the pile of gully dwarves and, cupping her hands around her mouth, shouted, "Fondu! Line them up! Line them up!"

Several seconds later, Fondu kicked and swatted his way out again and began hauling gully dwarves out of the fracas. Within minutes, everyone was sorted and lined up along the two ropes, which stretched over a quarter of a mile away from the cliff. Gisella reviewed her company, replete with bloody noses, blackened eyes, and swollen lips. No sooner did she turn her back than someone pushed someone else and the whole fray began over again until Woodrow collared the two troublemakers and held them at arm's length.

"All right, Woodrow," Gisella instructed, "you're in

charge of the ropes. With one horse and six gully dwarves on each, you should be able to lower the wagon nice and easy. Let's have that as our slogan today, shall we? 'Nice and easy.' Can everyone say that?"

A ragged chorus of "nice and easy," or variations on it, rippled up and down the two lines of gully dwarves.

"Right," said Gisella. "And Tas, you and your six husky lads have the guy lines. Your job is to guide the wagon off the edge . . . " Gisella's throat constricted slightly on the words " . . . and then steady it as much as you can on the way down."

For a moment, everyone looked at everyone else. Then Gisella winked at Tas and Tas kicked away the stone that was blocking the wagon's wheel. Slowly, guided by Tas, the six Aghar on the guy lines rolled the wagon toward the edge of the cliff. Meanwhile, Woodrow, who had three times as many gully dwarves to control and therefore three times as many problems, struggled to keep the lines taut through the pulleys.

Gisella's breath caught in her throat as the front wheels of the wagon dropped over the edge. The ropes on the forward pulley snapped tight at once, and the tree bobbed up and down. With its forward wheels suspended over six hundred feet of nothing, the gully dwarves inched the wagon ahead.

Gisella's heart was pounding. The wagon, the tree, the gully dwarves, all swam in front of her. Then the rear wheels of the wagon crunched across the brink, and the vehicle dropped six inches, swaying to and fro. The gully dwarves on the guy lines squealed and dug their heels into the packed dirt under the tree as the weight of the wagon, swinging out into line beneath the pulleys, dragged them toward the cliff. Gisella's hand shot out to a nearby boulder to steady her balance, and her knees chattered together like teeth.

"Hold on, hold on!" cried Tas, latching onto one of the guy lines. He realized then that the gully dwarves were squealing with delight, like children at a spook show. As the wagon reached its equilibrium the dwarves stopped sliding and the noise died down. Gisella swayed slightly, but was relieved that she was still on her feet. The wagon swung gently on its ropes, twisting slightly in the breeze.

"OK," said Gisella, swallowing a lump. "OK, that wasn't too bad." Cupping her hands to her mouth, she hollered, "Now, Woodrow, start letting it down. 'Nice and easy,' remember?"

"Lice and squeezies," grunted the dwarves in no particular unison. With a hand on each of the horses' bridles, Woodrow started walking them backward toward the cliff. After the first twenty-five feet, Woodrow could no longer see the wagon and had to rely on Tas to guide him from above, where he lay on a limb in the tree, watching to make sure the ropes glided smoothly through the pulleys.

"OK . . . OK . . . slow it down a little . . . the back end is a little high . . . oops, now the back is a little low . . . still low . . . no, the *back* is low . . . the back, the back!"

Gisella sprinted to the cliff. "What's happening?" she screamed, and then she spied the wagon, about one hundred feet down the cliff. One of the lines of gully dwarves had gotten ahead of the other. The front end of the wagon was at least four feet higher than the back, and still rising. "It's all cockeyed!" she shrieked, flailing her arms. "I can hear bottles breaking! Straighten it out! Straighten it out!"

But the gully dwarves, who had no concept of what was happening, continued their erratic march to the sea. In desperation, Woodrow let go of the slower horse's bridle and was hauling vainly on the faster-moving horse, trying to slow it down. Unfortunately the other horse, with no one guiding it forward, stopped in its tracks.

The wagon lurched suddenly as something inside it

broke free and crashed into the back wall. Gisella clapped her hands over her ears when a second crash echoed up the cliff face, then frantically slapped them over her eyes as the wagon's door flew open and a pot-pourri of melons, cushions, and personal items tumbled out of the doorway. Everything she owned spiraled, for what seemed to Gisella like an eternity, down the hundreds of feet to the sea.

By now, the wagon was hanging almost vertically. The door flapped in the breeze with one of Gisella's nightshirts, caught on the latch, waving like a flag of truce. Within moments, Woodrow brought the advancing horse and gully dwarves to a halt and raced back to the stationary line, then advanced it so the lines were again even. All this was accompanied by even more smashing and tinkling from below. Each crash made Woodrow wince, each tinkle made Gisella bite deeper into her lip.

Finally, Tas announced from above that the wagon was level again.

Peering down at Gisella, he called, "Maybe it's not as bad as it sounded." But when he saw her vacant stare fixed on the horizon, he gave it up. He shouted to Woodrow, "OK, try it again. You don't have to be *too* careful, I don't think there's much left inside." Out of the corner of his eye he saw Gisella's face twitch.

Once again the wagon started down the cliff in jerks and fits. Gisella no longer watched. Instead, she had positioned herself on an exposed tree root and was reciting a disjointed monologue that had more numbers than words in it. She was obviously trying to determine how she would recoup her losses of the last minutes.

"Slow it down, slow it down," Tasslehoff warned as the wagon neared the ground.

Woodrow was glad that the red-haired dwarf wasn't watching when he was unable to appreciably slow the wagon's momentum in the last one hundred feet. The gully dwarves clawed and tugged at the rope to little avail. The human could feel it in the ropes when the wagon landed with a heavy 'thump!' far below. He squinted up at Tas through one eye.

"Boy, what a landing!" the kender breathed. "The wheels look a little bowed out, but I think the wagon is OK."

Woodrow heaved a sigh and sagged against one of the horses.

Tasslehoff spotted Gisella. Climbing down from the tree, he approached her cautiously. "Well, it's on the shore," he said unceremoniously. "I guess I'll shinny down one of the ropes and unhook the pulleys so we can lower the horses and you and everyone who's going."

Gisella nodded her head and inhaled deeply. Tas took that as approval and hiked back to the tree.

Woodrow was waiting for him. "How is Miss Hornslager?" he asked.

"I think she'll be all right," said Tas. "She just needs to rest for a while. I think it was the nightshirt on the door latch that did her in. It's too bad you missed it, Woodrow. Stuff was flying everywhere. Boy, what a sight!"

"She'll never talk to me again," Woodrow moaned. "I wouldn't blame her if she fired me and left me stranded here with these gully dwarves. I don't know how I'd ever get home then."

"I could leave you a map," offered Tas. Woodrow blanched. The kender began tightening his belts, equipment, and pouches in preparation for his climb. "Anyway, it wasn't your fault," he added. "I'm sure Gisella won't blame you. She's just feeling lowly. That seems to be sort of common with dwarves. Apparently they can't help themselves. Whenever my friend Flint gets depressed, there's no cheering him up until he feels like being cheered up."

Stripped to his tunic, belt, leggings, and shoes, Tas

was ready to climb. He snaked across the branch to the pulleys and then swung down onto a rope.

"Good luck," called Woodrow.

"You, too," replied Tas with a wave as he started the long slide to the boat, six hundred feet below.

Chapter 8

Wilbur Froghair was on the deserted, cobbled street in front of his grocery shop at dawn, preparing for the early morning rush. The carrots and onions were in place on the vegetable carts and he was about to turn the rotten spots down on the two-day-old to-matoes when he noticed the body slumped in the bench before the haberdashery next door.

His first concern was for the human's health. Care-fully holding one of his small hands before the middle-aged man's nose, the kender was reassured by the even breathing. The man looked like he'd had a bad night. He wore a hat that was too small for his balding head, his pockets were turned inside out, the knee of his breeches was ripped, and his face had a layer of street dust on it. But what the kender saw next made him almost more concerned than before.

The perfectly good leather boot on the man's right foot lay carelessly in a puddle.

"He should be more careful with his possessions," Wilbur mumbled. "That very nice boot is going to get wet, and then shrivel up like an old, dried currant. I certainly can't sit by and watch that happen." With that, the kender crept forward and gingerly lifted the man's calf, slipping the boot from his foot. "I'll just keep it nice and dry in my shop," Wilbur whispered to himself, satisfied with his good deed. It was such a nice boot, in fact, that he decided it really deserved to be kept very safe indeed in the big, locked tin box under his grocery counter. He was about to take the other boot to maintain the pair, when the man stirred in his sleep. Wilbur tiptoed quietly into his shop, holding one boot.

Phineas Curick drifted half out of sleep, thinking that his foot felt cold. He tried to ignore the sensation because he knew his body would ache from top to bottom if he woke up fully. But when he realized his foot probably felt cold because it was also wet, he awoke abruptly.

The bone! He'd placed another rat bone in one of his boots to sell to Trapspringer in exchange for the rest of the map. He fished around frantically in his left boot and sighed with relief. The rat bone was still safely tucked away.

Disaster narrowly averted, Phineas was dismayed but not at all surprised to realize, too, that his other boot was missing. He saw his pockets sticking out and remembered that he had run through or lost all his money yesterday. He felt a headache coming on, as if someone had tied an overly tight band around his head. Reaching a hand up, he realized someone had done just that. His own hat was gone, replaced by a small, ratty-looking cap with a hole in the back, presumably for a topknot.

Kendermore was the kind of city in which a person could spend his entire life—or a number of years, as in Phineas's case—without ever leaving his own neighborhood. Everything he needed was near his home. When the human had come to Kendermore some years before, he had made his home in the first neighborhood he landed in. In the meantime, Phineas had forgotten how thoroughly confusing the city was.

There was virtually no such thing as a completed, or even a through, street. Roads just ended wherever their builders grew tired of them or, more often, wherever someone decided to erect a building. The city was a maze of dead-end streets that simply ran head-on into buildings and then started up again on the other side. Often you had to go several miles out of your way to continue on a road that you could have hit with a rock from where you started, if only you could have seen it.

Kendermore had an extensive street sign program. There were signs on every corner, naming roads and pointing the way to numerous landmarks, such as the homes of local celebrities or public squares. These signs would have been very helpful if they were updated in a timely manner when new roads were built or after buildings had been plunked down on existing roads. It was not uncommon to see a signpost with two arrows pointed in opposite directions and both reading, "The Palace." Part of the reason the sign changes came so slowly and inaccurately was the process used by city workmen to complete these tasks. The previous day, Phineas had watched a team of kender workmen replace the sign over a public square.

The foreman stood back from the rest, his arms crossed while he issued orders. "Now, Jessel, you get on Bildar's shoulders, Giblart on Jessel, Sterpwitz on Giblart, and Leverton, you're on top." The foreman tilted his creased face back and surveyed the distance.

Satisfied, he nodded. "Yep, that oughta be tall enough."

Like members of an acrobatic team, the kender set about forming a tower of bodies. Phineas knew kender owned ladders, but they seemed to prefer living kender pyramids. Deft as any circus acrobats, they passed one another upward until they reached the desired height and the kender named Leverton was on top.

"Oops, you forgot the hammer," the foreman called. One by one, the kender passed each other back down. Reaching the bottom, Leverton took the hammer from his foremean, and the stacking process had commenced again.

Phineas had been reduced to spending the night on a bench in front of a habberdasher's, having exhausted the entire day following one sign after another.

Begging an apple from a friendly greengrocer next to the haberdasher, he limped down the street now, his left leg more than an inch taller than his bootless right. He could have sworn he'd passed this way before, for he seemed to recognize shop fronts and even a little park across the way, but he followed an arrow that supposedly led to the palace.

Suddenly, in mid-block, an arrow pointed across the street and into a candlemaker's shop. Puzzled, Phineas stood in the stoop under the shop's sign and looked several times from the arrow to the interior of the shop strung with candles. Surely *this* couldn't be the palace—could it?

Abruptly the door swung open and a female kender in a wax-spattered apron stepped out. Kicking a brick into place to hold the door open, she said, "My first customer of the morning always gets a special on the big beeswax candles. Normally one copper a piece, but you can have three for six copper." She squinted at the human and added, "You look terrible, mister. Did you know you're missing a boot? Wanna swap for it?"

"Yes, I know," he said lethargically "And I'm not interested in swapping my boot for any candles this morning, thank you. But I would like to know why the sign across the street says that this is the way to the palace."

" 'Cause this is," she said curtly.

"This is the palace?" Phineas barked in disbelief.

"No, this is the *way to* the palace," she said with exaggerated forbearance. "It's a daytime shortcut when I'm open. If you want to go the other way, go way back to City Hall, take a left, then five or six more lefts, and a few rights after that. It should only take you a half-day or so to get there." She stepped back into her shop.

Phineas followed her, suddenly earnest. "I'll take the shortcut, then, thank you. Where do I go, right through this door?" he asked, pointing to an opening in the back of the shop.

"Yes, then just crawl out the window there. You'll be on Mulberry Street—or is it Strawberry Street? I can never remember. Keep going until you get to the statue of somebody or other. Or maybe it's a tree, sometimes they look so much alike, don't you agree? Anyway, just go past that and turn right. You'll see the palace at the end of the street." She held out her hand, palm up. "That'll be ten copper."

"Ten copper?!" he cried. "For letting me crawl out your window and telling me that trees and statues look alike?"

"It's a long way back to City Hall." She smiled.

"The fact of the matter is," noted Phineas unhappily, "I don't have any cash at the moment."

She looked at his feet. "As I was saying, that's a fine-looking boot you have there."

"Yeah, it sure was," he muttered to himself as he pulled it off and handed it to her, secretly slipping the rat bone into the cuff of his sleeve. "It used to be part of a matched set."

She rubbed the toe reverently. "This will be a superb place to keep my money. Here, take a candle, too," she said generously, thrusting a thick, lumpy, beige one into his hand.

Maybe he could use it for ear plugs, he thought. Holding the candle awkwardly, Phineas thanked her and left to find the window at back. Pulling a crate under it, he scrambled over the sill and dropped to the ground on the other side. Sharp, pointy stones bit into the tender flesh of his white soles as he hobbled through a weedy vacant lot toward the nearest street.

For one block, its name was, in fact, Mulberry Street. Then it became Strawberry Boulevard. The buildings were coming farther and farther apart, so he reasoned that he must be nearing the city limits, whatever side of Kendermore he was on.

At last he came to a lush, overgrown public square. The ground was blanketed in fallen leaves of every color. Perched on a pedestal was a tree. Or was it a statue? He was beginning to think like a kender! Stepping forward, he thumped it. Stone. It was a statue of a tree. Rounding the corner of the statue, he looked down the street to the right.

There, at the end of the short street, he saw the most unKendermore-like setting in the entire city. In the first place, the palace looked finished, at least from where Phineas stood. In the second place, it didn't share that "crates and barrels smashed together on a grand scale" look that so many architects in Kendermore seemed to favor. While the "smashed barrels" style was interesting to look at, it was not beautiful.

But this building was beautiful to Phineas's eye. It looked more like buildings found in the human cities he had visited and lived in before, but the flavor was slightly different, slightly exotic.

Stretching out before the front steps of the structure was a long, cool reflecting pool, edged by an expertly shaped topiary garden. Hedges were cut into the forms of animals, including dogs, cats, horses, and even mythical dragons. The shrubs were just beginning to turn brown at the tips, which made the animals look fuzzy.

Unconsciously, Phineas ran over the rough street to stand at the end of the reflecting pool. Eyes agog, he looked up at the palace. A central dome enclosed the body of the building, made of the smoothest white marble. An inestimable number of turrets surrounded the big dome, each capped by onion-domed minarets. Every landing—and there were dozens of all sizes— was supported by intricately carved arches that came to gentle points.

The whole vision was one of such consistent and soothing symmetry that Phineas could not help but wonder if he had, in fact, somehow departed Kendermore.

Then he saw an aged kender wearing muddy, knee-high boots, with a small hedge-clipper tucked into his white hair. The kender pushed a wheelbarrow up to a topiary of a bear and stopped.

"Excuse me," stammered Phineas, still awed by the building before him. "This . . . this is the palace, isn't it?"

The kender released the wheelbarrow's handles and turned around to look at the human. "This's it, yes, sir," he said. "Only one like it in Kendermore." Then his eyes narrowed. "Unless you know of another, that is."

"No," replied Phineas. "I've never seen anything like it before." The kender continued to eye him. "In Kendermore or anywhere else," he added.

"Well, that's good to know," announced the kender. "I like to keep on top of things like that. Enjoy yourself. Try not to break anything." The kender took the shears from his hair and snipped twice at the bear. Nodding with satisfaction, he replaced the clippers, picked up his wheelbarrow again, and continued on his way.

"Wait!" shouted Phineas. "Can you tell me something about this place? I've spent two days trying to find it!"

The kender stopped again and turned around. "Two days?" he exclaimed. "Where did you start looking— Silvanost? There are signs everywhere."

"Yes, I know," Phineas sighed. "I've seen them all. Unfortunately, the only sign that helped at all was an unlikely one that sent me through the middle of a candle shop."

"Oh, yes, down on Elderberry Street," said the kender, nodding. "That's an excellent shortcut. I like to get there first thing in the morning for their big beeswax candle special." He spotted a thistle in the grass, stooped to dig it out, then saw Phineas's feet. "Say, did you know you aren't wearing any shoes?"

"Yes, I know." The sun was beginning to peak over the palace, and Phineas had to squint to see the kender. "Is this the mayor's home? It's exceptionally grand."

"Nope," the kender said with a shake of his head, "the mayor doesn't live here. No one does, except prisoners now and then."

"That's why I'm here!" Phineas exclaimed.

"Oh," responded the kender, "are you checking in as a prisoner?"

Phineas scratched his chest for a moment, puzzled by the kender's question. "No," he responded simply. Spying a bench, Phineas hobbled over to it and plopped down. He rested a moment under the kender's curious gaze.

"My name is Phineas Curick," he began. "I've been trying for two days to find this palace because I need to talk to Trapspringer Furrfoot, whom I understand is being held a prisoner within. There. Now, who are you?"

"Bigelow Spadestomper, your friend and acquaintance." He extended his small, muddy hand. "I am the groundskeeper and gardener here at the palace, the

fourth Spadestomper groundskeeper in as many Spadestomper generations. And, yes, there is a Trapspringer in residence at the moment. I believe that's
him leaning out the window, there on the second
floor."

Phineas looked up and, sure enough, there was the
kender he recognized as Trapspringer Furrfoot leaning
out an arched window, casually cleaning his fingernails with a small knife. Phineas paused for a moment,
unsure what to make of this. The human had expected
to find the kender locked in a cell or some similarly unpleasant place. Yet here was Trapspringer, lounging
out an open window on the second floor of a palace.
Bigelow caught the baffled look on the human's face.

"Oh, yes, sir, I see you're wondering why he's there
on the second floor," he said. Phineas nodded slowly.
"Unfortunately for Mr. Furrfoot, the grand suite on
the third floor was unavailable, seeing as how it's being used by some visiting blue bloods in from Balifor.
Still, the second floor is comfortable enough, in an op-
ulent sort of way."

Phineas looked from Trapspringer to the gardener
and asked, "How do I speak with the prisoner?"

Bigelow looked at him strangely. "Why, you just
walk in that door, go up the stairs, and find him. How
do you humans usually talk to prisoners? Say hello to
dear Trapspringer for me. Pleasant fellow, and so
smart! I've finished weeding the flower beds here, so
I'm off. Good-bye!" In a few moments, Bigelow was
engulfed by the blinding yellow sunrise creeping
around the right corner of the palace.

"Good-bye," Phineas said limply, watching him go.
He set off for the door the gardener had indicated.
Passing a flower bed, he noticed that nearly all the
flowering plants had been uprooted and that weeds
grew abundantly but neatly within the confines of the
bed. The human would never get used to that peculiar
kender gardening technique.

Phineas walked quickly down the right side of the reflecting pool to the stairs at the base of the central dome. The cool marble was soothing on his blistered feet.

Before long, though, he pressed on up the flight of pristine, white stairs, which ended at a platform. The entrance to the palace proper was up one more short flight of stairs. An ornately carved archway at least as high as thirty men opened into another one at least half as tall. There was no door, only a recessed archway.

Abruptly, Phineas found himself inside the elaborate palace. The first thing that struck him was that, if possible, it looked larger inside than out, yet he was certain he was seeing only a fraction of the building. Way off in the distance above him, the inside of the dome looked like a crystal-clear night sky, either from black paint splashed with white to look like stars, or from an absence of light so far from the large but sheltered windows. Still, the effect was the same, tranquil and quiet and ice cold.

To either side of the dome, where the ceiling leveled off, two softly circling stairways led to the floors above. Phineas chose a staircase and began climbing. The marble was smooth and moist in the darkness of the palace, and Phineas was almost to the first-floor landing when he heard a familiar voice echoing from below him.

"Hellooo! Where are you going? Nobody up there but some boring snobs from Balifor. They aren't friends of yours, are they?"

Phineas leaned over the railing and looked to the bottom of the stairs. There stood Trapspringer Furrfoot, still dressed in his midnight-purple leggings and cape, but with a bright orange shirt and a large, floppy cap. The human flew back down the steps.

"Oh, it's you!" Trapspringer cried upon seeing Phineas's face. He took his hand and pumped it vigorously. "How wonderful to see you! And how friendly of you to come all this way for a visit!"

"You remember me?" asked Phineas, astounded. Hope blossomed. Perhaps getting the other half of the map wouldn't be as difficult as Phineas had feared.

"How could I forget the person who saved my life?" Trapspringer asked, almost offended. "That bone you gave me is marvelous, almost better than my last one. I've had nothing but good luck since I got it."

And I've had nothing but bad luck, Phineas thought to himself, but instead he said, "That's why I'm here, Mr. Furrfoot."

Trapspringer turned away possessively, his eyes wide. "You're not here to take it back, are you?"

"Of course not, Mr. Furrfoot!" Phineas assured him smoothly. "I'm a doctor! I would never jeopardize a patient's life, no matter what."

"Well, I'm certainly very relieved to hear that. You shouldn't fool around with a person's good-luck charm, you know," Trapspringer lectured. "Did you know that good-luck charms have existed since the beginning of time—as long as the Towers of High Sorcery, anyway. Back then, powerful magicians would endow worthless pieces of junk with slight magical abilities, or sometimes just good vibrations." Trapspringer accompanied his story with appropriately magical gestures. "Then they would sell them to anyone who happened by with enough money, just so they could eat."

"If these magicians were so powerful, why didn't they just conjure up some food?" Phineas asked, stumped by the moral of the story.

No kender had ever asked that before. "It's a story," Trapspringer replied temperamentally, "it doesn't have to be logical." But Trapspringer frowned; one of his favorite items of little-known information had been rendered suspect.

Sensing that he may have blundered, Phineas

rushed ahead. "You're probably right. Anyway, I didn't come here to take your luck charm, I came here to *add* to it."

The kender turned around and smiled, an interested gleam in his tilted, olive-green eyes.

With a gesture, Phineas let the bone fragment slip from his cuff. "I offer you this magnificent specimen, found frozen and preserved in the cold wastelands south of Ice Mountain Bay." Reverently, the human held the bone up in his palm. "The rare sixth metatarsal"—was that a bone or a tooth? he wondered—"of an extinct Hyloian woolly mammoth. Nothing short of a mage with great ability can provide a more powerful luck charm."

Scarcely breathing, Trapspringer gingerly lifted the bleached white bone and held it lovingly in his hand. "I can feel the good luck in it! Oh, thank you! How very nice of you. Say, doesn't it look a lot like my ly-canthropic minotaur bone?" he asked guilelessly, pulling a necklace chain from under his orange shirt. He held up the bone at the end for inspection.

"Yes, I certainly see some similarities," Phineas agreed quickly. "But it's not what the bone looks like that's important, is it? Its ability to provide good luck is what you're interested in."

"I see what you mean!" Turning both bones over and over in his hands, Trapspringer strutted happily. "Well, thank you very much again," he said in dismissal. "If there's ever anything I can do for you, don't hesitate to—"

"There is," the human interrupted him. "You collect bones. I collect maps. How did you know that when you gave me that expertly crafted one as payment the other night? I was wondering if you had any more from that period?" Here was where he had to tread lightly. "Actually, the map you gave me was of only *half* of Kendermore. Was that merely an oversight?"

Trapspringer looked genuinely surprised. "Are you

sure? I didn't think I had any 'half maps.' That was one of Uncle Bertie's, you know, although I'm not sure who he was, or if he was even *my* uncle. Isn't it rather odd for humans to collect things, particularly maps? My nephew's family collects them, but then that's what they do—make maps, that is."

Phineas's brain ached. His business was conning kender, not trying to figure out how kender were conning him.

"Yes, it is a bit of an odd hobby for a human," he agreed at last. "But I've been living among you kender for some time now, and I guess your better habits are rubbing off on me. Next to money, maps just seemed the most useful thing to collect. Particularly a map of Kendermore, since I live here. Now, how about the other half of that map?" Phineas pulled his section out and showed the kender how streets and their names were cut off midway along the frayed edge.

Trapspringer lifted his cap and scratched under his tight, silvery topknot. "Let me check."

Phineas's heart raced as he watched Trapspringer reach into his cape and pull out a four-inch stack of faded, folded sheets of parchment. How did he hide all that in there? Phineas wondered.

Trapspringer was leafing through the maps. "Endscape, Estwilde, Flotsam, Garnet, Lemish—how'd that get in here? It's out of order. Fascinating city, though; have you been there? It's very near Garnet—Kalaman, Kenderhome, Library of Palanthas—a wonderful place if you're looking for a good book, but they're a little strict about returning them—Mithas." He looked up from the maps. "We've passed the Ks and no Kendermore." He shrugged and moved to put the maps back in his cape.

Desperate, Phineas reached into the cape and snatched the maps away, adding a hasty, "May I?" Faster and faster, he flipped through the sheets. But none of them seemed to fit with his part of the map.

"I tell you what," Trapspringer proposed. "If I ever find it, I'll be sure to let you know. In the meantime, take any one of these. My personal favorite is this one here—" he said, randomly pulling a map out by its corner.

"I only want the one of Kendermore, and you know it!" Phineas growled in frustration. He was tired of this cat-and-mouse game. What did Trapspringer want from him? "What do you want from me? Money? A share? Name it! Just stop toying with me!"

Trapspringer stepped back, startled. "I don't want anything from you. You want something from me, remember? You aren't thinking very well, are you? It must have something to do with that ridiculously small hat you're wearing. You really should switch haberdashers. Wearing a hat that's too tight squeezes all the air out of your brain. Not to mention you aren't wearing any shoes. . . ."

"I know! I gave them away!" Phineas shouted.

Suddenly, Trapspringer's face lit up. "Gave them away! That's what I did with the map! Some years ago, I gave a bunch of my maps away. There!" Trapspringer looked pleased with himself for having remembered. "I gave them to my nephew, Tasslehoff Burrfoot. He's one of the Burrfoots I told you about," Trapspringer continued, without noticing that Phineas's eyes had gone blank. "He should be back here any day now. He's marrying the mayor's daughter, you know. When he gets back, they'll let me out of this depressing prison."

Phineas's vacant eyes traveled over the awesome beauty of his surroundings and his mind stumbled, trying to calculate its inestimable worth. He remembered the rickety bench where he had spent the night. Soundlessly, he repeated Trapspringer's last words. Light dawned in his eyes.

Some kender named Tasslehoff had the map, and he would be returning to Kendermore any day now.

New strength surged through Phineas's veins. He had only to wait until Tasslehoff showed up, and he'd have the map! But what if Tasslehoff never came back? The human remembered hearing, with some relief, that a bounty hunter had been sent after the wayward kender. And wasn't the council holding his favorite uncle? Oh, yes, he'd be back.

Caught up in his daydream, Phineas did not see Bigelow the gardener's approach. He was carrying a sapling in one hand and a note in the other. As he handed the paper to Trapspringer, the sound of his voice interrupted Phineas's thoughts.

"I couldn't help noticing as I was fetching it up here, sir, that it says Damaris Metwinger, the mayor's daughter, has run away," Bigelow announced before Trapspringer could unfold the message. "She wrote in a note that she got tired of waiting to marry someone she doesn't even know and that she's left for the Ruins and other parts unknown. You're free to go, Trapspringer, since she's welching on the marriage. Mayor Metwinger had to either give you a mayoral pardon or put himself or his wife in prison. Your nephew Tasslehoff is freed of his obligation, too, so he doesn't need to come back either. I'm sure they'll be sending word to his bounty hunter."

Phineas turned white and clutched at his chest.

"That's too bad," Trapspringer said. "I was looking forward to seeing him again. Oh, well, our paths will cross eventually."

"Too bad about the marriage contract," the gardener said absently, dirt falling in small clumps from the sapling's roots as he plodded through the archways that led to the steps outside. "Kids these days have no respect for rules. I don't suppose the mayor will be too keen on sending a bounty hunter after his own daughter, though." Bigelow disappeared through the last archway, and his words became indistinct mutterings.

But Phineas's mind was reeling, an idea, desperate

and dangerous, forming in his brain. Find Damaris and haul her back and Tasslehoff will still have to return—bringing the map with him. Phineas had no idea where Tasslehoff might be, but Damaris had said she was going to the Ruins, a favorite scavenging and picnic spot among the kender.

Phineas did not notice Trapspringer skipping happily down the palace steps until he realized he was alone. He hurried through the vast archs and spotted Trapspringer's reflection dancing in the rectangular pool.

"Hey, wait! Where are you going?" the human called after him.

The kender squatted on the shallow steps leading into the pool and deftly fashioned a paper boat from one of the oiled parchment maps in his cape. Wrapping a triangular piece of paper around a thin, straight stick, he attached it as a mast. Adding three small rocks as ballast, he gave the boat a gentle shove into the center of the pool.

"Trapspringer, you said you want to see your nephew again?" Phineas asked anxiously. "Bigelow was right. The mayor will never send a bounty hunter after his own daughter. But if someone else—say, for example, me—were to bring Damaris back from the Ruins, your nephew would still have to return for the wedding."

"That's awfully kind of you—what was your name again?—but not necessary. This sort of thing happens all the time with birthmates. One gets tired of waiting for the other. They'll either get around to it eventually, or they won't." He jabbed at the boat with a long stick.

"But I insist! It's no problem, really. It's the least I can do for that map," Phineas added cautiously.

"Oh, yes, the map." Trapspringer looked up from the boat and nodded. "Come to think of it, I haven't been to the Ruins in years. It might be fun."

"You needn't come along," Phineas assured him hastily.

"But you'll get lost without me," Trapspringer insisted. "Besides, you don't know what Damaris looks like, and I do."

All of this was true, Phineas had to agree. "We should leave as soon as possible. How about this afternoon after we collect supplies? And we must also make sure no one sends a message to Tasslehoff's bounty hunter."

"Don't worry about a thing, I'm a seasoned adventurer. Have I told you about the time I nearly went to the moon?" Trapspringer asked him. Phineas shook his head. "It's a great story for the road. You just get yourself ready, and I'll collect everything we need and meet you at your shop just past noon."

Phineas only hoped he could find his shop by the time Trapspringer showed up.

Suddenly the autumn wind picked up and sent a small wave crashing over the side of Trapspringer's little boat, sinking it in a second. Phineas wondered uneasily whether it was an omen or just a little maritime disaster.

Chapter 9

Tasslehoff, Gisella, and Woodrow stood on the bow of the ship: "the pointy end," as Gisella insisted on calling it. Behind them, her huge wagon was secured to the single mast, since there didn't seem to be much else to tie it to. The horses were tethered to the mast as well and hobbled to keep them from wandering about the deck. Their eyes rolled and their nostrils flared each time the ship rocked. Not even Woodrow could calm them completely.

"So, let's go," Gisella announced abruptly. "Let's get this thing moving."

Woodrow looked apologetic. "I was raised on a farm, ma'am. I don't know anything about sailing a boat. I thought you knew how."

"Me?" she squealed. "Dwarves don't even like water."

"I've noticed that," Tas began. "My friend Flint—you both remember him? Well, not very long ago, he had a bit of a boating accident. You see, Caramon—that's our big fighter friend—was trying to grab a fish with his bare hands, and he stood up in the little boat, and it tipped over, and Flint couldn't swim, and when Tanis fished him out, he was the most incredible shade of purple! Flint says it was from lack of air, but I say it was because he got so mad. It gave him lumbago."

"That's too bad," Woodrow said. "What does he do for it?"

"Flint says it helps to stay away from kender as much as possible," Tas mumbled reluctantly.

Gisella ignored Tas's story. "How hard can it be, anyway? You just put this cloth up," she proposed, fingering the white sailcloth wrapped around a stout, rounded piece of wood that tapered at the ends, "and then the boat goes where you point it, doesn't it?"

Woodrow frowned. "I don't think it's quite that simple, Miss Hornslager."

"Don't anyone bother asking me if I know how to sail," Tas said petulantly at the edge of their conversation.

"Well, do you?" Gisella asked skeptically.

"Of course I do!" he said, delighted to have their full attention. "I used to sail boats with my Uncle Trapspringer all the time." Tas skipped happily over to Gisella, looped an arm around the mast, and swung himself in a half-circle, grinning.

"You weren't too far from right, Gisella," he said, resting his hand on the piece of wood with the sail wrapped around it. "You raise this thing here—it's called the yard—up this thing here—the mast—and hang the sail from it. But you steer with those sticks dangling off the back end of the boat."

"I think those sticks at the *stern* are called sweeps,"

Woodrow said meekly.

"I knew that, but I was trying to simplify things for Gisella," Tas glared at him. "I thought you didn't know anything about sailing?"

Woodrow raised his hands defensively. "I don't. Sorry."

"All right then," Tas concluded his lesson. "All we have to do is figure out which direction the wind is coming from, catch some of it in the sail, and point our nose east. Sooner or later we're bound to find something."

Tas licked his finger and held it in the air tentatively. He turned it this way and that, licked it again, and held it up as high as he could.

Gisella leaned closer to Woodrow. "What's he doing?" she asked furtively.

"I think he's trying to find out which direction the wind is blowing," whispered Woodrow, afraid that noise would upset the kender.

"I think it's blowing from the north," Tasslehoff announced at last. He turned to Fondu who, along with a half-dozen other gully dwarves, had volunteered to come along as deck hands for the "pretty-haired lady." The deck hands were busy now spitting over the side and watching the bubbles drift on the waves. "Fondu, line up the crew."

With a resounding belch, Fondu grabbed his kinsmen by twos and propelled them toward the wagon. There, with their backs pressed against the side of the vehicle, they were able to form a line that was almost straight.

Hands clasped behind his back, Tasslehoff paced up and down in front of the ragged ensemble. One of the gully dwarves—Fondu had called him Boks—jabbed his finger into his ear and was vacantly gouging and scraping when Tasslehoff spotted him. "Stop that," the kender snapped, doing his best imitation of a fierce sea captain. "We'll have none of that when you're in ranks. This is a sailing ship, and you'll act like sailors."

The gully dwarf hastily withdrew his finger, glancing at it wistfully before wiping it on his shirt.

Tasslehoff began his orientation, walking around the ship and pointing out each item as he came to it. "That's the front end up there, and the back end back there. The sides are there and there. The little house in back is the cabin. Never mind that, we'll just call it the little house. That's where we sleep. This big stick in the middle is the mast. We're going to hang a big sheet of cloth on it, called a sail. Your jobs," he said, turning back to face the gully dwarves, "—and this is really important—is helping to raise and lower the sail by pulling on these ropes." Immediately the crew shuffled over and began yanking indiscriminately on ropes, sailcloth, and each other.

"No, no," hollered Tas, "not yet! Wait until I say!" The gully dwarves shuffled back to the wagon. "You can't just go hauling on ropes willy-nilly or the whole ship will come apart. Now, one step at a time, do exactly what I tell you. . . ."

Several hours later, at dusk, a kender, who was unaccustomed to giving precise instructions about anything, had managed to guide seven gully dwarves, who were unaccustomed to following instructions of any kind but especially unaccustomed to precise ones, through the complicated stages of hoisting a sail, raising an anchor, and launching an eighty-foot-long sailing vessel more or less across the wind.

Gisella and Tas sat on the roof of the cabin, their backs against the ship's rail. Because the cabin's roof doubled as the steering deck, Woodrow stood to their right, manning the starboard sweep. A gully dwarf named Pluk manned the port sweep under the human's watchful gaze. Looking like a boy about to stick his toe in icy water, Woodrow finally opened his mouth.

"I hate to wilt anybody's crops," he began, "but without a map, how do we know where we're going, and how do we tell when we get there?"

Tasslehoff popped open one eye. "I've been giving some thought to that very question."

Gisella groaned.

"There you go again," complained Tas, "criticizing my ideas before I even utter them. You ought to develop a little more tolerance."

"Oh, let's hear it," Gisella moaned.

"Thank you," said Tas. "It seems to me that we have a long way to go back to Kendermore, at least five hundred miles, I would say. The more ground—or should that be water?—whatever—that we can cover, the better off we'll be. So I think we should just sail east, or northeast or southeast, for as long as possible. When we finally run out of water, we'll know that we've gone as far as we can."

Gisella turned her head slowly and regarded the kender. "Those were *my* very thoughts! Sometimes you surprise me, Burrfoot," she admitted. "That settles it, then. We stay with the boat for as long as possible. Take care of the steering part, will you, Woodrow? Be a dear." And with that decision made, she retired to the confines of her wagon.

Woodrow looked to Tas. "For the time being, Woodrow, just steer away from the cliffs behind us. As long as they're getting smaller, we're moving away from them. Once they're out of sight, which won't be for some time, we'll have to rely on the sun."

"How do you know so much about navigating a boat?" Woodrow asked ingenuously.

"I don't know anything about navigating boats," Tas said matter-of-factly. "But I'm a mapmaker, and I rely a lot on the sun when I navigate on land. If it works on land, I can't think of any reason why it shouldn't work on water, too."

Woodrow nodded and watched the cliffs until they later disappeared in moonlight.

* * * * *

Early in the morning of their second day, Woodrow spied a land mass to the north, and by its narrow shape he knew it to be either a large island or a peninsula. He altered course to keep it in sight. "We can chart our progress by how quickly the land passes," he reasoned.

On the third day they passed through a channel that was perhaps ten miles wide, between the island and another spit of land. After narrowing gradually, the channel suddenly opened wide to the east. After a vote, everyone arbitrarily agreed that they should alter course again and parallel the east-west shoreline.

That evening, clouds hid the stars.

The sun never really came out the third day. Dawn was a dull gray, shrouded in fog. There was virtually no breeze, so the boat, christened *Loaner* by Gisella, made little progress. But to everyone's relief, the wind picked up at midmorning, clearing the fog away and raising everyone's spirits. The gully dwarves were happy enough anyway, having engaged in a game of "Gully Overboard," in which they kept jumping, falling, or pushing each other off the boat, leaving Woodrow and Tasslehoff to toss them a rope and drag them back to the ship. Even the long-suffering human threatened to leave them in if they continued the game. Only a word from the object of their fascination, Gisella, put a halt to their antics.

The wind continued rising steadily throughout the morning. By noon, Tas was standing in the bouncing bow of the boat, the long hair of his topknot flying over his shoulder, his tunic and leggings soaked by the spray blowing off the water.

"If this keeps up, we should be somewhere awfully soon," hollered Gisella, trying to be heard above the flapping canvas, slapping waves, and groaning ropes and timbers. Moments later, she retreated to her wagon to escape the wind and spray.

Like ducklings, four of the gully dwarves fell into line and trooped toward the wagon behind Gisella. "Where do you think you're going?" hollered Tas, collaring one of the deserters.

"Me cold," the gully dwarf bellowed. "All wet and blowy here. Warm and dry in little house."

"Oh, no, you don't," Tas warned. "You're all sailors now, and sailors don't abandon their posts because of a little wind and spray." At that moment, a thunderclap rolled across the sea and rain started pattering on the deck. "Or rain," Tas added doubtfully. He hesitated. "Although rain is a *lot* worse than a little wind and spray."

The gully dwarves looked at each other, then back at Tas, confused as ever. At least they weren't retreating to the cabin anymore, but neither were they returning to their positions.

Tas suddenly looked excited. "I know! I'll teach you a sea chanty."

Individually steering the gully dwarves back to their assigned spots, Tas started singing.

Come all you young fellows who live by the sea,
Kiss a fair maiden and then follow me.
Hoist up the sail and the anchor aweigh,
And run with the wind out through Balifor Bay.

Soon, all the gully dwarves were snorting and stomping along with Tas's song, singing, "Hoy tup the bale in the ankle a day," and tossing each other in the air.

Already straining to control the sweep, Woodrow was again concerned that the gully dwarves would start tossing each other over the rail. At the speed they were traveling, they'd never be able to stop and recover them this time. He was about to warn Tas of the danger when a flash of lightning struck the sea several hundred yards from the ship. Moments later, a tremendous gust of wind slammed into the little ship, heeling it over on its port side and sending the prancing gully dwarves scurrying for handholds. As the *Loaner* righted itself, a second gust hit it and with a loud tearing sound, a three-foot rip appeared in the sail.

Tas grabbed the nearest Aghar by the shoulder and hollered, "We've got to get it down! The sail! We've got to lower it!"

The gully dwarf dashed toward the cabin, too frightened by the storm's sudden fury to be of any help. Scanning the deck, Tas saw that his entire crew was stampeding toward the cabin or crawling beneath the wagon. The horses reared and snorted and strained against their tethers, and the wagon swayed menacingly.

Woodrow crouched on one knee with the sweep tucked under his left arm and both arms wrapped around the railing. Helplessly, he watched Tas stumble across the deck.

A third gust of wind sent waves crashing across the deck, washing several gully dwarves out from beneath the wagon and up against the opposite rail. They were crawling back to the wagon when a fourth gust filled the sail, stretching it like a balloon. The rip widened in a burst, and then another rip appeared, and then the entire sail split in half, tearing lengthwise and pulling free from the yard. The loose end billowed out over the sea until it reached the end of its sheet, then snapped, twisted in air, tore free from the rope, and dropped into the churning waves.

The remaining, shredded half of the sail slapped into the side of the wagon. The wagon's door flew open and Gisella appeared, wide-eyed. The wagon bounced and skidded across the deck, then slammed back into the mast. Gisella tried to climb down the stairs but the rocking threw her back into the wagon. Another wave crashed into the side of the wagon, and two of the three ropes securing the wagon to the deck burst under the strain.

"Miss Hornslager!" screamed Woodrow. He watched in horror as the wagon bearing Gisella slid across the tilting deck, straining at the remaining rope. But the rope held. Then, with a sound that almost stopped Woodrow's heart, a jagged, white crack appeared in the mast. The front end of the wagon smashed through the ship's rail, and the wheels dropped over the side. The ship rolled beneath the shifting weight until water washed over the deck. A second later, the entire wagon disappeared over the side of the ship, slipping beneath the waves, followed by the upper half of the mast.

The ship did not right itself, but bobbed and rocked with its deck awash. The horses screamed and pawed at the slippery deck. Seeing that the ship was lost, Woodrow leaped off the steering deck and scrambled to the stump of the mast. With his knife he sliced through the horses' tethers so they would not be dragged down by the sinking ship.

As the water rose in the cabin, Fondu and the other gully dwarves who had taken shelter there stumbled up on deck. A massive wave thundered down on the upturned hull and the deck rotated even more. Tas heard tumbling and crashing inside the ship as its ballast shifted.

"It's hopeless!" he shouted to the gully dwarves. "The ship is sinking! Jump off! Swim for it!"

Woodrow and the horses were already in the water when Tas dove after them. The few gully dwarves remaining on board were thrown in as well when the ship rolled belly-up. Moments later, it slipped beneath the churning surface, leaving only loose planking, knotted ropes, and a twisted, tattered sail behind.

Kender, human, and gully dwarves clung to the floating debris in the chilly water. The rain and wind continued for a short time, then suddenly died away. Before long, a dim sun poked through the gray clouds.

They bobbed on the debris in silence for several minutes. Neither Tas nor Woodrow wanted to speak, each thinking of Gisella. Fondu finally broke the silence.

"Where pretty-hair lady?" he asked. He looked first at Tas, then at Woodrow. "Fondu no see her."

Woodrow blinked furiously and would not meet Tas's gaze. "She's gone, Fondu," Tas said hesitantly. "She was in her wagon when it went over the side."

"When she coming back?" Fondu asked.

"I'm afraid she isn't," explained the kender.

Fondu stared at Tas uncomprehendingly for a second, then opened his mouth wider than any mouth Tas had ever seen and started bawling at the top of his lungs. "Laaaadyyy!" he screamed, with his nose running almost as much as his tears.

"Fondu, quiet!" Tas ordered. Between Fondu's wails, Tas was sure he had heard a voice. It sounded like someone yelling . . .

"Yoo hoo."

Tas looked over his shoulder. There, a couple hundred yards away, apparently sitting on top of the water, was Gisella, waving a soggy kerchief in his direction. A ragged cheer rose from the bobbing mob and in short order they were paddling toward her.

As they drew closer, Tas became convinced that Gisella was sitting on top of the water. The mystery was cleared up when she announced, "Guess what? My wagon floats!"

Fondu was so happy he broke into a garbled chorus of "Come maul yo-yo fellows, Shirley by the sea," that was soon picked up by the rest of the group. Boks spat a mouthful of sea water at Thuddo and before long the entire group was singing, laughing, spitting, and splashing.

Tasslehoff was almost disappointed when Gisella, standing shakily on the roof of her submerged wagon, hollered "Land, I see land ahead!"

"At last, a good omen," said Woodrow.

"That's no omen, boy, that's land," Gisella corrected. "That's dry clothes and something to eat and a place to sleep." And with those words of encouragement, they started paddling to shore.

Chapter 10

Phineas had little time in which to reach his shop and collect his things. He decided to risk a ride in a kenderkart, particularly since he had no idea where his shop was. Barefoot, Phineas hobbled to the first busy intersection and hailed one of the kender-pulled, two-wheeled conveyances.

Trotting between the two long handles that were attached to the cart's seat, the driver came to an abrupt stop. Phineas gave the kender his address. After jogging for some time, up stairs and down, and through a school yard full of kender children, the driver was forced to admit that he wasn't *exactly* sure where he was going.

"But a friend of mine has a map of Kendermore that will tell us *everything* we need to know," the driver assured him.

The kenderkarter met his friend, a vendor of roasted chestnuts, and after much conferring, several more flights of stairs, and a trip through the close-set stalls of a farmer's market with chickens flying in their wake, Phineas began to recognize the shops of his own neighborhood.

"There!" Unclenching his white fingers from the edge of the cart, the human pointed to the right. "There's my shop!" He looked longingly at the familiar storefront, which he had begun to wonder if he would ever see again.

The kenderkarter abruptly dug in his heels, sending the distracted human flying once more. His mouth twisted. "I wish you wouldn't *do* that!" The human jumped down from the cart and headed for his shop.

"Wait a second! Where's my thirty copper?" the kender asked, setting the handles of the cart down in outrage. "Thief! Help! Thief!"

Dozens of kender on the street looked up guiltily from whatever it was they were doing and put their hands back in their own pockets.

"Somebody get 'im!" the kender continued. "He's nothing but a shoeless, orc-faced, cheating, goat-sucker bird, and he owes me forty copper!"

Phineas, who was most offended by the orc comment, turned around and snarled, "I live and work in this neighborhood, if you don't mind! I'm getting your *twenty* copper right now."

The obnoxious kender stood at his elbow while Phineas searched his pockets for the key. It was gone, which came as no great surprise to Phineas. He knew it was useless to expect to find any money left in the cash drawer, but he had a secret place behind a wall board in the waiting room.

Locating the loose board, Phineas gave it an upward tug. The board slipped lose and a tin box fell out.

"Hey, that's really neat! I never would have thought to

look there!" the kender said, again at his elbow.

Phineas opened the box without comment. It was empty. "Well, somebody obviously thought of it," he said. That was all the money he had on hand. He cast his glance about the room, trying to spot anything that was left that might interest a kender.

Then an idea struck him. He intended to be rich soon, didn't he? "I don't have any money. Take anything that you like." He waved his hand at the room, then stepped into the dark examining room. "Shut the door behind you when you leave."

"Gee, thanks!" the kender exclaimed, his eyes wide. "Wow, look at these—"

But Phineas wasn't listening. He had very little time to get ready. He moved to a cupboard at the back of the room and found his spare pair of boots. They weren't nearly as comfortable as the ones he'd lost, he thought ruefully, slipping them on in the dark. Next, he took a satchel from a hook, making note of what clothing he'd need to gather from his rooms upstairs. Next, he pulled his half of the Kendermore map from his shirt and placed it in the satchel, then went upstairs to change his shirt, add a vest, and gather some other things.

Coming back down with his provisions and a haunch of dried meat, he decided not to light a candle while he waited for Trapspringer, so as not to attract customers. Sitting in the darkness, he started to snooze, weary to his bones.

A painful moan from the dark depths of the room brought him to his feet. "Trapspringer?" Shaky hands popped open the shutter partially, and a dim shaft of light struck the floor. Heart thumping, he peered in the direction of the moan.

Slumped in the examining chair, overlooked in the darkness, was the body of a large, muscular man with short, bristly hair, small eyes, and a flat, wide nose. Blood trickled down his right side from under a wad of red-stained white cloth.

"Who are you? What happened to you?" Phineas gasped, rushing to the man's side. "You should get some help right away!"

"That's what I'm doing. You're a doctor, aren't you?" the man managed through clenched teeth.

"Me? Sure. I mean, yes," he stumbled, caught completely off guard. Phineas tended to the aches and pains of friendly, city-dwelling kender. He saw lots of bruises, but precious little blood. This was a rather nasty-looking human, who was losing more blood each second than Phineas had seen in months.

Gingerly he lifted the bloody cloth from the man's side. The patient convulsed as the wet cloth caught on the raw edges of his wound. Phineas winced. "Sorry." Opening the shutter wider, he examined the cut, which was wide, deep, and about five inches long. Though he had never seen one, Phineas was certain he was looking at a sword wound.

"Who are you?"

"I'm called Denzil."

"Just Denzil?"

The man looked at him evenly. "Just Denzil."

"Well, what happened to you, Denzil?" he repeated.

"Nothing. Just a little household accident." His voice was getting weaker.

"You cut your meat with a sword?" Phineas scoffed.

"Who said anything about a sword?" the man named Denzil said harshly. He propped himself up slightly, somehow managing to look menacing despite his weakened condition. "Listen, just fix me up and keep your mouth shut about it."

Phineas looked at him helplessly. "I can't dress a sword wound. I'm not that good—I mean, kind—of doctor. You'll just have to find a surgeon." He pressed the dirty rag against the wound again, forcing another convulsion from the man. "Sorry."

"There *is* no one else. I wouldn't trust a kender doctor any farther than I could choke him." Phineas saw the man's fingers flex on the handrests. "Besides, I'm not in any shape to move."

"You can make it," Phineas said, sounding more desperate than encouraging. "Just hold this to your side and I'm sure—"

"I have enough strength left to choke an uncooperative doctor," the man said threateningly. Something in his small eyes told Phineas that this Denzil would happily spend his last ounces of strength making good on the threat.

Phineas poured three-day-old water into a wooden bowl and ripped some cleaning rags. "I'll do my best, but this really isn't a convenient time for me. My fee will be very high."

"I can pay it," the man said coldly.

"Would you mind very much paying in advance?" Phineas asked somewhat timidly, still not at all sure he could help the man. As he figured it though, if he was, well, unsuccessful, Denzil would not be around to choke him, and if Phineas was successful, everyone would be happy. Still, he was a businessman.

The man scowled at him. But with great effort, he raised a hand into his jacket and pulled out a pouch. Emptying approximately half the bag—at least twenty steel pieces, a veritable fortune—he sank back. "Now, get to work."

Phineas forced his mind away from the money and onto the man's wound. Seeing Denzil's pale, sweaty face, he snatched the half-bottle of wine he'd placed in his satchel, uncorked it, and offered it to the man. Expecting him to take a swig, Phineas watched as Denzil threw his head back and downed the contents in a couple of noisy, splashy gulps.

Phineas searched his mind frantically for ways in which he could close the wound, or at least stop the bleeding. His first thought was hot wax, but he discounted that. It might cauterize the wound and stop the flow of blood temporarily, but wax would fall away the first time the man moved after it cooled.

Perhaps he could wrap it tightly. But how? With the wound on his side like that, Phineas would practically have to crush Denzil's ribs to apply enough pressure to stop the blood.

His eyes fell on the twine the herbalist used to tie the bunches of fragrant eucalyptus used in Phineas's special elixir. Hardly stopping to think, he dug around in a drawer until he located the needle he used to sew patches over small holes in his boots. Wiping it quickly on his sleeve, he threaded the needle with twine and set it aside. Adding a few crushed leaves of eucalyptus to the bowl of water, he gently cleansed the wound. The man had already passed out and was beyond noticing.

Pinching the edges of the wound together, Phineas began at the back, using his most decorative cross-stitch pattern to draw the raw skin together. He concentrated on his neatness, because if he thought about what he was doing, he was certain he would feel the twine pulling through his own flesh. Sweat dripped into his eyes as he worked.

Denzil stirred and moaned beneath the needle. Phineas hastily finished up the last two stitches as his patient's eyes flew open. Tying a quick overhand knot in the end of the twine, Phineas stepped back anxiously and waited for the man's bellows of pain.

Understanding returned quickly to Denzil's eyes. Within moments even his color had turned better. Wincing only slightly, he looked under his arm at the hemp-colored twine in his side. "You do pretty fair work for a quack. Nice, thick stitches." His expression became soft and peaceful as he said, " 'Where we grow and decay no longer, our trees ever green.' Quivalen Sath, The Bird Song of Wayreth Forest."

Either the man was delirious, or astonishingly, he was in very little pain. His voice was steady, and so were his hands.

"You're familiar with his work, of course," the man in

the chair said. "Greatest poet that ever lived."

"Of course," Phineas agreed vacantly. This man was strange and creepy and Phineas wanted him out of his shop as quickly as possible. "I'm sure you'll be just fine now. I'm just on my way out of town, so if you don't mind—"

"I think I'll just rest here for a few more minutes," the man said. "I'm still feeling a little drained from the loss of blood." He flexed his fingers into fists so that the muscles in his arms wrippled under his blood-stained shirt.

"Sure, whatever you like," Phineas said quickly, stifling the impulse to bow as he backed out of the room. He would simply wait in the outer office for Trapspringer to arrive; by then this Denzil would probably be ready to leave.

What was such a man—obviously a vicious fighter—doing in Kendermore anyway, he wondered? Probably just a mercenary passing through. Looking out the small window, Phineas decided Trapspringer was already late. Though he expected it of kender, he wished the fellow would hurry up. He didn't want the trail of the mayor's daughter, Damaris, to get any colder. And he especially didn't want to sit around with Denzil.

A short time passed, spent shooing away curious patients, before Trapspringer Furrfoot arrived. The kender strolled in the shop's door with a flourish, twirling around to set his new crimson cape spinning in a colorful circle.

"Don't you think you're a bit overdressed for a trip to a place called 'the Ruins'?" Phineas asked.

"Hello to you, too. I always begin each adventure with new garb," Trapspringer explained. "Actually, the practice of dressing up for military maneuvers began in Tarsalonia—some place like that—long ago—"

"This is not an adventure," Phineas said firmly. "We're simply going to find Damaris Metwinger and bring her back so that your nephew Tasslehoff's bounty hunter will not be notified that he need not return to Kendermore from someplace named Solace with the other half of my map," he finished, out of breath.

"That's right. An adventure." Trapspringer's eyes glanced about the room. "Do you like being a doctor?"

Phineas noticed for the first time that the kenderkarter had cleared away what was left on the shelves in the waiting room. "I did." Suddenly he remembered Denzil. "I'm ready to go," he said, walking toward the dim examination room. "I just have to release one last patient, then collect my pack." He stepped into the back room and looked at the chair.

Denzil was gone.

Where could he have got to? Phineas wondered. There was no back door, only a small window, like the one in the candlemaker's shop. He listened for any noise above in his rooms, but there was no sound through the thin wooden floor. Denzil must have slipped out the window, the human decided at last, though he could not understand why. The steel pieces still lay where Phineas had set them, next to his satchel. The man's disappearance was easily as odd as his appearance, and that was odd indeed.

Shrugging, Phineas pocketed the steel pieces and took the leather handles of the satchel. He frowned suddenly, seeing his half of the Kendermore map sticking out the top of the bag. I must have pulled it up when I took out the bottle for Denzil, he concluding, placing the map in his vest for safe keeping.

Closing the shutters in the examination room, he led Trapspringer out the front door, made sure the "closed" sign faced the street, then set off toward the northeast corner of Kendermore with the elder kender, in search of Damaris Metwinger.

*　*　*　*　*

A dark figure lurked in the doorway for five long minutes after the kender and the human left on two small ponies. Holding his side to ease the pain of a recently won duel, the man walked the other way down the street. A mercenary by trade, he had just stumbled upon his next, and possibly last, job, if the spoils were all that were promised on the half-map. This time, he would be working for himself. Collecting his horse, a dark, menacing steed, from a nearby alley, he purchased enough provisions for one month; enough time, he figured, to find the village of Solace and a kender named Tasslehoff.

PART II

Chapter 11

"One, two, three, heave!

"One, two, three, heave!"

Tas, Woodrow, and the seven gully dwarves pulled with all their might, but the waterlogged wagon refused to budge. They had managed to drag it about halfway up onto shore. But now it was thoroughly bogged down in the mud.

Woodrow, standing waist-deep in the water, relaxed his grip on the rope and eased up to his full height. The movement aggravated a pain in his back. "I'm sorry, Miss Hornslager, but I just don't think we can do this. That wagon hasn't moved in the last twenty pulls."

"Never give up, Woodrow. Those are words to live by," responded Gisella, still seated atop the wagon. "Now everybody, one, two, three, heave!"

But even before she got to the word "heave," all nine heavers had dropped the rope and slogged wearily back onto the shore. The gully dwarves, who had been in the shallow water closest to shore, plopped down in a soggy heap. Tas followed, stretching out on his back on a small patch of grass growing on the sandy beach. Finally, Woodrow sat down beside him, resting his head on his knees.

"What's the matter with you? You're all a bunch of quitters, that's what's the matter with you!" hollered Gisella. She paced back and forth on the small roof of her wagon. "Do you think I came all this way to give up now? Do you think I'm just going to shrug my shoulders and say, 'Oh, well, things are getting a little tough now, so I think I'll sit down here and wallow in my own pity'?"

"C'mon, Gisella," responded Tas. "We're tired. We just survived a shipwreck—let us rest for five minutes, OK?"

Gisella surveyed her ragged crew. "Maybe you're right. So come and help me down off this thing already." She held out her hand demurely.

Wearily, Woodrow rose to his feet and splashed back to the wagon. Gisella sat on the edge of the wagon's roof and then, with a little hop, slid into Woodrow's arms. The thin human suppressed a grunt.

"Oooh," she purred, "you're stronger than you look. I find danger to be incredibly exciting, don't you?"

Woodrow's face flamed to a bright crimson, and he practically dropped Gisella in his haste to set her down and retreat to the shore. The dwarf was puffing as she finally waded onto dry land, several dozen paces behind the human.

"Really, Woodrow, it was just an innocent little remark. I don't know what gets into you sometimes," she complained. "Hasn't anyone ever flirted with you before?"

Woodrow was seated, hugging his knees and staring at the ground. "No, ma'am, I guess not," he mumbled.

This was beyond Gisella's comprehension, so she dropped the subject entirely and joined everyone else stretching out on the beach.

* * * * *

Woodrow woke up shortly after dawn. He was disoriented at first, until he realized that what everyone had intended to be a short nap had turned into twelve hours of sleep. Tas was curled up on his side, Gisella was snoring softly, the gully dwarves were in a heap, squirming occasionally. Woodrow's stomach growled, reminding him that he hadn't eaten since early the day before. He set off to the south along the beach in search of something edible.

The beach extended perhaps a mile before giving way to rocky outcroppings, gravel, and eroded dirt banks. Walking along the shore was too difficult after that point, so Woodrow moved inland. As long as I can still hear the waves, he thought, I shouldn't get lost.

Before long, Woodrow found a tangled patch of wild raspberry bushes. He filled his hat with the ripe, red fruit and sat down for a feast.

His meal was interrupted by the sound of movement somewhere in the tangle. Woodrow rolled onto his stomach and lay perfectly still, listening. Then he heard the sound again: the snorting of a horse.

Cautiously, he raised his head. In places, especially where the berries grew around gnarled trees and boulders, the bushes were taller than Woodrow. Slowly, he worked his way around the patch, then all of a sudden he laughed, stood up, and whistled. In the berry patch, contentedly munching, were Gisella's two horses. Eagerly they pushed their way through the tangled brush to where Woodrow stood.

"I sure am glad you two are all right," laughed Woodrow, throwing an arm around each horse's neck. "I was afraid I'd never see you again."

Both horses were nuzzling Woodrow's pockets. "I'm

afraid you've already found something better than anything I could offer you, right there in that berry patch," chuckled Woodrow. "Let's gather some of this up and head back to the others, eh?"

Woodrow refilled his cap and the entire front of his shirt with berries, holding the latter out like an apron. He and the horses turned north toward the beach.

Tasselhoff was just sitting up and rubbing his eyes as Woodrow arrived with the horses. In moments, everyone was awake and noisily slurping up berries.

While the others breakfasted, Woodrow walked the horses out into the shallow water and started hitching them to the wagon.

"Oh, good thinking!" hollered Gisella, looking up from her handfuls of berries. "I can't wait to get my things dried out so I can put on some decent clothes." She glared disdainfully at the simple drab work outfit she'd been wearing since before the shipwreck.

Woodrow finished adjusting the harness and walked around to the front of the horses. "I don't know whether pulling the wagon out will work, Miss Hornslager," he cautioned. "This harness is in pretty bad shape, what with spending the night underwater. The leather may split open under the strain."

Gisella crossed her fingers. Woodrow led the horses forward until they gradually put their entire strength into the harness. Slowly, the wagon rocked forward, then back, then forward again, and finally began rolling after the straining team. The horses picked up more speed as the wagon moved into shallower water and the water inside it drained out.

"Whoa," said Woodrow, placing a hand on each of the horses' muzzles. The wagon stood on the beach, water still running out through the door and around the floorboards.

"Hooray!" shouted Gisella, clapping her hands. "We'll be on our way in no time."

"I don't think so, Miss Hornslager." Woodrow stepped

from behind the wagon, shaking his head. "Both rear wheels are damaged, and the rear axle is cracked really bad. This wagon won't go more than a mile or two without falling apart."

"Well, can't we fix it?" Gisella waved her arms vaguely at the wagon. "People fix wagons all the time, right? I mean, everything looks fine to me."

Woodrow nodded his head. "Yes, ma'am, we could fix it . . ."

"Then let's get at it."

". . . if we had the right tools, ma'am. Like a forge, and a sledge, and an anvil. And maybe some jacks and woodworking tools. But we can't repair it with nothing to work with."

"Oh."

Gisella let her arms drop to her sides as she looked sadly at the wagon. Then slapping her hips, she said, "That's that, then. Let's salvage what we can and get moving. I still have one cargo left, and it still has to be in Kendermore by the Harvest Faire." She threw a glance at Tasslehoff. "I hope it intends to continue cooperating."

* * * * *

The day was more than half over when Gisella finally called for a short rest. The gully dwarves collapsed in exaggerated poses before the dwarf could even slide her leg over her horse's neck and drop to the ground. Riding the second horse together, Woodrow waited for the kender seated in front of him to jump down before slithering off himself.

The spot Gisella had chosen was the crest of a gently rolling hill, which continued eastward in ever-taller waves, becoming mountains within two miles. The hills were barren except for tall, wavering, wheatlike grass, and the occasional stark tree. The sun was warm, but there was a slight chill to the breeze, the only sign of autumn in the austere landscape.

"Pass around those berries, Woodrow," instructed Gisella. "But make sure I get some before those gully dwarves start stuffing their paws into them. And some water, too," she added as an afterthought.

Woodrow hefted from the horses two of Gisella's shirts, which had been salvaged from the wagon and stuffed with berries. The necks and waists had been knotted shut, and the arms were used to tie the makeshift sacks to the horses' necks. The human untied a shirt, paused, and peered into its neck.

"I could have sworn this was full when we started this morning. We must have jostled an inch of berries out of the top."

Guiltily, Tas shoved his red-stained fingers behind his belt. "How surprising," he noted, turning his back to Gisella's tight-lipped glare. But whatever she may have been thinking, Gisella said nothing, instead helping herself to a handful of raspberries.

"Does anything around here look familiar?" she asked Tasslehoff. "Anything at all? Does any of it even resemble anything on one of those ridiculous maps of yours?"

Tas shook his head. "I'm familiar with a lot of places, but this isn't any of them. Apparently none of my relatives has been here, either, because I don't see anything similar on the maps—no barren hills or tall grass anywhere." Tas's maps were spread around him in a semicircle. "Of course, we haven't traveled too terribly far. All the really good landmarks may be just ahead."

"Let's hope so," sighed Gisella. "We've got to find some sort of civilization soon."

Those words were barely out of Gisella's mouth when Woodrow's head snapped up from his meal and he cocked it to one side, listening intently for some barely heard sound in the distance.

But the gully dwarves were getting restless. Taking the silence as a sign of inactivity, Fondu chose that moment to start singing the gully dwarves' special version of the sea chanty Tasslehoff had taught them. Woodrow flapped his arms frantically at them, trying to get them to stop singing. But the Aghar took his gestures to be a new verse of sorts to the song, and they began flapping their arms to the music.

Helplessly, Woodrow looked at Tasslehoff. Acting on instinct, the kender took matters into his own hands and leaped in among the dancing Aghar, tackling Fondu. The two of them rolled across the ground and bumped up against Gisella's feet, Fondu still singing. But when the gully dwarf looked up, he saw his lady's face, her lips puckered and pressed to her finger. Instantly Fondu stopped singing and bellowed, "Red-hair lady says to shut up! Shut up! Shut up!"

The singing stopped abruptly, and the gully dwarves froze in place. Pluk, balanced precariously on one foot, wavered, jerked, hopped three times, and with his arms windmilling wildly, collapsed on top of his brother, Slurp. Both of them struggled back to their feet with their hands clamped firmly over their mouths.

Once again Woodrow bent his ear to the wind.

Several moments passed.

"Well?" whispered Gisella.

Without turning his head, Woodrow whispered back, "It's singing. I hear singing."

"Oh, that's marvelous," hissed Gisella. "It's probably another bunch of gully dwarves. Can't you tell any more than that?"

"No, ma'am. Either they're garbling the lyrics something awful, or they're singing in a language I don't understand, because I can't make out the words. Sounds like quite a chorus, though," he added.

"I can't see anything through these cursed weeds," spat Gisella, swatting at the dwarf-high grass surrounding her. "Woodrow, help me onto my horse."

Woodrow linked his fingers and formed a step with his hands, boosting Gisella onto the back of her horse. She shaded her eyes with her hand and scanned the horizon.

"I see a red banner moving across our path—it looks like someone's family crest," the dwarf said at last. "It's not too far off. There must be a road farther ahead. Let's try to catch up with whoever it is."

Gisella's horse loped easily through the tall grass. Woodrow and Tas hurried their horse to catch up, with the gully dwarves jogging along behind them.

Tas had an idea for attracting the attention of whoever was on the road. Twisting around on his horse, he yelled to the leader of the gully dwarves. "Sing! Fondu, sing!" The kender broke into the song he'd taught them.

"Come all you young fellows who live by the sea,
Kiss a fair maiden and then follow me."

And then came their reply:

"Hotel this ale and your uncle's a whale,
Wheel run with the Winifred ball of four bale."

Tasslehoff could see that the banner had stopped moving ahead, and he could no longer spot Gisella. Moments later, he and Woodrow broke through the grass and came upon the road. Gisella had dismounted and struck the same "come hither" pose she'd used in the inn: hands on her hips, hair tossed back. She was surrounded by a dozen male dwarves who were all stroking their beards and fumbling with their hats.

The troop was on foot—most dwarves distrusted horses. They stood in two straight lines of six dwarves, with a lone dwarf at their head. Wearing sparkling, polished chain mail and knee-high leather boots, each dwarf had a war hammer at his waist and a coil of rope draped over one shoulder. The leader of the troop wore an ornamental helm with a cluster of green rooster feathers in it.

Gisella threw Tas and Woodrow a coy look and batted her eyelashes when they at last emerged. "Boys," she said, "I'd like you to meet Baron Krakold of the village of Rosloviggen." She turned and blew a kiss to the dwarf who sported the green feathers. Tas couldn't tell whether the dwarf blushed—his already ruddy complexion was mostly hidden behind his enormous beard. He's not at all the way I pictured a baron, thought Tas, who, if he pondered the subject, conjured up images of shining armor, a flowing cape, and a prancing white charger.

Gisella hooked her arm around the baron's shoulder and gave it a squeeze. "The baron—I just love the sound of that, don't you?—and his men just finished some mission or other and they're on their way back to the baron's village. They'd love to have us join them. I don't see how we can refuse such a gracious offer." Gisella turned and stared deeply into the baron's eyes, simultaneously grinding her hip against his thigh. The baron's eyebrows—which constituted a considerable mass of hair—twitched up and down, and a murmur of vague, manly approval rippled through the troop of dwarves.

Just then, Fondu and his six kinsmen tumbled through the edge of the grass and onto the road. They froze for a second, looking at the noble entourage. Gisella closed her eyes and bit her lip—she knew that, as a rule, her own kinsmen were no fonder of gully dwarves than of horses. But when the Aghar broke into another spirited chorus of "Balifor Bay," the baron and his men laughed with delight. After a good round of guffawing and back slapping, the column was under way.

The procession hiked for several hours. Tas, Gisella, and Woodrow dismounted and walked in deference to the horseless dwarves. Woodrow took both sets of reins and dropped back to lead the animals at the rear of their party. The ground rose steadily as the road wound into the foothills of the upcoming mountain range. Tas, who thought himself uncommonly patient on this trip, finally voiced the question that had been occupying his mind all day.

"How much farther is the village? We've had nothing to eat but raspberries all day."

The dwarf directly ahead of Tas grunted good-naturedly. "We've a way to go. The town is across that spur, in the next gorge."

Tasslehoff eyed the spur with awe. "We have to cross

that? Those boulders look the size of castles! We'll be at it for hours!"

"We'll get to the other side, all right," replied the dwarf, maintaining the brisk pace set by his fellows.

"A friend of mine, Flint Fireforge—he's a dwarf, too—told me once to be more concerned about what lies on the other side of the hill than how I'm going to cross it," mused Tas. "I guess that applies right now. It isn't very often that sayings apply as well as that."

The dwarf grunted again. "It sounds like your dwarf friend is pretty smart."

The dwarf behind Tas blew his nose loudly, then asked, "Did I hear you right? You're a friend of Flint Fireforge?"

"Certainly," Tas said. "I saw him just a few days ago back in Solace. But it seems much longer ago than that. Why, do you know him, too?"

"No, no," replied the dwarf. "But we all know *of* him, if he's the grandson of Reghar Fireforge. The baron's father, Krakold the First, knew Reghar Fireforge during the Dwarfgate War. Of course, Krakold was just a young noble then and he's quite aged now, but he's one of the few who survived the blast of magic that ended the Dwarfgate War. Oh, yes, he was there the day Reghar Fireforge died. Fireforge is still revered among our people. We don't forget our heroes."

"Wow," declared Tas, scrambling to keep up with the marching dwarves. "If Krakold was at the final battle of the Dwarfgate War, then he must be over four hundred years old. Isn't that awfully old for a dwarf?"

"It is if you fought in the Dwarfgate War. I doubt there are more than a dozen survivors left," replied the dwarf, blowing his nose again. "My grandfather and granduncle were both killed there, too," he added proudly, his chest swelling with pride.

"Wow," Tas muttered. "It must be neat knowing where your ancestors went and what they did. I usually know where I am, but I usually have no idea where my family is, unless I'm with them. Except my Uncle Trapspringer. He's back in Kendermore, being held prisoner. That's where we're headed, to Kendermore to free my uncle. My name's Tasslehoff, by the way. Tasslehoff Burrfoot. What's yours?"

"I'm called Mettew Ironsplitter, son of Rothew Ironsplitter," answered the dwarf. "My father was the engineer who designed Rosloviggen's main gate."

Mettew raised his head to shout over the rapidly moving troop. "Excuse me, Your Grace," bellowed Mettew. "I was just speaking with this kender fellow, and I've learned something astounding. This one—calls himself Burrfoot—is a personal friend of Flint Fireforge, grandson of Reghar Fireforge."

The rest of the dwarves in the party stopped abruptly and fell completely silent, then looked toward the baron. He stomped back along the length of the line to stand before Tasslehoff.

"Is this true, what Mettew says?" asked the baron.

"Sure," Tas responded. "We're good friends. I was with Flint just a few days ago. He's a bit gruff, but I sort of miss him already."

"Well, lad, why didn't you mention you were a friend of the Fireforges right off?" boomed the baron. "That's not the sort of thing you should keep to yourself! You're doubly welcome now. You'll be guests in my home. And you've come at a good time. Our Oktoberfest begins tomorrow!" Turning back to his escort, the baron added, "It's going to be some fest this year, eh?" He was answered with a round of laughter and assent.

"Oktoberfest!" giggled Gisella, clapping her hands together. "I'd completely forgotten about that autumn dwarven tradition. This is too good to be true!"

Woodrow leaned close to Tasslehoff and whispered in his ear, "What's Oktoberfest?"

"I don't know," whispered Tas, "but judging from all of their reactions, it's bound to be exciting."

*　*　*　*　*

As they approached the ridge, Woodrow became more puzzled. "Does it seem to you," he whispered again to Tasslehoff, "that we're headed into a dead end? Mettew said we have to cross this ridge, but we're walking right up to the steepest part of it."

"I did notice that," Tasslehoff agreed, "but I assume they know what they're doing. Maybe they use ropes and pulleys to raise themselves up the cliff."

"I'd rather not get involved with any more ropes and pulleys for a while," Woodrow moaned.

By this time, the group had come to a stop. Looking around quickly, Tas saw that they were indeed in a box of sorts. Rugged, brush-covered walls sloped steeply upward on the right and left. Ahead, a sheer cliff towered at least fifty feet over the kender's head. Below the cliff were piles of brush and debris that had apparently cascaded down from above.

The dwarves went to work. Quickly they pushed aside a large pile of brush from the base of the cliff, revealing a roughly carved stone face with an open, gap-toothed mouth. Mettew rummaged inside his backpack and withdrew the largest iron key Tasslehoff had ever seen. "That must weigh at least twenty pounds," the kender exclaimed aloud to no one in particular.

"Twenty-two and a half, almost twenty-three," corrected Mettew. "It's nothing for a dwarven key. You should see some of the big ones we use for really important doors."

Tas whistled softly. Mettew slid the key between two of the face's teeth and, gripping it with both hands, gave a mighty twist. There was a puff of dust and a rush of air, then a crack appeared. As Mettew tugged, the crack widened and two more dwarves grabbed the edge and pulled. The face swung wide, revealing a dark tunnel leading into the cliff.

The group filed through the tunnel entrance. Inside,

the tunnel was cool and still, but dry. Mettew moved the key around to the back side of the face, and then the other dwarves helped him swing the door shut. With a final turn of the key, he removed it from the face and slid the massive tool back into his pack.

The tunnel was now completely black. The dwarves stood for a moment, allowing their keen dwarven eyes to adjust. Then, "Let's move!" shouted the baron, and the line set off again.

"Wait!" shouted Woodrow, halting abruptly. Tasslehoff collided with Woodrow's backside and dropped his hoopak. "The kender and I can't see in here. Can we strike a light?"

"Sorry," said Mettew, stooping to retrieve the fallen hoopak. "We don't carry torches, because we don't need them. Just put your hand on the dwarf ahead of you and you'll be fine. The floor is smooth enough."

Though she could see just fine, Gisella took the opportunity to rest her hands on the stout waists of two dwarves, who seemed happy to oblige.

Tasslehoff and Woodrow stumbled along behind the sharp-sighted dwarves. After some time, the line abruptly stopped. Tas heard a loud "thunk," and light streamed into the tunnel ahead. His eyes watered and smarted as he stepped through another leering face doorway into the light.

"There it is," declared Mettew proudly, spreading his thick arms wide. "Rosloviggen. The finest city in the realm."

Woodrow whistled through his teeth. Nestled deep in the valley between two steep mountains was a jumbled city of peaked roofs, gables, steeples, tiny, walled gardens, stone arches, colonnades, monoliths, and winding, neatly cobbled streets. The town was spotless, the buildings straight as arrows.

"This doesn't look like any dwarven town *I've* ever lived in," Gisella said, looking around her in awe. "Where's the roof?"

"Rosloviggen *is* unusual by dwarven standards," the baron agreed at her side. "My ancestors settled the village because of the rich mines in the surrounding mountains. The valley is so steep and protected that it affords us the comfort and safety of living underground that we dwarves need, along with the benefits of life on the surface, like sunlight for plants."

The procession set off down the valley, and the dwarves broke into a marching song of their own. The gully dwarves hummed and wailed along, but the powerful dwarven voices thankfully drowned them out.

Under the hills   the heart of the axe
Arises from cinders   the still core of the fire,
Heated and hammered   the handle an afterthought,
For the hills are forging   the first breath of war.
The soldier's heart sires and brothers
The battlefield.
Come back in glory
Or on your shield.

Out of the mountains   in the midst of the air,
The axes are dreaming   dreaming of rock,
Of metal alive through   the ages of ore,
Stone on metal   metal on stone.
The soldier's heart contains and dreams
The battlefield.
Come back in glory
Or on your shield.

Red of iron imagined from the vein,
Green of brass   green of copper
Sparked in the fire   the forge of the world,
Consuming in its dream   as it dives into bone.
The soldier's heart lies down, completes
The battlefield.
Come back in glory
Or on your shield.

The ragtag party marched through the massive gates of Rosloviggen at dusk. The sunset turned the stonework of the walls a vivid orange, and the mountain range threw long, purple shadows down the valley. The marching song of the dwarves mingled with the songs of the lamplighters, the matrons calling their charges home to dinner, and the hundreds of dwarves returning home from the day's work in the mines, the stonecutting and jewelry shops—plus the sounds of tailors, weavers, potters, candlemakers, and the vast number of other artisans, craftsmen, and laborers who made up a city. Tas was enchanted; Woodrow and the gully dwarves were overwhelmed.

"How they get so many people to be one place without fight?" Fondu asked aloud, setting off a rowdy debate among the gully dwarves.

Though the village was unfamiliar to Gisella, its sounds made her feel almost as if she'd returned home. Everywhere were the signs of the autumn harvest festival known as Oktoberfest, where goods were traded and sold, and food and drink were plentiful. Houses were freshly painted in bright colors with new thatch or shingles, flower boxes in full bloom, and gathered grains, potatoes, squashes, and gourds displayed in doorways. Benches had been erected in every square, and barrels of ale were stacked, ten high in places, awaiting the celebration.

Woodrow was still holding the horses' reigns, with the meager possessions that Gisella had salvaged from the wagon lashed across their backs, when they stopped before a large, open square. Dwarves from the town were busy setting up tables and tents.

"As you can see, Rosloviggen's Oktoberfest will be quite a splendid festival," Baron Krakold said with pride.

"Those workmen are having a time of it," commented Woodrow, nodding toward a crew of dwarves struggling in the square with one of the supporting beams of a tent. Two dwarves were trying to raise a beam upright with the help of a rope slung over a sturdy tree branch, while a handful more shouted directions.

"Pulley job! Pulley job!" chanted the gully dwarves.

The heavy beam swung round in a wide half-circle, threatening to crush several dwarves, all of whom dove to safety while the rest frantically tried to bring the massive timber under control. Grunting and straining, they wrestled the wayward beam into place between four other large supports. The workmen drew a collective sigh of relief and mopped their brows.

But Gisella's eyes were locked on the half-naked forms of two young dwarves, their shirts stripped off while they assembled a wooden bandstand. In addition to the obvious attractions, she thought the festival would provide an opportunity to replace her lost trade goods.

"I insist you accept the hospitality of my home," Baron Krakold boomed, repeating an earlier offer. "We are not far from it, and I should think that the telling of your travels over a sizzling haunch of aged beef, buttered gourd, and candied green apple would amply pay for a warm feather bed." It was not so much a statement as an order, and Gisella liked men who gave orders.

"That's very kind of you. By the way, is there a Baroness Krakbolder?" she asked bluntly.

"You could say that, yes," the baron said, his eyes twinkling at the dwarf's frankness.

Gisella winked at him, nonplused. "A minor point, really." She pushed a hand through her matted hair and straightened her clothing, although she still looked like someone who had been through a shipwreck. The red-haired dwarf looped her arm through Baron Krakold's.

Giving her hand a fatherly pat, the baron withdrew his arm reluctantly. "Not to my wife, it isn't!" he laughed.

Gisella's face pouted a little.

"Be of good cheer!" he said. "It is not often we have such unusual visitors in Rosloviggen. We are eager to hear how you came to our land."

"I can tell you that," Tasslehoff offered. "I was sitting in the Inn of the Last Home, and—"

"He meant *me*, and he meant *later*," Gisella said tersely.

Tasslehoff pulled a sullen face. "I don't remember him being that specific," he said. "I'm just as unusual as you are, Gisella, and I've done some interesting things, too."

"I'll just bet you have," the baron said kindly, "and I'd like to hear all about them after we've all had a chance to rest. My trip to the shore has drained me more than I thought it would."

"Look at that!" Tasslehoff cried. His attention was riveted on a large, circular platform with a round, pointed roof. A menagerie of brightly painted animals carved from wood crowded the platform. Each animal was mounted on a pole that ran from the platform to the roof. Tas recognized a griffon, a dragon, a unicorn, a horse with a fish's tail, and an enormous wolf with the head of a man. Eyes as wide as a full moon, the kender ran from one to the next, convinced that each was more beautiful than the last: stroking their manes, peering in their mouths, counting talons, eyes, and in some cases, heads.

"I'm most interested in that contraption myself," the baron said, rubbing his square jaw thoughtfully. "I am told that it is called a 'carousel.' It is being constructed for Oktoberfest by a gnome, another unusual visitor to our city."

"What does it do?" the kender asked.

"I'm not sure," Baron Krakold confessed. "I believe one rides it." A look of fatigue crossed the baron's weathered face. "But we can see it in action tomorrow. Now we will go to my home, dine, and rest before tomorrow's festivities." With that, Baron Krakold signaled his party forward. Tasslehoff followed reluctantly; Woodrow trailed silently. Behind them, Gisella was deep in thought. This was an opportunity of tremendous potential but she had to make the most of it. The gully dwarves reverently tripped over their shoelaces in her wake.

They wound through Rosloviggen's narrow, immaculate streets until Tas was certain they had traveled every alley in the town. When he was just about to announce that they must be lost, they emerged into a large, open space containing only a single house and several outbuildings. The front yard, like every other front yard in Rosloviggen, held a neatly manicured garden of small, flowering shrubs and perfectly shaped trees. The baron's yard had an additional circular fountain surrounded by heavy stone benches.

The ground floor of the house was constructed of enormous blocks of granite, polished to show off the rocks' natural colors. The upper floors were the more typical red dwarven brick. White-trimmed gables of all different sizes poked from the roof of the fifth floor, although the building was the same height as a three-story human dwelling. The last rays of the day's sun glanced off colorful stained glass rather than the usual oiled parchment. Flower boxes filled with multicolored geraniums lined every window. Servants in white aprons were busy closing the shutters on the first floor.

The baron tipped back his head and planted his hands on his hips. "This is my home," he said simply. He waved his guests forward into the neat garden, nodding and saying, "Welcome," to each. Then a look of surprise crossed his wide face. "It seems that your poorly dressed friends have left."

Engrossed by the sight before them, Woodrow and Tas looked behind Gisella and noticed for the first time that the gully dwarves were no longer with them. No one was particularly dismayed, especially the baron, though he seemed to be inordinately openminded about Aghar. Still, he was not sure he wanted them running loose in his village, but he decided that was better than having them lounging about in his home.

"It's no problem," Gisella said vaguely. "I'm sure they'll turn up again eventually. Or maybe not."

Woodrow's attention had already returned to the

house. "I didn't know houses could be made that tall," he stammered. "I thought those tree houses in Solace were something, and now this. Is it held up by magic?"

"No," laughed the baron, "just ordinary stone and wood and brick. But, of course, it was built by dwarves." There was no arrogance in his voice.

"Now," he continued, stepping toward the door, "if you'll collect your things from your horses, some of my escort will see the animals to the barns for the night."

Quickly Woodrow pulled two bundles from the backs of the horses, one containing the clothes Gisella had salvaged from the wagon, the other a few of his own and Tasslehoff's belongings. Several of the baron's guards then led the horses away around the side of the house.

"Miss Hornslager," Woodrow said, indicating that she should go before him.

"Thank you," Gisella replied, batting her eyes demurely at the baron as she sauntered through the front door.

Once inside, Baron Krakold instructed servants to lead the three weary visitors up the sweeping, circular staircase to their rooms on the third floor. "We'll sup in one hour," he said, then disappeared into a door below the stairway.

"Boy, this is like being home in Kendermore again," Tas breathed as he hurried up the stairs after the somber servant. The servant raised his eyebrows questioningly. "All the doors and knobs are at the right height," explained the kender, stopping to trace a finger over a particularly intricate carving of a rose on the banister. "This is very pretty, though my friend Flint would have added a few more petals, and you would swear you could see drops of water on his roses. He's a much better woodsmith."

"Hush!" Gisella hissed, afraid the baron might hear Tas's criticism.

At the top of the second flight of stairs, the liveried servant led them into a long, door-flanked hallway. Starting

with the first door on the right, he issued rooms to Gisella, Tasslehoff, and Woodrow.

"I'm making it your responsibility to watch Burrfoot
while we're here, Woodrow," Gisella called before she
disappeared behind her door.

"Yes, ma'am, and don't you worry," he answered.

But both human and kender were forgotten when her
sharp dwarven eyes spotted the copper tub in the middle
of the room. Two dwarf maids in gray muslin dresses
poured water from a single, enormous wooden bucket
into the spotless copper basin. A purr of pleasure escaped her lips as she flew into the room, already peeling
off her grimy clothing.

Tasslehoff's explorations carried him from room to
room. He was on his third one on the third floor, and just
thinking about heading to a different floor for variety,
when he felt a strong hand grip his shoulder. Tas whirled,
ready to pounce on whoever had sneaked up on him. His
eyes fell on stringy blond hair.

The kender's face reddened with something short of
anger. "Don't sneak up on people like that, Woodrow.
You might have startled me!"

"And you might have thought about staying in your
room," the young human said evenly. "You know I'm responsible for you. How am I supposed to keep track of
you if you're running around? I thought we were becoming friends."

"We *are* friends," Tas said patiently. "But I was so
bored in my room."

"But you weren't even in there for ten minutes,"
Woodrow pointed out. He looked around at the room in
which he'd found the kender. "This one looks just like
yours—they all look alike, for that matter."

"Really, Woodrow, it's not my fault they're all the
same," Tas sulked. "Nothing interesting in the drawers,"
he said, pulling one out of a dresser and holding it up to
demonstrate. "See? Empty, just like all the others."

He opened his arms wide to show off his new outfit. "I

found these clothes on the bed in my room." Tasslehoff plucked at the sides of the tunic. "It's a bit big, but then so are dwarves, at least sideways. The trousers sure feel weird," he continued, giving them a tug as well, "but my leggings were so dirty that clouds of dust whooshed out every time I took a step. I washed them in my basin and left them to dry.

"These pockets are very roomy, though," he added, jamming his hands into their depths to demonstrate. Tas's fine brows shot up in surprise. From his pockets emerged an elaborate silver candlestick, a delicate, glass bud-vase, a bar of soap, and a boar-bristle hairbrush.

"Whoever wore these before me sure carried a lot of stuff in his pockets," he said matter-of-factly. Examining the items more closely, he added, "I saw some things exactly like these in the other rooms. . . . Baron Krakold should be more careful about the people he invites into his home. Someone might have walked away with all this if I hadn't found these pants. I'd better keep my eyes on these until I can mention it to him." Tasslehoff stuffed the items back into his pockets and started for the door.

"Maybe you should leave them here so Baron Krakold doesn't think you took them," Woodrow suggested. "After all, he's only just met you."

Tasslehoff's eyebrows arched again. "Yes, I suppose you're right." Almost reluctantly, Tas pulled the items from his pockets, letting his hands linger on the shiny vase. He set them on a table near the door.

Heaving a sigh of relief, Woodrow led the way out the door and down the stairs. He, too, had found in his room a clean, white tunic, just a little bit short in the sleeves— it must have been made for an unusually tall dwarf—and a pair of black breeches, also just a touch too short.

They met the baron at the base of the stairs. He was dressed formally for dinner in a stiff, blue tunic with a red sash and bright red breeches, all layered with tremendous amounts of yellow piping and gold braid.

Shortly, Gisella appeared at the top of the stairs,

where she paused momentarily for effect before gliding down the stairway and alighting with a flourish, swirling her skirts. Red hair flowed down her back in luxurious waves, and her round cheeks were flushed with hints of crimson. The bodice of her saphire-blue dress was cut dangerously low, and well she knew it.

Everyone was still admiring her entrance when she threw herself into the baron's clumsy embrace, locking her arms around his head and nearly stuffing his red face into her ample bosom. Lifting his head, she kissed him full on the lips.

"Young woman, I—" blustered the baron.

"Thank you, you wonderful man!" she cooed as he backed away, coughing and sputtering. "The bath was absolutely marvelous! How did you know I practically live for them?" She caught him wiping away traces of lip rouge from her kiss. "Oh, I'm so naughty and impulsive! I hate myself, I do!" She charged forward with a silk kerchief and began dabbing at his face.

Gisella's performance was abruptly interrupted by a loud cough from the base of the staircase. Everyone turned, and the baron's face drained of color and he gasped. Pushing Gisella's hands away, he rushed to the side of a broad, squat, bearded, dark-faced dwarf in a high-necked, drab-colored dress.

"Hortense, dearest!" the baron squeaked. "I'm so glad you're here!" He tried taking her elbow but she held it tightly to her side.

Scowling, she glanced over at Gisella. "I can see that you are," she said pointedly.

"Let me introduce our guests," he said, a bit too eagerly. "Everyone, this is my wife, the Baroness Hortense Krakold." He directed her attention to Woodrow.

But Tasslehoff stepped up first. Thrusting out his small hand, he said "Tasslehoff Burrfoot, at your service. This is a very nice place you have here, although I think it might be improved by removing some walls. Have you ever been to Kendermore? Also, it seems that someone has been—ouch! What is it, Woodrow? Stop stepping on my foot! OK, I'll introduce you!" Frowning slightly, Tasslehoff turned back to the baroness. "This is my good friend, Woodrow . . . I'm sorry, I don't know your last name."

"Ath-Banard," the young human mumbled. He extended his hand awkwardly to the baroness, who ignored it.

This time Gisella coughed behind them and pushed her way forward. "Oh, yes," said Tas, "this is—"

"Gisella Hornslager," the dwarf announced herself, locking eyes with the baroness. There were only two things Gisella liked better than a contest of wit and will, and those were making money and a good roll in the hay. Since business was going down the sewer fast and the appetizing baron had turned out to be milquetoast, she decided to channel her energy into a good catfight with the baroness. The ugly, sour-faced old matron obviously wore the pants in the family, Gisella thought to herself. Rubbing her hands with glee, she fell in behind everyone else as the group followed the baron into the dining room.

The evening passed very uncomfortably for everyone but Gisella, as the two women passed barbs across the dining table, the game table, and finally the sitting room. All the while the mighty baron squirmed and fidgeted like a beetle in a birdcage.

"You really must tell me where you do your dress shopping, Baroness," Gisella gushed, shoveling strawberry tart into her mouth. "I find men leering all the time so annoying, don't you?" She smiled into the matronly dwarf's face. "Anyway, I think some dull, drab, highnecked dresses like yours might help, though I'm certain they won't be able to hide my obvious attributes."

The baroness pursed her lips and rang a little bell to signal a servant. "We'll need another ten tarts for our guest," she told the starched butler. "Speaking of strawberries," she turned to Gisella, "do you color your hair that unlikely shade to hide the gray, or simply to attract attention?"

Feeling restless, Tasslehoff tried several times to change the direction of the conversation. He couldn't quite understand the two women. They smiled at each other and were polite, but somehow he didn't think they liked each other much. When finally the baron suggested that everyone retire for the evening, they discovered Tasslehoff already asleep before the fire.

Chapter 12

"*Ouch!*" *swore Phineas.* "*There is absolutely no* comfortable way to sit on this damned, dinky animal."

Phineas stood in the stirrups, raising himself to his full height, which was at least two and a half feet taller than the hairy kender pony he was riding. He rubbed his backside.

Trapspringer chuckled aloud. "Still convinced it's chewing on you?" he asked. "I'll be happy to trade."

Phineas gave him an acid glance. Trapspringer laughed again.

"It might help if you could stop laughing about it!" shouted Phineas. "By the time we reach this place, assuming we ever do, I'll be crippled."

"I can't help laughing, Phineas. It's funny. You should

---

see yourself. Why, you're twice as tall as that pony, who probably is not enjoying this ride any more than you are. Besides, I thought you said you'd ridden horses before."

"Sure, I've ridden lots of horses before, but this beast is a first cousin to a night hag. And whoever made this saddle didn't pound the nails all the way in."

Trapspringer whooped and rocked in his saddle at that. "Nails! Oh, that's funny! I should have met you years ago. I never would have settled down if I'd had a traveling companion with such a rich sense of humor."

Phineas gingerly lowered himself back into the saddle with a wince. With his feet in the stirrups, his knees rose almost to the level of his elbows. With his feet out of the stirrups, his toes dragged on the ground. At least with my feet in the stirrups, he thought, I can massage my calves more easily. "How much farther do we have to go?" he whined.

"Not far," replied Trapspringer. "Maybe another hour. We'll be there by dark."

"Fine. You just lead the way and keep your laughter to yourself," grunted Phineas through gritted teeth.

"The time will pass better with a story," Trapspringer announced. "I'll tell you about my expedition to Hylo and you'll feel better. It was back in 317 . . . or was it 307? It was the year that mosquitoes infested Darken Wood so bad that you could hardly inhale without sucking a couple dozen up your nostrils. We had to wear gauze sacks over our heads just to travel along the fringe of the woods. Of course, the only place to get really good gauze was from the elves and they lived *in* the woods. Since none of us could speak their language, we had to hire a translator before setting out. This fellow that we hired was—"

"Excuse me, Trapspringer, but what does any of this have to do with Hylo?" asked Phineas. As if I really care, he thought to himself.

"I'm just establishing what year it took place," he explained. "Proper chronology is very important to a story like this. If you don't want to know what year it takes place, I'll just skip the whole story. I know it by heart anyway. I was telling it for your benefit."

Phineas sighed. There seemed to be no way out of this situation. He was stuck with Trapspringer until they found Damaris and returned her to Kendermore. Were Uncle Trapspringer's whoppers, all with identical themes and morals, too high a price to pay for the riches Phineas expected as his reward? Probably not. "Please, go on," he said stiffly. The words caught slightly in his throat.

As Trapspringer resumed his narration, Phineas's mind wandered ahead to the Ruins and what he might find there. Soon Trapspringer's voice had faded into the background like the multitude of other pains afflicting Phineas.

The sun was well below the treetops when the two travelers finally approached the Ruins. The trees cast long shadows across the tumbled columns and low, standing walls. The bleached white blocks of stone stretched away and disappeared in the twilight.

"I didn't expect them to be so—extensive," murmured Phineas. He had expected something on typical kender scale; small, chaotic, and thoroughly vandalized. Instead, he found a size and symmetry in the Ruins that astounded him.

Trapspringer dismounted his pony at the edge of the area. "We'll camp here for the night. Tomorrow we can start looking for Damaris."

"Why can't we do some looking tonight?"

"It's too dark already," Trapspringer explained. "This area's pretty safe in daylight, but I wouldn't want to wander through it at night. There's no telling what you might fall into or knock down. Worse still, you never know what might find you wandering around."

That's reassuring, Phineas thought. Then aloud, he asked, "What was this place before it became ruined?"

"Now that's an interesting story," said Trapspringer, collecting sticks for firewood. "Eight interesting stories, actually. The past of this place depends on who you talk to. Some say that the elves built it as a shelter for their dead. Others say that it just sprang up as a natural result of the Cataclysm. I've talked to people who—"

"To shorten what is shaping up as a very long story," interrupted Phineas, "what you're trying to tell me, in as few words as possible, is that no one knows what these ruins once were."

"That about sums it up," agreed Trapspringer. "I think it's safe to assume it was once a city of some size, though." He gathered a load of firewood and let it roll unceremoniously from his arms.

"I'll start the fire," Phineas offered, feeling awkward and out of his element. The kender handed him a piece of flint and he found some good, splintered kindling to catch the spark.

Trapspringer took several paper-wrapped packages from a pack on his pony. Kneeling, he carefully unwrapped the larger one and proudly held up two roasted rabbits. Stripping the cooked meat from the bones, he dumped it into a crusted, black iron pot, added some whole carrots and potatoes from the other package, sloshed in some water from a skin, and set it to boil over Phineas's fire.

For once, Trapspringer didn't launch into a story. Instead, they ate the stew in silence and fell asleep before the fire.

Phineas tossed and turned anxiously all night in his sleep, great fuzzy things flapping at him in his dreams.

Chapter 13

Tasslehoff awoke in Baron Krakold's home to the musical strains of a tuba floating in his window from somewhere below. Oktoberfest! Leaping up from the feather bed—which was a little too soft for his taste—the kender ran a hand over his blue leggings, checking to see if they had dried from their washing the night before. The few damp spots left would dry quickly next to his skin, Tas decided, and slipped them on with a satisfied sigh. He never felt quite comfortable without them. A night's airing had done the rest of his clothes a world of good, and he donned them with glee. Finally the kender strapped on his belt-pack, picked up his hoopak, and strode to the door.

The hallway was silent and empty as he stole down the

stairs. He listened for sounds of life and heard pans rattling somewhere at the rear of the house. None of his friends seemed to be awake yet, nor did he see any sign of the baron or his dour wife.

"I'll just go see what's happening with the festival," he said softly as he let himself out the front door. "By the time they wake up, I'll have a lot to report. They'll be so pleased when I tell them where all the best food halls and magicians are. Maybe I can even find other traders for Gisella to do business with."

The sky was partly cloudy but it did not look like it would rain, Tasslehoff thought. He decided to find the tuba player first and, after stopping to listen for the direction, he set off straight down a cobbled street.

Shutters and doors were beginning to open, and cooking hearths were being stirred to life. Tas paused in front of a bakery and looked inside for the baker. Not finding him, the kender counted twenty-eight pies cooling on shelves just inside the windows. There was blueberry, cherry, rhubarb, apple, currant, and mulberry—Tas's favorite—plus a large tray of raspberry cinnamon tarts.

A few doors from the bakery, a knife-grinder was setting up his display cases along the sidewalk. Still licking mulberry from his fingers, Tas paused to admire the keen edges on the blades of every size and description. His own little belt knife could use a good sharpening, he thought, continuing his stroll. A few moments later, the grinder was puzzled to discover an unfamiliar dagger with a worn blade sitting prominently in his case where an elegant, stag-handled clasp-knife should have been.

The tuba sounded very close as Tas rounded a corner and found himself back on the edge of the square where, on the previous evening, they had watched the workmen. His mouth dropped in surprise. Overnight the square had been transformed from a jumble of timbers into a wonderland. The bandstand, with its polished, carved timbers and rounded roof, looked as if it had been rooted to that spot for generations. The side toward the spectators' bleachers was open, affording an excellent view of the band.

Actually, 'band' was a bit of an overstatement. Seated on the stage were two rotund dwarves in colorful, short-sleeved shirts and black knickers with embroidered suspenders. The tuba player's cheeks and moustache puffed in and out in time with the music. His face was as red as his hair. The other dwarf, his moplike black and gray hair and beard bobbing in time, was strapped to an instrument like nothing Tasslehoff had ever seen before. Though straps supporting the instrument criss-crossed the dwarf's broad back, his stomach was so round that the contraption rested on it like a shelf. His stubby fingers danced happily over a row of square, wooden keys, carved alternately from white and black wood. Above them were round, black buttons, which he would occasionally push or pull. On top of all that, the instrument was connected to a bellows which the musician had to pump furiously the whole time he played. Its honking tone reminded Tasslehoff of a duck in flight.

For the next hour and a half, the kender wandered around and through the festival grounds, continuously discovering new things of interest, such as the locations of all the metalsmiths' booths; where and when the axe-throwing competition would be held; the judging standards for the rock-splitting contest; which ale tents were best; and where the tastiest dwarven stews could be purchased. He even met the oompa band members, Gustav and Welker, who let him blow into the tuba and play the instrument Welker called an "accordian."

Tasslehoff was having such a good time that he lost track of how long he had been at the square. The festival was now in full swing. The kender stood at one of the ale tents, slurping from his second flagon, when he felt a tap on his shoulder.

"Good morning, Mr. Burrfoot."

Tasslehoff spun around, slopping ale on Woodrow's cleaned and buffed shoes. "Woodrow! I'm glad I found you! I've met the most marvelous people this morning!"

"Found me?" Woodrow's voice cracked. "Mr. Burr-foot, did you stop to think what Miss Hornslager would do to me if I lost you? She'd fire me for sure! Not that it's such a great job, but I need the money."

Tas's voice filled with concern. "Gee, Woodrow, I'm sorry. I've never heard you sound so angry."

"I've never had to watch a kender before," Woodrow almost snarled. "When I woke up and couldn't find you anywhere, I had to lie to Miss Hornslager at breakfast. Do you know how much I hate lying? I told her you were still sleeping and that we would meet her here later. Then I slipped away and prayed that I'd find you."

"Well, here I am. And if you must know," Tas said, trying to sound indignant, "I've been exploring the festival and talking to people to determine the fastest route to Kendermore." Or at least I intended to, Tasslehoff reasoned.

Woodrow's ire lessened a bit at that news. "What have you discovered?" he asked anxiously.

"Oh, I know where the richest ale is—would you care for some?" Woodrow shook his head impatiently. "And I've found a silver bracelet with gold filigree that I simply must have—actually, it looks a lot like this one here on my wrist." He paused, studying a band around his wrist in puzzlement. "Anyway, I've just had a mug of the tastiest stew ever!" Dropping his voice, he added, "Please don't tell Flint I said that."

"Mr. Burrfoot," Woodrow interrupted, "what have you found out about *Kendermore*?"

Tasslehoff fidgeted under his friend's gaze. "I was just about to start asking people, actually."

The wiry human took the kender by the arm. "Let's hope Miss Hornslager has learned something, because she's waiting for us right now over by the carousel."

Excited, Tasslehoff slipped from the human's grip, dancing by his side. "Have you seen the carousel yet? If you haven't, brace yourself. It's the most magnificent thing you'll ever see."

Woodrow glared at Tas. "Please, Mr. Burrfoot!"

Woodrow looked so worried that Gisella would find out about Tasslehoff's solo adventure that the kender made a mental note not to let the human down. They found the shapely dwarf glancing around anxiously near the strange ride. She wore a skin-tight, sand-colored shirt and slacks that made her look, in certain light, like she was wearing nothing at all. A broad-brimmed hat perched on her pomegranate-colored hair shaded her fair skin from the autumn sun.

"Woodrow, Burrfoot!" Even their names sounded like a scold on her tongue. "I was beginning to get worried."

Gisella suddenly turned her attention to the festival, and her eyes scoured the stalls, the tents, and the men. "I've got a lot of deals to make today if I'm going to come out of this fiasco with a copper to my name, aside from what the kender is worth to me. I make my best deals in this outfit." She was half-talking to herself as she unconsciously smoothed the tight fabric over her rounded hips.

Suddenly she remembered the kender and grabbed him by the collar. Her small, dark eyes burned into his. "This is work, and I need to concentrate. I don't want to be distracted by fretting about you. So stay close—but not too close. Better yet, stay close to Woodrow. Keep your eyes open and learn something."

Adjusting her hat to a jaunty angle, she strode up to the first booth next to the carousel, that of a fabric merchant. Tasslehoff and Woodrow both noticed that she put a lot more wiggle in her walk than before. She paused for a few moments among the tables filled with bolts of brightly colored fabric, running expert fingers over each one.

"Good morning, handsome," the red-haired dwarf purred to the buck-toothed, hunch-backed dwarf seated inside the booth. She judged his age to be well in excess of three hundred years. His crossed arms were so hairy that Gisella couldn't tell where they ended and his beard began. "May I speak with your father, the proprietor?"

The old dwarf's eyes roamed across Gisella's tightly clothed form. "I am the proprietor," he announced, his lips rolling back over his teeth in a grotesque smile.

Gisella's hand flew to her mouth in a masquerade of shame. Somehow she coaxed color to flood her cheeks. "I don't believe it! Oh, now I've insulted you! I'm usually not such a blunderer at guessing a person's age!"

She clucked her tongue and shook her head gravely. "I've ruined everything. You won't want anything to do with me, and you have the best merchandise at the fair! Please accept my apology." She touched his hairy arm gently and turned to leave. "I won't bother you further." She took a step from the booth, putting more wiggle in that one step than either Woodrow or Tasslehoff thought possible.

"Please, don't be sorry, Miss—?"

"—Matron Hornslager," Gisella supplied, letting a grateful smile grow on her face as she turned to him again. This was one of the easiest fish she had ever reeled in. "Then you will deal with me? Oh, you dear man! To show you how guilty and grateful I feel, I'll buy twice as much as I can afford! Mr. Hornslager will surely be angry with me, but I don't care!" she said defiantly.

"By Reorx," he responded, "I'd hate to think of you in trouble with your husband, whoever the lucky fellow is. I can't imagine any greater tribute to my wares than for them to adorn your lovely figure. I'll gladly sell you twenty bolts for what they cost me, if only you promise to tell people where you got them."

"Any twenty bolts?" cooed Gisella.

"My shop is yours," he replied, with a sweep of his hairy hand. Gisella knew his eyes were glued to her swaying bottom as she brushed past him. Even though she found him repulsive, she did love the attention.

Now the hard dealing began. Gisella flipped through the bolts, casting aside anything she judged to be of inferior quality and grilling the merchant over weavers, cost, dyes, and age.

"This isn't real silver thread!" she snorted, raveling a strand from the end of a bolt.

As Tasslehoff watched the dwarves bargaining, a whooshing, clanking, grinding symphony started up behind him. Turning, Tas realized that it was coming from the carousel! He immediately started forward, but Woodrow's hand stopped him.

"But the carousel is starting," the kender pleaded. "Look at it! Animals going up and down and around in a circle. And it's playing music!"

Woodrow stood fast.

"OK, then come with me and I won't be lost," reasoned Tas.

Woodrow eyed the carousel, intrigued but unsure. "I don't know . . ."

"I do!" Tas cried. "Come on. Gisella will be looking at cloth all morning. She's still arguing about the third bolt." He pulled at Woodrow's sleeve. "Just one ride. We'll be back before she even notices we've left. Come on, Woodrow!"

At last, Woodrow's own curiosity overcame his better judgment. He looked back at Gisella, then trailed behind the kender toward the carousel.

Next to the carousel was a churning mass of gears and pulleys and knobs and chains that obviously made the whole thing go. Even though the ride was in motion, a short, bald gnome wearing an ankle-length, white coat and goggles on a cord around his neck, scurried to and fro with a handful of wrenches, twisting this screw, pulling that rod, and banging on that other gear.

"It'snotrightyet; themusicistooslow," the gnome mumbled almost incomprehensibly fast, as gnomes do. He yanked out a knob and the music, a dirgelike stew of whistles, honks, and clanks, slowed down even more and went flat. Then suddenly it sped up until it was so high-pitched that dogs in the city howled in pain. The gnome pushed the knob back in, and the music returned to its normal blare.

Arms crossed, the gnome stood back and nodded with satisfaction. His expression suddenly fell. "That'sfixed-buttheunicornismovingtooslowly. Where'smy wrench; IknowIleftitrightthere. Someonetookit!" He rummaged through the pockets inside his long, white coat and produced the missing instrument, nonplused. He poked it into the gears blindly, giving another bolt a twist.

As he did, the carousel's wooden statue of a dog-faced kobold started pumping up and down faster and faster, moving so violently that the kobold figure's head smashed through the roof of the carousel, giving its young dwarf rider the fright of his life and an instant headache to boot.

The gnome scratched his bald head in puzzlement. "Thatshouldbetheswitchfortheunicornnotthekobold," he murmured, reaching in blindly again and giving another switch a twist. The kobold kept on bashing through the roof.

"Sorry," he mumbled. "Sorry." He released the lever and the kobold slowed down. The dwarf on its back swayed dizzily.

"Where'sthatoffswitch? IknowIputonein." Extending his arm through the grinding gears in a way that made Woodrow wince, the gnome groped around in the gear box and pulled things seemingly at random. The swan flapped its wings, boxing its rider's ears, while the leprechaun pinched a passing matron and the unicorn bucked its rider completely off.

"IknowIputoneinheresomewhere. Orwasthatonmy-boatsharpeningmachine? Ohdearohdearohdear. . . ." Frantically, he began pulling even more switches, making things worse with each tug.

"Maybe it's this one marked 'OFF,' " Tas suggested at his side.

"Itcouldn'tbethat—" The gnome shook his head, but before he could say more, Tasslehoff reached out and flicked the lever down with his index finger. The ride ground to a halt.

"Wellwhatdoyouknow?" The gnome's face stretched into a surprised smile, which grew as he considered Tasslehoff.

"Your carousel is fantastic," Tas breathed, trying to decide which animal to ride. "If you can fix a few things, like the animals smashing their heads through the carousel's ceiling, it will be perfect. Did you think this up yourself? Is this your Life Quest?"

Tasslehoff knew that gnomes were born inventors. Each was assigned a quest at birth—or inherited it—that they were expected to complete before they died so that they and their ancestors could sit next to their god Reorx in the hereafter.

"You could say that," the gnome said, deliberately slowing his speech for Tasslehoff's benefit. "You're a kender, aren't you? I've never seen a kender around here before." The gnome smiled at Tasslehoff in a strange way, until the kender began feeling like a bug under a glass.

"I've only seen pictures of dragons and hippocampuses—that's the one that looks like a horse with a fish tail and flippers for feet, isn't it? Your animals look so real, like you've actually seen them up close, but of course that's impossible, since dragons exist only in stories."

"Many people think that, yes," the gnome said absently. He looked closely at Tasslehoff's face, then reached out a hand to squeeze his waist, as though checking for something. "You're not very old for a kender, are you?"

Tasslehoff pushed the gnome's hand away. "Do you ask everybody this many questions before letting them on your ride? If you're worried that I'm too heavy, I'm sure I weigh less than a dwarf, wouldn't you say, Woodrow?"

The human was looking back with concern at Gisella, who was nearing the end of the first of two tables of fabric. The carousel ride was taking far longer than he'd thought it would. "I'm sure you do, Mr. Burrfoot," he said distractedly.

"Are you going to start the carousel up again soon?" Tasslehoff asked. "I have to be going, and I really would like to ride on that dragon."

"Of course, right away; let me help you," the gnome said excitedly, gripping the kender by the shoulder and leading him onto the platform. "And may I say that the red dragon is an excellent choice?" He hurried Tasslehoff halfway around the carousel until they stood next to the dragon.

Tas knew that, as a race, dragons had been banished from Krynn by a legendary knight, Huma, long before he or any of his friends had been born. His eyes opened wide in wonder as he beheld the statue of the mythical creature. The dragon had been carved with painstaking detail. Six long, rubbery-looking bones, linked by fleshy webbing, formed the creature's mighty wings. Its powerful, deadly claws had horned hocks. Spikes ran down its long, spade-shaped tail and continued up the dragon's entire length, ending at the base of the horned skull. The monster's face was a lumpy, frightening mass of bulging muscles and veins. The jaws were parted in a vicious snarl, displaying two rows of double-edged teeth, each sharper than a butcher's axe.

Tas was most taken with the paint job. Each rounded scale was daubed with such precision that it looked as if the dragon could lift and flap its wings if necessary. The ruby-red color was rich, vivid, and glistening. Tas was reminded of tightly packed, juicy pomegranate seeds.

Looking at the spikes on the dragon's back, Tas was relieved to find a saddle of a sort carved into the creature's neck. Putting his booted foot into the stirrups that dangled from it, the kender hopped aboard the dragon's back.

Woodrow selected the centaur statue behind the dragon so that he could keep an eye on his charge. Settling himself on the centaur's lifelike, chocolate-brown-haired back, the straw-haired young man waited for the ride to fill up with dwarves so that it could begin.

Standing by the gears, the gnome rubbed his hands with glee and threw a big lever. The carousel jerked to a start, and the slightly flat, peppy bell tones of the carousel's music roared from somewhere in the ceiling above the statues, drowning out all other noise. The animals bobbed alternately on their poles—when the dragon soared upward, the centaur plunged. It seemed that the gnome had everything under control this time. He hopped up and down by the gears, clapping his hands happily.

Tasslehoff was delighted, too. As the dragon rose and fell, its wings glided upward, then lowered again, as if the monster were truly flying.

"What fun! I hope this ride never ends," Tas said to himself fervently. "I'm sure this is how it would feel to ride a real dragon—it's too bad there aren't any more on Krynn."

Just then, Tas felt the dragon statue shift under him and rock slightly. "The gnome should attach these statues more firmly," the kender thought. "I'll just mention it to him when I get off."

But to Tasslehoff's surprise, the ride didn't slow down one bit. Worse still, the shaking and shifting under him intensified, until it was difficult to stay on the dragon's back. He wondered if Woodrow was having similar trouble, so he glanced behind him at the human riding on the centaur statue. Woodrow's expression was bored, but turned to concern when he noticed the kender.

"My dragon is coming loose!" Tas called to him.

Tas felt his grip slipping even further. He pressed his chest to the dragon's back, locked his arms around its neck, and wrapped his legs around the pole behind him. Why wouldn't that silly gnome stop the ride? Had he forgotten where the off switch was again?

Behind him, Woodrow saw the kender's lips moving,

but couldn't understand what he was saying. Woodrow, too, had had more than enough of the ride. He gestured at the gnome as the carousel spun past. Wearing a strange smile, the gnome waved back.

Just then, there was a sharp sound of splintering wood, and the poles connected to the dragon statue ahead of Woodrow tore loose. Woodrow opened his mouth to shout a warning to Tas. Then his blood froze as he saw the red dragon's head swing around to look at the kender on its back. The human's jaw dropped when he saw the dragon flick its tail and flex its wings. The muscles in the monster's back rippled beneath its red scales!

The dragon was alive!

Woodrow shook his head, unsure whether he'd imagined the dragon's movement or really had seen it. When he looked up again, the centaur he was riding was staring into his face. "The dragon is getting away with your friend," it said.

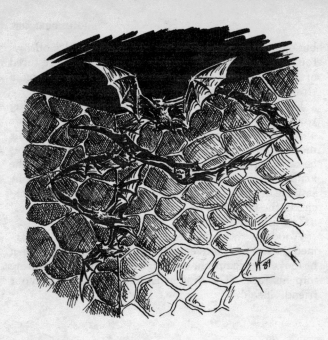

Chapter 14

Phineas awoke the next morning feeling as if he had dreamt all night, but unable to recall anything specific. The sky was overcast, and a strong wind blew. Phineas shivered in the cold autumn air and drew the blanket tighter around his shoulders. Dry leaves rustled against his face. Reluctantly, he sat up. His face was covered with grit, his back ached from the cold, damp ground, and each tooth felt like it was wrapped in its own wool sweater. All in all, he was in a foul mood.

Scrubbing a finger vainly over his teeth, he looked to where Trapspringer should have been sleeping and saw that the kender had already awakened and packed up the camp. Peering around, Phineas spotted his 'guide' sitting nearby on the remains of a stone wall. He was kicking his heels happily while chewing on a stale chunk of thick, grainy bread.

Hearing Phineas's approach, Trapspringer sang, "Good morning!"

"That's one opinion," snarled the human, slapping his arms to warm them up.

"Someone woke on the wrong side of the bed today," Trapspringer said glibly, observing the human's dark expression.

"If I had slept in a bed, I wouldn't be in this mood," was Phineas's sullen response. "Do you have any more of that bread?"

Trapspringer broke off a hunk, handed it to the human, and looked up at the gray sky. "This should be a great day for exploring the Ruins. Sunny weather brings out more kender from the city and all sorts of creatures from underground."

Phineas's open mouth stopped in mid-bite. "Creatures?"

The kender nodded vigorously. "Oh, you know, the sorts of monsters you find in ruins: lizards, snakes, rats, bats, beetles, spiders, goblins, giant slugs, norkers, owlbears, goat-sucker birds . . ."

"I get the point."

Trapspringer shrugged. "Care for some water?" He extended the skin to the human.

Phineas swallowed hard. The bread felt like a lump in his stomach. He took the skin and half emptied it in two gulps. "Why didn't you tell me about the monsters?" he asked at last, his voice unnaturally high.

Trapspringer gave him a peculiar look. "What did you think you'd find in the ruins of a city? The local bakers' guild?"

"No! I expected to find empty ruins."

"Oh, this place is lousy with monsters," Trapspringer said plainly. "Once, out here, I saw an owlbear bite the head off a pony. And the rider, well . . ."

Phineas felt the bread coming back up. He concentrated on keeping it down and on not hearing the details of Trapspringer's story.

". . . But you're a doctor—I don't have to tell you what the inside of a person looks like." The kender blithely jumped down from the wall and took his pony by the bridle. "Are you ready? Say, you don't look very well."

Phineas pressed two fingers to the bridge of his nose, trying to massage away a spreading headache. "The bread just didn't sit well," he said feebly.

"We can go back to Kendermore anytime you like," Trapspringer offered. "I've been here plenty of times— not much left to discover, really."

"Then why did Damaris come here?" the human asked.

Trapspringer shrugged. "Why not? It used to be a great place to find relics, but it's been picked clean for decades. Now it's just a sort of unofficial rite of passage to survive the Ruins."

"Survive?"

Trapspringer peered closely at Phineas. "You sure are the skittish type, aren't you?"

"I hardly think it's being skittish to worry about having your head bitten off," Phineas sniffed defensively.

"Oh, that," Trapspringer said, dismissing the incident with a wave of his hand. "The pony probably asked for it. So, are we going or staying?"

Phineas dug his knuckles into his eyes and rubbed. He'd come awfully far to turn back now. With Damaris gone, Tasslehoff had no reason to return to Kendermore with the other half of the map. The human felt his tenuous grip on the situation, and the treasure, slip away. He heard himself say in a hollow voice, "Going."

"That's the spirit!" Trapspringer said, clapping Phineas on the back. "I just hope we don't run into any undead. I forgot my holy water, and skeletons and ghouls and the like are so persistent." The kender secured his hoopak to the saddle, squared his shoulders, and led his pony into the Ruins.

Phineas took a deep breath and followed, tugging at his own diminutive mount.

From what Phineas could see, the city that had once stood here had been extensive. The ruins stretched for hundreds of yards in both directions, fading gradually into the surrounding woods and sloughs. The kender and the human picked their way along the large, loose cobbles of an old, weed-choked street. Along the winding street were the crumbling foundations of ancient buildings and jumbled piles of rectangular, white stones. Perhaps one out of every ten buildings was nearly intact, its walls still standing, doors and roofs missing.

Trapspringer, who was standing with his pony a dozen or so paces ahead at the junction of two streets, stopped and turned to wait for Phineas. The street they were crossing was at least three times wider than the one they'd been following, and stretched off to the right and left in a gentle, graceful curve.

"This must have been one of the main streets, back when this place was alive. It circles all the way around the Ruins," Trapspringer said. "As long as you can find this road, you can't get lost, because eventually it will bring you back to where you started. Remember that in case we get split up somehow.

Trapspringer set off to the right. "In the meantime, you watch the far side of this road, and I'll watch the near side."

"What are we looking for, exactly?" asked a confused Phineas, pumping his legs to keep up with the nimble-footed kender.

"Signs of Damaris, of course."

"What sorts of signs?"

"You know, *signs*! Footprints, hoofprints, turned-over rocks, bits of trash, campfires, whatever. Just keep your eyes open."

Phineas shrugged. He'd tracked his little sister through fresh snow once when he was seven years old and almost lost the trail. He suspected he was not going to be much help in this search.

They followed the road slowly for some time, finding nothing but chipmunks and field mice, when Phineas heard Trapspringer calling his name. He looked over his shoulder and saw the kender standing several yards down a side street, motioning to Phineas to follow. The human led his pony behind Trapspringer as they approached a large, virtually intact building.

Shortly, they stood among the crumbled columns of a large portico. "What was this, a temple perhaps?" asked Phineas, squinting up at the tall stone building. The front doors were twelve feet high, the side walls at least twenty feet. Arched windows lined the walls in graceful rows, and a round window stood out against the top of the peaked front wall. The roof of slate had survived centuries of neglect.

"Perhaps. Let's see if Damaris is in here," Trapspringer suggested. Wasting no time, he took a small lantern from the limitless pack on the pony, lit it, and strode into the structure. Phineas followed anxiously, leaving the ponies behind.

They stood in what must have been a vast, tall antechamber, which looked like it once had a second floor. Long lengths of pitted stone hung suspended midway between the ground and the roof. Indirect light from the gray day filtered through the window holes and lit the room. Not even a block of stone littered the floor.

"The most intact stones from these ruins are the rage among builders in Kendermore," explained Trapspringer. "They come out here in wagons and completely disassemble what's left of some of the buildings. I'm surprised this one's still here." Trapspringer's voice echoed in the hollow stone room. Swinging the lantern at his side, he walked to an opening on the far side of the chamber.

The next room was smaller. Less sunlight reached the ground here, since the windows were smaller, too. Trapspringer held the lantern over a black square of marble against the left wall, making the shadows dance. "You were probably right about this being a temple. I'll bet this is where the altar was." He started toward the next opening at the far side of the room.

"Can't we just call to her from here?" Phineas suggested, feeling less secure with each step. Cobwebs tickled his nose annoyingly.

"Sure, if you want everything in the area to know we're here, go ahead," was Trapspringer's reply. "But me, I'm the cautious type," he added as he stepped through the next door.

A thunderous roar rose up in the next room, accompanied by screeching, Trapspringer hollering, a loud crash, and then both rooms plunged into darkness. Phineas froze, unable to see or think. Something struck him in the chest, then struck him again. Suddenly, he was surrounded by a storm of shrieking, flapping, hairy things. He squeezed his eyes shut and flailed mindlessly at the unidentifiable horror that assaulted him from every direction. "Trapspringer, help me!" he screamed. Phineas felt something settle on his neck. Terror tightened around his rib cage, and his breath came in shallow gulps. He slapped furiously in the darkness at the thing on his neck, nearly knocking himself senseless.

Suddenly, the attack slackened. He felt fewer and fewer creatures banging into him. He heard their distant cries as they found their way through the rooms to the outside.

"Trapspringer?" Phineas said tentatively. He heard movement to his right. The human froze.

"Wow," breathed the kender's voice at last. "That was something, eh? Those bats sure were anxious to leave." The kender struggled to his feet. "The lantern must have gone out when they knocked me down and I hit my head. Are you all right?"

Phineas could feel his cheeks growing warm. He hoped the kender hadn't heard his foolish cry for help. "Fine, fine," he said lamely. "Don't worry about me."

Trapspringer fumbled with the lantern. In moments, it

blazed again. The side of Trapspringer's face was bruised, his graying topknot in disarray as he looked around the room. "No more doors. Damaris obviously isn't here."

"Obviously," Phineas repeated. "Let's get out of here."

"I'm sure it's safe now. Don't I feel silly!" He laughed. "An experienced adventurer like me getting flustered by a gaggle of bats," he said, walking back through the temple and out onto the portico.

"Say, do bats come in gaggles?" he asked, turning back toward Phineas. "Maybe its a brood. A drove? A herd? Flock? Hmmmm."

Through the rest of the day, Phineas followed the kender into several more ruined buildings. His body ached with tension, and he expected something to spring on him at any moment. But nothing did. The worst thing they saw was a couple of giant centipedes, which seemed almost as anxious to leave as the human was to see them go.

A hazy sun burned through the gray at about midday. Kender and human looped the ponies' reins around the stump of a column near what once must have been a reflecting pool. They collapsed and nibbled a bit of dried beef Phineas had brought. Finally, Phineas asked a question that had been haunting him the whole, fruitless morning.

"Is it possible that something has happened to Damaris? Could she have . . . disappeared somehow? Had an accident?"

Trapspringer considered that, lips pursed. "It's possible. But more likely she got bored already and left. As you can see, there's not a lot here anymore."

Phineas thought that the constant possibility of a monster attack ought to be exciting enough for even a kender. He asked, "Where would she have gone, then? Are there more ruins near here?"

"No, this is it," Trapspringer responded. "I take that back," he corrected himself instantly. "There is one more place she could be near. It's actually part of the Ruins, but I don't know anyone who's ever actually gotten into it."

Trapspringer had already jumped up and was leading them toward a wooded area on the north side of the Ruins. The woods looked like a nearly impenetrable tangle of trees, brush, brambles, roots, and vines. Phineas could not see far into the gloom.

"Why would anyone go in *there*?" he asked Trapspringer as he followed the kender's lead and tied his pony's reigns to a tree. Trapspringer took his hoopak from his saddle and started chopping his way through the green density. Phineas sprang forward to follow.

"I understand that the brush thins out quite a lot once you get inside," explained Trapspringer unhelpfully.

"What's inside?" asked Phineas, gingerly picking a thorn-covered branch from his pant leg.

"The tower, of course—the fifth Tower of High Sorcery. It was one of the five original Towers of High Sorcery, but it must have been ruined shortly after the Cataclysm. The tower isn't really the problem. The problem is that an enchanted grove was planted around each tower to keep out unwanted visitors. No one I know of has ever reached as far as the tower."

Phineas stopped dead in his tracks. He turned around and practically ran back to the ponies. "What are you doing, leading us into a magical grove? And a Tower of High Sorcery at its center! Are you crazy?" Just as suddenly, he stopped again and gave the kender a skeptical glare. "I don't see any tower. And I don't see anything magical about these woods. Besides, how do you know all this?"

"The grove's effect isn't physical," Trapspringer explained. "The grove just sort of . . . makes whatever you're feeling at the moment seem more intense and hard to control."

"Gods, that's stupid, Trapspringer! You obviously think I'm a simpleton!" His eyes narrowed as he confronted the kender. "I know what you're up to, though. You think you can scare me into running away so *you* can find Damaris. Then you'll go back to Kendermore as the big hero and get the map from your nephew for yourself!" He poked a finger into Trapspringer's chest. "You're not dealing with some silly kender, you know." Phineas's head was throbbing fiercely, and he'd never felt so angry and frightened at the same time.

Trapspringer's almond-shaped eyes grew wide with unaccustomed fury. "Silly kender! You smelly, bug-infested sack of straw! You're nothing but a cowardly, toadying hobgoblin! And I'll bet it comes from your mother's side of the family! I never thought any human could be stupid enough to reproduce with a hobgoblin, but if there was one, he'd be your father! And he'd still be smarter than you!" Trapspringer raised his hoopak threateningly.

Phineas didn't wait to see what the kender intended to do with his forked weapon. The human spun around, dropped to his knees, and crawled furiously through the brush and into the depths of the grove. He had to reach the tower and find Damaris Metwinger before Trapspringer!

"Phineas, come back!" Trapspringer called, tears welling in his eyes. "Was it something I said? Whatever it was, I didn't mean it. I haven't meant anything I've said for years. Except what I just said. I think." Trapspringer was terribly confused.

The kender's heart was near to breaking. He wiped the tears away angrily. Phineas is all alone in the grove, and it's my fault! he thought. Huge, hiccupping sobs racked his small frame. He crashed through the tangled growth of the forest after the human, blinded by his tears.

Branches slapped him, thorns tore at his clothing, his hoopak thumped behind him, banging against his right heel. Then, "Whoooofffff!" All the air exploded out of the kender's lungs as he slammed into another living, running creature.

Trapspringer was thrown backward by the force of the blow. He landed on a small bush, its stiff branches stabbing his back. His eyes were closed as he struggled for a few ragged gulps of air. But whoever had hit him jumped on top of him now, swinging and clawing at him like a tiger.

"Phineas?" he gasped, fending off the blows.

Whoever it was pressed him flat to the ground and slammed its mouth down on his and stayed there, the kiss becoming more and more insistent. Trapspringer hoped his assailant wasn't Phineas. The kender cracked one eye open hesitantly, gripped by the unfamiliar sensation of fear.

Damaris Metwinger!

Trapspringer's wrinkled old face spread into a delighted grin. He hadn't remembered her being so pretty, hadn't remembered her much at all. Her waist-long hair had the color and scent of meadow buttercups. Though it was tangled and ratty now, she wore her topknot in six braids woven with colorful bird feathers. Her eyes were the pale, pale blue of winter ice on a clear day. Phineas's arms were around her now, and he could feel that her figure was slim and well-toned; Trapspringer was certain she'd have no trouble scaling a building with him.

Her heavy wool vest was matted and dirty, with dozens of twigs and leaves tangled into it. The sleeves of her cotton blouse were torn, her red leggings were crusted with dried mud and covered with burrs.

Her only flaw was that her face had not yet developed the network of fine wrinkles Trapspringer found so attractive in a woman, but she was still young so there was hope.

"I don't know who you are, but you're not a bad kisser," she mumbled. Trapspringer thought her voice sounded like soft, melodious bells. "But you'd be a whole lot better if you—"

Trapspringer silenced her with a crushing kiss of his own, as his passions took over his mind.

There was even less conversation after that.

"What was that?" Trapspringer demanded all of a sudden. He wrestled Damaris away from his face and tilted his head to the side. "Don't you hear something?"

"I hear something, all right," she giggled. Damaris whispered something obscene in Trapspringer's ear.

"Good gods, girl!" Trapspringer breathed in admiration. "You're too much of a handful for my young nephew!"

Damaris held herself away from Trapspringer and inspected his face. "You're the uncle of that worthless no-show, Tasslehoff Burrfoot?"

Trapspringer saw the lusty fire in her eyes growing into an angry blaze. Perhaps he'd made a mistake mentioning the name of the kender who'd jilted her.

"Well, sort of," he equivocated. "But we're not close, really. If you want to know the truth, I don't like him much, never have! Why, I'd spit on him if he were here now!" To show his sincerity, the graying kender spat on the ground in disgust. His hands sought Damaris again.

But his words came too late. Damaris was already well on her way to boiling over. She thrust his hands away.

"Spitting wouldn't be enough for the likes of him. Why, if he were here, the first thing I'd do is stake him out on the ground. Then I'd pluck out his eyelashes and nails, and then I'd slice off his fingers one at a time so he'd never be able to pick a lock again!" Her voice was rising hysterically. Trapspringer scuttled backward like a crab.

"Hmmm, yes, well that should show him you're upset," Trapspringer said weakly, not wanting to excite her further. He wanted only to resume their previous activity.

Damaris was on her haunches, rubbing her hands in glee, her eyes glowing with hatred. She smiled at him maniacally. "That's just the beginning!" She quickly went on to outline the order in which she would remove Tasslehoff's major organs. "Then I'd stuff his nose and mouth with cloth and watch him blow up!"

"Be sure to leave his lungs in for the finale," Trapspringer pointed out helpfully. He jerked his head to the side once more. "There it is again!"

At that moment a huge, loping form crashed through the brush. It might have looked vaguely human if not for a sloping forehead that led to a pointy brow and greasy, slicked-back, dark hair. It had unusually long arms, no chin, and horned feet. That, and it was nearly ten feet tall. Damaris stared in amazement. But Trapspringer wasn't amazed at all; he recognized an ogre when he saw one.

"Too much noise!" it howled. Snatching up a startled kender under each arm, it advanced a dozen yards through the brush. Suddenly, Trapspringer saw a gaping hole in the ground with steps cut into the side. The opening had to be at least six feet across. Certainly big enough for . . .

The ogre, without pausing, leaped into the emptiness. The walls rushed past as they plunged down the twenty-foot pit and slammed into the packed dirt at its bottom. The ogre landed on his feet, the kender still safely tucked under his arms. Twisting around, Trapspringer was able to see that the ogre was charging down a tunnel. Damaris was squirming and punching, while Trapspringer was enjoying the bumpy ride.

The damp, musty-smelling passage poured out into a round, cluttered room, old but apparently still sound. A stairway zigzagged upward on one side of the room. With a grunt, the ogre dropped his burdens to the floor.

Dazed by the wild ride and by the fading effect of the grove's enchantment, the two kender sat on the uneven, sandy floor, recovering their wits. In the flickering torchlight, Trapspringer saw a crude table consisting of a large board laid over two equally large boulders. Sitting on the table—or tied to it, actually—was Phineas Curick. The human's head slumped onto his chest. The little halo of hair that nature had left him at the base of his skull stuck out wildly now. There were scratches on his face and hands, but otherwise the human looked unscathed.

"What have you done to him?" Trapspringer asked, inclining his head toward Phineas.

The ogre drew back as if insulted. "Aw, I barely nicked him. He was flailing about so much that I had to tie him down to keep him from hurting himself." He poked the human, and Phineas groaned. "He'll be OK."

"Wait a minute! How come you can speak the Common tongue?" Damaris demanded.

The ogre rolled its big, baggy eyes. "I should know by now not to expect simple courtesy from kender." He heaved a deep sigh, blowing a puff of foul air through the gaps between his teeth, and shook his head sadly. "Let's start at the beginning, shall we? My name is Vinsint. Who might you be?"

Damaris and Trapspringer looked at each other in disbelief. A polite, articulate ogre? This was very interesting indeed.

Trapspringer's hand disappeared in the ogre's meaty palm. "Trapspringer Furrfoot, at your service," he said politely. He gestured toward the other kender. "And this is Damaris Metwinger."

The ogre took her tiny hand. "Charmed, I'm sure," he said and giggled, sounding like someone choking on a fish bone. "Get it? 'Charmed'? You just came from the enchanted grove!" His mirth turned to frustration. "Never mind. That one always passes right over kender."

Vinsint moved away and busied himself among some crates. "Will smoked fish, baby carrots, and bread pudding be acceptable for dinner?" he asked over his shoulder. "Oops, sorry, I'm out of bread pudding. How about fresh, roasted apples instead?"

Trapspringer's mouth watered, but he was a bit worried about Phineas.

"While that sounds delicious, Vinsint," the gray-haired kender said, "my friends and I really must be going." Trapspringer stood, taking Damaris's hand, and headed for Phineas's unconscious form on the table. "Thank you very much for rescuing us from the grove. We'll be sure to tell all our friends about it."

"Sit down!" the ogre roared, poking Trapspringer in the chest and knocking him to the ground. Damaris tumbled down next to him.

Trapspringer's eyebrows shot up in surprise. This wasn't going to be as easy as he'd thought.

"You're going to stay here and keep me company until I say otherwise!" Vinsint thundered, standing above them with his legs spread wide, his massive, muscled arms crossed.

Phineas stirred on the table, choosing that unfortunate moment to awaken. Expecting that there would be a scene, Trapspringer almost wished he had something heavy he could use to put Phineas back to sleep. As it turned out, he did not need it anyway.

Phineas moaned, squirmed and twisted until he was sitting upright on the table, and opened his eyes. He looked at his own bound hands and feet, at Trapspringer and Damaris, and then squarely at Vinsint, standing to his full height with his arms folded and the veins in his neck bulging. Phineas opened his mouth as if to speak, then closed it again as if he had thought better of it. Without making a sound, Phineas's eyes rolled back in his head and he collapsed back onto his side in a dead faint.

Chapter 15

WOODROW WATCHED THE ANIMATED DRAGON STRETCH its wings below the kender. "That thing will take Mr. Burrfoot over my dead body," he announced unconsciously. He wished he'd chosen other words as he sprang forward, the centaur obligingly ducking its head. The straw-haired man flailed desperately at the dragon's swishing tail. Rough scales and pointy horns slashed and scraped at his exposed flesh but he held on, thinking only that if he lost the kender, Miss Hornslager would be furious.

The dragon seemed to grow larger as it flapped its mighty wings and rose higher. Moments later, when Woodrow came to his senses, it was far too late to think about jumping off. He clung with all his might to the thrashing, flicking, mighty tail.

Tasslehoff, meanwhile, had already overcome his initial shock and was sitting upright in the saddle. He happily bounced and kicked with his heels as the dragon climbed into the morning sun. Suddenly, the creature lurched and the wings stopped flapping. Its climb leveled out and the beast nosed to the left and began to dive furiously back toward the carnival. Tasslehoff squealed and Woodrow shrieked as the wind screamed past their ears. Tas's long hair whipped into Woodrow's face, and probably would have obscured his vision if Woodrow's eyes had been open. If anything, Woodrow's eyes were shut tighter than his grip on the dragon's tail.

Faster and faster they dove, straight down toward the carousel. Dwarves scattered in every direction as the terrifying beast plummeted toward them. At the last moment, the dragon pulled out of its dive and raced across the green, raising a cloud of leaves and dust in its wake.

Tasslehoff had spotted the tiny gnome dancing a jig near his controls. "I guess it's working the way it's supposed to," he hollered to no one in particular. Mere inches from the ground, the dragon expanded its wings and pulled up into a nearly vertical climb. Tasslehoff threw his arms around the saddle to keep from falling off backward.

The piercing scream from behind alerted Tas that he was not alone on the wild ride. Twisting in the saddle, he saw Woodrow, white as an elven shroud, wrapped around the dragon's tail. Directly behind Woodrow was the ground, receding at an alarming rate, and Gisella, shaking a finger at the gnome. "Woodrow! What are you doing here?" bellowed Tas. "Hey, Gisella looks much smaller from way up here! Isn't this great!"

But Woodrow knew that if he opened his mouth he would scream. So he just shook his head furiously, until he felt himself rolling over on his back. Too frightened to keep his eyes closed, he opened one to find out what was happening. He saw the dragon's back, Mr. Burrfoot—

who had apparently gone quite insane from terror—and the sky, which rolled past from top to bottom. Then the sky gave way to ground, but the ground seemed to be coming from above. If I don't scream, I am going to vomit, thought Woodrow, and I don't have any idea which way it will fall. He opened his mouth, but all that came out was a hoarse, croaking sound.

"What did you say?" shouted Tas. As the kender leaned back in the saddle, the dragon finished its roll and once again dived straight down toward the ground. "C'mon Woodrow, loosen up!" shouted Tas, tugging at the human's shirt. The dragon leveled out, eight feet off the ground, and shot down a narrow street with buildings crowding in on both sides. It turned a corner, side-swiped a row of flowerpots right off a balcony with the tip of its wing, and then rose just enough to swoop across the rooftops and slalom between chimneys.

"This is better than going over a waterfall," shrieked Tas. "What a ride! That gnome is a genius! Here we go again!"

The dragon climbed steadily, its wings beating rhythmically. Long after Tas expected it to swoop or roll again, it continued climbing. Tas looked back over his shoulder and let out a long whistle. "We sure have covered a lot of ground. I can barely see Rosloviggen anymore."

"Where are we?" Those words were the first Woodrow had spoken since leaping onto the dragon's tail several lifetimes ago.

"I'm not sure, but we're way above it," Tas said matter-of-factly. As if that was its signal, the dragon banked steeply and circled to the right, spiraling down toward the mountains. Moments later, Tas could make out the silhouette of a tower against the white snow background. Then he spotted another tower, jutting out from the face of a cliff, then three more structures: another tower, a square keep, and what appeared to be the front half of a castle, built into the side of the cliff.

The dragon skidded to a stop on top of the second

tower. Tas looked back to check on Woodrow, who raised his head and looked at the kender with swollen eyes, as if he had just woken up. Both of them blinked at their surroundings.

The top of the tower, where the dragon had landed, was flat and surrounded by a raised wall about two feet high. The tower itself was cylindrical. Rising behind the tower, however, was a sheer cliff that topped out at least sixty feet above Tas.

"I think it brought us here on purpose," said Tas.

"What makes you say that, Mr. Burrfoot?" Woodrow asked weakly.

Tas knocked his fist against the dragon. "Because our mount is plain, old wood again. I wonder where we are." The kender swung his left leg over the front of the saddle and slid down onto the dragon's wing, then jumped from there to the stone floor. Woodrow followed, clutching his stomach and leaning against the dragon for support.

"Who'shere?" sounded a hasty, nasal voice from the far side of the dragon. "Doesmybrotherknowyou've-beenridinghisdragon?"

Tasslehoff peered around the front of the dragon. He saw a gnome, dressed in baggy, green pants, a dirty, yellow shirt, a blue apron, and an orange hat. A pair of spectacles balanced on the tip of his nose. The pockets of his apron were stuffed full of carpentry and stonecutting tools. He stood near an open trap door, peering over his spectacles at the dragon.

"Comeon, comeon, thedragonnevercomesbackby-itself. Youmightaswellshowyourself."

Tas watched from behind the dragon, fascinated. He knew that kender were distantly related to gnomes, and he could see a little of it in this one's slender hands.

"You really should speak more slowly, particularly if you're going to be that bossy," said Tasslehoff, stepping around into the gnome's view, followed by Woodrow.

"Oh ho!" chortled the gnome. "We seem to have an air-sick human and a short, wrinkly, humanoid thing.

Hmmm, wrinkles, topknot, rude, lots of pouches and pockets, short; must be either a kender or a meerkimo. No, meerkimos have been extinct since before the Cataclysm. Must be a kender. We've been looking for one of those for decades—not many of them around here. You might as well come in; no sense standing around up here exposed to damaging sunlight."

"Tasslehoff Burrfoot," said the kender politely, extending his hand. "And you are—?" The gnome took his hand, peered at it intently, found it empty, and dropped it without interest. Turning, the gnome clomped back down the staircase and out of sight.

Tas and Woodrow stood for a moment, trying to digest what was happening to them. The gnome's face reappeared above the stairs briefly. "Come on, I said. There's no other way down except the quick way," he noted, looking over the side of the tower. "And very few specimens of any sort choose that." He disappeared again.

Woodrow cleared his throat, then spoke to Tasslehoff in a low tone. "I don't have a good feeling about this, Mr. Burrfoot."

The gnome reappeared again, this time dangling an apple on a stick toward them. "I've got foooooood," he chanted, waving the stick from side to side. "Red, juicy aaaaaaaapples. Caaaarrots. Raaaabbits. Dishes of buuuuugs. Whatever you kender eat, we've got it. Just follow me."

"Apples?" Tas was not actually hungry, but he was always ready to eat. "I love apples. I could use something to eat, come to think of it." Tasslehoff headed toward the door.

Woodrow took the kender's arm and swung him around. "This sounds *very* bad to me, Mr. Burrfoot," he whispered. "What kind of place serves bugs?"

"Well, it's not the Inn of the Last Home," Tas conceded; he liked the gnome. But, noting Woodrow's concern, he forced himself to be serious. "There's only one way to find out where we are." He stepped through the door before the human could protest further.

Abruptly, they were in a very narrow, dark stairway that leveled out into a long stone corridor. Ahead, waving them on impatiently, was the gnome.

"Come on, come on! I have things to do, too, you know." He pushed up his spectacles distractedly.

Tasslehoff skipped ahead to his side. "Where are we going? And who are you, if you don't mind me asking again?"

"Well, I do. Didn't my brother tell you anything?" the gnome growled. "He's always leaving that to me. Well, I just won't do it this time. You'll have to wait until he gets here," he said petulantly.

"I sure hope he'll be here soon," Woodrow said earnestly, "because we really must be getting back to Rosloviggen. Miss Hornslager must be very angry with us for leaving." He followed the gnome and the kender around a corner into a cavernous room.

"Wow!" Tas gasped. "What is this place? It looks like the museum in Palanthas."

Every inch of the large room, except for its narrow aisles, was covered with long, horizontal, glass display cases set up on high, thin legs. Row upon row of dead insects lay on white velvet cushions inside the cases. There were five cases filled with nothing but blue butterflies, each one slightly different, each with its name neatly penned on a card next to it. Then there were whole cases of red butterflies and white butterflies, then another case of red and white ones. Every color in the rainbow was represented.

There were two cases with black ants.

Two more for red ants.

One for dragonflies.

Ten for wasps.

And on and on.

"Do you collect insects?" asked Tas, running from case to case, pressing his nose to each.

"What makes you ask that?" the gnome said sarcastically, rolling his eyes. Using his sleeve, he rubbed nose prints from the cases after Tasslehoff had passed.

Tas opened his mouth to respond when Woodrow leaned into him and whispered, "I think he was joking, Mr. Burrfoot."

Tasslehoff's brows knit in confusion. Oh, a joke! Gnomes sure are funny, he thought.

The gnome hustled them through an archway with a letter "C" above it at the far end of the room, and into an even larger room with a ceiling at least three stories high. The display cases here were much taller and held one stuffed creature each.

"These are all dinosaurs," Tasslehoff said, breathless with awe. "I never realized they were so big." He threw his head back to run his gaze the full length of the largest dinosaur, its incredibly long, muscular neck fully extended. He took note of the plaque at its feet: 'Apatosaurus.' Next to it was the number 220.

"You collect dinosaurs, too? What does that number mean?" Tas asked.

"Of course we collect dinosaurs," the gnome said in exasperation. "We collect everything. The number means that it, uh, came into the collection in the year two hundred twenty."

"But that was more than one hundred twenty years ago!" Tas gasped. "You can't be that old."

The gnome beamed. "Why, thank you for saying so!" He lifted his orange hat and slicked his hair back with his hand. "I'm not." Suddenly his eyes narrowed. "You're trying to get answers out of me, and I told you you'd have to wait for my brother."

"You could at least tell us who you are and why that dragon came to life and what this place is," Woodrow demanded, his voice shaking.

In reply, the gnome clamped his lips shut and herded Tas and Woodrow into a small, torch-lit laboratory off the dinosaur display room.

Water dripped down the cold, stone walls in the circular room. From floor to ceiling on the walls were shelves. The shelves were packed with empty glass jars, and seemed to be organized by color more than shape or function. Tall, thin, red ones were perched next to short, squatty bowls, which ranged in size from one inch in diameter to two feet. Every color imaginable was present.

In the center of the laboratory was a tall alchemist's table cluttered with more colorful jars, though these were filled with little creatures of one sort or another suspended in liquid. White wisps of smoke bubbled from the tops of two beakers. The room had a faintly unpleasant, medicinal smell.

Woodrow looked around aprehensively, feeling a shiver tickle his spine. "On second thought," he said hoarsely, "we don't really have any questions we need answered. If you'd just be kind enough to show us the door, we'll be on our way back to Rosloviggen and won't trouble you any further." Latching onto Tasslehoff's arm, the human began backing toward the door.

"Good!" someone exclaimed from the doorway behind them. Tasslehoff and Woodrow jumped straight up and spun around as one. "Youmadeitsafely. Whatarelief."

The gnome from the carousel stumbled in, looking exhausted. Removing a pair of tight, black leather gloves one finger at a time, he collapsed into a chair next to the door. "Whataday!" he wheezed, his speech slowing as he relaxed. The gnome pulled a pair of goggles from his eyes and let them snap down around his neck. "How are we going to get the carousel back, Ligg? I forgot. It wasn't working right anyway, then that teleport ring misfired and I ended up in—"

"Whatdoyoumean?" the bigger gnome with the baggy, green pants demanded, his voice reaching proper gnome velocity in his agitation. "Itwasworkingjustfine! You-weren'tfiddlingwiththemusicagain, wereyou? Well?"

His brother looked sheepish.

"You did!" the second gnome clutched his head and

spun around in anguish. "Oooh, that makes me so mad! Which one did you bash through the ceiling this time, Bozdilcrankinthwakidorious?" His face fell as a thought struck him. "Not the kobold?"

His brother looked even more sheepish.

"He was my favorite!" the second gnome cried. "That's it! From now on I, Oliggantualixwedelian, will get the specimens!"

"Are those your *names*?" interrupted Tas.

"And what's wrong with them? They're very common first names," Bozdil said defensively, toying with his goggles.

"But they're so *long*," Tas complained.

"Bozdil and Ligg?" the one named Ligg said, puzzled.

Woodrow's mind was locked onto one terrible word. "Specimens?" he squeaked, repeating Ligg.

The others turned to him, and three sets of eyebrows arched in surprise.

"What do you mean, 'specimens'? "

Ligg gave Bozdil a perturbed look. "I've been waiting for you to get back to explain things to them. I think I'll go build another display room or something." He turned to the kender and the human. "Nice knowing you."

Bozdil reached out a hand without looking and caught Ligg's collar as he tried to leave. "You'll forgive my brother, but this part is always so difficult," he began with an apologetic smile to Tas and Woodrow. "I know, we'll show you! I find visual aids so helpful, don't you?" he asked pleasantly.

"Actually," Woodrow said, looking around the room frantically, "we would find the front door most helpful right now. I don't know why you've brought us here, and I'm not sure I want to know. Live and let live, I always say." He tried to shield Tasslehoff.

"It's my job to keep Mr. Burrfoot safe. No offense, Mr. Bozdil, Mr. Ligg, but this is all very strange—and unacceptable. It would be a good idea if you allowed us to leave right now, before we have to hurt you." Flexing his muscles, Woodrow wished his voice had not cracked as he spoke.

"Yeah, you've got a lot of explaining to do!" Tasslehoff cried, leaping around the human in his excitement. "Like . . . like how you made that dragon fly—did I tell you how much fun that was—better than—" Woodrow jabbed Tasslehoff in the ribs. "Clunk 'em, Woodrow!"

Ligg gave Woodrow a severe look. "There's no need for any clunking around here. Let's at least be civilized about this."

"Ohdearohdearohdear," muttered Bozdil nervously. "We're handling this all wrong! Just come with us, and you'll understand everything."

"I'd like to understand *something*!" the kender said, shaking his head. "Come on, Woodrow, they're not going to let us leave until we look at whatever it is they want us to see. As long as we're here, what's the harm of taking a little peek?

Woodrow pursed his lips. "OK," he said at last. "But we're leaving right afterward." What choice did he have, really?

The gnome brothers looked at each other, giggled conspiratorially, then grew serious.

"Now, is it under 'K' for kender, or 'D' for demihumans?" Ligg asked Bozdil.

"No, I think it's under 'T' for 'things with thirty-two ribs,' or perhaps 'B' for 'upright bipeds'. "

"Wouldn't that be 'U'?"

"Oh, you're right, you're right," muttered Bozdil. He scratched his balding head. "Let's look it up." Moving a lit candle closer, he pulled a big, cobweb-covered tome from a shelf, sending dust flying. He coughed, and Ligg patted him on the back. Chewing his lip, Bozdil flipped the book open and ticked his index finger down the table of contents until he found what he was looking for. "Ah ha!" He licked his thumb and flipped to the appropriate page. " 'K' for kender!" He let the book thump shut.

"No, that's where it *used* to be," Ligg said wearily.

"Don't you remember? We reorganized everything ten years ago, so we could keep track of inventory better? *After* I built the third tower . . . ?" he continued, trying to jog his brother's memory.

"Yes!" Bozdil said. "Now I remember! We put it in Display Room Twelve."

"So is it 'D' or 'U' or 'B' or what?" Tas nearly exploded.

Ligg looked at the kender as if he were a bug. "Why would it be any of those?"

"But you said—oh, never mind!"

Bozdil led the way and Ligg brought up the rear through at least twelve rooms filled with display cases of all sizes. Tasslehoff stopped in a room that contained aquatic specimens displayed floating in liquid-filled jars. He paused before the jar containing an Eye of the Deep. The evil creature's large central eye in its round, blobbish body and its two small eye stalks looked so deadly, floating like that in its natural environment, that it brought a shudder even to the fearless kender.

Woodrow lingered by a display of stuffed and mounted hunting birds. The hawks reminded him of his training as a squire, and he stood in front of the rows of unblinking owls and falcons, remembering his time at his Uncle Gordon's home.

Tas and the gnomes didn't miss him as they stopped in a room whose glass cases varied in size, shape, and color. They walked slowly past stuffed creatures with plaques proclaiming their species: dryad, gully dwarf, wood sprite, mountain dwarf, and elf.

Bozdil stopped before an empty display case with a plaque at its base that read "kender." He smiled ruefully and said, "Now do you see why it's so difficult?"

"I see an empty kender case," Tas said stupidly.

"Not for long," Ligg sang.

Tasslehoff still looked puzzled.

"Don't make me say it!" Bozdil cried in anguish. "It's nothing personal, mind you," he continued quickly, noting Tasslehoff's growing awareness. "But it's our Life Quest. One of everything on Krynn, so generations from now our descendants will know what a *kender* looked like, just for instance.

"Oh, don't look so revolted!" he continued, noting the expression on Tas's face. "You think we like doing this? This isn't what *I* would have chosen as a Life Quest! How about you, Ligg?"

Insulted, his brother snorted, "Certainly not! I'd almost rather count the number of raisins in muffins, like Cousin Gleekfub, for the rest of my life! Hmmphh!" He lifted his nose imperiously.

Bozdil peered at the captives accusingly. "You have no idea how difficult this job is. Take trolls, for instance. What do you do with a troll? It can only be killed by burning or immersing in acid—," he snickered without humor "—and you can well imagine what that does to their appearance." Bozdil's hands raised in a gesture of helplessness. "And if we kill one, we certainly can't display it. So how can we get a proper-looking troll for display without killing it?" He frowned. "I still haven't figured out a solution to that one. Have you been thinking about it, Ligg, like you said you would?" Bozdil cocked one eyebrow at his brother.

"Troglodytes!" Ligg barked suddenly.

"I beg your pardon?" said Tasslehoff, startled.

"Troglodytes!" Ligg repeated. "They can change color at will, you know. If the one we select decides to make itself green at the last moment and we've selected a nice green jar, we'd have to change it." He grew very serious. "Selection of water and jar color is very tricky, and can change at the last minute."

"Details, always details!" Bozdil had worked himself into a real frenzy on the subject. His face was beet red, and he was hopping about in his ill-fitting shoes. "New breeds, half-breeds—it's impossible to keep up! But we have to try."

"You mean you're going to pickle me?" Tasslehoff exclaimed, sucking in his breath.

"Oh, heavens no," Bozdil kindly reassured him.

Tasslehoff exhaled.

"We always *stuff* the mammals. Now, I'll need your full name and date of birth for our records." He watched disbelief grow in the kender's face. "I told you," Bozdil said slowly to Tas, as if speaking to a child, "it's nothing personal—you seem pleasant enough. But it's what we do."

"Well, I'm *taking* it personally!" Woodrow squeaked hysterically from the doorway, his face pale, his eyes wide.

Bozdil peered darkly at the straw-haired man. "I didn't even want *you*—we already have a human male specimen. You just sort of latched yourself onto my dragon and barged your way in uninvited."

Woodrow didn't know how to react to that statement. That there wasn't an empty display case bearing a plaque with his race on it was only marginally good news. He knew he had to do something. He could think of only one thing to do.

"Run for it, Mr. Burrfoot!" the human screamed, grabbing the kender and yanking him out of the room, into a hallway. Stunned, Tasslehoff stumbled over his hoopak, recovered, and then landed on his feet. Woodrow ran down hall after hall, the kender in tow. Then, he came to a door, twisted the knob, and flung the heavy wooden door open. For a moment, he saw sunlight, then he heard the most awful roaring. Into the doorway shot the open, drooling maw of an enormous mountain lion.

Woodrow slammed the door shut and leaped away from it, panting, waiting for either the gnomes to reappear or the mountain lion to shred the door while he thought.

"What are we running for?" Tasslehoff asked, never one to flee a fight. "I've got my hoopak—we'll send that lion packing!" Tasslehoff reached for the doorknob.

Woodrow's hand stayed him. "I have nothing to help

you but a tiny dagger! A lion would tear us apart and eat us for dinner, hoopak or no hoopak! No offense," he panted.

"I'm not afraid," Tasslehoff said, jutting out his chest proudly.

"That's good, because I'm frightened enough for both of us," Woodrow said seriously. "What I can't figure out is where Bozdil and Ligg are."

"They're probably tired from running and haven't found us yet," Tasslehoff suggested.

"Good guess." Woodrow pulled the kender after him.

Woodrow and Tas tried five other doors and were met by a crocodile pit, a huge ape with fangs like daggers, something that looked like a walking lump of garbage, a five-foot-long scorpion—Tas wanted to stop for a good look at that oddity but Woodrow forbade it—and a room so filled with spiderwebs that Woodrow did not even want to know what was living there. They saw no sign of Ligg and Bozdil.

At last, they entered a large, one-story chamber that was empty except for huge, regularly spaced support pillars. It appeared to be an unused display chamber.

"There's no way out through here," Tas warned. But the door had already slammed shut, practically in their faces. Kender and human rocked back on their heels and both felt a sense of dread.

"We're sorry you made us do this." Bozdil's whiny voice filtered through a small grate in the large, wooden door. "We would rather you had been a little more civilized about all this. You could have remained free to wander about the place and dine with us this evening. We certainly would have given you a nicer room, too. I would have liked that—we don't get too many visitors who can talk, you realize."

"But you've ruined it by being selfish," finished Ligg in an accusing, nasal tone. "We can't be blamed." Tas could see Ligg's shoulders through the grate, shrugging. "Now we have things to prepare." With that, they disappeared.

"I've got to say, Woodrow, that this sure makes getting married look attractive," Tas sighed, sliding down the wall into a heap.

Woodrow parted his limp, sweat-soaked hair from his eyes and collapsed next to Tasslehoff on the floor. "You could say that again, Mr. Burrfoot." He was quickly asleep.

For once, the kender seemed to know a joke when he heard one. Tired beyond caring, he extinguished the spark in his brain, like a flame snuffed out by wet fingers.

Suddenly, Tas heard something.

What was that noise?

Something was whimpering behind the pillars. Tasslehoff crept past Woodrow's sleeping form and tiptoed from pillar to pillar, peering carefully around each. Near the back of the dark room, he leaned around a pillar and gasped.

Lying in the shadows in a disconsolate heap was a large—enormous, actually—hairy elephantlike creature! It lay on its side, thumping its trunk in an unhappy rhythm, while tears coursed down its thick, gray coat, settling in a puddle by its fierce-looking tusks. Suddenly it raised its head and peered at Tasslehoff around the pillar.

"I'm sorry, I didn't know anyone was in here," it said in a high-pitched, sing-song voice.

"You can talk!" gasped Tas, stepping from behind the pillar.

"Of course I can. Don't all woolly mammoths talk?"

Tasslehoff blinked, taken aback. "I—I'm not sure. I've never met one before. Still, I'm fairly certain they don't talk, as a general rule."

A sigh like a trumpet blast erupted from the mammoth's trunk. "I've never met one either." The creature's head dropped back to the stone floor, and a big tear squeezed out of one large, pink-rimmed, gray eye.

The tender-hearted kender knelt by the animal's massive shoulder and patted it comfortingly. "What's wrong?" he asked. "Don't cry, you'll flood the place and we'll all drown!" he giggled.

Another large tear plopped onto the ground. "What does it matter if we drown? The gnomes'll kill us eventually anyway," the mammoth moaned.

Tas was beginning to understand. He patted the creature again. "Don't worry, we'll find some way out of here," he said hopefully. "Then Woodrow and I will take you with us."

The mammoth's eyes opened wider. "You would do that?" he said shrilly, then slumped back down unhappily. "It wouldn't matter if you did think of a way out. I'm too big to get through the doors. This is the only room left in the whole place that's big enough to hold me."

"Then how did they get you in here?" Tas inquired, looking from the enormous mammoth back toward the tiny doorway.

The mammoth raised itself half-heartedly up onto one knee-joint, and the floor shook. "I was brought here when I was very little," he said simply, his voice weary.

"How long ago was that?"

"Bozdil and Ligg tell me it was more than fifteen years ago."

"They've kept you locked up in here for fifteen years?" Tasslehoff was incredulous.

The mammoth's eyes clouded with concern. "Oh, it's not their fault," he said unexpectedly. Seeing Tas's confusion, he said, "Let me start from the beginning. . . ."

Tas made no effort to interrupt.

"Bozdil found me on one of his specimen expeditions fifteen years ago. I was just a pup at the time, wandering around in the hills south of Zeriak, or so he says, with no sign of my mother. He brought me back here, and he and Ligg thought I was too small to be their woolly mammoth specimen. So they just decided to let me grow up." The mammoth let out another buglelike sigh. Tas took a handkerchief from his pocket and held it to the end of the creature's trunk.

"Thank you," it sniffed. "Anyway, they fed me and played with me—so I wouldn't become too flabby to be a good specimen, they said. And I learned to speak. They treated me like the family pet!" Another shattering snort of anguish ripped through the room.

The noise jolted Woodrow awake. Moments later, his white head poked tentatively around the pillar. "Mr. Burrfoot?"

"Woodrow, meet—?" Tas looked at the mammoth blankly.

"The gnomes call me Winnie," it said. "Even I can't pronounce the full name they gave me."

Tasslehoff patted one of Winnie's flat-bottomed feet in a modified handshake. "Tasslehoff Burrfoot."

"Woodrow," the human said dubiously, eyeing the mammoth.

"Glad to meet you," replied the long-haired mammoth courteously.

"Woodrow, we've got to think of a way to help Winnie escape! Bozdil and Ligg mean to kill him!" the kender said earnestly.

"That seems to be their overall plan, all right," said the human. "Us included." He began pacing, his hands clasped behind his back.

"I know! Let's jump them when they come back with our dinner, and clunk their heads together!" Tas suggested.

Winnie perked up at that, and his eyes opened wide in fear. "Oh, I couldn't let you do that to Bozdil and Ligg. They're all the family I have!"

Tas's lips pursed in irritation. "Well, they're ready to pack *you* full of cotton!"

Winnie's large head shook slowly from side to side. "That's just the problem. They haven't been able to bring themselves to do it! I can't get out; they can't kill me. But they still need a woolly mammoth specimen! They haven't spent much time with me lately, so I think the end is near. Oh, it's all so hopeless!" Winnie pressed his trunk to the ground and wailed and wailed, until every cloth Tasslehoff had was soaked with mammoth tears.

This has to be much worse than getting married, Tas thought unhappily. "We'll do something, Winnie, don't worry."

The kender only wished he knew what that something might be.

Chapter 16

"*You don't actually expect me to believe this is* real silk," Gisella scoffed, casually tossing a robin's-egg-blue bolt of cloth to the side, boredom on her rouged face.

"But of course it's silk," the hairy old dwarf said. He hefted the bolt and lovingly held a corner of cloth in his hand. "Look at how few imperfections are present," he said, flicking a small, thick, raised nub in the fabric. "You don't usually find such perfection in cotton weaving."

Gisella knew he was right. Cotton was coarser and often contained many more thread imperfections, which professionals called slubs. She wanted that fabric—badly. The airy, genuine silk would feel like butter against her fair skin, and its rich hue would complement her fiery hair. In her mind's eye she saw herself in a clingy gown of blue-green, not to mention that she could sell the remaining fabric at a substantial profit. The vision made her smile like a cat in the sun. But she didn't want to pay what the merchant was asking.

She had gulled this old, buck-toothed dwarf, but she feared he was reaching the limit of his patience and his greed.

She wanted that fabric.

"OK, three steel, but not a copper more," she exhaled.

"Three and a half," he intoned, wagging his head.

"Sold!" Gisella hugged the fabric to her chest. It was not the best deal she had ever made, but the fabric was worth the cost. Now all she had to do was get him to extend her some credit until she could bargain her way into some cash. She was wetting her lips for the performance, when she heard shrieks.

Woodrow and Burrfoot! She suddenly remembered them and spun around. They weren't in the booth. She heard the shriek again and she looked over at the thing the baron had called a carousel. Dwarves were fleeing like trolls on fire, jumping from the carousel and running for their lives. There was an empty slot in the carousel, as if one of the creatures had been ripped from its place. Hearing more shrieks of terror, she noticed that more and more people were looking up, so Gisella raised her eyes.

The beloved fabric slid from her fingers to the dusty ground. Gisella could scarcely comprehend what she saw.

Tasslehoff Burrfoot was soaring and diving over the city on the back of a red, winged creature that looked vaguely like a dragon from legend, except for the pole intersecting its body. A human—*her* human, she realized—clung to the creature's thrashing tail, snapping like a weight on a kite's streamer.

"Tasslehoff Burrfoot, I demand that you return here at once!" the flame-haired dwarf screamed, running over to stand by the carousel. She shook her fist at the sky. "You, too, Woodrow! You were supposed to watch him! You're fired!"

Where on Krynn had the red creature come from?

"Ohdearohdearohdear," a voice moaned nearby. "Whereisthatring?"

Gisella looked down and saw a bald gnome in baggy pants and a long, white jacket, with goggles strung around his neck on a cord. The gnome's hands were covered by black leather gloves, and he was frantically rummaging through the pockets on the inside of the coat and turning them inside-out.

"Are you the gnome who owns this contraption?" she demanded. Without waiting for a response, she continued, "What on Krynn happened here?" She snatched him. "I'm holding you responsible. Where is that thing going with my friends?"

"Ah ha!" The inventor slid out from under her hand and victoriously held a small ring aloft. "Ireallywould enjoyexplainingeverythingtoyou, especiallysinceit appearsIcouldstartanywhere, butImustbegoing." The gnome deftly lifted his goggles and let them fall into place over his eyes with a loud "snap." "Anothertime, perhaps," he added, poking his thumb through a neat little hole in his right glove. Quick as a flash he slipped the ring over his thumb, squeezed his eyes tightly shut, and then was gone!

Gisella's hand dropped uselessly. She whirled around, scanning the crowd, but she saw no sign of the gnome. The dwarf squinted up into the sky at the now-distant, black dot that was Tasslehoff and Woodrow.

Just then she spotted a uniformed dwarf with strawberry-blond hair and beard doing his rounds and swaggering in her direction.

"Excuse me, Colonel," she began.

The dwarf blushed under his beard. "I'm just a captain, ma'am." He eyed Gisella appreciatively.

"Isn't that wonderful. I was wondering if you have any idea where the gnome who owns this carousel lives?" She sidled up to him, and he blushed again.

"Not officially, no, ma'am, I wouldn't," he said. "I know of a tower in the mountains to the east, but I don't know who owns it. You could try the festival officials, but their office is closed until after Oktoberfest."

"Well, someone must know who he is!" she exploded.

"I'm sure someone does," the officer said, "but the records are locked up for the next three days."

"One of his creatures just flew off to the east with my friends, and I have to sit for three days waiting to find out where he lives?" Gisella's face was red with fury.

"I'm afraid so, ma'am," the officer said apologetically. "I could send a patrol out after them, though."

She smiled broadly and clapped him on the back. "That's more like it!"

"But they can't leave for three days, however. The first team is just ten days into a three-week sweep to the south. The second team left just last night for three days to the east."

"This is an emergency! Call them back, or whatever it is you military types do."

"I'm afraid I can't do that, either, ma'am." The captain was looking very sad. "By the time anyone reached the group and returned, the patrol would be scheduled to arrive anyway. But if you care to lodge a complaint . . ."

"Never mind, Private, I'll take care of it myself!"

The dwarf officer beat a hasty retreat from the fiery dwarf.

Damn!" Gisella cursed, stomping her foot petulantly. Now what was she going to do? She couldn't wait three days.

"Excuse me, milady, but you look like you could use some help," a deep, male voice suggested.

Gisella looked up in irritation. Suddenly, her eyes widened with appreciation, and she exhaled softly. The speaker was a tall, well-muscled human. His features were strong, his jaw square and jutting, as if the bones beneath had been chiseled from cool marble. His eyes, appraising her as well, were deep set and dark, faintly unfriendly in a challenging sort of way that excited Gisella. His hair was dark and coarse, almost bristly. His clothing—an olive-colored tunic, fawn breeches that tucked into calf-high leather boots, and skirted, scaled brigandine armor—was expensive and immaculate.

The only feature she could find fault with—and she looked hard—was his nose. Not that it was bad, she told herself, just a little less than perfect. Round and somewhat large, and turned up slightly, it gave him a slightly porcine look.

"Milady? I am Denzil, at your service." He held his hand out.

Her eyes snapped up from his biceps to his face. "Huh?" she grunted, tongue-tied in the presence of such physical magnificence. "Oh, hello! I'm Gisella Hornslager." She held her hand and her breath as his lips lingered over her white knuckles. She giggled like a schoolgirl and reluctantly extracted her hand.

"Just Denzil?" she asked, batting her eyes coyly.

"Do you require more?"

"N-no!" she stuttered, off balance. "Just curious."

"May I be of some assistance, then?" he offered. "I could not help overhearing your distress."

The red-haired dwarf blushed.

"Were those your friends on that monstrosity?"

"Yes and no. Woodrow is my employee. The kender is baggage. I was delivering him to a customer."

"So the flight wasn't planned?"

She snorted inelegantly. "Not by me, it wasn't." She thought about that for a moment. Woodrow was too naive and innocently loyal to dream up such a plan, the kender too frivolous. It had to be the work of someone else. "The strangest thing about it is that no one is investigating the disappearance. I can't get a patrol to go out for three days! Don't these people think that flying away on a wooden animal is a bit unusual?" she finished, gazing challengingly at the unconcerned crowd.

Denzil's tone was ironic. "No one is ever surprised when a gnomish invention goes awry."

Her eyebrows rose in agreement. "I've got to find them. I could have squeezed some answers out of the gnome who owns the carousel if he hadn't disappeared on me."

"Perhaps he left to find and return your, um, friends," Denzil suggested.

Gisella shook her head firmly. "I can't take the chance and wait. I must return Burrfoot to Kendermore in a week. If I have to find him and fetch him back by myself, I will!"

"He must be very important for you to risk your own life to find him," Denzil said, watching her closely.

Gisella laughed with genuine mirth. "I wouldn't say he's *that* important, no. He means a lot of money to me, that's all. I certainly don't intend to die looking for him."

"Then you must let me help you," Denzil insisted. "The mountains are no place for a lady alone. There's no telling what you'll encounter."

Gisella's eyes widened in surprise, then delight. This was an unexpected turn of events. She was not about to point out to her attractive new acquaintance that she had spent most of her life traveling alone.

"I have no money to pay you for your time," she said coyly. "Perhaps we could make another arrangement suitable to us both?" she said, clarifying her offer with a suggestive smile.

"I've never found it necessary to trade for *that,*" he said without bragging. "Anyway, no payment is expected in this case. I was tracking someone who had a map that I needed, and my search lead me to Roslovig-gen. But now I would enjoy the company—and a new mystery."

Gisella gave him her most enticing smile, which he returned. She noticed with a twinge of regret that his smile did not reach his eyes. It was something she looked for in a man. However, that he was willing to help her for nothing more than compensated for his cold eyes.

"We should waste no time," he stated. "My horse is just at the edge of the square. We could ride to your lodgings, collect your things, and be in the mountains before midday."

Gisella ignored the calls of the fabric merchant, whom she had no money to pay anyway, and followed Denzil to a stable just off the square. He emerged with the largest, blackest horse she had ever seen.

Something about the animal disturbed her. Its nostrils were unusually red, and its breath seemed to steam more than it should, in the cool, mountain air. It was as if the animal were powered by coal. The horse, obviously high-strung, pawed the ground. Its lips moved but no noise came from them, and when it walked, its hooves did not clatter. The animal was eerily void of sound.

The stable master stood back from the creature, counting the coins Denzil had pressed into his hands. Meanwhile, Denzil swung nimbly into the saddle and patted the monstrous horse affectionately. Then he held out his hand to the russet-haired dwarf.

Gisella's arms hung at her side. "Is it magical?" she asked tentatively.

"Yes," he said matter-of-factly. "Scul is a nightmare.

Give me your hand and I'll help you if you're frightened."

"I'm not afraid of anything," she said with determination, taking his hand anyway. He pulled her up behind himself effortlessly, leaving her breathless. She gave him directions to the baron's home.

Gisella looped her arms around Denzil's waist armor and leaned into his muscular back. Drawing a long, contented breath, she filled her nostrils with the familiar, manly scent of leather and sweat, and something else—peculiarly Denzil's. She pressed her face into the arch behind his shoulder blade and forgot about anything troubling.

Despite the nightmare's intimidating appearance, the black animal's ride was the smoothest she'd ever experienced. Riding Scul was what she imagined it would be like to ride on a cloud—a frigid storm cloud. Beneath her hands and seat, the animal felt as cold as death, right through the heavy leather saddle. She snuggled into Denzil, sighing blissfully as they rode.

"We're here." She heard the words rumble through his chest, and she looked up reluctantly.

Gisella knew the baron and baroness would be busy with official festival duties all day. She ordered one of the servants to take care of her horse while she returned to her room, than changed into her most revealing traveling clothes—a calfskin jerkin worn without a blouse, and laced pants—gathered the rest of her belongings, and hurried back to the front step. Two of the baron's grooms were flanking her saddled and bridled horse, trying to keep it calm. Its eyes were wide, its nostrils flared. Every time it caught sight of the nightmare it tossed its head and pawed the ground.

"She'll calm down before long," Denzil announced. "They always do."

With that, he turned and rode from the baron's yard. Gisella followed, thinking about what the evening might hold in store.

They climbed into the mountains, over a carpet of crunchy, fragrant pine needles, riding until late in the afternoon. Long shadows soaked the ground beneath the heavy, sweeping bows of the mountain fur trees. Sunlight seldom poked through the thick treetops. No breeze stirred the branches. No birds chirped. Gisella became acutely aware of a growing stillness in the air, which she attributed to the nightmare, although she could not explain why.

Eventually they stopped in a small clearing. Gisella shivered in the silence and the cold. "How do we know we're looking in the right place for this tower?"

"We don't," Denzil said simply. "I watched the dragon until it was a distant speck. I believe we're on the right track." His eyebrows knit as he squinted toward the sun, which had dropped below the summit. "We'll stop here tonight." He swung down from Scul's back, speaking a few tender words into the anxious animal's ear. The horse trotted to a nearby tree to graze.

"That's quite a trick." Gisella's voice was filled with admiration as she held out her hand demurely.

Denzil took it and helped her down. "Scul and I have an understanding," he said mysteriously.

Turning his back to Gisella, he took stock of what needed to be done. There were plenty of pine needles and dry branches at hand, and before long a small, cheery fire blazed within a circle of rocks.

Clapping his hands to remove dust and needles, Denzil rummaged through his saddlebags until he found the bundles of dried meats and fruits that would be their dinner. Only when he was finished did he turn and notice that Gisella was nowhere in sight.

Anger, the only emotion Denzil ever displayed, flushed his cheeks.

But within moments, the dwarf stepped through the ring of trees surrounding the clearing, wearing a thin, red wrap and a smile. "I found a little mountain stream not far from here. The water was wickedly cold, but I—"

Denzil strode forward and viciously jerked her by her wrist into the clearing. "Don't ever do that again."

Gisella's smile fell. "I was only gone for a few minutes. Who made you the boss, anyway?" She tried to pull her arm from him. "Hey, you're hurting me!"

His strong fingers tightened around her wrist, until dark, finger-shaped shadows appeared on her skin. Stifling a cry, she tugged again, and Denzil released his grip. Gisella rubbed the bruises, staring at him speechlessly.

"Your little adventure was rash and dangerous. You never know what you'll find—or what will find *you*—in the woods," was his only explanation.

The dwarf's anger and confusion subsided somewhat. Could it be that this handsome human was worried about her? Setting her chin, she tugged her wrap more closely and arranged herself on a boulder near the fire.

"What's for dinner?" she asked, keeping a distance in her tone.

Denzil tossed her a small, cloth-wrapped bundle of dried rations. Gisella stared at the unappetizing pile briefly, poking through it experimentally. While it certainly looked dull, it didn't look unhealthy, and she had not eaten since breakfast. Gisella shrugged, and soon was gnawing absentmindedly on a strip of beef, made sufficiently tantalizing with spicy thoughts of Denzil.

Afterward, Denzil settled back on one of the bedrolls he'd spread before the fire, picking his teeth with a small, sharpened stick. Staring into the flames, he said, "This night reminds me of my favorite poem. Do you like poetry?" Without waiting for an answer, he began reciting in a reverent voice, speaking in lively bursts:

Easeful the forest, easeful its mansions perfected
Where we grow and decay no longer, our trees ever
    green,
Ripe fruit never falling, streams still and transparent
As glass, as the heart in repose this lasting day.

Beneath these branches the willing surrender of move-
    ment,
The business of birdsong, of love, left on the borders
With all of the fevers, the failures of memory.
Easeful the forest, easeful its mansions perfected.

And light upon light, light as dismissal of darkness,
Beneath these branches no shade, for shade is
    forgotten
In the warmth of the light and the cool smell of the
    leaves
Where we grow and decay; no longer, our trees ever
    green.

Here there is quiet, where music turns in upon silence,
Here at the world's imagined edge, where clarity
Completes the senses, at long last where we behold
Ripe fruit never falling, streams still and transparent.

Where the tears are dried from our faces, or settle,
Still as a stream in accomplished countries of peace,
And the traveler opens, permitting the voyage of light
As air, as the heart in repose this lasting day.

Easeful the forest, easeful its mansions perfected
Where we grow and decay no longer, our trees ever
    green,
Ripe fruit never falling, streams still and transparent
As air, as the heart in repose this lasting day.

Denzil stopped with a sharp exhalation, still staring
into the flames. " 'The Bird Song of Wayreth Forest.'
Quivalen Sath," he said solemnly.

Gisella watched his stony profile from her own bed-
roll. What a complicated package this man was—at

once violent and sensitive. A surplus of feeling bubbled up inside her, rising in her throat. She had only
one response to that sensation.

She leaned forward, took Denzil's face in her hands,
and crushed her rouged lips against his. Startled, he
began to pull away, but she would not let him go. Gisella held the dark-haired man still with the force of
her kiss until she felt him relax. His arms surrounded
her, tightening until she thought her lungs might burst
from her chest. She liked the feeling of being pos-
sessed, so she didn't struggle. Instead, she pushed him
onto his back, rolled onto his chest, and let her wrap
fall away.

Chapter 17

Damaris touched the screaming human's shoulder tentatively. "If you don't mind my saying, you sound a little unhinged, whoever you are."

Phineas was pressed against the wall of Vinsint's room, still seated on the table, whimpering and gibbering with fear. When Damaris spoke to him, he closed his mouth and for the first time his rheumy eyes looked up at her. "Damaris Metwinger, I presume?"

"That's me," she said pleasantly. Her light blue eyes were as large as her smile. "Who are you?"

Trapspringer hastily made the introductions.

"I'm glad that's settled," the ogre said mildly, continuing his meal preparations as if nothing untoward had happened. "You'll find the accommodations quite comfortable, and I'm told I'm a good cook. You'll like it here, once you get used to it."

"We can't stay!" Phineas wailed, frantically straining against the bonds at his wrists.

"And why not?" the ogre demanded, gnarly hands on his hips.

"Not now, Phineas," hissed Trapspringer. As a rule, the elder kender wasn't particularly cautious. But he was a little concerned that the human's rising hysteria might bring an abrupt end to what might prove to be a very interesting experience—the remainder of his life.

"What Phineas means," Trapspringer explained, "is that we wouldn't want to intrude or take advantage of your good nature."

The ogre smiled broadly, displaying a mouthful of uneven, jagged, and broken teeth. "You wouldn't be intruding! I love company! That's why I'm here!"

"You're here just for the company?" Even Trapspringer was confused by that.

Vinsint put a whole golden, dried fish on each of four tin plates. "Indirectly, yes. You see, many years ago, I came to this area with a raiding party from the Ogrelands, just north and east of here." He ladled a steaming white sauce over the fish. "I was wounded by an arrow from one of my own people, and they left me to die. I don't know how long I lay there, delirious with pain.

"Anyway, the next thing I knew, I was lying in the softest bed on Krynn. Some kender had found me, brought me to their home just beyond the Ruins, and were healing me with herbs." Vinsint's eyes misted over with the warm memory. He shook his head happily, and a tear splashed onto a plate.

"My wound was serious and took a long time to heal. The kender treated me like family and taught me their language, which answers your earlier question," Vinsint said, looking at the blond-haired female.

"Why didn't you go home after you were healed?" Damaris asked, taking a bite of the delicious, steaming fish.

Vinsint winced. "You kender certainly are nosy, aren't you? Well, if you must know, it was no accident that one of my own people shot me." The thought obviously still pained the ogre. "Apparently my people thought I wasn't bloodthirsty enough for an ogre. Killing and terrorizing is OK every now and then, but I don't *live* for it the way they do, you know what I mean?" The ogre hunched his massive shoulders. "They took the opportunity to get rid of me." He sighed heavily. "So, you see, there was nothing to return to."

"But that still doesn't explain why you ended up here," Damaris pointed out a bit snottily. She didn't like being called nosy.

Vinsint glared at her and spoke to Trapspringer. "I decided to help the people who had helped me. And what better way than to rescue kender from the magical effects of the grove? I'm sort of a self-appointed sentinel."

At the mention of the enchanted grove, each of Vinsint's visitors colored and squirmed. Phineas was a bit hazy on the subject, but he was fairly certain he'd been barking like a dog when Vinsint found him and dragged him into the tunnel. The human closed his eyes slowly now and shuddered.

Trapspringer and Damaris both suddenly realized that the ogre had caught them in the middle of something very intimate. Remembering now, the kender locked gazes, then looked away uncomfortably.

Phineas pushed aside his shame to say, "But I thought you said you wanted to help kender. Doesn't holding them captive sort of work against that?"

"I don't keep them *forever*," Vinsint said darkly. "Besides, I think keeping me company is a small price to pay for being saved from the grove. I get lonely here! I'm always polite and friendly, and I serve good food."

"I suppose it's important to be polite when you're plug-ugly," Damaris agreed with a kender's usual alacrity.

Vinsint looked at her ominously. In silence he laid out dinner, and everyone but Phineas ate with great enthusiasm.

After dinner, the ogre pushed his tin plate back and belched loudly. "What shall we do after dinner? Cards? Dice? Marbles? I have them all."

"Let's play 'Let the prisoners go', " Phineas suggested under his breath. Trapspringer flashed him a look of warning.

"You name the game," Vinsint insisted of Trapspringer.

The elder kender glanced uneasily at Phineas. "All right. Pick-up sticks!"

Vinsint clapped his hands together with a crack that reverberated in Trapspringer's chest cavity. "I love pick-up sticks! It's my favorite game!"

The ogre leaped to his feet, knocking over his stool and rattling the room, then clomped toward a pile of boxes in a corner. Vinsint pawed through the boxes, flinging all manner of things to the floor in his haste. Trapspringer saw manacles, a jeweled necklace, a scroll case, a chunk of a mildewed saddle, and other things that he could not identify. When Vinsint stomped back, clutching an intricately carved ivory tube in his enormous hand, he cleared the dishes from the table with one swipe of his large hand.

"Ahhhhh," he crooned, easing his bulk back onto his righted stool. "I'll bet you've never seen a pick-up sticks set like this one." With exaggerated care, he slid the lid off the tube. Then, with a flourish, he slowly upended the cylinder until the long, slim sticks tumbled out onto the table. "Gold plated!" purred Vinsint.

Damaris, Trapspringer, and Phineas stared at the painted sticks on the table. After a long moment's pause, Trapspringer said, "Those aren't gold. They aren't even painted gold."

Vinsint flicked at the end of his nose self-consciously. "No, they aren't," he agreed, "except for these two." He mauled the delicate sticks with his melon-sized hands, eventually plucking out two that were vaguely gold colored. "The real gold sticks disappeared one by one over the years. These two are all that I have left. But it used to be a complete set of gold-plated sticks. It sure was something to see."

Vinsint scooped up the sticks and stood them on their ends, ready to begin the game. But then his head twisted to the side abruptly. "Did you hear that?" He smiled and clapped his hands. "Someone else is walking through the grove. More company!" He jumped up and began leaping excitedly in circles.

Vinsint stopped suddenly, and his smile fell. "I must hurry before they somehow find their own way out." He stomped over to a large cupboard that sat on the floor. Opening the door, he hauled out yard after yard of heavy, rusty chain, coiling it about his arm. His three guests cringed, thinking he meant to tie them up. Instead he took the chains to the door and dumped them on the other side, in the tunnel.

"I know what you're thinking," he said in a sing-song voice. "You're thinking, 'why does he need so many chains to lock this door?' I'll tell you. I've left a lot of kender in here in my time. Always when I went into the grove I'd lock the door, come back not ten minutes later, and they'd be gone, 'poof!'" He snapped his big-knuckled fingers.

"Maybe they escaped another way," suggested Trap-springer.

"There is no other way," the ogre said simply. "The funniest thing is that the kender always lock the chains back up again, and they don't even look like they've been touched. So, I add more chains each time. Maybe I can slow 'em down enough until I can get back."

He took the last of the chains from the cupboard and slipped through the door. "I'll just be gone a few minutes, and when I come back we'll have a fifth player for pick-up sticks. Don't try to get away, now." With that, Vinsint closed the door, and they could hear chains being strung on the other side.

Phineas stood up and began to pace nervously. "Do

you suppose he'll let us go now that he'll have new people to keep him company?"

Damaris shook her head and her blond hair flew in a half-circle. "It didn't sound to me like he had any intention of letting us go. You go first," she offered Trapspringer, pointing to the jumbled sticks on the table.

"Are you just going to sit there and wait for him to come back?" squealed Phineas.

"No, we're going to play this game," said Trapspringer, concentrating on lifting a stick perfectly from the tangle.

"Why aren't we looking for another way out?" the human demanded, glaring at the kender on the floor.

Trapspringer shrugged. "Vinsint said there wasn't one. But it would be interesting to explore the rest of this place," he had to admit.

"You're just saying that because you made that blue stick move and have to give up your turn," sulked Damaris.

Trapspringer laughed. "I did no such thing! That was a clean draw."

The blonde kender stuck out her lip in what she hoped was an adorable pout. "Well, at least I can beat *him*!" She pointed at the red-faced human.

Trapspringer's laughter turned into full-blown snorting. He liked the way the torchlight brought out the yellow in Damaris's hair. "Sure you could, but humans are lousy at pick-up sticks. Vinsint could probably beat him, and Vinsint's hands are bigger than my head."

"That's not the point," she said with mock indignation.

Phineas rolled his eyes in disgust. "If you two would stop billing and cooing at each other, we might find a way out of here!" He looked to the stairway. "Those steps have to lead somewhere!"

Trapspringer helped Damaris to her feet. She self-consciously rubbed at her cheeks with her sleeves to remove any grime and straightened the broken feathers in her hair.

Phineas and Trapspringer each took a lit torch from

the walls. "After you," the human said, jerking his head from Trapspringer to the steps.

The older kender, holding Damaris's hand, set off at a carefree pace up the stone steps that spiraled upward beyond the reach of the torchlight. Moss and fungus grew through cracks in the stone walls. Phineas followed closely, hunched over defensively, his eyes darting everywhere at once.

"You know, from the circular shape of it," Trapspringer said, "I'll bet this is the Tower of High Sorcery. I don't know why I didn't think of it earlier." Damaris gave his hand a squeeze.

"Does it matter?" Phineas asked cynically.

"It means we might run into some leftover magic," Damaris said, obviously excited by the prospect.

Phineas stumbled over a loose stone in the ancient stairs and grabbed for the wall. "Leftover magic? What does that mean?"

"His voice is getting more shrill than a harpy's," Damaris pointed out to Trapspringer.

"This single tower is all that's left of the complex that was created here at the dawn of time," explained Trapspringer, "along with the other four Towers of High Sorcery—Wayreth, Palanthas, Istar, and some other one I can't remember now. Several of them are still used as centers of magic, but this one was abandoned shortly after the Cataclysm."

"Which means?" Phineas asked impatiently.

"Magic was once performed here regularly. There might be some of it still lingering, like a spell that never met its mark—"

"—Or magical monsters might still be guarding the upper floors!" Damaris suggested enthusiastically.

"Spellbooks, scrolls, magic rings, bracelets, potions, wands, staffs, gloves, swords—"

"I get your point," Phineas gulped. Perhaps he'd been rash to suggest exploration. They continued spiraling upward.

"Maybe a wicked sorceror, abandoned—*banished*, that's better!—by his peers lives at the top of the tower," Damaris continued her daydream. "Lonely and bitter, he's practicing his art on kender! Maybe we'll get magicked!"

"Except for the magic, you just described Vinsint," Phineas scoffed.

"I knew I heard it somewhere," Damaris mumbled.

"I haven't been magicked since I tangled with that goat-sucker bird," Trapspringer said wistfully.

"You met a goat-sucker bird?" Damaris asked enviously. Goat-sucker birds were legendary among kender. "I've never known anyone who's seen one! I didn't realize they were magical. What did it look like? Did it try to peck your eyes out?"

"Oh, yes!" Trapspringer said, a swagger in his voice. "Of course they're magical! That's why they're so fierce. This one came at me out of a murky swamp—they live in them, you know. Well, it . . ."

Phineas's legs ached, and he was finding it difficult to catch his breath. They'd been climbing for some time before he thought to start counting, and even without that he estimated they'd covered more than three hundred steps without a rest. Wheezing, he collapsed on a step.

"I'm beginning to think Vinsint was right: There is nothing else in here. Maybe we should turn back. There's no telling what he'll do if he returns and sees that we've slipped away." The human shuddered, picturing the ogre's bulging muscles.

But the eager kender were already out of earshot. Afraid to get too far behind, Phineas struggled to his feet and forced himself to continue upward. Holding the torch aloft, he thought he could see a ceiling at last.

Abruptly, the stairway emptied out into a chamber that was slightly larger than the one far below. There the human found Damaris and Trapspringer running to and fro in the sumptuously appointed room.

Phineas frowned. Wasn't it odd that this place, so obviously visited by light-fingered kender for centuries, still had any furnishings at all? He placed his torch in a sconce on a wall and looked about the room. One thing quickly caught his attention.

The human stared, open-mouthed, at the large, wooden, intricately carved desk against the wall to the right of the stairs. Behind it was a stuffed leather chair with a wooden carving of a dragon's head on its high back. On the desk's blotter was a quill and a dried-up bottle of ink, a pair of spectacles, and a wine glass, all covered with an inch of dust.

He looked in admiration at the leather-bound volumes that circled the room. They were all dust-covered, too, but undamaged. Twisting his head to read the spines, he spotted one called "Herbal Medicine," which sounded interesting. He took it down and slipped it under his arm.

Damaris and Trapspringer both were busy tapping here and there in search of hidden drawers, which they hoped might hold gems or other interesting items.

Suddenly, Trapspringer snapped his fingers. "Something about this place looked familiar, and now I remember what it is. This room looks just like the drawing on the other half of the map I gave Tasslehoff."

Damaris looked up from behind the desk with a self-satisfied grin. "I found a lever for something!"

Phineas's eyebrows rose. But before he could form a question he heard a loud "ping!"

Suddenly, the room filled with roiling, purple mist streaked with rich emerald green. The mist extinguished the torch in the sconce, then Trapspringer's as well. But it produced a dim glow of its own.

"What did you do, Damaris?" thundered Phineas, crawling behind the desk.

"I'm not sure," she breathed anxiously. Even in the fog her eyes looked as big as tea plates. "But isn't it pretty?"

A vicious wind grew on the other side of the mist, evaporating it in seconds, leaving behind a huge burn scar that seared a large, rectangular hole through the stone wall. Beyond, more purple and green mist roiled in a shapeless tunnel.

Hand-in-hand, Trapspringer and Damaris were advancing toward the hole.

Phineas watched in horror. He could not move his feet. He could only scream. "Stop! Don't go in there!"

Being kender, of course, Trapspringer and Damaris did not stop. "We're going to be magicked!" was all they said as they disappeared into the fog.

Though the human was physically frozen by fear, his mind raced. He saw himself with two options. He could either go back down the tower and face a very ugly, very angry ogre who didn't seem to like humans as much as kender to begin with.

Or, he could throw himself into the mist after Trapspringer and Damaris, who seemed to be inordinately lucky, at least where life and death were concerned.

Biting his lip, Phineas ordered his legs to move around the desk. Unconsciously drawing a deep breath and holding it, the human flung himself into the cold, swirling mist.

Chapter 18

"Dear Flint," Tasslehoff began, stroking each letter with great relish. He stopped and held the paper up for inspection. The kender was very proud of his penmanship. Tas tapped the tip of the borrowed quill against his chin, not quite sure what to write next. He'd never written a "solongforever" letter, as Ligg had called it when he brought the quill, ink, and parchment Tas had politely requested.

Woodrow and Winnie lay in the shadows on the far side of the pillars, still asleep this morning after the previous night's delicious meal of marinated, grilled chicken, fresh, boiled turnips, bread pudding, and home-brewed ale. Actually, Woodrow had passed out, having finally taken Gisella's advice—"Let loose,

Woodrow!"—to heart. By his own confession, the fresh-faced young man had never done more than sip ale at the family table, so it hadn't taken much to lay him low. Woodrow's arms stuck out at odd angles, his left cheek was pressed to the cold floor, and blond hair fanned his face as it rose and fell with his snoring.

Propped on his elbows on a straw mat, Tasslehoff kicked a syncopated rhythm against the stone block wall. The large, empty room was quiet except for the sound of his boots against the hard wall, Woodrow's ragged snoring, and Winnie's deep, even breathing.

Tas chewed the end of the quill, then pressed its tip to the parchment again. "So long forever." He shook his head immediately and scratched through the words. Too depressing, he decided. Tasslehoff crumpled the paper up and threw it into the center of the room.

He pulled up the next sheet, quickly penned the greeting, then, "You're my best friend and I'll miss you a lot." He shook his head again, his topknot bouncing on his thin shoulders. Too mushy. The gruff, old dwarf would surely hate that. Tas crushed the note again and sent it flying.

Flint was a hard one, Tas decided. He would have to think about the letter to the dwarf a little more before writing it.

The kender pulled out another sheet of paper and noticed with alarm that he had only three more left.

"Dear Tanis," he began anew. For some reason he knew that he could say anything to the half-elf, and Tanis would understand.

Woodrow and I—you met Woodrow, do you remember? He's the human who works for Gisella Hornslager, the red-haired dwarf who came to fetch me back to Kendermore. He can talk with animals, and he knows a lot about boats, and he doesn't yell at me like Flint.

Tas paused, then carefully crossed out the yelling part in case the dwarf read the note over the half-elf's shoulder. He could picture them by the fire at the Inn of the Last Home, tears flooding their eyes, clinking their mugs together and toasting his memory.

A few interesting things have happened since I last saw you. We met a bunch of gully dwarves who dumped everything out of the wagon as it was going down the cliff, then we got in a shipwreck and nearly drowned.

But the most exciting thing was riding on a dragon! You'd like riding a dragon, Tanis. This was not a real one, it was built by a gnome named Bozdil—or maybe his brother Ligg built it. I never asked. They made this machine called a cara . . . carus . . . a round thing that plays really loud music and has statues of animals that go up and down and around in circles.

Tas looked over the description of the carousel. He was not completely satisfied with it but he couldn't think of an easy way to make it better, and he did not want to start the whole letter over again.

So I was riding the dragon at Oktoberfest in Roslovig- gen and it took off! Bozdil won't tell me how he made it come to life, and I know it didn't really, but it was neat anyway.

The bad part is that the dragon brought us to this tower way up in the mountains where those two gnomes I mentioned live, and they are going to kill me and put me on display in a glass case to fulfill their Life Quests. They're going to do the same thing to their pet woolly mammoth, Winnie, which I think is terrible! Ligg is bigger and gruffer than his brother, and he builds everything around here. Bozdil is more sensi- tive, but he's the one who usually collects the speci- mens.

I asked Woodrow whether a person could see things after dying, if he's been stuffed. I mean, will I be able to see the people who stare at me in my display case the way I stared at the dinosaurs? Woodrow didn't think so, but I think the next few centuries might be more interesting if I could.

With only one sheet of paper remaining, Tas decided to conclude his good-bye.

I'm running out of paper, so I have to go now. It was really nice knowing you. I had a lot of fun with everyone (even Raistlin, I guess), while we were all together in Solace. Please tell Flint that I never believed him when he called me a doorknob and that I really like him, too.

Tas read that sentence over and decided he liked the way it sounded. He knew he was going to have to close soon, or he'd burst out crying, which would smear the ink and he'd have to do it all again.

Biting the tip of his tongue in concentration, he signed it, "Your friend, Tasslehoff Burrfoot." Choking back a sob, he fanned the last page to hasten its drying, then stacked the pages and folded them in half as one. On the back of the last page he wrote "Tanis Half-Elven, Solace." He knew that someone there would get the letter and hold it until Tanis returned from wherever he was.

Tasslehoff was not crying because he was afraid of dying; there was very little any kender feared. Though they did not welcome it, they thought of death as the last big adventure. Still, Tas hated the thought of leaving his good friends, Tanis and Flint, forever.

Just then there came a knock at the door, which seemed ridiculous considering that the occupants of the room were prisoners. The wooden door swung open and Bozdil's head appeared around it.

"Time for the kender's jar fitting!" he said merrily.

Woodrow and Winnie both snorted themselves awake at the sound of the gnome's voice.

"Jar fitting?" Tas repeated dully. "What's that?"

"LiggandIweretalkingaboutwaystoimprovethe-exhibits, somethingtomakethemmoreinteresting." He was speaking very quickly, avoiding Tasslehoff's eyes. "We thought perhaps putting more of the specimens in interesting-looking jars might help." Bozdil's voice trailed off, and he continued to fidget.

"Uh oh," Winnie mumbled in the shadows. The sound reached only Woodrow's ears. "This is just an excuse to get him out of here without suspecting anything. No one ever returns from a fitting."

Woodrow looked up through bleary eyes and gulped. "Oh." Woodrow's foggy brain began to slowly clear, and he was frozen with helpless indecision.

"Come with me, Burrfoot," instructed Bozdil. Seeing the kender reach for his hoopak he said, "Leave your forked weapon here. You won't need it where you're going. You can retrieve it later."

"Where's Ligg?" Tas asked the smaller of the two gnomes, peering past him into the silent hall.

"He's preparing some things," Bozdil said vaguely, "but he'll be along shortly."

Tasslehoff set his chin firmly, said good-bye to Winnie and Woodrow, who seemed to be a bit muddled still, then followed Bozdil into the torch-lit hall. The kender walked without his usual bounce, his arm held firmly by Bozdil's small but strong hand, a torch sputtering in the gnome's other hand.

"So, how are you going to do 'it'?" the kender asked. "Bonk me over the head, poison my food, hold a pillow over my face?" He'd been thinking about "it" very clinically in the last hours.

Bozdil cringed. "Don't you think talking about 'it' is, well, in bad taste?" He patted Tas's hand. "You're better off not knowing."

They fell silent. Tas heard a rooster crow in some far-distant room. He could hear the near-silent "swish-swish" of a pendulum slicing through air.

The kender did not know how far they'd walked when they stopped before a closed door. "This is it. The jar-fitting room," Bozdil said, his voice clipped. He pushed open the small, simple wooden door.

Tasslehoff ducked his head in hesitantly. He let out a high whistle of wonder and delight. Multicolored glass

from thousands of jars winked and sparkled in the torchlight.

"They look like gems," he breathed. The kender
dashed into the room and skipped between two rows of
knee-high jars of all shapes and colors, gaping at every
one in unabashed fascination: sky blue, bird's egg blue,
water blue, sea green, grass green, leaf green, amber,
ruby, and dozens of other colors. "I haven't seen this
many colors since the stained-glass windows fell out of
the Rainbow Inn in Kendermore. I didn't know glass jars
came in so many shades!"

"They don't generally," Bozdil said smugly. "We blow
our own glass, so it's very clear and sturdy, but thin
enough so you can still see through it clearly. Nothing is
too good for our specimens. Do you see anything you
like?" He waved a hand to include the whole area.

The room was so full of jars that it was impossible to
tell how large the room was, or even to hazard a guess as
to how many jars were actually there. Tasslehoff sprang
from one to the next like a bee between flowers. He
stopped momentarily by a long, low amber jar with a
wide mouth cocked up at an angle.

"Go ahead, try it on for size," Bozdil encouraged the
kender.

Nodding happily, Tasslehoff hitched up his vest,
leaned over sideways, and slipped a foot into the mouth
of the jar. He was in to his hips when his feet scraped the
bottom.

"I'd have to lie down to fit in here, and I don't think I'd
like lying down forever," he said, looking about for another jar to sample.

"No, no," Bozdil said agreeably. "I'm not sure amber is
your color, anyway."

Tas buzzed around the room and located some taller
jars. He slid into and out of all shapes and sizes. He elimi-
nated the fishbowl shape quickly; he was afraid he
would slop from side to side in it, which was not the im-
pression he wanted to give of kender. He liked the ele-

gant design of the ginger-jar. Its narrow bottom gently curved out toward the top, then closed back up again at the mouth. But he hated the way it felt on his neck, like he was suffocating. He discarded the straight, thin style as too conventional. Besides, sitting down in it would be impossible, he reasoned.

Weighing the options carefully, he wandered back to a jar he had considered early on. It was cobalt blue, with simple but classic lines: sleek yet roomy, from its slightly flaired mouth to its tantilizingly rounded bottom. This was a jar a kender could be proud of. Tasslehoff studied it and tried to picture himself in it. Would he look happy in this jar? he wondered.

"Ah, hah!" Bozdil exclaimed, clapping his hands in delight. "I thought you'd select blue. It looks so nice with your leggings. By the way, is this pretty typical dress for a kender?" he asked bluntly, plucking at Tasslehoff's clothing.

"Sure. I guess," the kender said haltingly, caught off guard by the question. But looking at the rich blue shade made him happy again. "You think blue is my color?"

"Oh, definitely!" Bozdil declared vehemently. He locked his fingers together to form a step and nodded toward Tasslehoff. "Here, let me help you up."

Enraptured, Tas eagerly placed his foot in the gnome's clasped hands. He reached for the top of the jar and nimbly swung himself up to sit on its wide lip. Then, with his arms at his sides, he straightened his body and slipped to the bottom with a sharp "tink."

The kender's breathing echoed in the jar. Tas shuffled his feet softly, and it sounded as if his feet were right next to his ears. He pressed his hands and nose to the blue glass and yelled, "What do you think?" Reverberations rang in his ears, so he muffled the sound with his fingers.

"Perfect!" Bozdil clapped his hands again happily. "You don't even need a size adjustment. Absolutely perfect!"

"Huh?" Tas squinted through the glass. He could see

the gnome's lips moving but all he could hear was a faint murmuring. Eternity might be a little indistinct and difficult to understand from inside this jar, Tas decided. But this thought was interrupted when Tas felt the jar shudder, as if the ground, or at least the building, were shaking. The expression on Bozdil's face turned to confusion. When it happened again, much more violently, the gnome's expression turned to anger and he spun and bolted from the room, his puffy sleeves billowing behind him.

Tas pounded on the glass anxiously. "Wait, Bozdil! What's going on? Where are you going? I can't get out!" The sound of his own shouts ricocheted around the inside of the jar.

Something exciting was obviously happening, and Tas was not about to sit inside the glass bottle and miss the fun. The problem was how to get out. While the jar itself was roomy enough, the opening at the top was quite small, barely large enough for Tas to slip through. He reached up and grasped the edge and pulled himself up. With his head and shoulders through the opening, there was too little space left for his arm. No matter how he twisted and pushed, his elbow just wouldn't fit through the jar's mouth.

Irritated at the delay, Tas dropped back into the jar. Pointing his arms straight above his head, he sprang from his toes. His eyebrows came level with the rim of the glass, then he dropped back into the jar. Undaunted, he sprang again. This time his shoulders cleared the lip of the jar and as they did, Tas threw his arms to the sides, catching the rim of the glass under his armpits. He then proceeded to wriggle and squirm his way up and out.

Then, suddenly, the castle shook even more violently than before, and Tas heard a terrific crashing from somewhere nearby. The jar, now impossibly top-heavy, teetered and rocked menacingly. Tasslehoff froze. The jar did not. It swayed and tottered, wavered and wobbled across the small, low shelf on which it stood. Just as it tipped over the edge, Tas sprang clear to land on his fingers and toes. The jar smashed into the floor behind him, showering Tas with broken fragments of glass.

A hasty inspection proved to Tas that although he was blanketed with tiny slivers and a fine powder of glass, he was unhurt. Snatching a polishing rag from a nearby shelf, he quickly brushed away the splinters, then dashed through the door after Bozdil.

The gnome stood in the hallway, his back turned to Tasslehoff, his gaze fixed on the end of the hall. There was a loud thump, the castle shook slightly, and the door creaked and groaned, followed by a tremendous crash. Pieces of splintered door showered the floor, along with chunks of rock smashed from the stone door frame. Through this jagged breach stormed the woolly mammoth, Winnie. The slight human, Woodrow, was spread-eagled across the mammoth's back, hanging on by two handfuls of fur.

"Whatisthemeaningofthis?" shrilled Bozdil. "Thisisamuseum, notanarena! Inthenameofscience, stopthisrampage!"

Woodrow sat up unsteadily. "We're leaving," he announced, "and we want Mr. Burrfoot." The human shook the kender's hoopak over his head threateningly.

"Youcan'thavehim," Bozdil shot back.

"He'sanexhibit," added Ligg, scrambling over the wreckage behind Winnie. The skin of some small lizard, complete with feet, tail, and head, was clasped in his left hand. "It'sanhonortobeanexhibit. It'slikeimmortality!"

"You haven't pickled him already, have you?" Woodrow asked anxiously.

"Yes, you're too late," Ligg said quickly.

Woodrow gasped, swallowing a lump in his throat.

"Now give this foolishness up, and we'll deal lightly with you," the bigger gnome continued, pushing up his spectacles.

Winnie shook his head furiously, forcing Woodrow to tighten his grip. "I won't make any deals," the mammoth said firmly.

"Look at all the damage you've caused," implored Bozdil. "At least help us repair this and clean up the mess."

"We may be too late for Tasslehoff," Winnie sobbed, forcing his voice to be firm, "but Woodrow and I are coming through anyway. I've decided I don't want to be pickled for posterity. Don't make me hurt you, Ligg, or you either, Bozdil. You've treated me pretty well these fifteen years, but I've decided I want to leave, and I'm taking my new friend with me. I'll do what I have to do to get free."

Winnie advanced rapidly toward the two brothers, who were now side-by-side in the hall. Just then Tas emerged in the hallway from the jar-fitting room. He could immediately see how angry the mammoth was. Fearing for the two gnomes, who stood resolutely in the path of the charging behemoth, but anxious to get away with his friends, Tas made a quick decision. Dashing into the hall behind the brothers Ligg and Bozdil, the kender used his favorite trick: he knocked their heads together, which clunked like two coconuts. The startled gnomes slumped into Tas's arms, and he dragged them to the wall, out of Winnie's way.

"Tasslehoff!" both human and mammoth cried at the sight of their friend. "We thought you were dead!" The woolly mammoth slowed down, allowing Tas to grab two handfuls of thick fur and haul himself up the animal's flank. The kender plopped down behind Woodrow, and Winnie continued to hurtle down the hallway.

"Boy, am I glad to see you guys, too!" Tasslehoff exclaimed, craning his head around to get his bearings. "Which way is out?"

Woodrow grinned foolishly with relief. "We don't know. But if we try enough doors, we're bound to find one that leads outside."

"Wahoo!" screamed Tasslehoff as Winnie lowered his head and smashed through another doorway.

"Uh oh," said both Tasslehoff and Woodrow as the dust cleared and they saw what was in the room they had just broken into. On the far side of the room was a large door that appeared to lead outside. Between the door and the woolly mammoth stood a giant cat—a mountain lion, guessed Tas—connected to the wall by a thirty-foot chain. "Turn around. We'll find another door," urged Tas.

But Winnie stood fast. "C'mon, Winnie, that's a mountain lion," pleaded Woodrow. "You've been locked up in here all your life. You don't know what a mountain lion can do. Just back up and we'll find another way out."

But Woodrow underestimated the woolly mammoth. In spite of years of imprisonment, Winnie's instincts were still honed. He charged straight toward the mountain lion, which had never seen anything as massive as Winnie. The cat crouched on its belly and slinked to the side, expecting to leap on Winnie's flank when the wall forced the mammoth to stop. Winnie passed the lion, hit the wall, and kept right on going, smashing completely through the brick and out into the sunlight beyond.

And he did not stop there, either! The frantic woolly mammoth bounded down the slope, away from the castle, skidding in the dirt, whooping and hollering and waving his trunk.

* * * * *

Farther down the mountain, Gisella and Denzil rode single file, Gisella in the lead, along the narrow, winding trail. As they rode out from the shadow of a towering boulder, Gisella looked ahead and spotted the silhouette of a tower against the morning sky. She halted, waiting for Denzil to catch up.

They rounded yet another bend in the twisting, rock-strewn trail. Gisella spotted something and stood in the stirrups to get a better look. A structure, or series of structures, like no other she had ever seen—four towers thrust upward from the side of the mountain, staggered irregularly. Beneath the towers, a castle appeared to grow out of the side of the mountain, or perhaps the mountain had crumbled down on top of the castle. She thought she saw two figures riding atop a boulder. Then she realized that the boulder was, in fact, some sort of enormous, shaggy animal. In a few moments, Denzil reined up alongside her. He, too, straightened up and shaded his eyes with his hand.

"Some sort of creature, carrying two riders," he said. "They seem to be running from that stronghold. Could they be your companions?"

Gisella squinted. Fortunately, the sun was behind her. "It's hard to be sure at this distance. The one in front looks a lot shorter than the other one . . . and he's definitely carrying a hoopak. OK, that's Woodrow and Burrfoot. Do you suppose that's another wooden animal they're riding?" Gisella laughed girlishly at her own joke.

Denzil ignored her question, saying only, "We'll wait for them here."

"Want to make the time pass more quickly?" Grinning, Gisella slid her hand across Denzil's leg and patted his rump.

Denzil lowered himself to his saddle. Gisella snatched her hand away to keep it from being pinned beneath him. "No," he replied. With a flick of the reins, he directed his horse forward to a spot where he could edge off the trail behind an outcropping.

Pouting slightly, Gisella rode up to him. "What's the matter with you? You've been acting strangely all morning."

"Get off the road," ordered Denzil. "Back here, behind me." He unslung his crossbow and cocked it, then drew a bolt from a pouch attached to his saddle. "Keep your mouth shut and stay out of the way."

Gisella's arms dropped to her lap and her petulance disappeared, replaced by indignation. "When did I enlist in your army? And what have you got in mind here, anyway? Those are the people we came up here to rescue. Start waving that shooter around cocked and loaded— and you'll end up hurting somebody."

"Hurting people is what I do best!" he snarled. "Now

get behind me unless you want to be the one hurt."

"Well, isn't this typical?" fumed Gisella. "Give a guy a tumble and right away he thinks he's been knighted. I've got some news for you, Dunce-el. Gisella Hornslager doesn't bow, scrape, or take orders, especially from somebody whose eyebrows meet in the middle. Now you can either change your tone with me or turn around and trot back to town."

Denzil swung the crossbow to point directly at Gisella's chest. His face betrayed no emotion. "I'm here for the kender. As long as I leave with him, what happens to everyone else is unimportant. Whether you live or die is the same to me. Now toss the little dagger I know you keep strapped to your thigh on the ground, be quiet, and keep out of sight, or I will silence you."

Gisella sucked in her lip for a long moment. Was this real? She had spent a terrific night with this man and a moment ago she was looking forward to quite a few more. Now he was pointing a crossbow at her and telling her he would pull the trigger with no remorse. He was also talking about Tasslehoff as if the kender was a valuable commodity. Was Denzil some kind of bounty hunter? Gisella decided that defiance might be inappropriate, for now. Cursing herself for getting involved with someone she knew so little about, she obediently dropped her weapon and guided her horse into the nook behind Denzil's.

Ignoring her, Denzil pulled a strip of cloth from his pocket and tied it around the leather protecter on his left forearm. Fishing a handful of crossbow bolts from his saddle pouch, he deftly slid them, one by one, under the cloth band. With growing horror, Gisella realized that Woodrow and Burrfoot were riding into an ambush.

Heroics were not Gisella's stock in trade. In her travels, she'd had to defend herself more than once. But drunken guildsmen and starving goblins were a far cry from a trained killer. Wistfully, Gisella eyed her dagger, lying on the ground. There was nothing she could do.

*   *   *   *   *

Tasslehoff was laughing.

"Did you see the look on that mountain lion's face when Winnie smashed the wall? It was one of the funniest things I've ever seen. He looked like he'd bitten into an overripe skunkberry."

"I wasn't scared!" wheezed Winnie. "I was sure I'd be scared, but I wasn't. I just put my head down and, smash!"

Woodrow was twisted halfway around on Winnie's back, peering back up toward the castle. "I don't see anybody following us. Why do you suppose they aren't following us? They have a dragon, after all."

"Maybe they're invisible," suggested Tas, twisting around to see for himself. "I don't see anything either. That's usually a good sign that something is invisible, when you can't see it. What do you think, Winnie? Could they make themselves and their dragon invisible?"

Winnie considered that for a few seconds. He really didn't know much about invisibility. "Well, I never saw them while they were invisible. Does that mean anything?"

"It's not definitive," said Tas. "Although, if you'd seen them invisible, then at least we'd know for sure."

Winnie had been loping along at a good rate since leaving the tower. Abruptly, however, he slowed. "There's something ahead of us. I can smell it. It's different . . . There is something alive up there."

*   *   *   *   *

Gisella tugged a lock of her hair. Denzil, still seated on his horse, had his crossbow braced on top of a rock and was sighting on something. She could not reach her dagger, and she had nothing else to attack Denzil with. But she had to stop this foul deed.

Suddenly, she had an idea. Gisella spurred her draft horse forward, waving her arms. Denzil was caught completely off guard.

"It's Miss Hornslager," shouted Woodrow, pointing down the trail some fifty yards. "She found us! Hooray!"

But even as Woodrow cheered, Gisella grimaced and clutched her side. The human's joy turned to horror when Gisella cried out, swayed in her saddle, clutched her side, then slumped backward and tumbled to the ground.

"Winnie, get over there, fast!" pleaded Woodrow. "We've got to see what's wrong with her!"

Winnie took two tentative steps forward, then stopped. "We don't know what's there."

"Miss Hornslager is there, and she's hurt!"

Woodrow swung his leg across the mammoth's back and slid to the ground. As he dropped below the animal's furry back, a crossbow bolt whistled past Tasslehoff's ear and shot harmlessly through the space Woodrow had just occupied. Tasslehoff had heard the sound enough times before to know what it was.

"Crossbow!" yelled the kender as he flattened himself across Winnie's back. Lifting the mammoth's ear, Tas told him, "Rush forward, Winnie. If we stand back, they'll pick us off one by one. Rush forward, now!"

The huge animal hesitated for a moment; then, with a toss of its shaggy head, bounded down the trail. Tas was almost thrown to the ground by the unexpected burst of speed. He clutched tightly to the thick fur of Winnie's back, bouncing furiously.

As they closed in on Gisella's still form, Tas spotted a face behind a crossbow, perched atop a rock, only a heartbeat before another bolt was loosed. Tas heard the "thud" and felt Winnie stumble slightly. Looking down, he saw the feathered shaft sticking out of Winnie's flank, just inches from Tas's thigh. But Winnie pressed on, and in seconds they had covered the remaining distance to the assassin's niche.

After firing his third bolt, Denzil had dropped the crossbow and yanked his heavy, curved sword from its scabbard. The metal-shod end of Tas's hoopak whistled toward his skull. Denzil's scimitar deflected the attack, knocking a divit from the wooden shaft of Tas's weapon. But he had no easy means to attack the kender himself, as the woolly mammoth stood at least four feet taller than Denzil's horse. The kender's height advantage reduced Denzil to fending off attack after attack as his horse backed slowly down the trail.

Woodrow reached Gisella at last. Her horse was pawing the ground nervously several feet away. Woodrow knelt beside the dwarf and gingerly rolled her from her side onto her back. Then he saw the small, red hole in her wool vest, just below the armpit. At such short range, the crossbow bolt had buried itself completely in her side. Choking on his own emotion, Woodrow pressed his ear to the dwarf's still chest, then held his cheek over her mouth, hoping to feel even the slightest breath.

But there was nothing.

Spinning around, Woodrow saw a burly man on a horrid horse—a nightmare—locked in a vicious melee with Tasslehoff. The man's sword was not long enough to reach the kender atop Winnie, and Winnie could not get close enough to the man's thrashing horse for Tasslehoff to strike effectively.

Leaving Gisella's body, Woodrow dashed toward the fight, snatching up the dwarf's dagger on the way. As Tas aimed another blow at Denzil, Winnie struck out with his trunk, wrapping it around the man's heavy boot. With a tug, he wrenched Denzil's foot from the stirrup, throwing him off balance. Seeing his opening, Tas thrust the pointed end of his hoopak, spearlike, straight for Denzil's chest. The metal point struck just below his rib cage, forcing the air from the man's lungs and toppling him from his saddle. Armed with Gisella's dagger, Woodrow stabbed toward the falling body and felt the blade sink in. Denzil hit the ground with a thump. There was blood on Woodrow's dagger.

Tasslehoff was ready to slide down from Winnie's

spine when Woodrow scrambled back up. "Let's go!" the human barked. "We've got to get out of here before the gnomes catch us again. They couldn't have missed all this racket."

"Oh, oh, I can't be captured again. I just can't," Winnie moaned, launching himself back down the trail.

But Tasslehoff shouted, "Wait, who was that guy? And what about Gisella—don't we have to wait for her?"

"Gisella's dead," spat Woodrow, fighting back angry tears, "and so is the man who attacked us!"

Tasslehoff looked stricken. "Gisella can't be dead! How do you know?"

"She's dead, Mr. Burrfoot!" Woodrow sobbed. "She was hit in the side by a crossbow bolt. I stabbed the man who killed her—the one you were fighting as you knocked him off his horse. See, there's still blood on Gisella's dagger! Please, Mr. Burrfoot," he begged, "let's go! We can't do anything for either of them, so the best thing to do is get away."

"He's right," Winnie whimpered, sad for his new friends. "We can't let Bozdil and Ligg find us here."

"I don't care about the gnomes!" hollered Tas. "We can't just leave her back there. Stop, Winnie! Turn around!"

But Winnie continued charging down the mountainside. "I can't, Tasslehoff. I just can't. It's too risky! The gnomes. . . ."

"Kender don't leave their friends!" Tas cried in anguish. Quicker than Woodrow could react, Tasslehoff tossed his leg across Winnie's back and was on the ground, rolling to break his fall. In a flash he was back on his feet and charging uphill toward Gisella's body.

Woodrow's hands shook as he tried to slow Winnie. Every nerve in the human's body told him to fly from this place as quickly as possible. Yet Tasslehoff Burrfoot was his friend, and if Woodrow could not go back, at least he would wait.

As Tasslehoff approached Gisella's body, his breath

caught in his lungs and his eyes blurred. Her horse trotted forward to meet the kender, who gathered up the animal's reins. The red-haired dwarf's limp body lay some ten paces from the man who had shot her. His horse stood over him. The animal snorted and stamped as Tas drew near. When Tas saw the wound in Gisella's side, he knew she was indeed dead. Summoning his strength, he gently lifted the body of Gisella Hornslager into his arms and laid it across the saddle on her horse.

His steps leaden, Tas turned and directed Gisella's horse, bearing her body, back down the trail to where Woodrow and Winnie waited anxiously. No one spoke as Tas tied the horse's reins to Winnie's tail and climbed back on the mammoth, behind Woodrow. Tas could hear nothing in his mind but the lone, droning drum beat of a kender funeral procession as they rode to the east down the mountainside.

They did not look back.

If they had, they would have seen a large man stir on the dusty road near the gnomes' tower.

* * * * *

They buried the flame-haired dwarf by moonlight in a wooded clearing within earshot of a babbling stream. Tasslehoff's voice broke over the strains of the Kender Mourning Song.

Always before, the spring returned.
The bright world in its cycle spun
In air and flowers, grass and fern,
Assured and cradled by the sun.

Always before, you could explain
The turning darkness of the earth,
And how that dark embraced the rain,
And gave the ferns and flowers birth.

Already I forget those things,
And how a vein of gold survives

The mining of a thousand springs,
The seasons of a thousand lives.

Now winter is my memory,
Now autumn, now the summer light—
So every spring from now will be
Another season into night.

"I'm glad Fondu isn't here to see this," said Woodrow.
"He's better off rampaging through Roslloviggen." Wiping away a tear, the human straightened Gisella's auburn tresses and brushed the dust from her pale cheeks because it would have mattered to her.

Tasslehoff's hoopak served as a simple marker for the grave.

"We're going on to Kendermore—for Gisella."

PART III

Chapter 19

TRAPSPRINGER REACHED FOR DAMARIS, but he couldn't find her in the swirling green and purple mist. He felt as if his lungs were being pushed out the front of his chest. Butterflies seemed to be swarming inside his stomach, fluttering their wings all at once and tickling him unmercifully. He giggled, but he heard no sound. He could see nothing but roiling, white mist streaked with amethyst and emerald, as his limbs flailed helplessly. Wherever he was, he was not touching ground, yet he did not feel as if he were quite floating, either.

Suddenly Trapspringer became aware that the hair on his body was growing, and his fingernails were stretching. He felt weightless and unattached, but at the same time an enormous pressure bore down on him.

Then, as if a great harness had been unbuckled and the doors flung open, the pressure and the mist disappeared and Trapspringer lay sprawled on top of Damaris Metwinger. She pushed him away frantically, and together they stood and looked around, unconsciously holding hands.

Both kender dropped their jaws in amazement, and Trapspringer shook his head. We've plummeted into a child's shadowbox diorama, the elder kender thought.

For that is what the land around them most resembled. They stood at the crossing of two narrow, shiny black streets that looked and smelled remarkably like anise licorice. Neat little houses of golden brown with scrolling, white trim—iced gingerbread?—were set at regular intervals along the streets. Every house was identically landscaped with multicolored gumdrop bushes, lollipop trees, nut-cookie sidewalks, and all-day-sucker flowers. Everything was in perfect kender scale.

Though there was plenty of light, there was no sun—no sky, for that matter, just a swirling mass of pastel mists that formed a ceiling of sorts over the strange landscape. It was as if the town had, in fact, been constructed in a box.

Trapspringer and Damaris spun about, their excitement growing.

"Can it be real?" she breathed.

"Only one way to find out!" Trapspringer said brightly. He led them to a small, pink-and-white striped bush and broke off a crunchy leaf. Snap! He popped it in his mouth. "Strawberry and vanilla taffy!" he proclaimed, snapping off another piece for her.

"Harkul Gelfig, what do you mean, eating my bush?" an angry voice called from the depths of the nearest house. Trapspringer and Damaris jumped back guiltily.

"Why, you're not Gelfig!" The man peered through a little grate in his taffy front door. The door swung open and a heavy-set kender waddled down the cookie walk.

"The name's Trapspringer Furrfoot, not Gelfig What-ever-you-said," Trapspringer said pleasantly. "Pleased to meet you." He held out his hand. "Where are we, by the way?" He looked around at the small village.

"I'm Lindal Hammerwart." The kender, one of the most obese either Damaris or Trapspringer had ever seen, took Trapspringer's hand and broke into a jowly grin. "And you're in Gelfigburg! Hey, everyone, we've got newcomers!" he hollered.

It was as if the cry opened floodgates. Doors flew back, their lemondrop knobs slamming into ginger-bread siding. The box-world shook as dozens of the fat-test kender ever seen waddled and jiggled themselves toward Trapspringer and Damaris. The two were sur-rounded in no time and bombarded with an unintelligi-ble stream of high-pitched, excited questions.

"What are your names? The Welcoming Committee needs them for the cake."

"Are those boots pigskin or cowhide?"

"Are you bothered by indigestion?"

"Where are you from?"

"Do you have any food made from anything besides sugar?"

"What an interesting color for a cape! May I borrow it sometime?"

Laughing and shaking hands, Trapspringer tried his best to answer all the questions, unable to squeeze in one of his own.

Suddenly a multicolored streak of light shot down from the swirling clouds above and touched the ground for a heartbeat or two, as if it was solid. Then, as quickly, it receded back into the mist, leaving a very un-steady Phineas standing a few yards from the cluster of kender.

"What in hell was that foggy tunnel?" he grumbled, while jarring the side of his head with the heel of his hand. He looked at the black licorice beneath his feet and jumped backward. "And what in hell is this?" Then he heard the chatter and looked up, his face turning crimson. "Who in hell are you?"

"A human," one of the kender muttered above the twitter. "I don't think we have one of those, do we? And a vulgarian! I don't suppose he can help being a human. Still, didn't we outlaw vulgarity?" The crowd of weighty kender turned in on itself to discuss the matter.

Phineas pushed his way through the fleshy crowd surrounding Trapspringer and Damaris. He looked more than a little relieved at the sight of them.

"Where are we?" he asked, trying hard to control his voice so that Damaris could not accuse him of sounding "unhinged."

He had never even imagined such a place. Who would build an entire village out of candy? Who, indeed, he mused, watching the throng of unusually massive kender. Perhaps this was the stage for a play, and these kender were but actors with padding in their clothing? But then how do they get their cheeks to puff out so convincingly? he wondered.

No, these were genuinely plump kender, he concluded after bumping into a few of them. Then he noticed something that made his breath catch in his throat. These kender were nonchalantly breaking off pieces of houses, plants, and fences and stuffing them into their mouths while they continued their discussion.

"I believe that one there—" Damaris pointed to the first kender they'd met, the one who looked to be wearing two pair of pants sewn together "—said this place was called Gelfigborough, or something like that."

"That's right, Miss," said the very man who'd told them that, spinning around. "Gelfigburg. Named after our founder here, Harkul Gelfig." The kender put his meaty arm around the shoulder of a gray-haired kender wearing pants similar to his friend's. Both men beamed.

"But where is 'here'? " Trapspringer asked.

The kender named Harkul stepped forward, his face serious. He rocked back and forth, heel to toes, his hands unable to clasp behind his back. "We're not sure about that, exactly. There are those of us who think that we're dead and that this is Reorx's pantry."

"But I don't worship Reorx," said Phineas.

The village's founder frowned. "That's interesting. Somebody write that down."

"But the human was with these kender when he entered the foggy tunnel," said a voice from the crowd. "Maybe he was just sucked along in their vortex."

"Another good point! Somebody write that down, too." Harkul rubbed his hammy hands eagerly. "I think we're on to something here! We haven't had a good paradox in . . . oh, a long time, I'd say."

"How long have you all been here?" Damaris asked, noticing the range of ages in the faces of the crowd.

"Three days!"

"A fortnight!"

"One week!"

"Four months!" That came from Gelfig.

"You're the founding father, and you've only been here four months?" asked Phineas.

Gelfig looked insulted. "It's been a very productive stay, thank you! Why, I've accomplished more in that time than that silly leprechaun mayor, Raleigh, has done in nearly a year."

"You mean 'did' in a year," Damaris Metwinger, the mayor's daughter, dutifully pointed out.

Gelfig looked annoyed. "Has Raleigh been replaced already? I knew he wouldn't last the year!"

Damaris looked confused. "But my father, Meldon Metwinger, has been mayor these last several months. I've seen the likeness of this Raleigh you mention on the wall in the council chamber. He was mayor just after the Cataclysm, wasn't he?"

"That's right," Gelfig agreed. "Personally, I had no problem with Raleigh; he seemed effective enough, for a leprechaun. And he once treated me fairly on Audience Day. You say there's a Mayor Metwinger now?"

Phineas was focusing on Gelfig's words. *"Are you trying to tell us you knew Raleigh?"* His voice was barely above a whisper.

"Of course I knew him!" Gelfig snorted. "I was nearly elected to his council, being one of Kendermore's premier chocolatiers. Of course, the city is so young, competition isn't too bad yet," he felt compelled to admit.

"What year do you think this is?" Phineas asked, his eyebrows knitted together.

Gelfig looked at him as if he were an idiot. "Why, it's 6 A.C., of course. What year do *you* think it is?"

Flabbergasted, Phineas opened his mouth to speak when five of the stout kender leaped forward to give answers of their own.

"27!"

"45!"

"68!"

"129!"

"234!" the throng of kender chorused.

"Try 346," Phineas said dryly when the hubbub quieted down. "But none of you have been here for more than four months?"

The kender all shook their heads silently.

"Sounds like a time warp to me," Trapspringer announced.

"Huh?" Phineas grunted.

"Sure, it's an old trick," Trapspringer explained. "You take a pocket dimension or a demi-plane, or break a chunk off a regular plane, surround it in its own singularity, and then either slow down or speed up the local time. Or even make it run backward."

"So are you saying we're all a lot older than we think?"

Biting his lip, Trapspringer nodded. Several of the female kender swooned.

But Phineas looked skeptical. "How do you know all this?"

Trapspringer pumped himself up proudly, hooked his

thumbs in his collar, and rocked back on his heels. "When I was a prisoner of the frost giants, they locked me up with a wizard from another dimension. He told me all about this stuff."

"When were you held prisoner by frost giants?" asked Damaris, wide-eyed.

"It doesn't matter," Phineas snapped.

"I disagree," joined Gelfig. "I'd very much like to hear about the frost giants." A murmur of approval swept through the crowd, along with cries of "Story! Story!" Trapspringer readjusted his pouches and belts to get comfortable and seemed about to begin when Phineas interrupted.

"I would much rather figure out what this place is and how we get out of it," he shouted. The human glared at the assembled kender, who grumbled and shuffled their feet by way of complaint. "Who's been here the longest?"

Gelfig raised his hand. "I was the first one here."

"When you first got here, did you find any clues suggesting where all this . . ." Phineas groped for a word, waved his arms around him, and gave up. ". . . all this, came from?"

"Oh, it wasn't like this *then*." The kender chorus supplied a round of "No's" and a good deal of head shaking.

"Now we're getting somewhere. What was it like, 'four months' ago?" asked Phineas.

Gelfig plucked a chocolate tulip and sipped the thick syrup collected in the flower, then launched into his story enthusiastically. "You should have seen this place then. What a dump! There was almost nothing here, nothing at all. Just a flat, featureless, gray nothing."

The kender chorus shook their heads and sighed.

"I wandered around for a few hours and was just thinking about leaving when I tripped over something. I might have fallen and broken my nose if not for my catlike reflexes." Gelfig assumed a stealthy stance, up on his toes with his pudgy arms out, to emphasize his grace. It seemed to be a crowd pleaser, though at his current bulk, the pose looked mighty ridiculous to Phineas. The human took advantage of the timely pause to pluck a tulip, curious himself as to how it might taste.

"I spun around to see what I had tripped on, but there was nothing there! 'This is strange,' I said, so on my hands and knees I groped around a bit. And sure enough, what do you suppose I found?"

"AN INVISIBLE CHEST!" shouted the assembled kender, startling Phineas so badly that he crushed the tulip in his fingers. Thick, sticky, chocolate goo oozed down his forearm.

"That's right, an invisible chest," continued Gelfig. "Bound with invisible chains and sealed with three invisible locks. Now, there was something to do!"

The kender chorus oooed and aaahhed.

"Removing the chains didn't take long; a child could have done it. The first lock was simple enough, too. I tripped it open with my needle file."

As he was licking his hand clean, Phineas began getting caught up in the story. He knew the tower was supposed to contain a powerful, magical treasure. And here was Gelfig, describing an invisible, three-lock box concealed inside a pocket dimension! What better hiding place could there be?

"The second lock proved a bit more difficult," the kender continued. "It being invisible only made things worse. I worked at it for over an hour, and finally I heard those tumblers click.

"By now, I was getting hungry and thirsty, but there was nothing here to eat or drink. I cut a flap of leather from my map pouch and chewed on that so I could concentrate. And that last lock took every ounce of concentration I could muster. It seemed impervious to needle files, invulnerable to penknives, invincible against wires. Finally, the only tool I had left was 'old number three,' my charmed pick. I gave it a kiss for luck, slipped it into that lock, and gave it a twist."

The group of kender gasped in anticipation.

"Nothing happened. I twisted it left, and I twisted it right, and I pushed it in and pulled it out, I tried it backward and upside down. That lock was locked and that's all there was to it.

"At least that's the way an ordinary kender might have looked at it. But I'm no ordinary kender. I kept at that lock. I had that piece of pouch leather chewed down to nothing, so I cut off another. I worked until I'd chewed that down to nothing, and another, and another, until I'd eaten my whole map pouch. And still that lock wouldn't open.

"Then, suddenly, all in a flash, the answer hit me. Since that lock was invisible, I could see my pick inside it. That didn't do me much good because I couldn't see the lock. But in my tool pouch I had a tiny tube of powdered lead. Putting the tube into the keyhole, I blew into the exposed end and shot just the tiniest bit of lead into that lock. Lo and behold, for just a second, before that lead powder turned invisible like the rest of the lock, it outlined the tumblers! I could see how that lock worked, and oh, it was a beauty. It took 'old number three' two flicks and a nudge, and that lock popped right open."

The crowd of kender stared, their mouths hanging open, breathing in every word. Undoubtedly they had all heard this story dozens of times before—many of them mouthed the words along with Gelfig—and they would hear it dozens of times again, and each telling would be as exciting as the first.

"What was in the box?" asked Damaris, unable to stand the anticipation any longer.

"When that lid sprang open, the enchantment was broken and the whole thing turned visible again. My hands had already told me what the box looked like; a smooth pine box with an arched lid reinforced by thick iron bands. Inside it was a single item: A fine, steel chain necklace, with a steel triangle suspended from it. I picked it up and slid it over my head. That's when it happened."

"What happened?" prodded Phineas, the hardened sticky mess on his hand long forgotten. "What did it do?"

Gelfig straightened up, put his arms at his sides. "Suddenly I was surrounded by a field of caramel apple trees. I was terribly hungry, and coincidentally that is what I'd been thinking about before I put the necklace on—caramel apples."

At the mention of food, the tubby kender all reached without looking, snapped off a piece of landscape, and popped them into their mouths.

"Without really understanding what was happening," Gelfigburg's founder continued, "I thought about how nice it would be to have some peppermint schnapps to go with those caramel apples and, poof! A stream of peppermint schnapps appeared, bubbling right past my feet. I don't think I need to say that this was pretty exciting!"

Phineas sprang forward and grabbed the short, wide kender by his tightly stretched lapels. "Where is the necklace?" he demanded, pawing through the folds of clothing around Gelfig's neck. "What have you done with it?"

Trapspringer leaped between the two, prying Phineas's hands loose and pushing the human away. "Settle down, Phineas," he soothed. "Don't interrupt the story."

Gelfig smoothed down his ruffled shirt and settled his shoulders while the rest of the kender scowled at Phineas. "It's right here, if you must know. I used to wear it, but it won't fit around my neck anymore."

Phineas's eyes were as big as Gelfig's caramel apples when the kender pulled a slender chain from an inside pocket of his vest. A small steel triangle, no bigger than Phineas's thumbnail, dangled from it. Phineas turned white.

With his voice trembling, Phineas asked, "Could I see it? I know a little about such things. I may be able to tell you where it came from," he lied.

Gelfig looked at the chain, then shrugged and extended it to the human. "Sure, why not?" Phineas reached out a shaking hand, snatched the chain, and immediately wished himself into an enormous, gem-encrusted castle filled with rich tapestries and beautiful women and servants to cater to his every whim. When he opened his eyes, he saw Gelfig still peering at him, saying, "It doesn't work any more anyway."

Phineas collapsed to the ground near some cotton candy bushes, squishing an intricate mosaic made of cream-filled pastries.

"It doesn't work," he mumbled. Then he glared at Gelfig. "You used it up! How could you use up the whole thing? What could you have wanted that was so important you used up all the magic?"

"Hey, look at this place," Gelfig boasted, sweeping his arm to take in the whole panorama. "You think this was easy? It took a lot of tries to get this just right."

Phineas doubled over and hugged his knees, sobbing gently. He was surrounded by bloated kender in an unbelievable candyscape. He'd risked everything to get here, and it was all for nothing. Now he was penniless, homeless, and hopeless.

It wasn't the first time.

The kender drifted away, absorbed in retelling Gelfig's famous story and devouring the scenery, getting the latest news of Kendermore from Damaris, who, from her enthusiastic munching, seemed to be fitting right into Gelfigburg society. Phineas felt a hand on his shoulder and looked up to see Trapspringer munching on a piece of cinnamon fence. The kender plunked down next to him. They sat that way for several minutes. Finally, Trapspringer broke the silence.

"That's what you were looking for all along, wasn't it?" he asked. "I finally put all the pieces together. My nephew, the marriage, the map—it was all because that map I gave you said something about 'a treasure of powerful magic'."

Phineas heaved a heavy sigh.

"Don't take it too hard," advised the kender. "Treasures come and go—I should know—but this . . . ," he said, holding up a solid butterscotch mushroom, ". . . is the sort of thing you don't find every day."

Phineas raised his head and stared at the mushroom through unblinking, red-rimmed eyes.

"I'm leaving," the human said flatly, and struggled to his feet. "Where's the exit?" He started walking down the licorice street toward Gelfig and the laughing, joking cluster of kender, who were trailing bits of pastry behind.

"Hey, Gelfig," Phineas shouted, "here's your trinket back. Now, how do I get out of here?"

Suddenly the kender, who had been jovial and boisterous moments before, grew sullen and quiet. They paused before Gelfig's gingerbread house. Gelfig coughed self-consciously and pretended he had not heard the question.

"What's the matter?" asked Phineas, suddenly nervous. He glanced at Trapspringer, who shrugged and looked back to Gelfig.

Finally, Gelfig turned toward them. "Umm, I guess I forgot to mention this, but we haven't found any way to leave."

"What!?" screamed Phineas.

"I said, there . . ."

"There's no way out!?"

"I didn't say that, exactly," explained Gelfig. "I said we haven't found any way out."

"That's a damned fine distinction to be making at this point!" thundered Phineas. He turned and stomped back up the licorice street, then spun back to face Gelfig. "And I hate licorice!"

Chapter 20

The morning after burying Gisella, Woodrow, and Tasslehoff rode Winnie in gloomy silence. The Khalkist Mountains gave way to foothills. At dusk the human and the kender reached the exotic port city of Khuri Khan, across the Khurman Sea and far away from their final destination of Kendermore.

The brilliant rose-orange sunset at their backs reflected off the gold-leafed onion domes that rose majestically into the darkening eastern sky. Date and coconut palms swayed gently in the breeze. Women in colorful, gauzy outfits hurried through the streets on their way home, baskets perched on their heads. Merchants in batik head scarves, wraplike garments, and blousy pants gathered at the ankles, made their final deals of the day, perched from the backs of their elephant mounts.

"See, Winnie, you won't look too out of place in this city," Tasslehoff pointed out. The mammoth had been expressing concern since they spotted the city in the distance. "These elephants don't have nearly as much hair as you do, but then, I don't know anything that does. Maybe you can meet more of your own kind here."

"I don't think so," Winnie whined. "Lig and Bozdil always told me that I was the last one like me." A giant tear rolled down the mammoth's big, rubbery cheek. The city frightened him, and being reminded that he was all alone in the world made him even more despondent.

"That's terrible," Woodrow said, genuinely sympathetic. He gave the mammoth's neck an affectionate pat. The big fellow had saved their lives twice already, and the young human hated to see him cry.

"Maybe some food will cheer us up," Tas suggested.

They pooled their resources, which amounted to two copper pieces from Woodrow and an emerald ring, a small cut of amber, and some pointy teeth from Tasslehoff.

"That looks just like the baroness's ring, from back in Rosloviggen!" Woodrow exclaimed.

Tas looked surprised, then colored slightly. "Why, I think you're right. I wonder how it got in my pocket? It must have fallen in somehow, perhaps when she passed me a roll at dinner. Anyway, we may as well pawn it," he said, without breaking stride.

"We can't do that!" Woodrow's shaggy blond mane shook furiously. "It's not ours! That would be stealing."

"No it wouldn't," disagreed Tas. "Stealing is when you take something, not when you pawn it." Winnie agreed with the cockeyed logic.

Woodrow's face was dark. "You're both right, the pawning comes after the stealing."

"Exactly! Since I didn't steal it—"

"—it just fell into your pocket—"

"That's right. We'd just be borrowing it. We can buy it

back when we have more money, and then return it to the baroness."

"I don't know," the human hedged.

Tasslehoff grew tired of Woodrow's reluctance. Jutting his nose in the air defiantly, he said, "Well, do what *you* want, but I'm going to sleep in a nice, warm bed tonight, and Winnie will be staying in some comfortable stable filled to the brim with . . . well, with whatever he wants it filled to the brim with."

"Oh, all right!" Woodrow gave in. Another night in the woods didn't appeal much to him, either.

Pawnshops were plentiful in Khuri Khan, as was usual in a port city. Tasslehoff received seventy steel pieces for the emerald ring, which he thought was much less than its true value, but still a lot of money. In any case, it would more than cover their immediate needs.

They found an inn by the waterfront, with a very large stable around the corner willing to board a woolly mammoth. Though frightened to be without his new friends, Winnie seemed relieved to be sheltered from the noise and evening bustle of the city.

After a filling repast of curried pork with yellow rice and exotic plum wine, the kender and the human dragged themselves upstairs to their quarters above the taproom, sparsely furnished with two beds and a chamber pot. Both fell into an exhausted sleep, fully clothed, their breathing in sync with the deep-throated harbor bells outside their window.

* * * * *

It was well past midmorning when Tas and Woodrow stumbled out of bed and retrieved an anxious Winnie from the stable. The day was warm and clear, the sky azure blue. A strong breeze blew across the wide, central dock, where they sat eating honey-glazed sweetbuns and sipping thick coconut milk they'd purchased at a bakery.

Tasslehoff removed his blue leggings and dipped his toes in the cool, black water. He tore off a piece of sticky bun, stuffed it into his mouth, and licked his fingers with gusto. Then, after a few moments of pawing through his pack, he removed his ever present roll of maps. Woodrow eyed the bundle skeptically.

"They're not *all* from before the Cataclysm," Tas said, noting the human's pained expression. He unrolled the maps and thumbed through them. "Here's one of Southern Solamnia; I know that one's OK, 'cause I made it myself when I teleported there with a magic ring. Did I tell you about my teleporting ring?"

Woodrow was not in the mood for one of the kender's stories today. "I believe I've heard something about that, yes," he mumbled, telling himself that this particular lie was really a very small one.

"I haven't heard it," Winnie said. He was not keen about water, and particularly disliked the way the dock groaned when he moved across it. Despite coaxing, he would not venture far from solid land.

"Sorry, Winnie, but we really should discuss if we're going to Kendermore by boat or by riding you overland."

Tasslehoff's face fell; the teleporting ring story was one of his favorites. But the kender continued searching through his pile of maps; it had been a long time since he'd examined them closely. Nordmaar, Estwilde, the islands of Northern and Southern Ergoth and Enstar—he had maps from all over.

Woodrow elbowed the kender suddenly. "I think we should travel to Goodlund on that," he said, squinting into the morning sun and pointing to a sleek, two-masted ship docked at the end of the pier. Its sails were furled, but a gaudy, red-and-gold flag snapped smartly from the top of the taller mast. The long, thin ship looked much more elegant than the round, squat ships that crowded the quays. Despite the shipwreck, Woodrow thought longingly of the sea—he was not keen for any more bumpy riding on Winnie's back.

"What would we do with Winnie?" Tas asked.

"I'm sure we could bring him aboard. Ships carry livestock all the time."

"You're going to put me in a compartment with cows and pigs and chickens that are waiting to be butchered?" Winnie squealed. A passerby looked at the talking mammoth in stunned disbelief, then hurried by.

"That's the wrong attitude, Winnie," Woodrow said in his most solicitous voice. "Look at it as a chance to save your feet miles of stumbling over unfamiliar ground."

"All ground is unfamiliar to me. Remember where I've been for the last fifteen years."

Tasslehoff stood up and stamped his feet on the dock to dry them. "Let's go find out how much it would cost to cross the Khurman Sea with a mammoth. Or even where the ship is headed." Woodrow agreed with this suggestion and stood up to join the kender when Winnie's frightened voice stopped both of them.

"Wait, Tasslehoff, Woodrow," he said, his tone reluctant. "I don't think I can ride on a boat." The mammoth looked embarrassed.

Tas hugged one of Winnie's massive legs. "If you're frightened by water, we'll travel overland so you can go with us. Won't we, Woodrow?" the kender offered generously.

The human's "Sure," was not as enthusiastic, but no less sincere than Tasslehoff's.

Winnie shook his massive head, his trunk swinging wildly. "It's not just the water, Tasslehoff." The mammoth paused as if thinking, then blew a big sigh. "For years—ever since I was captured—I've thought about where I came from. The gnomes said they found me abandoned, and I believe them. But I had to have parents sometime, didn't I?"

"But how will you know where to look?" asked Woodrow.

"I have one clue," said Winnie, taking a drink of water off the side of the dock. "Bozdil told me that they found me south of someplace called Zeriak."

"South of Zeriak . . . that's Icewall," Tasslehoff muttered to himself, tapping his chin. "I think I can help you." The kender took out his roll of maps and found one that satisfied him. "Yes, here it is, a map of the South." Tasslehoff rolled it back up and slipped it into the tight curl in the end of Winnie's trunk. "A farewell present," the kender said, swallowing a sniffle. He hugged the mammoth's trunk and stepped away, his eyes welling.

"I have no gift for you except my gratitude, friend," Woodrow said, reaching out to pat the hairy pachyderm. "Good-bye, and good luck."

"I'm the one who must thank you," corrected the mammoth. "But if I don't go right this minute, I'll lose my courage. Thank you, and so long!" Winnie the woolly mammoth called with a wave of his trunk as he left the dock and disappeared into the bustling city streets. Biting his lip, Tasslehoff stood and waved long after the mammoth had disappeared.

"Shall we see when the ship at the end of the dock leaves for Port Balifor?" Woodrow suggested gently.

Tasslehoff's blue mood passed as quickly as it appeared at the mention of another sea voyage. Kender and human hurried down the pier. A gangplank led onto the ship. Finding no one on the dock, they boarded the ship. As they crossed the gangplank, Woodrow noticed a barge floating behind the ship and tethered to it. The barge was loaded with heaps of wilted produce.

Once aboard, Tas hung back to explore while Woodrow spoke to the steward, a hunch-backed, grumpy human in salt-stained, black wool breeches.

With his arms crossed (he thought it made him look older), Woodrow concluded a deal with the steward, who seemed reluctant to allow a kender aboard. Woodrow was looking for Tasslehoff when his eyes focused on a sight on land at the end of the dock. There, amongst a small gathering of men, was an unusual but familiar horse with red nostrils, and its well-muscled owner. Walking with a bit of a limp, the man and his huge, black horse were striding down the dock toward the ship.

Gisella's killer!

Woodrow made himself small and ducked behind the large mast, his eyes scanning the deck frantically for the kender. He swore.

Where was that kender?!

Woodrow wondered briefly how the man they'd fought near the gnomes' tower and who had murdered Miss Hornslager could have survived his wounds. Obviously he had, for there was no mistaking either him or his frightening horse. But now Woodrow had a greater mystery to solve.

Such as where the damned kender was, and how both of them could hide from Gisella's ruthless killer.

Woodrow spotted the kender when Tas suddenly popped up a narrow stairway near the stern, his mouth open in an impending exclamation. Woodrow launched a low, flying tackle and clamped his hand over the startled kender's mouth. He ducked between a water barrel and the ship's rail, dragging a struggling Tasslehoff along.

"I'm sorry, Mr. Burrfoot, but I've got terrible news. That man who killed Miss Hornslager is about to board this ship with his horse. We can't get off without him seeing us, and I can't think of any place to hide where he won't eventually find us."

Tasslehoff's face burned with anger and he bit Woodrow's hand, which the human hastily snatched away. "I thought you said you killed him!" accused Tas.

The human looked sheepish as he rubbed his smarting palm. "I thought I did. I don't have much experience at that sort of thing, Mr. Burrfoot."

Tas's anger ebbed somewhat. "I'm not going to hide from him," he announced firmly. "That troll-spawn is going to pay for what he did to Gisella!" The kender struggled against Woodrow, trying to get to his feet.

Tas's fearlessness only heightened Woodrow's fear. The human had seen this stranger in combat and knew that one kender, however determined, and a runaway squire like himself were no match for such a man.

Woodrow peeked around the corner. Denzil spoke with the steward, then handed him a small bag full of jingling coins. He had obviously booked passage for himself and his monstrous horse.

Fear squeezed Woodrow's heart. He and Tas couldn't leave the ship without being seen, and they couldn't stay where they were without being discovered.

Then the human remembered the barge containing wilted produce. Assuming it hadn't drifted too far from where he'd seen it, it should be only a few feet away. A pile of lettuce and carrots would make a soft landing.

"I'm sorry, Mr. Burrfoot, but this is for your own good." With one arm around the struggling kender's shoulders and another over his mouth, Woodrow threw Tasslehoff and himself over the ship's railing, praying that his aim was true, that the vegetables were as cushiony as they looked, and that he didn't land on and squash the kender.

Woodrow hit the barge with a wet, sloshing slap and released the kender. Tumbling and rolling side to side, he slid down a hump of slimy refuse and tumbled up against the side of the barge. With horror, he realized that the garbage on the barge was a lot older and more rotten than he'd thought—mounds and mounds of rotting lettuce, tomatoes, carrots, meat, rags, and worse.

After spitting over the side a dozen times and wiping his lips and face as thoroughly as possible, Woodrow scanned about for Tasslehoff. "Mr. Burrfoot?" he whispered loudly, trying not to swallow. "Tasslehoff, are you all right? Please answer me!"

Woodrow heard a soft groan nearby. Raking through the awful-smelling garbage, he found the kender lying in a heap against the side of the barge, a large lump forming in front of his topknot. Woodrow felt awful, but he was glad too that the kender was unconscious, because he would surely kick up a fuss otherwise.

Woodrow curled up into a ball in the mess, forming a plan. He knew from speaking to the steward that the ship was scheduled to sail as soon as the crew returned from shore, which would be very soon. If he and Tasslehoff could remain hidden, the ship would leave and tow them along. Then they could keep an eye on the man who killed Gisella without worrying about bumping into him accidentally. Working as quickly and quietly as possible, he buried himself and Tasslehoff in the garbage.

Within the half-hour, the crew was reassembled on deck. Sails were unfurled, the anchor weighed, and mooring lines cast off.

The sun was just past midday when the ship slipped away from the dock and headed out to sea, trailing the stinking barge. Woodrow peeked his head out at the first sign of movement and caught sight of the evil man standing at the stern of the ship. Woodrow shivered involuntarily. Excitement and fear had left him exhausted. With nothing else to do, he fell asleep next to Tasslehoff.

A wave slapped over the barge and Woodrow awoke with a start, gagging on water. A putrid taste clogged his nose and mouth. His heart pounded furiously until he remembered where he was. The sky was bright orange and white, the sun a giant half-circle on the horizon. He could see no land in any direction.

When Woodrow looked toward the ship, his panic returned.

A sailor was bent over the rail, a hatchet in his hands. With a soft "thunk," the sailor's hatchet chopped through the rope that linked the barge to the ship. Tas's and Woodrow's garbage barge slowed and fell behind. The beautiful, two-masted ship glided through the water toward Port Balifor as the barge glided to a stop and rolled gently on the waves.

* * * * *

"For the last time, Woodrow, I'm not mad!" Tasslehoff snapped. Tempers were short on the garbage barge. The kender had cleared himself a little, slimy patch of boat, which he'd rinsed as best he could by scooping up seawater with his hands.

"I just wish you'd warned me before you tossed me on my head, that's all." He gingerly touched the bruised knot that had formed just above his brows. "I'll bet it looks like a third eye."

"You can hardly see it," Woodrow said kindly, privately amazed by its size.

"Not see it!" Tas cried. "I can see it myself without looking in a glass!" To demonstrate his point, he crossed his eyes and looked up, only managing to look demented. They broke into ridiculous, hysterical laughter, hiccuping slowly to a stop.

The barge fell unnaturally silent. Not even a whiff of a breeze crossed their heap of fermenting, rotten, stinking garbage. The midday sun beat down on them, and the sea was as still as bathwater.

"I'm hungry," Tas said at last, rubbing his growling stomach. He remembered their sweetbuns back on the dock.

Woodrow's boyish face scrunched up in disgust. "How can you think of eating in the middle of this stench?"

"I eat when I'm bored, OK?" Tas said defensively.

"We haven't been out here that long," Woodrow said.

"How long is long enough?" Tas asked genuinely. "I wasn't bored during the shipwreck, though." He smiled fondly at the memory. "Things were flying and crashing about on the deck, the gully dwarves were, well, being gully dwarves, and Gisella was rolling off the side in the wagon—" The kender's eyes misted over at the mention of their fallen friend. The memory of her sacrifice was fresh in his consciousness.

"Remember before, how we thought she had drowned?" Woodrow was trying to sound inspirational. "It turned out she was just fine!"

"That time," Tas said sorrowfully.

"I miss her, too, Mr. Burrfoot."

Tasslehoff set his chin with determination. "I pledged to return to Kendermore, for Gisella—to complete her job—and to rescue my Uncle Trapspringer." His eyes sparkled fiercely. "I must!"

"We'll get there somehow," Woodrow promised, his unblinking eyes staring into the neverending horizon. Gulls swooped overhead, squawking in their distinctive voices.

Tas's nose lifted in the air as he sniffed. "Something smells like my mother's furniture polish. Or maybe it was her broth." He shrugged. "They may have been the same thing."

Woodrow picked up the corner of a soiled piece of parchment. "What could possibly be causing such an awful smell, anyway?"

"I don't know. Maybe if we find it we can throw it overboard."

Woodrow picked up a sturdy-looking piece of lumber and started poking through the refuse. After turning over several piles, both he and Tas retreated, holding their noses.

"We must be getting close," Tas said.

Two more reluctant pushes with the piece of wood revealed the gray, decomposing carcass of a beak-faced owlbear buried beneath the more usual sorts of garbage. Both Woodrow and Tas dashed for the farthest corner of the barge and hung their heads beneath the level of the gunwale.

"We've got to dump that thing overboard, Mr. Burrfoot," gasped Woodrow.

"I don't think that would be wise," the kender answered. "I'm sure it would attract sharks."

"Would a shark eat *that*?"

"Oh, yes. Sharks eat everything, dead or alive, but mostly alive, and mostly humans and kender and such. And they're enormous and can chew a boat apart if there is something aboard they want to eat. Which is—as I said—everything."

"But we're not in the ocean," objected Woodrow. "This is the 'Bay' of Balifor. So we're all right, right?"

Tasslehoff flopped back into the bottom of the barge and inhaled deeply. "They *call* it a bay, but it connects right up to the ocean. Ships that sail on the ocean come in and out of Port Balifor all the time. We're definitely safer with a dead owlbear than with a live shark."

Wordlessly, Woodrow sank down beside Tas. In the quiet, windless heat, the stink hung over the barge like a shroud. Together they sat and stared at the offensive owlbear carcass and wished themselves elsewhere.

Tas was soon bored again, so he absently watched a distant dot grow against the horizon. "What is that, land?" he asked at last, pointing for the human's benefit.

Woodrow squinted down the end of the kender's finger. "It can't be. We're not moving, but the dot is getting bigger."

"It's a boat!" Tas cried suddenly, his sharp kender eyes catching a glimpse of movement. Rowers, he guessed from their constant motion. Tas jumped up and down, waving his arms excitedly and screaming at the top of his lungs.

Woodrow stilled the kender's arms and said, "We may not be happy to see who's on this boat."

Tasslehoff looked at Woodrow as if the human had lost his mind. "Not happy? But they can rescue us! Anything has got to be better than riding around on here, particularly since there's nothing very interesting in the heap." He squinted at the speck again. "Besides, I think it's too late. They've spotted us." As the rowers drew closer, Tas recognized bull-shaped heads—minotaurs.

Minotaurs were one of Krynn's most unusual—and unfriendly—races. Before the Cataclysm, their history was filled with prejudice and slavery, first by the Kal-Thax dwarves, (according to legend, at least), and later by the Istar Empire. Their bovine appearance and incredible strength made them both despised and coveted as slaves.

No one but another minotaur ever called one of their number beautiful. Both bulls and cows were seldom less than seven feet tall. Short, black or red-brown fur covered their heavily muscled, human/bovine frames. Though they walked upright and had hands like men, their ankles, or tarsal joints, were the hocks of quadruped animals with cloven hooves. Horns as much as a foot long grew from their temples or browbones.

Though they usually wore clothing, particularly outside their island nation, they were scantily covered by human standards. Their outfit of choice was a harness studded with weapons and decorations, and a short leather skirt.

Before long, the small, gleaming, beautifully crafted longboat, propelled by sixteen powerful oarsmen, glided gracefully up to the barge, barely leaving a wake. Everyone aboard the minotaur boat looked worse than unfriendly—angry, almost. They stared unabashedly without speaking, their collective gaze primarily on Tasslehoff.

The kender was beginning to feel like one of the bugs in Lig's and Bozdil's display cases, and it made him squirmy. "Hello," he called, flashing his friendliest smile. "Tasslehoff Burrfoot. And you are—"

"Goar. We've had much trouble of late with the kender on the Blood Sea Coast." The speaker and apparent leader, if his lone red harness was any indication, was a head taller than the other oarsmen. "They are an infantile and thievish race. You are not, perhaps, like the rest?" His words sounded awkward but were phonetically correct, as if he had learned the common tongue from a textbook.

Tasslehoff was too busy staring to hear the insult at first. Woodrow watched the kender's cheeks grow hot as the words sank in. He cut in before the kender could launch into one of his spine-tingling taunts.

"My friend and I are stranded out here, having mistakenly boarded this barge without knowing that it would be cut adrift." Woodrow licked his lips nervously, knowing that this pronouncement sounded unlikely. "Perhaps you could give us a ride to the nearest port, or at least tow us? We would be most grateful."

Goar turned his back and engaged in a loud series of moans and harsh grunts with his crewmen. Suddenly, one of them, a red-furred minotaur whose horns stretched two feet if they were an inch, growled long and low in the back of its throat. The monstrous creature shook its heavy head twice, pointing an accusing finger at Tas, and crossed its arms defiantly.

But Goar's answer was a vicious snort, his lip curled back in an ugly sneer. The gesture left no room for debate. The other minotaur averted its head in angry shame and stormed to the back of the small boat.

Goar turned back to Tas and Woodrow, regarding them as he carefully prepared the unfamiliar words. "We have decided to believe that you are, indeed, *stranded.*"

Woodrow and Tas waited for the minotaur to continue, both thinking, *What an odd way to agree to help us!* When it appeared the silence would stretch on indefinitely, Tas said, "Well, we *are*—stranded, that is. So are you going to help us or not?"

"We did not say we would, no."

Tas and Woodrow exchanged puzzled looks. "Surely you can't leave us out here to die!" croaked Woodrow.

"We cannot?" Goar's voice was without guile. "We are unaware of any law regarding this."

Tas gave an uneasy laugh. "Of course there's no law, but . . ."

Goar arched an eyebrow at the kender, who decided to try a gamble.

"We can pay you!"

Goar's furry ears perked up, but he looked dubiously at the pile of garbage. "I doubt you have anything we would find of value." His attention was abruptly commanded by a tug on his arm from another of his crew. Goar turned away from the barge again.

"Mr. Burrfoot," Woodrow whispered hoarsely, "I'm not sure it was a good idea to promise them payment. Remember, we paid for passage on the other ship, which, after breakfast, leaves us with next to nothing."

"You shouldn't worry about things so much, Woodrow," Tas said in that lecturing tone kender used so frequently. "Something will come up. It always does."

"I don't know," Woodrow said slowly. "They don't seem like the trusting type."

"Human and kender," Goar rumbled behind them. Tas and Woodrow spun around. "My . . ." He seemed to be searching for a word. ". . . my cook tells me that he detects the scent of seasoned owlbear coming from your boat. We would accept that in payment for delivering you to the nearest port."

Tasslehoff and Woodrow were dumbstruck.

"However, if you are unwilling to relinquish such a valuable item in exchange for your lives," Goar continued, "regrettably we would continue on our way."

"Take it!" kender and human cried in unison.

* * * * *

Minotaurs made incredible oarsmen, Tas concluded, watching the strange bull-men pulling at their respective oars. Driven by the cadence of their leader/coxswain, their rhythm never faltered, their strength never flagged. It was mesmerizing to watch, back and forth, back and forth, corded muscles rippling in their thick arms and necks.

The ride was smoother than any Tasslehoff had ever encountered, on land or at sea. The sleek, streamlined minotaur ship cut through the still waters of the Khurman Sea like a hot knife through butter. The speed of sea travel was difficult to gauge, since there were no landmarks to follow, but Tas was quite certain he had never before traveled as swiftly on land. It was more like flying on a dragon, he concluded.

They had been at sea with the minotaurs through two

sunsets and sunrises. The garbage barge had been cast adrift after the removal of the owlbear. Life aboard the minotaur ship was all work and no play. When the rowers were not at the oars, they were sanding and polishing the gleaming chestnut-colored deck to remove any imperfections in its surface.

The two passengers were treated with barely veiled distaste by all but the leader, Goar, who seemed to be the only one able to communicate with them. Tas tried speaking with the others in fragments of several languages and concluded that they spoke only Minotaur. Woodrow doubted from their attitudes that they'd acknowledge a human even if they could understand him.

On the third morning, Goar announced, "We are nearing Port Balifor," though neither Woodrow nor Tas saw any sign of land.

"How long will it be before we reach the port?" Woodrow asked.

"We will not be reaching the port," Goar growled. "We have no wish to mingle with human sailors, nor they with us."

"So you're dumping us?"

"We will provide you with a floating conveyance that should maintain you until another ship passes by. Many ships pass this area. You should not have long to wait."

Tasslehoff was about to protest when the minotaur cook came forward hefting a large, lidless barrel.

"You don't mean for us to float around in that," Woodrow said, shaking his head in disbelief and backing away.

The minotaur's hairy lip curled up. "It is waterproof. We can provide you with paddles, if that would assist you."

"Look at it as an adventure," Tas said to Woodrow, his eyes sparkling eagerly. "This might be fun. I've never been set adrift in a barrel."

"An adventure? Haven't you had enough of adventure for a while?" Woodrow asked impatiently.

"How can you have enough adventure?" asked Tas as

Goar lifted him effortlessly. The cook rolled the barrel over the gunwale and Goar deposited Tas, and then Woodrow, into the pitching, bobbing tub.

Tasslehoff splashed merrily in the lapping water as the minotaurs pulled rapidly away. Before long, they were once again just a speck on the horizon. Woodrow slumped down to the bottom of the barrel.

While Woodrow sulked, Tas experimented with the barrel's balance and buoyancy. He rocked from side to side, jumped up and down, and made the barrel spin in slow circles by paddling with one hand.

Occasionally Tas took a break from his research to scan the horizon for sails. After hours of seeing nothing, he suddenly began jumping up and down in the barrel with a purpose, tossing it from side to side and frantically waving his arms above his head. Soon he was shouting at the top of his lungs, "We're over here! This way! Are you blind or stupid? We're over here!"

Woodrow leaped to his feet and squinted across the water. He, too, saw the approaching sail. "You know, something about that ship looks familiar," he said, grasping opposite sides of the wildly swaying barrel, trying to steady it.

"I know!" Tas snapped his fingers. "I recognize the captain's red flag with the golden cloverleaf symbol. It's the ship we booked passage on, and then you threw me on my head!"

Woodrow's blood froze in his veins. How could that ship have got behind them?

"Paddle, Mr. Burrfoot!" Even as he made the desperate cry and stabbed his own oar in the water, Woodrow knew that the attempt was useless. He closed his eyes and steadied his nerves for the inevitable.

When the human opened his eyes again, he could see the ship was much closer—close enough for him to pick out the dark, sinister form of Gisella's killer at the bow, looking like its figurehead. His cloak flapped around his knees, and he was flanked by two sailors who scurried about, one with a long pole with a hooked blade and the other with a rope.

As the ship approached, it did not reduce its speed. Instead, the sailor with the long pole hooked its blade onto the barrel. The barrel tipped dangerously and some water spilled over the rim as it swung toward the ship. As the barrel bumped against the hull of the ship, the second sailor tossed a rope down to the two castaways. "Climb up quick!" he barked. "We ain't got all day."

Keeping one suspicious eye on Denzil, both figures clambered up the side of the boat. The barrel was set adrift. Through all of this, Denzil stood in the forecastle and watched, perfectly playing the role of the disinterested stranger.

The steward, holding quill and parchment, found them moments after they boarded. The hunch-backed, grumpy-looking human wore the same black wool, salt-stained breeches he'd worn almost a week before, when Tas and Woodrow had first booked passage on the ship. He recognized them at once.

"You paid for your passage, then disappeared," he said, his glance suspicious. "If you have enough coin to be throwing it away, what are you doing sailing Balifor Bay in a barrel?"

Tas shifted while he thought fast. "See, after we paid for passage, a friend of ours came along and offered us the use of his boat. We couldn't say no, could we? But we didn't think it was right to ask for our money back from you—a deal's a deal, isn't it, Woodrow?" The human nodded his blond head.

"Anyway, neither of us really knows how to sail a boat, so we ran into a bit of trouble—a hurricane, I think—lot's of wind, anyway. We escaped in the barrel before the boat sank." Tas finished his story, out of breath. That one had been a real test of his storytelling skills.

The steward looked dubious, but he shrugged. "This close to land, who cares why you're really here? You paid for the whole ride, anyway. You may as well finish it out with us."

"One more thing," injected Tas artlessly. "That man up front," he pointed, "standing next to the anchor rope, is a murderer. He should be arrested and turned over to the constables in Port Balifor."

The steward was taken aback by the turn in the conversation, then at the claim. "You are confused," he explained. "Master Denzil is a model passenger. I'll take no action against him on the whim of a couple of castaways." The steward laughed at what he considered to be a silly request.

Walking away to resume his duties, the sailor shot back over his shoulder, "We should reach Port Balifor in a few hours. Until then, stay on this deck and *don't bother any of the other passengers.*"

"But he's—"

"*I said, don't bother any of the other passengers!*" roared the steward. Then he turned and strode back to his post at the stern of the ship.

As soon as the ship tied up and the gangplank was lowered, Tasslehoff and Woodrow were ordered off. They retreated into the beehive of barrels, bundles, sacks, and urns that covered the wharf.

"We can follow Denzil easily in all this bustle without being seen," proposed Tasslehoff. "Let's wait here and see what happens."

Shaking his head dazedly, Woodrow kept walking through the throng. "No, Mr. Burrfoot. I don't mean to be disrespectful, but I intend for us both to get as far away from that murderer as possible." Suddenly the human was dragged to a stop by the surprisingly strong arms of the kender.

"Wait, Woodrow," Tasslehoff insisted. "That Denzil guy is dangerous, and we can't just let him walk away. If not for Gisella's sake, then for our own safety we'd better keep track of him. He'll be a lot more dangerous if he gets out of our sight."

Woodrow stood silently behind the kender. He was still jittery, but his friend's confidence soothed his nerves somewhat.

They watched the ship for several minutes. Denzil emerged from belowdecks leading his monstrous nightmare. He led the huge, black animal down the gangplank and across the wharf. The crowd parted before him, people edging away from the snorting, red-eyed nightmare. Still within view of the ship, Denzil strode directly past Woodrow and Tasslehoff, ignoring them, and continued into the town.

"What do you suppose he's up to?" murmured Woodrow, tearing a fingernail to the skin with his teeth.

"Maybe he just doesn't care about us," Tasslehoff said, though he didn't sound convinced himself. "Maybe what happened outside the gnomes' castle had nothing to do with us personally. He doesn't seem interested in us at all anymore."

"Maybe you're right," Woodrow agreed warily.

"Let's follow him anyway," suggested Tas. "Maybe we can get something to eat while we're at it."

Tas led the way down the street, trailing Denzil. Before long, however, the kender was absorbed in the sights, smells, and sounds of the bustling seaport. Strange languages, exotic dress, people with unusual features and tattoos, and dozens of merchants all trying to sell him something (or keep him away from their stalls) proved too distracting for the irrepressible kender. By the time they left the second market square, Tas no longer knew where Denzil was, nor was he very concerned.

Instead, Tas paused to buy some smoked fish, admired the merchandise in a map seller's booth, and was chased away by a silversmith after the merchant caught him making funny faces in the side of a teapot.

Even Woodrow had begun to relax as they passed an alley, munching on the last chunks of smoked fish. Suddenly, two powerful arms shot out and grabbed the startled kender and human. One hand wrapped around Tas's neck, the other grasped Woodrow's shirt. The human was flung against the wall at the back of the alley. Tasslehoff felt himself being hoisted face-down across the pommel of a saddle. The pommel gouged painfully into his ribs. Then someone else leaped into the saddle beside him. Woodrow scrambled to his feet, only to be met by the ringing sound of a sword being drawn.

Denzil!

"This doesn't concern you, farmboy!" growled the assailant. "Stay out of it." With that, the dark-cloaked assailant swung the flat of the sword viciously down on top of Woodrow's head, and the human crumpled. A powerful hand on Tasslehoff's back pressed him tightly to the saddle as the mount and rider turned and dashed from the alley.

Chapter 21

Denzil threw Tasslehoff on the hay-strewn dirt floor of a warehouse near the docks. Dusty light streamed through knotholes in the walls' wide boards. The room contained only large wooden barrels held together with rusty bands, and stank overpoweringly of herring.

With his hands tied together at the wrists, the kender had to struggle to get into a sitting position. He gave the sinister-looking human a murderous glance. "You're going to pay for what you did to poor Gisella, and now Woodrow!"

"Give me your maps."

Tas met his challenging gaze. "I wouldn't give you a bucket of spit!"

"Lucky for me, I'm not asking for one," Denzil said. He grabbed the kender by the neck of his tunic, lifted him off the ground, then rummaged around in Tas's vest until he found what he wanted. Letting his mouth crack slightly with an expression that was half grimace, half smile, he held a roll of parchment up victoriously. Denzil dropped the kender absently and turned away.

Kneeling on the ground, he unrolled the maps and regarded them in a stream of light with the tender gaze of a lover. After scouring the top one with his eyes, he grunted angrily, then viciously threw the map over his shoulder. He repeated the scene with each of some six maps, rose to his feet, then scowled darkly. Turning to find the kender, he nearly tripped over Tasslehoff, who had been spying over the human's shoulder.

"Where is it?!" Denzil stormed, reaching for the kender's throat.

Tasslehoff backpedaled quickly. Even he was a bit alarmed by the murder in the human's eyes. "Where's what? I'm sure there's a useful map in there somewhere. Are you having trouble reading them? You needn't be embarrassed. I could read them for you—"

Denzil closed the gap between Tas, and his black-gloved fingers tightened around the kender's throat.

"Of course you don't need any help reading them," gurgled Tasslehoff.

"Don't jerk me around, ken-dirt," Denzil growled. "I want the other half of a map that covers the territory east of Kendermore."

"Withh twwr—?" Denzil loosened his hold on the purple-faced kender somewhat. "Thank you." Tasslehoff gave a raw cough. "The only area worth mapping due east of Kendermore is the Ruins. And even that isn't really worth mapping, since it's ruined." Tasslehoff gave a resigned shrug, then another thought struck him.

"Hey, I once had a small map of the Tower of High

Sorcery there, and the magical grove surrounding it."

Denzil leaned into him, his fetid breath fanning the kender's face. "What do you mean, 'had'?"

"Well, as I recall, there wasn't much detail on the map—just a bunch of trees with a beware sign on them, then this tall, round tower, with lots of steps. I don't remember how many rooms there were.

"Anyway, one day I was out of parchment and I wanted to draw a new map—of Neraka, I think. So I sorted through the maps I had and I decided to use the back of the one with the Tower on it.

"So where is *that* map?"

Tasslehoff shrugged again. "I haven't seen it in a long time. I must have given it away." The kender could see the human's hands trembling with rage.

"What's so important about that map? I've got plenty of others."

"I might as well tell you," Denzil said, "since you're about to die anyway. I stumbled upon *half* of that same map in the office of some quack doctor in Kendermore. *Your* half of that map showed the location of a treasure. I want that treasure, and provided someone else doesn't already have it, I'm going to get it!" With that, he pushed the kender to the floor against the wall and prepared his crossbow.

"Well, then, if you're going to the tower, you're going to need to know how to get through the grove," Tas said quickly, squirming away from the crossbow's sight.

"You're trying to stall me," Denzil said in a distracted, low voice, his fingers nocking the crossbow bolt.

Tas kicked and flailed, trying to keep moving. "That may be true, but it's also true that you have to know the secret of the grove to get through! Ask anyone! Every Tower of High Sorcery is surrounded by a magical grove."

Denzil let the crossbow slip from his shoulder as he

considered the kender's words. "What can a bunch of trees do?" he snarled at last, raising the bow again.

"Plenty!" Tas said hoarsely. "This particular grove tends to make people go crazy! I'm sure you've heard how, uh, resourceful kender are when it comes to getting into difficult places. Well, even most kender haven't been able to get through this grove. Only those who know its terrible secrets have ever made it into the tower!"

Denzil lowered the bow again and squinted at Tasslehoff. "And I suppose you're one of those kender?"

"I might be," Tas said coyly. "Remember, I saw the map."

Denzil thought about that for a moment. "If you know the secret—if there is one—tell me now."

Tasslehoff looked offended. "How stupid do you think I am? I'd tell you the secret, and you'd kill me! I'd rather die without having told you, thank you!"

Denzil wiped his face wearily; he couldn't take the chance that the kender was telling the truth. Snatching at Tas's bound wrists, he jerked him to his feet. "I'm going to kill you no matter what, you know. This way you'll get a nice, comfortable ride on my nightmare." His small eyes narrowed to little slits. "And if you're lying, the quick death I would have given you here will seem luxurious compared to what you'll get later on."

Tasslehoff swallowed hard as Denzil dragged him out of the warehouse and to an alley where his black mount pranced anxiously. This Denzil and his fierce, fire-breathing creature were enough to make even the stout-hearted kender wish he really did know the secret to the grove.

*　*　*　*　*

They rode on the cold-as-ice nightmare from Port Balifor, around Kendermore to the north, and to the Ruins. At least that's what Tas assumed, since he couldn't see more than the ground as it flew by the nightmare's right flank. Denzil had tossed the kender before him on his stomach and lashed him to the saddle.

"Wouldn't want you to fall and get hurt," he chortled.

When they reached the outskirts of the Ruins, Denzil dismounted. He issued an order to the nightmare in an ugly, guttural language that Tas had never heard before. Then, with Tas still tied across Scul's back, ahead of the saddle, Denzil strode down the main, rundown road that ran through the Ruins. Tas thought it strange that they encountered none of the usual vermin that inhabited the area, but then he realized that the nightmare probably scared most of them away.

Satisfied at last, Denzil approached the grove, leading his monstrous mount.

With a wicked-looking, curved knife, he cut the rope securing the kender to the nightmare. Tas fell to the ground like a sack of grain. His back seemed permanently rounded and his leg muscles cramped painfully. Denzil jerked him upright by the wrists.

"It's time to reveal the big secret, ken-dirt," Denzil said nastily. "Put up or shut up, as they say."

I can't tell him something I don't know, Tas thought grimly. If I did know, he'd kill me the minute I told him. But if I only tell him a little bit at a time, he'll have to keep me alive for the rest of the information. Once we get into the grove, maybe I can get away. Once it starts to take effect . . .

"Don't you mean 'put up *and* shut up'? " Tas retorted. "Oh, no. You're just going to have to follow my lead." Tas took one step into the trees.

"I'm getting real tired of you, Burrfoot," Denzil growled. He held fast to the kender's bonds, but strode in next to him. "So what do we have to do?"

"Well, there's a whole series of things that must be done in the proper order," Tas ad-libbed. "The first is coming up just inside the grove's edge. We have to crawl on our hands and knees to avoid springing a trap."

Denzil looked skeptical. "I thought this grove was magic, that it inspired craziness."

"It does!" Tas said. "But that doesn't mean there aren't traps, too."

"You go first," Denzil said, slinging his crossbow across his back. "I'm going to have a hand on your ankle the whole time."

So much for losing him in the grove, thought Tas. Still, there was hope. The kender dropped to his knees and began crawling awkwardly because of his bound wrists, Denzil right on his heels as promised. Tasslehoff's knees got sore and he stopped. The kender could feel the grove's magic encouraging him to suggest crazy things.

"Now, we have to walk backward," Tas announced. He assumed that the human would still insist on watching him, which meant Denzil would have to go first and he'd probably trip.

"If you're playing me for a fool, Burrfoot . . ." Denzil growled. The grove was making him even more suspicious than usual.

Tas managed an unconcerned shrug. "Go ahead. Don't listen to me, the one person who's seen the map of this grove, and see how far you get!" Secretly, Tas was more than a little surprised that they'd gotten as far as they had. The grove's effect had seemed much stronger the last time he had been there. How long ago had that been, he wondered—ten years?

"I'm going first this time so I can keep my eyes on you," Denzil said predictably. He wound his hand through Tas's topknot and began dragging him backward, bringing tears to the kender's eyes. Worse still, Denzil was surprisingly sure-footed. He didn't trip. He didn't fall. He didn't even stumble. When Tasslehoff could stand no more, he told the human to stop. Tas clumsily pulled his hair back into place with his tied hands, massaging his tender scalp with the heel of one hand.

"I must be doing something right," Denzil said. "We're more than halfway in."

"You're welcome," Tas said sourly. The human's smugness brought the next idea into the kender's mind. He could not see how it would help him get away, but he could not resist the opportunity to make Denzil look silly. "Next we have to hop like bunnies."

"Huh." It was no question.

Tas pulled his bound hands up before him, letting his wrists hang limp to look like rabbit paws. "Hop. Like bunnies." He lifted Denzil's hands to the proper position. "Come on!"

Looking at the human's face, Tas wondered if he had gone too far.

Denzil raised his arms together, fingers locked, and slammed both fists into Tasslehoff's stomach. The diminutive kender flew through the air like a ball, landing in a heap ten feet away. He could not even break his fall, with his hands still tied in front of him. Eyes glowing as red as Scul's nostrils, Denzil stalked toward the dazed kender.

The grove was obviously still working very well.

Denzil launched himself. Reacting with true kender speed, Tas rolled out of the way and tried to scramble to his feet. But with his hands tied, the kender could get no leverage. Denzil was on him in a second.

"I warned you not to lie to me," the wild-eyed human snarled. "Now I'm going to snap your limbs off, one by one. This is going to take such a long time, little fellow, that you can't even imagine how much it's going to hurt! All I ask is that you don't die before I finish."

"I didn't lie!" Tas shot back, suddenly enraged. "I said you couldn't reach the tower unless you knew how to get through the grove, and that's the truth. I never said I knew how to do it. Your six-foot-tall greed made you assume that!"

Tasslehoff stuck his nose into Denzil's face. "And another thing: I'm sick of everyone calling me a liar and a thief, and putting me down, just because I'm a kender! Being tall doesn't make you right, and it sure doesn't make you smart! It doesn't even make you tough! Why, if my hands were untied, I'd pound you until you were lumpier and more miserable than a toad! You'd—"

Denzil's right hand closed around Tas's throat, cutting off his tirade. His other hand tightened around Tas's upper right arm, and he began twisting, a sadistic smile on his face. "I'm tired of your voice, kender. But I'll enjoy hearing your joints pop!"

The pain was intense and growing more acute every second, but Tasslehoff would not allow himself to cry out. His eyes were squeezed shut, but the pain and tears forced him to blink.

It was then that he saw the face appear behind Denzil. It belonged to a huge, ugly, hairy creature, as ugly as anything Tas had ever seen. With a sloping forehead, bulging teeth, pockmarked nose—an ogre! As if in a dream, Tas watched the creature's enormous, knob-knuckled hand close around Denzil's right shoulder. The huge hand twisted and there was a loud "pop!"

Denzil flopped to the ground in pain and surprise, releasing Tas's arm at the same time. Before he even saw his attacker, the human let out a loud, shrill whistle.

The large, powerful human spun around, but his fury died when he stared up into the face of the even larger ogre.

And then Scul was there, slicing with his sharp hooves through the web of brush and vines behind the ogre. Denzil maneuvered quickly so he was behind the nightmare. Tasslehoff, still caught up in kender militancy, rushed forward and kicked Denzil behind the knee. The surprised human toppled sideways. Tas landed another kick to his lower back, yelling, "That one's for Gisella!" then scurried away from the human's reach.

The ogre ducked and dodged away from the windmilling hooves. The nightmare, its eyes even wider than usual—probably the influence of the grove, thought Tas—lunged after its prey, but became momentarily tangled in the thick undergrowth.

One moment of hesitation was all Vinsint needed. The ogre swung his massive fist in a roundhouse punch that caught Scul fully between the eyes. The stunned animal staggered, almost recovered, and then its legs buckled and it thudded to the ground at Denzil's feet. Its blood-red eyes rolled back in their sockets.

Without breaking stride, the ogre plucked Denzil's crossbow from his back, snapped it in half, and flung it into the depths of the woods. Then he grabbed Denzil himself and stuffed him under one arm. Before Tas could scramble more than a step, he was scooped up and slung under the ogre's other arm. The creature lumbered off into the grove with his two prisoners.

*   *   *   *   *

"What shall we have for dinner?" Vinsint asked pleasantly.

The usual introductions after an abduction had been made. Vinsint showed them around the small, circular room that contained a table, a bunch of crates, and a stairway. The ogre explained his presence in the Ruins and told the two newcomers what was expected of them.

"I've been awfully busy here lately," the ogre continued, "so I'm a little short and there is not a lot of variety, but I've been told I'm a very good cook." He placed a tin plate of little sandwiches before Tasslehoff and Denzil. Tas was reaching for one of the tasty-looking morsels when Denzil furiously swept the plate from the table.

"I don't need any of your stinking food!" He stood up and paced furiously.

Vinsint was mildly offended. "Perhaps you don't, but your friend might have liked some. That was good, aged skunk!" He picked up several of the morsels, brushed them off, reassembled them as small sandwiches, and placed them back on the table. "Though I should have expected this sort of behavior from a half-orc!"

Denzil froze. His gloved hands clenched and unclenched. "You are mistaken. I am a human."

The ogre was unswayed. "Yes, but you're also an orc." He wagged his finger. "I know my species."

"Yeah!" Tas chimed in, studying Denzil's face. "That nose, those eyes: I always thought there was something strange-looking about you, but I just figured it was because you were so mean all the time."

Denzil's face was as dark as a thundercloud, and he said nothing for a moment, just clenched and unclenched his fists. Tasslehoff found that gesture more frightening than any words he might have uttered. But when he spoke, his tone was clipped, measured, and a threat. "I do not resemble that part of my, uh, parentage."

"Speaking of animals, where did you get that nightmare?" Vinsint continued conversationally while he went on preparing the main course.

"You're such a smart ogre," Denzil said sarcastically. "You tell me."

Vinsint chose to ignore the sarcasm. "I am rather smart, aren't I?" He tapped a wooden spoon against his chin as he thought. "Let's see, nightmares are usually owned by demons and their kind, but however bad you may be, you're no demon. So my guess is that you stole it."

Denzil looked impressed despite himself. "I won it when I bested the demon, Cthiguw-lixix," he said proudly, continuing to pace.

"Wow! You fought a demon?" Tas breathed. Denzil ignored him.

The half-orc studied the walls of the circular chamber while Tas and the ogre ate a companionable dinner of fried onions and pony.

"That was delicious!" Tas exclaimed in satisfaction, pushing himself away from the feast. "I'm quite a good cook myself, so I should know."

"Have more, have more!" the ogre invited, ladling more onto the kender's plate, despite his feeble protests. "I do so love it when my guests appreciate my cooking. I had some very nice kender here several days ago, a pretty, blonde girl and her beau. He was an older, flashy guy—" Vinsint squinted in the lantern light at Tas. "Come to think of it, you remind me of him."

Tas waved his hand merrily. "Oh, we all look alike."

"I suppose," the ogre said, unconvinced as he looked closely at Tas. Finally he shrugged and began cleaning up.

"They had a nasty human with them," Vinsint continued. He shrugged his broad, bare shoulders. "It must run in the breed or something. Kender are usually rude and nosy, but they're seldom nasty. I hate nasty!"

"There are some who think being nasty runs among ogres," Tas pointed out, not meaning to be insulting. He found himself liking the unlikely ogre.

Vinsint nodded. "That's why I left the Ogrelands."

They finished cleaning up and spent the rest of the evening drinking herbal tea, playing pick-up sticks, and talking by the fire. Denzil crawled into his own corner and pretended to fall asleep, actually planning his escape from the much larger ogre.

When Vinsint asked Tas what such a pleasant kender was doing with such a nasty half-orc, Tasslehoff told the ogre about Gisella; he had to stop momentar-

ily to wipe his eyes. He finished by telling him about
Denzil striking down Woodrow in Port Balifor, and
ended with their trek for the treasure.

"You know, this *is* the Tower of High Sorcery," Vinsint whispered to the kender. "We're in the basement.
But I've never seen any treasure here."

"Have you explored all of it?" Tas whispered excitedly, leaning forward. He cast an anxious glance toward the sullen half-orc. Denzil lay on his side in the
distant shadows, his breathing shallow and regular.

"I went about half-way up those steps once," he said,
nodding toward the circular stairway. "But the passage got tighter and tighter, until it was a real struggle
to squeeze through. And, I don't mind telling you, I
don't like heights! Even though there weren't any windows along the stairs, just knowing I was climbing
gave me the woozies. But I never even came to one
landing, so whatever is up there must be way up, or
ruined like everything else here."

Tas thought about that long after Vinsint fell asleep.

When Tasslehoff himself awoke, it felt like morning,
but he couldn't be sure; there was no natural light in
the chamber, only a single, lit candle. He felt rested
and refreshed. He stood up, brushed off his leggings, and
looked around. Denzil was still sleeping in the
shadows, but Vinsint was nowhere to be seen. On the
table the kender found a folded piece of parchment
with his name awkwardly penned on the front. He
supposed the ogre's big hands were awfully clumsy to
write with.

Tasslehoff unfolded the note. It stated, simply,
"Gone for food. Back soon. Vinsint." He pocketed the
note and picked up the candle.

Everything in the room looked just as it had the
night before. Tas examined the locked doorway. He
counted eleven chains and sixteen locks of all different
sizes and styles. That would take hours to unravel, he
decided. And anyway, why escape when there is an

unexplored Tower of High Sorcery upstairs?

Tas took stock of his gear. His hoopak was gone, marking Gisella's grave. Denzil had confiscated all of his knives and daggers, and Vinsint had taken them all from Denzil. His maps were back in his pouch: something of a gift from Denzil before they set out from Port Balifor. Sorting through the silverware, carefully so as not to wake Denzil, Tas borrowed a small fork and a butter knife that looked like useful tools for opening the sorts of locks one might encounter in a Tower of High Sorcery. Vinsint had said there were no windows in the stairwell, so a candle was also a necessary item.

Thus equipped, and tingling with the anticipation of impending adventure, Tasslehoff Burrfoot tiptoed up the stairs.

Beyond the lowest steps, the stairwell was blanketed in dust. Dipping the candle, Tas saw clearly the prints of three people ascending the stairs. There were dozens of others, but these three were fairly fresh. With curiosity devouring him, Tas bounded up the stairs so quickly he almost extinguished the candle.

It seemed to Tas that he had climbed far beyond the tower's apparent height when he finally spotted a door blocking the stairs. He crept up to it and listened, but heard nothing. He tried the latch and the door swung quietly inward, astounding the kender with its smooth operation after so many years. Without a pause, Tasslehoff stepped through the doorway.

The room where he found himself was obviously someone's study. Light streamed in through leaded windows in the ceiling. The circular, outside wall was lined with books, except for a few open spaces where pictures had fallen to the floor. A heavy desk and carved chair did not nearly fill the rest of the room.

The footprints Tas had been following now scattered through the room. Picking out the largest set, he traced them, one step at a time, along a winding course to one of the bookshelves. Just above eye level was an empty spot on the shelf. "Someone's been taking down books," Tas said to himself.

The footprints changed course suddenly. Tas noticed an odd thing. All three sets of footprints converged on a bare section of wall, then vanished. The kender paused for a moment, lost in thought. With a sudden thrill he realized that among all the footprints ascending the stairs, both new and old, he had not seen a single print going back down. He strode over to the wall and studied the tracks there until he was satisfied that they did, in fact, end at the wall. Whoever came up here, he thought, went out right here.

"There must be a secret door!" he cried aloud.

Tas groped across the cobweb-covered surface, searching for a hidden trigger or latch to open the door. He prodded and wiggled the bricks, twisted them and tapped them with the handle of the butter knife. Nothing happened. After several fruitless minutes, he dusted off his hands and decided to try a different tack.

"Perhaps the trigger isn't here at all," he told himself, "but somewhere else in the room." He scanned the room. The missing book? Not very likely. If the book was the trigger, it would need to be attached to something and could not be taken from the shelf.

It took several minutes before Tas's experienced eyes picked out the lever behind the desk. He gave it a quick flip and looked toward the wall. Already each of the bricks was outlined with a bright green glow and mist was pouring through the cracks. Colors swirled across the floor, up the walls, and around Tas's ankles and knees. Then the wall disappeared completely, replaced by a pulsing, flashing, pearl-colored pane. The mist roiled inside the pane and poured out the edges, blanketing the walls and ceiling. Tas's heart thudded against his ribs. This was no ordinary secret door! This was magic, and it could lead anywhere! Tas took two quick steps toward the portal but was stopped by a voice from the stairwell.

"You found it! I knew you'd be good for something!" Tas turned and saw Denzil, framed by the doorway and the swirling mist. The pulsing green and yellow light of the portal made the half-orc's harsh features even more terrible and cast shifting shadows across his frame.

"Stay right where you are, ken-dirt," Denzil warned. "The treasure of this tower must lie through that portal and whatever it is, it's mine. But before I claim it, I have unfinished business with your bones."

The snarling assassin advanced across the room toward Tas. Fully aware that he was no match for the half-orc, the kender took the only other option open to him. He dove for the portal.

And almost made it.

Chapter 22

A ROCENT—*a* LARGE RAT—SCURRIED ACROSS THE BURN-scarred, debris-strewn floor. Stealing from shadow to shadow, the rodent knew it risked its life. Each time it moved, it glanced toward the far end of the room, toward the cracked and crumbling throne carved from a single block of volcanic stone, the throne once used by the Kingpriest of Istar, which now resided in the dark, evil Abyss. Even after centuries, the fires still flickered faintly within the throne, casting their red glow against the pocked surface.

The rodent feared that throne, for on it sat, in her five-headed chromatic dragon form, the Dark Queen, She of Many Faces, Mistress of Evil, and one of the three creators of the universe, along with Paladine, the God of

Good, and Gilean, the neutral god who kept the balance. If a being of such evil power should notice the rodent, the best it could hope for would be death, sudden and final.

But the Dark Queen was certainly aware of the rodent—nothing happened in her chamber without her knowledge and permission—but something else was far more interesting than the fate of a semi-intelligent scavenger. The Dark Queen was occupied with other thoughts.

On the world known as Krynn, on the continent of Ansalon, just south of the Blood Sea, near the once-powerful city of Istar, a magical gate was opening.

An intrigued rumbling escaped the Dark Queen's five reptilian throats as she relished the awareness of the gate. Writhing, two of her heads spit fire in delicious anticipation, scorching the tail of the rodent. This gate was very special, very powerful. It resided in a Tower of High Sorcery, and joined that tower to a pocket dimension of inestimable age. The Dark Queen craved the power of that gate. She wanted to slip through it and reenter the Prime Material Plane, which she had been driven and forbidden from entering these many human centuries past. But Takhisis had no notion or need for time; hours to her were as centuries to the inhabitants of Krynn. Thus, though Huma, that detestable Knight of Solamnia who had led the fight to banish her, had been dead in the grave for centuries, the wound of her embarrassing defeat was still as fresh in her mind as if it had occurred just yesterday.

Takhisis's many tongues lashed out between her razor-sharp teeth as she tasted the thought of final victory. She decided its flavor was even better than the flesh of her enemies.

It was an added bonus, of course, that this Tower of High Sorcery had libraries and laboratories filled with secrets that might be useful to her in the war she intended to wage once she secured her return to the Prime Material.

Ages ago, she had learned the secret of the pocket dimension. She had found a 'back door' into the Prime Material Plane. The door's use was limited, and pointless unless the gate was opened. Now, every time the gate was activated, the secret signs and wards she had placed there alerted her to its use. But it always stayed open for such a horribly short time, and her preparations consumed time. But she knew, as certainly as she loathed Huma, that at some point, the gate would open and remain so long enough for her to intervene.

She knew this and had been patient and ever-watchful, and now her chance had come to pass.

* * * * *

With astounding speed, Denzil's powerful legs drove him across the chamber at the top of the tower. Snarling, the half-orc took a swipe at the kender, who was lunging for the gateway, and managed to snag the shoulder strap of Tas's pouch. Intercepted in midair, Tasslehoff crashed to the ground.

Shaking off his surprise, Tas quickly realized that he was being dragged back across the dusty floor by the leather thong.

Reaching up desperately, Tas's fingers closed around the thong and he gave a powerful tug. The leather strap broke at a seam. Before Denzil could comprehend what had happened, Tas was on his hands and knees and was scrambling toward the mist-shrouded opening. His arms, head, and shoulders disappeared in the swirling mist.

To Denzil, it looked as if the top half of the kender's body had been neatly sliced off, his legs protruding from a wall of pearl. He grabbed Tasslehoff's kicking heels and began to tug.

The body did not budge. But neither did it disappear. The blue-covered legs flailed wildly and twisted from side to side, but the torso did not emerge from the wall one bit. Denzil tightened his grip and pulled again, hard this time. Tas's body slid toward him several inches, still thrashing.

Encouraged, the half-orc looked around for something to help him gain purchase. He spotted the bookcases on either side of the opening and, still holding fast to the kender's legs, Denzil braced his feet against the bookcases.

* * * * *

Swirls of color and texture engulfed Tasslehoff, spinning around him and turning him end-over-end. His lungs swelled up as if something were alive inside them, tingling and tickling him pitilessly. He could see nothing but spiraling clouds of white and emerald and lavender. They reminded him of cotton candy. How pretty, he thought.

He felt at once chilled to the bone by the fog, and moist and sweaty from humidity and exertion. Hot, cold, hot, cold! He shivered as if in a fever, his teeth chattering.

Abruptly he stopped spinning and now he began floating, though he still couldn't tell which way was up. He was no longer capable of struggling or moving himself at all. He still felt as if he were being stretched until he would rip into pieces. His feet and his head felt as if they were miles apart.

Suddenly, he burst through a curtain of rainbows and landed face down in a pile of pointy, deliciously tart-smelling gravel. Sputtering and scrambling to get back on his feet, he learned two odd and intriguing things.

First, spitting what he thought were rocks from his mouth, he tasted lemon and realized that he had not landed in gravel, but in a mound of hard, lemon-flavored candies. The confections skittered like marbles under his hands.

Second, he could not stand up. Something was still trying to pull him apart, holding his legs and yanking on them ferociously. Tasslehoff twisted around to see what the problem was and was confronted not by an antagonist, but by a swirling, silvery pane of light that swallowed the lower two-thirds of his body.

Tas tried crawling forward, but he was stuck fast. Then he felt a sharp tug and slid backward an inch or two. Tasslehoff's heart constricted uncharacteristically.

Denzil is still trying to drag me back from wherever I'm at! Tas realized. The kender redoubled his effort to escape. He looked about for anything to grab and hold onto that might give him leverage.

Meanwhile, Tasslehoff's arrival in Gelfigburg had not gone unnoticed. The young kender looked up to see three of the stoutest beings—they looked like orbs with arms and legs attached—waddle over to where he lay on the ground, struggling for a handhold. The eldest of the two, wearing a sacklike smock over his round body, introduced himself.

"Good day, friend! Harkul Gelfig's the name." He extended his pudgy hand. "It's always nice to see a new face around here. You'll have to tell us your name so we can put it on the cake."

"Why are you lying in the lemon candies like that?" asked the second.

"And where's your other half?" demanded a third kender.

Tas reached frantically for Gelfig's outstretched hand. The kender shook Tasslehoff's hand and released it before Tas could explain his desperate situation. Struck dumb for the first time in his life, Tas held up his hand again in a silent plea for help.

But the onlookers simply continued to gape at him, smiling.

Tas looked around them anxiously, taking in his surroundings for the first time. His mouth dropped open and he nearly lost his tenuous grip at the sight of taffy trees, peppermint fences, gingerbread homes with graham-cracker shutters and shingles of chocolate shavings.

Just then, Tas felt another mighty pull on his legs; one

more inch of his torso disappeared back into the portal. Waving his arms frantically, he finally managed to cry, "Help me, please! Someone who wants to kill me is trying to drag me through this doorway! Please hurry and grab on!"

What intrigue! the three kender thought. They took hold of Tasslehoff's arms but, try as they might, they could not pull him free of the wall. Somewhat to Tas's relief, he did stop sliding backward, though he could still feel Denzil tugging and yanking on his legs.

The commotion quickly attracted a crowd. Among the gathering onlookers was Trapspringer Furrfoot, who recognized his errant nephew at once.

"Tasslehoff!" he shouted, pushing his way to the front of the throng. "Is that you, you young delinquent? What on Krynn are you doing in Gelfigburg, when you're supposed to be in Kendermore getting married?"

"Uncle Trapspringer!" his nephew cried in surprise. Despite his current danger, the kender couldn't help but smile at the sight of his favorite uncle. "I didn't expect to see *you* here. Actually, I didn't expect to be here myself, wherever here is. Say, I'm sorry about your having to go to prison on my account."

"You've got some explaining to do, young kender," Trapspringer said sternly, shaking an accusing finger at his nephew. He paused and frowned at Tasslehoff's prone half-form. "Stand up when I'm speaking to you!"

Tasslehoff gritted his teeth against another tug. "I can't, Uncle. And I can't explain it all now," he grunted, "but I seem to be stuck in this portal. It would help me immeasurably if you would pull me through."

"What kind of trouble have you gotten yourself into this time? Always the one to find trouble, weren't you?" Trapspringer clucked his tongue, then chuckled.

Denzil gave Tasslehoff's legs yet another pull, forcing Tas to snarl impatiently, *"Not now,* Uncle!"

Trapspringer looked momentarily befuddled. "Yes, well, I suppose you're right. All of Kendermore has been searching for you these two months past, and they'd hang me if I let you slip through my hands now. Grab on, everyone!" he hollered.

Dozens of kender trudged forward, wrapping their hands and arms around Tas's limbs and torso, around each other, and around other, presumably immobile, features of the landscape. Soon, at least a dozen kender were pulling, straining, and sweating against some portion of Tas's upper body.

* * * * *

Denzil propped both feet against the bookcases on either side of the portal. He looped his belt around Tasslehoff's ankles and encircled his own wrist four times with the remaining length of leather. Grasping his bound wrist with his free hand, he took a huge breath and used the strength of his braced legs to heave with all his might. The kender's body slipped back at least three inches.

"You're mine, kender," laughed Denzil, flexing his fingers in preparation for one last pull.

* * * * *

Suddenly, the air in Gelfigburg filled with flying bits and shards of hard candies and fine sugar and cinnamon dust. Sneezing, many of the kender pulling on Tasslehoff paused to rub their eyes and clear their vision.

Just then, a bright purple whirlwind appeared nearby on Gelfig's front lawn, twisting and writhing and tearing up great hunks of the carefully landscaped terrace. The kender watched in fascination as the storm tore apart their homes and whipped sharp, stinging particles of candy wreckage into their faces.

Just then Damaris emerged from Gelfig's house, munching on part of a sucker bush. "What's going on?" she demanded, licking her fingers with great enjoyment. Damaris was fitting right into Gelfigburg. She spotted Trapspringer at the wall, tugging on a pair of arms. "What are you doing with those arms?" Without waiting for an answer, she elbowed Harkul Gelfig out of the way and grabbed onto Trapspringer's waist. "Whatever you're doing, it looks like fun!"

"This is certainly shaping up into a busy day," Gelfig said, grunting as his stubby fingers closed around Damaris's tiny waist. "You got here just in time before you starved, girlie."

Then, with no warning but a loud "pop," Tasslehoff disappeared back through the portal. Along with him went his Uncle Trapspringer, Damaris Metwinger, Harkul Gelfig and the two other kender who'd witnessed Tasslehoff's arrival in Gelfigburg, and several other bystanders who had joined in the tug-of-war. Those left at the new front of the kender chain were pulled partway through the foggy curtain and left in much the same predicament as Tas.

* * * * *

Summoning all his considerable strength, Denzil straightened his back, bore down, and hauled on the leather belt attached to the kender. Muscles and veins stood out in his neck, and beads of sweat broke out and ran down his forehead and temples. Gods, but this kender was surprisingly strong! thought the half-orc. He'd obviously underestimated him, and the kender, in fact, seemed to be getting stronger still.

"There you are!"

Denzil nearly lost his grip in surprise. Struggling to look over his shoulder, he saw Vinsint the ogre from below stomping toward him.

"You're not going to get away this time!" Vinsint crowed, looping one of his long arms around Denzil's bent waist.

"Ooofff!"

Vinsint gave a great yank that almost cut the half-orc in two.

Abruptly and without warning, the resistance on the strap tied to the kender disappeared. Denzil tumbled heels-over-head across the floor, bowling over the surprised ogre. The half-orc slammed into the hard, unyielding desk. In a heartbeat, both Denzil and Vinsint were stampeded by an enormous, wriggling weight.

Forcing his eyes open again, Denzil saw that the room, as if by magic, was filling with stumbling, obese kender. They tumbled forward and crashed into the walls and bookcases, into the desk and Denzil and Vinsint. And more were pouring through the portal every second!

* * * * *

"A way out! We've found a way out!"

The cry rose from every kender's throat moments after Tasslehoff and Trapspringer slid back through the portal. Slipping over lemon drops, they began diving headlong into the swirling mist, dragging friends and loved ones along.

As they fled, the purple cyclone grew in intensity. The eddies at its top coalesced and became forms, which gradually took on the shape of a woman's face, severe but beautiful. The Dark Queen's cruel, dark eyes surveyed the scene of panic and destruction, but fixed on the gate. The last kender had barely fled into it when the cyclone gathered up its tails, coiled almost like a spring, and streaked into the doorway between dimensions.

Chapter 23

"We're free! We're free!" squealed the multitude of kender, rampaging through the opened portal and flooding into the chamber at the top of the ruined Tower of High Sorcery. In minutes, the room was nearly bursting with obese refugees from Harkul Gelfig's candy dimension.

The ogre stood with his long arms crossed expectantly as he surveyed the tiny room. "So this is where you went," he growled at Tasslehoff, who was pushed up against the desk at the far side of the room, next to his uncle. "And who are all these other kender?" he demanded. He peered closely at Trapspringer. "Wait a minute, I remember you! Weren't you here several days ago? I was very cross with you when I found you'd run away." He looked disparagingly at Damaris and Phineas. "I see Nosy and Nutsy are still with you."

Damaris's chin rose haughtily, and Phineas scowled. Vinsint was abruptly swept away by the sea of kender, many of whom wanted to get reacquainted, having been helped through the grove by him over the years.

Tasslehoff turned to Trapspringer, his face a puzzled mask. "I'd like to know where these kender came from myself," he said. "Especially you, Uncle."

"And hello to you, too, Nephew. You're looking well!" the elder Furrfoot exclaimed, clasping Tasslehoff to him in an embrace.

After returning the hug, Tasslehoff drew back. "Uncle Trapspringer, what *are* you doing here at the Tower of High Sorcery? Is this where you're being held prisoner? I'm supposed to marry some silly little minx, but I'll do it happily if it means you'll be set free."

"Uh, Tasslehoff," Trapspringer interrupted, coughing uncomfortably as Damaris elbowed her way through the crowd to them, "I'd like you to meet your birthmate. Damaris Metwinger, this is Tasslehoff Burrfoot."

The surprises were mounting up so fast that Tasslehoff didn't notice Damaris's angry glare. "Pleased to meet you," he said, extending his hand.

The blonde kender pushed him away angrily. "Silly little minx, eh? I wouldn't marry you if you were the last man on Krynn!" With that, she stormed off and was swallowed up by the swirling mass of flesh filling the room.

Tasslehoff's eyebrows arched. "She's pretty enough, but a bit hot-tempered, isn't she? What is she doing here, anyway? Is she being held prisoner, too?"

Trapspringer quickly recounted the events of the last several weeks, drawing Phineas from the teeming crowd for an introduction. The human, who had been trying to make his way to the stairs, eyed Tasslehoff from top to bottom. "So you're the one we've all been chasing after," he grunted. "Well, I'm glad I lived long enough to finally meet you, even if there wasn't any payoff." Phineas abruptly began elbowing his way toward the stairs, leaving Tas to puzzle over his strange comments.

"Now, Nephew," Trapspringer said, "why don't you tell me why you're here, instead of in Kendermore?"

The question reminded Tasslehoff of Denzil, and the kender hastily scanned the room for the half-orc. Denzil stood less than three feet from the mist-shrouded portal, hemmed in by milling kender, his back pressed against the wall. Tasslehoff could see from the look in Denzil's eyes that the half-orc was still trying to make sense of everything that had happened. Tasslehoff was about to warn his uncle about the assassin when one of the large kender silenced the chattering in the room with a piercing whistle.

"Who's got the treasure box?" boomed the speaker, none other than Harkul Gelfig. "I was pulled through that tunnel so fast I wasn't able to retrieve it." He looked around expectantly at the tightly packed throng. All movement stopped. "No one?" the kender squealed. "Everyone just marched out and left such a valuable box behind?" An embarrassed silence enveloped the room.

Hearing the word "treasure" seemed to have a rallying effect on Denzil. He snapped out of his stunned fog. At last, the object of his hunt was within his reach. Never one to hesitate, the half-orc pushed and punched his way through the kender until he stood before the pulsing, multicolored portal. Casting one more look around the room, he stepped into the purple and green clouds that marked the gateway and disappeared.

"Say, is he going back to get the box?" asked one of the kender in the crowd. "Who is he, anyway?"

Before Tasslehoff could answer either question, a terrific gust of wind blasted out of the portal, sending the kender smashing into each other in an even more tightly packed clump on the far side of the chamber.

Once again, purple mist boiled out of the glowing rectangle on the wall. But the mist darkened and grew sinister, and felt cold to the touch. The kender crowded away from it where they could and cringed where they could not. Black lightning streaked through the void, accompanied by vague sounds that resembled nothing so much as shrieks and groans of torment. Everything in the room was charged with electricity. The long strands of hair from Tasslehoff's topknot stood out from each other, and everyone was outlined with a ghostly yellow glow. Then lightning crackled across the compartment and struck the far wall, but it did not dissipate. The bolt hung in midair, and was joined by another, and another, all splitting and writhing in a dance of impossible symmetries.

Suddenly, with a great gust of hot wind, gobs of the purple mist pulled together and took shape, forming themselves into the likeness of a human visage, a woman's face. Its complexion was white, the lips thin and gray. The sharply ridged nose and harsh cheekbones gave the face a disturbing severity. The eyes were yellow and cold, and darted from person to person like a snake's tongue beneath razor-thin brows.

The head weaved from side to side and bobbed slightly atop the vortex of purple mist that trailed back to the portal. Webs of lightning played around it and enclosed it.

"Great Reorx!" whispered Trapspringer. "What is that?"

The face continued hovering, but its tail of purple-and-green-streaked mist reeled out of the wall as if drawn by some magical vacuum. The mist piled up in great heaps beneath the head, twitching and flicking like the tail of some nightmarish reptile. The mounds of mist reeked of sulfur and ammonia.

"I'm not sure," Tasslehoff whispered slowly to his uncle, unable to remove his eyes from the horror growing in front of him. He covered his nose with his sleeve, then added, "It's almost beginning to look like the dragon I rode back at Rosloviggen."

"You rode a dragon?" asked Trapspringer, suddenly heedless of the horror confronting him. "Good show! That's more impressive than even some of my adventures. Promise to tell me all about it?"

"Now is not a good time to discuss this," sang Phineas, his voice and eyes crowded with fear. "I suggest we run before this thing, whatever it may be, completes its genesis." Acting on his own suggestion, Phineas tried forcing his way through the mass of kender, but they were all far heavier than he and transfixed by the sight developing before them.

Then from behind him, Tas heard a loud "ping!" followed by the sound of cracking wood. "I found the lever again!" cried Damaris, poking her head up from behind the desk. "It wasn't made very well, either," she said critically. "I think I may have broken it," she confessed, holding up the fractured end of a thin, smooth piece of wood.

A strangled cry erupted from the creature in the mist. The woman's face turned stormy and thrashed about as if in pain. Suddenly the face disappeared and was replaced by five dragon heads on a single neck, snarling and spitting fire. But the heads dissipated into mist as quickly as they had formed, and the mist was sucked back through the glowing passage from which it had poured. Lightning bolts unweaved themselves and glowing outlines disappeared. The portal faded until the outlines of the wall bricks were visible again, and finally the room looked as if nothing had happened. Even the dust and cobwebs on the blank section of wall were undisturbed.

Still standing behind the desk, Damaris blushed furiously. "Oh, dear, did I do that?" she squeaked.

* * * * *

Abruptly dragged back to the Abyss, the Dark Queen's fury surpassed anything she had felt in the three and a half centuries since the Cataclysm.

She had been so close!

Centuries of banishment could have ended this day. Takhisis's throne flamed bright crimson, its internal fires fanned by her hatred. Columns split and walls cracked open as she vented her anger. A new layer of rubble was added to her throne room as a reminder of yet another frustrated attempt to return to the world she held in such contempt.

She had been there!

And then a kender who did not even know what it was doing had closed the gate! All five of her dragon heads spat flames and acid and ice. Her domain withstood the onslaught only because she willed it so. Without her will, it would crumble to dust and ash.

Then, all ten of the Dark Queen's leathery eyelids drooped in an expression of pure evil. She was struck with an idea. She was foiled this day, but she could still exact revenge. Those kender—better yet, all kender— would suffer for slamming the door in her face. Though she could not physically appear on the Prime Material Plane, she was not powerless there. Plagues were beyond her control, but she held considerable influence over Nuitari, the moon that could be seen only by creatures aligned with evil. Thus she could affect Krynn's weather. . . .

* * * * *

"I'd say that about hangs it," puffed Harkul Gelfig, out of breath from the exertion of kneeling in the small space behind the desk, his massive stomach doubled and tripled over. "You broke it, all right, girlie." He glared at Damaris. "Now I can't get back to retrieve my treasure box unless we fix this lever."

Damaris's face was stormy, her hands were on her hips. "Don't bother thanking me for driving away only the most evil, awful, icky-looking frightosaurus that was materializing right here. Or for rescuing everyone from Garfigtown—"

"Gelfigburg!"

"Whatever." Seeing Tasslehoff's and Trapspringer's questioning looks over her last claim, Damaris added humbly, "Of course, Burrfoot helped a little. However, let me point out that had I not run off to the Ruins to escape marriage, Trapspringer would not have been here to recognize his nephew when he popped through the dimensional curtain, and *you*—" she poked Harkul's massive chest "—wouldn't have found a way to keep the portal open." Damaris finished her tirade out of breath but with her nose held high.

"I'd like to point out that it was *my* idea to come looking for Damaris in the first place," Phineas sniffed. His jacket was stained with chocolate and candied cherry juice, his hair still standing on end from its brush with static electricity.

"They're both right," Trapspringer concluded, stepping between Damaris and Gelfig. "But there's an even bigger problem here. Tasslehoff's friend, that big, nasty-looking fellow, is trapped in Gelfigburg. With the lever broken, we can't activate the gate to get him back out. And frankly, after what just happened, I'm not sure it's a good idea to play around with this thing too much more."

But to Trapspringer's surprise, his nephew looked delighted. "Don't worry about that. His name is Denzil and he isn't my friend at all. He was going to kill me, in fact, or at least break all of my bones and then pull my arms off. He did kill a friend of mine, a dwarf named Gisella."

"But why?" Trapspringer asked.

Tasslehoff's face went blank, making his creaseless face look even younger. "I think it had something to do with a map you gave me before I left on my Wanderlust. Denzil believed there was a fabulous treasure here, and he thought the directions on my map would lead him to it."

"There isn't any treasure," scoffed Phineas, pointing at Gelfig. "This architect of obesity managed to squander it all making licorice roads and chocolate tulips."

"That depends on your perspective," Gelfig huffed. "Many would consider Gelfigburg a utopia."

But Phineas was already thinking about something else that Tasslehoff had mentioned. The human snapped his fingers and his face brightened in sudden understanding. "Denzil! I *knew* I recognized that man from somewhere! We're so smashed together in here, and he was on the other side of the room, so I couldn't get a really good look at him. That's why he disappeared so quickly from my office!"

"You're sounding unhinged again," remarked Damaris. "You're not making a bit of sense."

"But I am! That man—"

"He's a half-orc," Tas corrected him.

Phineas's eyebrows lifted and he nodded. "That would explain the snout. Anyway, minutes before you picked me up for our expedition out here," he said, addressing Trapspringer, "this oddball character—now I find out he's a half-orc—showed up in my office, bleeding like a stuck pig from a gash in his side." Phineas quickly related the rest of the story, including Denzil's sudden disappearance from his office.

"That also explains why I didn't find my half of the map where I'd left it. Denzil must have looked at it while he was recuperating after his stitches, and that's how he found out about the treasure. He obviously decided to track Tasslehoff down for his map with the directions."

Trapspringer was watching Phineas closely. "That's why you offered to find Damaris, too, isn't it? You wanted the treasure, just like this Denzil."

Phineas drew back. "Don't make me sound so evil! I didn't *kill* anyone over it—quite the opposite, since I was almost killed myself several times. And let me point out that I didn't get any treasure, either," he finished, wagging his finger in Trapspringer's face.

"Well, there's no point in lingering around here," Damaris pronounced abruptly. "Coming, Trapspringer?" she called, looking up demurely from under her lashes.

Trapspringer's head snapped up. The room was emptying quickly. Looking toward the door, he saw the last dozen or so of the kender squeezing through the narrow exit.

The elder kender's facial creases multiplied with a lovesick grin. "I'm right behind you," he sang, setting off for the stairs.

Hurrying after him, Tasslehoff touched his uncle's shoulder. "My fiancee may not think much of *me*, but she seems to like *you* well enough," he said ingenuously. "You'll have to tell me more about this place where Denzil is trapped. Made entirely of candy, you said? I hope it's all anice licorice. I *hate* anice licorice!"

I couldn't agree more, Phineas thought, following them out the door.

*　*　*　*　*

"Well, I'm sure you'll be wanting lunch," said Vinsint when they reached the bottom of the long staircase. Without waiting for a response, the ogre easily plowed a path through the dozens of stout kender in his small room and began pawing through crates of food. He looked up uneasily. "I'm not sure I have enough to feed the whole lot of you. My, you're all awfully large for kender, aren't you? You're all as round as balls." He shrugged his massive, muscled shoulders. "I'll just have to make do. We'll have a rousing pick-up sticks tournament afterward." The ogre began humming happily to himself.

Tasslehoff looked at the door to the tunnel that led outside. It was covered in chains.

"I'm not going to stay here one night," muttered Phineas under his breath.

"I have an idea," Tasslehoff announced, making his way to the ogre's side. He stopped the ogre momentarily with a hand on his thick arm. "Look, Vinsint, we appreciate your offer, but we really must be going. It's nothing personal, mind you, but many of us have not been home to Kendermore in some time."

Tasslehoff paused and took a deep breath. "Which brings me to my next point. Why don't you come with us? You say you get really lonely here. Kendermore is a big, exciting place, and things never get dull there!" He nudged the ogre. "What do you say?"

"Oh, I could never go to a big city like Kendermore," Vinsint argued, shaking his head. From his tone, though, Tasslehoff could tell that the ogre was at least mildly intrigued. "I wouldn't fit in there any better than I did in my own home city of Ogrebond."

"Don't be silly!" Tasslehoff laughed. "Kendermore isn't like Ogrebond. We're much more, uh, democratic. Why, we even had a gynosphinx as mayor once. Even you could be the mayor someday!"

Vinsint smiled, showing his crooked, missing teeth. "Mayor? You really think so? I've always thought I'd make a good politician. . . ."

Trapspringer stepped up. "I'm certain you would," he said, "though I understand that the position is filled at the moment," he added, catching the eye of Mayor Metwinger's daughter. "Come on along, Vinsint. What have you to lose? If you don't like it, you can always come back here."

Vinsint fidgeted with barely contained excitement. "I have been feeling a little bored lately. . . . But who is going to help kender through the grove?"

A twinkle came to Traspringer's eyes as he remembered the grove, and he gave the blond kender a sidelong glance. "You know, the grove's enchantment can have some positive effects, too," he said wistfully. "In any event, kender will have an interesting time there, which is really all they seek."

The ogre bit his lip. "OK, I'll do it!" Vinsint shuffled over to the chains on the door and yanked them down without removing their locks. "I won't be needing these anymore." The locks fell heavily to the floor, and Vinsint swung the door wide. "Come on! I know a tunnel that will deposit us on the other side of the grove!" The ogre bounded through the door in excitement.

Fast on his heels, Tasslehoff, Trapspringer, Damaris, and Phineas made sure they got to the tunnel before the other, slower-moving kender. Ahead of them, Vinsint took a right turn and waited for them, waving them on. In minutes, they saw dim light at the end of the tunnel.

It was still morning when they emerged from Vinsint's secret passage, covered by thick branches at the edge of the Ruins. They were not prepared for what they saw.

The land was engulfed by a thunder and wind storm the likes of which none of them had ever seen. Stout trees bent in the wind. Stone blocks could be heard tumbling and crashing even above the roar of the wind. Thunderclaps cut through the heavy air. And though the air held the moist, earthy scent of rain, none fell from the sky.

It was the sky that was the most alarming of all. Daytime looked almost like night, the angry black and purple sky cut by jagged streaks of wicked white lightning. The sun was an undistinguished, dull glow straight overhead.

Harkul Gelfig, chocolatier who founded and lived in the time-warped Gelfigburg for more than three-hundred years, pushed past them as he emerged from the tunnel. His bulky form was tossed about by the wind, so he clung to the trunk of a stout tree. "My, they sure let this place fall into disrepair," he said, clicking his tongue in dismay as he surveyed the nearby ruined buildings. "In my time, this was a beautiful city, which sprang up around the Tower of High Sorcery. Goodness, the weather certainly is fierce, isn't it? Is this usual?

"No," said Tasslehoff, not knowing quite what to make of the strange weather, "this is most certainly *not* usual." Tas turned into the wind and scrunched up his face.

Trapspringer peered around in the dim light and swirling dust. "We left a couple of ponies near here before we entered the grove. I think they're just a ways to the left." Head bowed, he set off, with Damaris, Tasslehoff, and Vinsint following behind.

Phineas gaped after them, then shouted, "Surely you don't intend to travel in this! Let's just wait it out in Vinsint's tunnel."

Tasslehoff looked back over his shoulder and hollered, without stopping, "Why? It's just wind. I think it's kind of fun trying to stay on your feet in it."

"You're crazy! You'll be blown to Kendermore!"

Tas shrugged. "That would sure speed things up. If you're afraid, though, stay here. There's Vinsint's larder and plenty of company. We'll see you later in Kendermore."

"Fine! That's what I'll do," yelled Phineas to no one in particular, as Tas was beyond earshot in the howling wind. The human turned back toward the tunnel exit. He was confronted by a dozen or more very wide, very disoriented kender, deep in a discussion about the merits of mushroom husbandry on a hypothetical city made of small boats lashed together.

Several minutes later, Phineas caught up with Tasslehoff and the other three just as they were preparing the ponies to leave. Grumbling to himself, Phineas got on his dreaded pony behind Tasslehoff.

The group struggled through the wind without speaking, since words were lost in the storm anyway. Travel was slightly easier in the occasional forests, since the trees provided some protection. But the expanses of open fields, crops tearing from the ground around them, taxed their endurance beyond their expectations.

They had traveled about halfway back to Kendermore when they decided to break for the day on a small, clear, grassy rise with a view of Kendermore, still almost ten miles to the west. Sliding off the ponies to the ground to rest and enjoy the first glimpse of the view, Tasslehoff, Trapspringer, Damaris, and Phineas each jerked up again when Vinsint, pointing to the city, cried, "Fire!"

Kendermore was burning.

Chapter 24

Tasslehoff's party reached the edge of Kendermore before dawn, Damaris and Trapspringer on one pony, Tas and Phineas on another. Vinsint, with his long, powerful legs, easily loped along beside them through the dark fields and wind-blown forests surrounding the burning city.

No smoke hung over the city; the howling wind scattered it before it could rise above the peaked roofs. Only the light from the flames, reflected off the mist and fog, gave away the fact that Kendermore was ablaze. The dull orange halo flickered, rose, and fell.

"It's like an aurora," mumbled Trapspringer.

"A what?" Damaris asked.

"An aurora—strange lights in the sky. You have to

travel south a good distance to see the effect."

The five companions stared at the glowing sky, entranced, until Tasslehoff jolted them back to the present.

"I'm sure there are a lot of people who need help. Let's find out what's happening."

As they moved up the main road toward the city, they passed kender fleeing into the countryside. Flames danced above the cityscape on the distant west side, where the worst fire appeared to be raging. Here on the east side, they saw evidence of small spot fires: blackened storefronts and homes, charred trees, flame-swept grass. A few blazes still burned in isolated spots, but small groups of kender fought them with water, dirt, brooms, and blankets.

A short distance inside the city, Tasslehoff spotted a kender dressed in a mackintosh, galoshes, and a broad-brimmed rain hat. He was caught up in securing his ornate windows and door of polished wood against the raging wind by nailing sheets of canvas across them. But each time he got a sheet almost attached, a gust of wind tore it off again.

"Look's like you could use a few more hands," shouted Tas. With their heads bowed against the wind and biting rain, he, Vinsint, and Trapspringer pushed their way through the storm to help the beleaguered kender.

While stretching one corner of a canvas sheet across a window opening, Tas asked, "Where are all the people?"

The homeowner plucked another nail from between his lips. "Fled, mostly. Out that way, where you came in. Or fortifying and getting ready to ride it out, like me. This thing looks unstoppable, though. There aren't many of us left."

Phineas shook his head. "There'll be even fewer if you think you can survive a city-wide conflagration just by tacking some wet leather over your windows. Abandoning the town is your only option, and I suggest doing so right now!"

"No!" shouted Tas, setting his chin stubbornly. "Kendermore is my home! I didn't travel all the way across Ansalon just to see it burn down. There has to be some way to stop this thing. Haven't any of you ever seen a real fire-fighting team at work?"

Glancing uneasily at the others, Vinsint raised his hand, then looked at Tas expectantly. Tasslehoff, who had never seen this sort of behavior before—he was accustomed to kender, who simply shouted their suggestions at the tops of their lungs—finally realized that Vinsint was awaiting some sort of signal before speaking. He shrugged and said, "Go ahead, Vinsint."

The ogre cleared his throat and, with one more nervous glance at his fellows, explained fire-fighting as he understood it. "When I was still living in the Ogrelands, my tribe used to raid the neighboring human settlements. Sometimes, places we attacked caught fire. By accident. You know how those things happen." Vinsint shifted his weight uncomfortably.

"Anyway, sometimes as we were leaving, we would stop on a hill and watch the humans try to put the fires out. They'd form lines to a stream or a well and then pass buckets of water from hand to hand and throw them on the fire. That usually didn't work very well on a really big fire, so some of the places that caught fire a lot built big barrels in the middle of the town and kept them full of water. Then when a fire broke out, they could get water from the barrel and not have to pass it so far, or they could even just chop a hole in the barrel and let the water flood through the streets to put out all the really hot embers on the ground.

"Of course, if the fire did go out, then my cousins would shoot some burning arrows into the town to start it all up again. They thought that kind of stuff was pretty funny."

"Nice bunch," muttered Damaris.

"Yes, well, you don't see me with them now, do you?" Vinsint grunted. "I knew somebody was going to make a nasty remark." The bristles on the back of his neck stood up like a bootbrush.

Tas jumped in, trying to calm the ruffled ogre. "That's OK, Vinsint. We trust you. And that story gives me an idea. Uncle Trapspringer, do the water towers still have water in them?" Tasslehoff squinted against the smoke and spotted several of the tall, bucket-shaped devices above the city.

"They sure do," he replied. "I went swimming in one just the other day."

"Good! Lead the way to City Hall."

The group wound its way through the twisting streets, with Trapspringer in the lead, to City Hall. The streets were clogged with kender trying to get out of the city, into the city, to their homes, to their shops, to the city's wells with empty buckets, and to the fire with full buckets. Kender were racing in every direction with pails, washtubs, pitchers, battering rams, urns, ladders, bowls, stuffed animals, chamberpots, and cupped hands. Others were pushing carts or pulling wagons loaded with their own or other people's belongings. There was no panic—no one seemed frightened at all, thought Phineas. But there was pandemonium on an unimaginable scale.

Tasslehoff chose as his goal City Hall because he knew that it was, approximately, in the center of the city. The building was a very valuable symbol to Kendermore's democratic citizens. It was a good place to stop the fire from spreading to the east side of the city. Tas didn't recognize any of the civic landmarks on the way to City Hall. He'd been gone only a few years, yet the town seemed completely changed. Everything's different—it feels like home, he thought.

The howling of the wind suddenly dropped away to nothing as they rounded a corner into a very small square. Tas looked up at a four-story building. Dark support timbers crisscrossed its face and strengthened the whitewashed wood and stucco walls. The familiar, gaping hole on the second floor showed Tas that not everything had changed in his absence.

Looking at it, everyone knew that the one-hundred-year-old building would burn like dry tinder.

How could they stop the fires from raging?

As Tas pondered that question, two things happened. First, a straw-haired human with his head bowed down strode out of City Hall.

Second, Tas realized that it was not just the sound of the wind that had died away, but the wind itself. The air in the square was calm. But the noise of the wind was replaced by a different sound; a distant rumbling that reminded Tas of the approach of an avalanche. He had no idea what an avalanche sounded like, really, but he had a good imagination.

Tasslehoff watched the figure hurry out the big door in the front of City Hall and head down the street, directly toward the kender and his companions. Apparently sensing their presence in the street ahead of him, the man looked up.

"Woodrow!" Tasslehoff cried, flinging himself at the startled human.

The straw-haired young man's face exploded into a smile. "Tasslehoff Burrfoot! I thought I'd never see you again!" Woodrow picked up the kender and spun him around, both laughing joyously.

"How did you know to find me here?" Tasslehoff asked, shouting to be heard above the avalanche.

"After Denzil knocked me out and kidnapped you, I didn't know what to do. I had no idea where he took you or even which direction he would go in. No one in Port Balifor would even listen to me.

"But I knew that Kendermore's council was waiting for you and holding your uncle. I figured maybe the council had sent Denzil to take over for Gisella, so I came here. But after four hours with that council," he continued, slapping the side of his head with his palm, "all I learned was that they didn't know where you were, either, and that you didn't need to come back anymore because your fiancee had run away.

"And then this storm hit the city," Woodrow said. "Wind, rain, lightning everywhere—worse than the storm that sank our boat. The lightning started fires all over the city. I hear it's a real inferno west of here. We'd better get out of the city while we can!"

"What's the hurry?" Tas exclaimed. Pushing his uncle forward, he announced, "Uncle Trapspringer Furrfoot, meet my friend Woodrow Ath-Banard."

Trapspringer thrust out his hand. "So you're the fellow my nephew's been talking about since we left the Ruins. Glad to meet you." Abruptly Damaris coughed. "Oh, yes," Trapspringer said, "this is Tasslehoff's birthmate, Damaris Metwinger—" he extended his gesture to Phineas and Vinsint "—and these are my friends, Phineas Curick and, uh, Vinsint—the ogre." Woodrow looked questioningly toward Tasslehoff.

"I'll explain it all to you later," Tas assured him.

Woodrow turned to Damaris. "Metwinger—isn't that the mayor's name?"

"Yes, it is," Damaris beamed. "He's my father." Her eyes narrowed suddenly and glared at Tasslehoff. "And I am no longer *his* birthmate," she scoffed. "I've divorced him, or disowned him, or disavowed him, or whatever it is you do to someone you were going to marry before you marry him. I've un-fianced him."

"I hate to break up all these happy hellos," Phineas said loudly, "but the town is still burning down."

Tasslehoff inclined his ear to the west. "What I want to know is, what's that weird noise I'm hearing? And what's happened to the wind all of a sudden?"

Everyone paused for a moment and listened. The sky to the west was a bright orange and yellow palette. Red shadows flickered and danced on the sides of nearby buildings. In the calm air, a massive column of twisting, black smoke climbed upward to blot out the gray dawn.

After a moment's thought, Phineas said, "The fire must be a real cooker to roar like that. What's happened to the wind is anybody's guess."

"Too late," Vinsint boomed. "Look!"

They followed his pointing finger to the north of City Hall. Sweeping toward them was a dark, spinning cloud, its pointed tail snapping back and forth like a whip. Everywhere the tail touched ground, buildings exploded or were shredded like straw, trees were ripped from the earth, boulders flew into the air and hung suspended, then crashed down like the hammer of Reorx.

"Get down, in the gutter!" Tasslehoff shouted, pushing Woodrow and Phineas to the ground before diving between them himself. He had seen a cyclone once before, in Neraka, where the people knew that the safest place to be in such a situation was huddled in low, sheltered ground. Trapspringer, Damaris, Vinsint, and even the multitude of kender scurrying about in the street followed suit, diving into the mud and muck.

The tornado twisted and jigged toward them. Tas felt himself being lifted off the ground. Gobs of muddy water swirled around him, then suddenly he was thrown back to the gutter. Quickly he scraped the mud from his eyes and saw the tornado veering to the west of City Hall. It tore a swath around the building and pelted the walls with lumber, rocks, and pieces of furniture. The smashing of stained glass and wood and copper echoed in the streets, mingling with the incongruous squeals of kender. In spite of mortal danger, a tornado was something that happened once in a lifetime and these kender were as thrilled as if Paladine himself had dropped in for a visit.

In the space of a minute, the tornado had passed through the area and was on its way toward the edge of the city. Laughing with glee, Tasslehoff rolled onto his back. "What a ride!" he yelled. Trapspringer and Damaris were equally giddy, flushed from toes to topknot.

"Are you all crazy?" Phineas shrieked. "Every one of us could have been killed, turned inside out by that thing, and you're laughing as if it was nothing more than a pillow fight!" Phineas climbed to his feet and opened his mouth to say more, but was suddenly dumbstruck by the kenders' attitudes. He spun back and forth in a half-circle, working his jaw and waving his hands, but no words came out. Finally he strode to a nearby building and slumped to the ground, his back against the wall.

Tasslehoff, meanwhile, had stopped laughing. Frantically he walked the street where Woodrow had fallen. There was no sign of the human! "Woodrow!" he cried. "Woodrow is gone!"

Vinsint, Damaris, and Trapspringer sat up, blinking, and looked around. Even Phineas lifted his head and scanned the road. But there was no sign the young man had ever been there.

Tasslehoff shouted Woodrow's name, then shouted it again. The only answer was the creaking and groaning of weakened timbers, the roar of the fires, and the rising howl of the returning wind. But then, Tasslehoff heard his name. He looked around, yet saw nothing. When he heard it again, he looked over and saw Woodrow around the corner, looking to the west.

Tasslehoff sprinted to his side. "Woodrow, I thought you'd been swept up by the tornado!" Tas exclaimed, punching his arm in mock anger. "I was really worried!"

Woodrow knew that was quite a statement for a kender. "I'm sorry, Mr. Burrfoot, but I wanted to find out how far the fire had gotten, so I jumped up before everyone else, after the twister. I really hate to upset anyone further, but our troubles aren't over yet," he announced. By now, everyone could see flames licking at the buildings immediately to the west of City Hall and across the tornado's path. "We've got to move now."

"We can't just abandon the city to the fire!" Damaris cried.

"We can't stop those flames," said Phineas, looking uneasily at the approaching inferno.

Everyone, including the other kender in the square, turned to the east. But they stopped when a voice commanded, "No, we're staying here."

All eyes turned toward Tasslehoff.

The young kender felt a strange sense of self-consciousness. He shifted his weight from foot to foot. Swallowing hard, he tasted only soot. But everyone was waiting to hear what he had to say next.

"I think we can stop the fire and save at least part of the city. Vinsint's story about fire-fighting gave me an idea, and the tornado showed me how to make it happen. But we're all going to have to work together"—a murmur of resistance passed through the crowd of kender—"and we're going to have to get a lot more help."

A kender wearing a long, blue, fur-trimmed robe with lots of pockets stepped forward from the crowd. As he drew a deep breath in preparation for a speech, Damaris squealed "Daddy!" and rushed forward, throwing her arms around the man's neck. There was a brief burst of applause from the crowd while he readjusted his robe, planted a peck on Damaris's cheek, and cleared his throat nervously.

"People of Kendermore," he intoned, "as your mayor, I think it behooves us to listen to what this young wanderer has to say, no matter how shabbily he treated my daughter. If he thinks he has a plan, let's hear it. And if it turns out he doesn't have a plan, we can always skedaddle afterward. After all, 'there's no danger so pressing that it couldn't be worse', as they say." With that, he turned to Tas and folded his arms.

No sooner had Tasslehoff outlined his plan than the tiny assembly fell to putting it into effect. Several crates were piled up for Tas to stand on so he could oversee progress and be heard by everyone.

"Uncle Trapspringer and Damaris and Mayor Metwinger," he ordered, "go round up more help. We can't do this with two dozen people.

"Woodrow and Vinsint, take two-thirds of the kender already assembled and start pushing all that debris from the tornado's wake up against those buildings on the far side.

"Is there anybody here who knows lumber?" A dozen fingers pointed to a kender in the crowd who was staring intently at Tasslehoff. "Are you a carpenter?" asked Tas.

The kender stared.

"Do you run a sawmill?"

No response.

"What's the matter with him?"

A small girl stretched up and plucked a wad of paraffin from the older kender's ear. "He wants to know if you're a carpenter or a woodcutter, Papa," she chimed.

The kender beamed. "Both," he replied. Then he recovered the paraffin from the girl and stuffed it back into his ear.

Tas cupped his hands around his mouth and shouted, "Then you go with Phineas and build the flumes!" Again, the kender smiled at him blankly. Tas motioned to the girl, who removed the paraffin once again.

"He wants you to go with this man and build some flumes," she told him.

"Fine," responded the kender, grinning. "I'll help all I can." As he turned to join Phineas, his face lit up even more.

"Doctor Ears!" he cried. Phineas winced. "It's me, Semus Sawyer! I've been following your prescription exactly, and it's miraculous. Everytime I take out these plugs, my hearing improves a thousandfold!"

A murmur of sudden recognition passed through the crowd. Phineas took a short step backward as kender closed in on all sides, arms outstretched. Before he could break free, they had closed in, and dozens of hands were pummeling and yanking at him, pushing him this way and that, and—hoisting him on their shoulders? Phineas's heart nearly thumped out his mouth before he realized that these kender were happy to see him, were actually overjoyed to recognize their beloved doctor!

"Take him to the lumberyard! Build flumes!" Tas shouted over the cheering. "And lift him up higher! His toes are dragging on the ground!"

Soon more kender were streaming into the square, shepherded by Trapspringer and the Metwingers. Leaving several behind to direct latecomers, Tas led them some distance up the tornado's path, then turned off toward the water tower.

Kendermore's three water towers were the products of a civic project carried out four years earlier. The mayor and city council at that time decided that if the town had water towers, life would be much easier for people who had to make numerous trips to the city's wells every day. Instead of drawing water up, they could simply let it run down.

Unfortunately, the towers' designer neglected to put a spout of any sort on the towers and, even less fortunately, this defect was not discovered until the newly appointed water tower replenishment crews had spent several weeks filling the towers. At that point, the only possible way to repair the deficiency was to chop a hole in the tower bottoms, letting all that water drain out, and then afterwards, to add the spouts. The prospect of seeing several weeks' work gush away to make up for someone else's goof so infuriated the water tower crews that they threatened to resign.

This gross mismanagement pushed public opinion about the project to such a low point that it was clear that even if the spouts were added, no one would apply for the certain-to-be-vacated spots on the water tower replenishment crews. In what was perhaps the only clear-sighted decision of the entire affair, the council decided that empty towers with spouts were no more useful than full towers without spouts, and voted to maintain the status quo. Thus, for the last four years, the water towers remained full but spoutless.

By the time the flumes arrived, well over a thousand kender stood assembled under the largest of the three water towers. Flames raced along the debris and threatened to leap across to City Hall and the largely intact portion of the city that remained on the other side.

Tasslehoff had climbed to the top of the tower, where he could see everything and everyone could see him. After surveying the various stations and satisfying himself that everything was ready, he shouted, "Vinsint! You're the biggest and strongest! You be at the base of the pyramid, right under me! Everyone else, pile up on Vinsint!"

Hundreds of kender of all ages rushed forward, scrambling up over the ogre and each other. Four kender wide at the base and three rows of kender high, with the top row holding Semus's flumes overhead, they formed a living aqueduct that stretched from the water tower, eighty yards to what had been nicknamed "Tornado Alley." Trapspringer, who was part of the very end of the aqueduct, felt blasts of heat curling the hairs on his arms and eyebrows.

With the aqueduct complete, Semus scaled the water tower, axe in hand, and began chopping a hole in the side of the enormous, wooden tank. Seconds ticked by, running into minutes. Flames roared along the debris wall, singeing Trapspringer's tunic and scorching the sides of buildings across Tornado Alley. Semus's axe, which initially had torn fist-sized chunks of wood from the water tank, now bounced ineffectually away from the rubbery, water-soaked inner layers.

The kender beneath Trapspringer fainted from the heat, sending the front edge of the aqueduct tumbling to the ground. As the flames licked their ankles, the next file struggled heroically to hold up the flume. Tasslehoff, still atop the water tower, cupped his hands around his mouth and shouted at the top of his lungs the only thing that came to mind: the sea chanty that had worked so well with the gully dwarves.

Come all you young fellows who live by the sea,
Kiss a fair maiden and then follow me.
Hoist up the sail and the anchor aweigh,
And run with the wind out through Balifor Bay.

One by one, and then by tens, and then by hundreds,

the kender picked up the song. A thin stream of water trickled across Semus's axe. Another blow started it flowing, and the third created a gush that thundered down the flume. The kender supporting the flume swayed and staggered, but stayed on their feet, and they kept singing.

As the water poured off the end of the flume, enormous clouds of steam jetted skyward and blanketed Tornado Alley. Along the length of the burning debris, flaming beams and glowing embers hissed and sputtered and were extinguished. The water ran in all directions until the wall of steam extended as far as Tasslehoff could see.

Fifteen minutes after the first trickle of water had appeared, the water tower was empty. Exhausted kender collapsed under their flumes into a squirming, snakelike pile, and crawled slowly out to lie panting on the smoking ground. Tasslehoff wiped his arm across his brow and it came away black with soot.

Slowly he picked his way down the water tower and went searching for his friends.

* * * * *

"Tasslehoff! Tasslehoff! Over here!"

Tas and Woodrow looked up from the frothy mugs of warm ale they were sharing outside the newly renamed Scorched Scorpion Inn to see Trapspringer and Damaris approaching, linked arm in arm, leaning into the wind.

"Tas, my favorite nephew! I've got wonderful news for you," bubbled Trapspringer. "Assuming you don't object, that is," he added with a mischievous wink to Damaris.

"Damaris Metwinger—your birthmate—and I propose to become engaged, and to be married as soon as possible. You're off the hook! Ha! What do you think of that?"

Tasslehoff stared at his uncle and his birthmate for a moment. Woodrow thought he detected a hint of sadness in the kender's expression, though it could have been exhaustion. Then Tas rose, threw his arms around both of them, and hollered, "Tap another barrel; my uncle's getting hitched!"

Chapter 25

The tornadoes and lightning slowly departed the region of Goodlund during the night, and the following day dawned bright and clear over Kendermore. Trapspringer Furrfoot and Damaris Metwinger were wed at noon in the chamber of the Kendermore Council. The bride's father, Mayor Merldon Metwinger, presided over the ceremony.

Damaris wore a butter-yellow dress that perfectly matched her soft hair and that was adorned with tiny seed pearls and creamy brown cat's-eye agates. Woven into the six braided strands of her topknot were lengths of gold-spun thread, and at the crown of the knot was an arrangement of the finest feathers ever sported by a bluebird. In her fine-boned hands was a bouquet of clover, crabgrass, and lavender bull thistles.

Trapspringer wore his finest cloak of black velvet, a sparkling, white tunic, and wine-colored pants. His head was bare, as were both the bride's and groom's feet, a kender symbol of the many roads that would be traveled (and shoes worn out) during a long and happy marriage.

Tasslehoff, dressed in clean, blue leggings and his usual vest and tunic, stood attendant for his uncle. In the pocket of his vest were two wide bands of shiny, polished silver. Under such short notice, Damaris was attended by a blushing Woodrow, who was wearing a new muslin shirt with properly long sleeves.

Smiling proudly, Mayor Metwinger straightened his purple mayoral robes and gulped in a big breath, preparing to ad-lib the traditionally long but unwritten kender marriage ceremony.

"Daddy," Damaris said, holding tightly to Trapspringer's hand, "could you give us the condensed version? We'd like to get on to the party at the Autumn Faire."

"That starts today, does it?" said the mayor, actually relieved. He was still having a bit of trouble, after his bump on the noggin, remembering anything longer than three or four sentences.

"So, will you marry her, and you marry him?"

"Yes!" they both cried at once.

"Done!" the mayor announced joyously. "Now let the celebration begin!"

* * * * *

Tasslehoff lay in the warm autumn sun, his back propped up against a tree on the grounds of the Palace. Moving the Autumn Faire to the relatively unscathed setting on the northeast side of the city was the population's only concession to the devastation visited upon Kendermore. But the unspoken kender motto, "There's always more where that came from," certainly applied to homes. Members of the city's Department of Housing had been out early with reams of parchment, planning Kendermore's "new look." "It'll be like getting a whole new city!" they all agreed happily. Unfortunately, so far not a one of them agreed with another's designs.

In the meantime, the rearrangement of buildings into rubble gave the city's inhabitants whole new places to explore.

Nearby, Tas could hear Phineas and Vinsint.

"With your muscles and my brains," Phineas was saying, "we could clean up as tour guides on the trail from Kendermore to the Tower of High Sorcery."

"I don't know," said Vinsint, rubbing his large, flat forehead.

"I'm telling you," wheedled Phineas, "this is a goldmine waiting to be harvested! I arrange the tours, and you take them to the Ruins and lead them safely through the grove. We collect enough money to retire in two, three years, tops!"

"How come it sounds like I'd do most of the work?"

"Are you kidding me?" squealed Phineas. "I'd be stuck doing the tedious stuff—making schedules, taking reservations, advertising, buying supplies—while you're out taking walks! But I'd be willing to do it for only a slightly higher percentage of the profits—say, eighty percent?"

"You would?" Vinsint asked, his voice edged with eagerness.

Just then, Woodrow sat down next to Tas on the green grass and handed him one of two cups of fresh-squeezed strawberry juice. The human looked out wistfully at the merchants' tents, the vegetable vendors, the small wedding party nearby at an open foodhall.

"I keep seeing Miss Hornslager here," he said softly. "She was hoping to get her melons to this faire before they went bad."

"I know. I miss her, too," said Tasslehoff. They were quiet for some time.

"What are you going to do now?" Tas asked finally, taking a long sip of the fresh berry juice.

Woodrow chewed on a thick blade of grass. "I've been thinking about that a lot since I lost you in Port Balifor," he said. "These last weeks have taught me a lot, but mainly that life is very short, at least for a human," he added seriously. "I want to have some fun, but I can do without the danger. I was thinking maybe I'd take over Miss Hornslager's import business. I pretty much got the hang of it watching her." He gave Tas a questioning glance. "What do you think?"

"That sounds like a great idea!" said Tas, clapping his hands.

Woodrow nibbled the grass pensively. "Someday I'll have to go back to Solamnia and make peace with my Uncle Gordon, though. Just not yet." With a toss of his blond head, he shook the gloomy thoughts away. "How about you? What are you going to do?

Tasslehoff plucked a full-blown dandelion and blew the seeds into the air. "I've been thinking about that myself. I haven't seen my parents in years—since I left on my Wanderlust, actually. I would have tried to find them here in Kendermore yesterday, but things got a little busy, what with the fire and the tornadoes and the wind."

Tasslehoff sighed, and an uncharacteristic look of concern crossed his face as he spoke. "Anyway, Uncle Trapspringer told me where my parents were living, so I went to find them and invite them to Trapspringer's wedding." The tiny creases in his face deepened. "Their house survived the fires and the tornadoes, but they weren't there. I asked some neighbors about them, but no one knew anything."

"They were probably out helping friends clean up," suggested Woodrow. "Or maybe they were among the kender who fled the city."

"Probably," Tasslehoff agreed reluctantly. But he didn't mention that the neighbors hadn't seen his parents in some time . . . strange, because they were a bit old for Wanderlust. Tas abruptly decided to hold his concerns at bay on such a happy occasion.

"Look!" he said, pointing to the wedding party clustered around Trapspringer and Damaris, who stood by a silversmith's booth. "I think the newlyweds are preparing to leave on their honeymoon. Let's go say good-bye." The two jumped up and hastened to rejoin the wedding party.

"—And so I bought it," Trapspringer was saying. "All we have to do is stretch it over both our wrists, say the magic words, and we'll go to the moon!"

"Oh, do you really think so?" Damaris breathed excitedly. "What a marvelous honeymoon that would be! Let's try it!"

With that, Trapspringer produced an inch-wide, etched silver band. Snapping it over his own wrist first, he stretched the right side out to enclose Damaris's own fine-boned one. "There!" he exclaimed in satisfaction. "That ought to do it, dearest. Good-bye, everyone!" Trapspringer's face became a mask of concentration as he tried to remember the magic words. "*Esla sivas gaboing!*"

"Good-bye, Uncle Trapspringer!" Tasslehoff sang happily. "I hope this trip to the moon works out better than the one with your first wife!"

Damaris's face fell into a stormy glare. "What first wiiiiiii—!" In a poof of smoke, Trapspringer and his second wife were gone.

"Oops," mumbled Tasslehoff, giggling behind his hand.

At dusk that evening, Tasslehoff sat sipping a mug of ale, contemplating the events of his life since leaving the Inn of the Last Home. Gazing at the moon, he thought fondly of Trapspringer and Damaris. Suddenly, his eyes narrowed and he squinted at the full, glowing orb. Could it be? Staring intently, a smile grew on his face. Tasslehoff was certain he saw two tiny shadows racing over the pocked surface—or was it three?

Preludes Trilogy

Darkness and Light
Paul Thompson and Tonya Carter

Darkness and Light tells of the time Sturm and Kitiara spent traveling together before the fated meeting at the Inn of the Last Home in *Chronicles*. Accepting a ride on a gnomish flying vessel, they end up on Lunitari during a war. Eventually escaping, the two separate over ethics.

Brothers Majere
Kevin Stein

Much to Raislin's irritation, Caramon accepts a job for both of them: They must solve the mystery of a village's missing cats. The search leads to murder, a thief who is not all that he appears, and a foe who is not what Caramon and Raistlin expect.

THE LONG-AWAITED SEQUEL TO THE MOONSHAE TRILOGY

Druidhome Trilogy
Douglas Niles

Prophet of Moonshae   Book One
Evil threatens the islands of Moonshae, where the people have forsaken their goddess, the Earthmother. Only the faith and courage of the daughter of the High King brings hope to the endangered land. Available March 1992.

The Coral Kingdom   Book Two
King Kendrick is held prisoner in the undersea city of the sahuagin. His daughter must secure help from the elves of Evermeet to save him during a confrontation in the dark depths of the Sea of Moonshae. Available October 1992.

The Druid Queen   Book Three
In this exciting conclusion, the forces of the Earthmother are finally united but face the greatest challenge for survival ever. Available Spring 1993.

Saga

Elven Nations Trilogy

FIRSTBORN
Paul B. Thompson and Tonya R. Carter

Sithel, the leader of the Silvanesti elves, struggles to maintain a united elven nation, while his twin sons' ambitions threaten to tear it apart. Kith-Kanan leads the Wildrunners, a group of elves that stirs tension by forging contacts and trade with the humans of Ergoth; Sithas strongly allies himself with the elven court. When their father mysteriously dies, Kith-Kanan is implicated and Sithas, the firstborn twin, is enthroned.

The Kinslayer Wars
Douglas Niles

Kith-Kanan commits the ultimate heresy for an elven prince and falls in love with a human. Soon after, his twin brother, the firstborn ruler of all Silvanesti elves, Sithas, declares war on the humans of Ergoth, and Kith-Kanan finds himself caught between two mighty forces.

The Qualinesti
Paul B. Thompson and Tonya R. Carter

One of the most fabled of all of Krynn's legends—untold before now—is the founding of Qualinost and the creation of the magnificent society of the renegade elves, the Qualinesti. Kith-Kanan becomes the first Speaker of the Suns, but he is haunted by his failures: the unfaithfulness of his wife, and the mysterious behavior of his son and successor.

DragonLance® Saga

Meetings Sextet

Kindred Spirits　　　　Mark Anthony and Ellen Porath
The reluctant dwarven hero Flint Fireforge is invited to the elven kingdom of Qualinesti, where he meets a young, unhappy half-elf named Tanis. When the elven princess Laurana declares her love for Tanis, a deadly rival for her affections frames Tanis for murder.

Wanderlust　　　　Mary Kirchoff and Steve Winter
When Tasslehoff Burrfoot accidentally pockets a magic bracelet, he becomes the target of a mysterious mage who covets the bracelet's power. Flint and Tanis form an alliance with a sea elf princess and the fabled phaethons to save both Tas and the Black Robes from a fate far worse than death.

Dark Heart　　　　Tina Daniell
At last, the story of beautiful, dark-hearted Kitiara Uth Matar, from the birth of her twin brothers, the frail mage Raistlin and the warrior Caramon. Kitiara's growing fascination with evil and ceaseless search for her father throw her into the company of a roguish stranger whose fate is intermingled with her own.

Meetings Sextet
The Adventures Continue

The Oath and the Measure
Michael Williams

Sturm leaves his friends Raistlin and Caramon to seek a place with the Knights of Solamnia. In searching for the truth about his father, he discovers an old enemy and a new friend, both of whom hide their true intent.

Steel and Stone
Ellen Porath

On his way back from Qualinesti, Tanis encounters the beautiful Kitiara and rescues her. As the two travel together rapport grows, creating a special bond that is later threatened by misunderstanding and conflict. On sale September 1992.

The Companions
Tina Daniell

Caramon, Sturm, and Tasslehoff are transported by a magical windstorm to the eastern Bloodsea, and Raistlin convinces Flint and Tanis to journey with him to rescue them. Once in Mithas, however, the companions must battle the Nightmaster of the minotaurs, who plans to conquer Krynn. On sale January 1993.

DRAGONLANCE Saga

Tales II Trilogy

Volume Three: *The War of the Lance*

All of the best-selling DRAGONLANCE authors—
Margaret Weis and Tracy Hickman,
Richard A. Knaak, Dan Parkinson,
Nancy Varian Berberick, Michael Williams,
and more—together in a fantastical
short story collection.

Among the tales to be told . . .
A dragon snookered by gully dwarves.
A blood sacrifice at sea.
A deathcurse overcome by love.
Plus, a new novella in which Tasslehoff Burrfoot
tells a tale he promised never, **ever** to tell!

Be sure to read *The Reign of Istar* and
The Cataclysm. Available now.